Dead Hunger VII
The Reign of Isis

By Eric A. Shelman

Dead Hunger VII: The Reign of Isis
is a work of fiction By
Eric A. Shelman

All characters contained herein are fictional,
and all similarities to persons living or dead
are purely coincidental.

This text cannot be copied or duplicated
without author or publisher written
permission.

©2014 Dolphin Moon Publishing

ISBN 978-0-9891416-3-5

Edited by Linda Tooch

Cover Art By Gary McCluskey

Interior DHVII Cover by Jeffrey Kosh

DEDICATIONS

At this point in the series, there are so many people to thank it is just ridiculous. I must always begin by thanking my wife, Linda. She endures my many long hours sitting at this damned keyboard creating these stories, and I love her for that and for so much more. Thanks, babe. (See where all the "babe" nonsense comes from?)

Thanks to my brother Don Shelman. The guy is there for me when I stumble and don't quite know where to go with a story; sometimes it's not even input, but a sounding board. He doesn't need to say anything because I see the light go on when he thinks I've had a good idea. Thanks, Don. I love you and am thankful I have you as a brother. Thank you, too, Marion. You love the shit I write like a sister-in-law should.

Jean Middleton deserves thanks, because she's my mom and the English teacher who made sure I knew how to string a sentence together. Mom, you did a better job than you know. You also taught me hard work pays off, and I love it. I love you, too. While I'm at it, I want to thank Ed Middleton, my dad from the time I was fourteen years old. He passed away and I miss him.

Last but not least, there's you. Yep. The person taking the time to read this dedication page and the remainder of the book. You have come along with me on this crazy ride with some awfully strange zombies and some characters I've grown to love. THANK YOU. Some of you have read my books in advance and fixed my screw-ups! THANKS, Jesse Donovan, Megan O'Hara, Dave Gammon, Carrie Herbel, Debra Allen, Chris and Sharon Berget and others. You all Rock. Jeff Clare, Danielle Pascale, Anna Dolhancryk and Gavin Cooksley from All Things Zombie on Facebook? You ALL deserve a mention. You rock hard!! ☺

Prologue

My name is Isis.

As I begin to tell you this story, the year is 2027. There are no flying cars, poverty has lost its meaning and peace on Earth has not been, and likely never will be, achieved. All members of humankind – and I include all men, women and children in that category – will likely be required to commit violent acts for the rest of their lives in order to survive.

Not against one another; never against one another. To the ones known as rotters and infecteds and abnormals. The ones that a film creator named George Romero introduced to the world through his movies as zombies; also called the living or walking dead.

The ones that I call the Mothers and the Hungerers.

I've read about a man who died long ago named Nostradamus who was said to be a prophet and one who could foresee the future. I'm of the understanding that nobody ever credited Mr. Romero with this distinctive talent, and yet his work came eerily close to painting a portrait of the world in which we're now forced to live.

I've known nothing different. This *is* my world, unchanged from that into which I was born.

There are six chronicles preceding this one. The fifth volume tells the story of my father and of the group of survivors who helped us just over thirteen years ago. Within this tiny band of heroes was my cousin Dave

Eric A. Shelman

Gammon. He and his friends sought out my father, Brett Ulrich Gammon – with no knowledge of my existence.

We were essentially trapped in a bunker in northern California. Without their help, it might have been several years before I would have been able to look upon daylight for the first time without perceiving it through a computer monitor.

You may have noticed above that I said *humans* will be required to commit violent acts for the rest of *their* lives.

While I look very much like them, and I was born of man and woman, I'm different. My mother, Angela Gammon, was pregnant with me when she was exposed to the eye vapor from one of the Mothers, or what Uncle Flex and the others call red-eyes.

These Mothers are female abnormals who were pregnant when they were infected by the gas leaking from the very planet upon which we live. The increased levels of estrogen surging through their brains, firing neurotransmitters and enhancing their brain function, caused them to become more evolved than the others.

They continued to evolve and at one time nearly exterminated all those who eventually saved my father and me.

As for the gas coming from the planet, nearly fifteen years later, the clear, odorless gas still emits from the surface of the Earth with no significant reduction in volume.

Hemp Chatsworth, our resident scientist and former CDC contractor, has determined some important things through testing over the past decade. The most important discovery – in his eyes – is that the gaseous element slowly leaves the planet's atmosphere. Additionally, he has determined that it will someday cease.

As for the most important discovery, it is that when the gas flow does stop and the gas slips out of our atmosphere, the zombies will die.

You may ask what becomes of me when this happens.

I'm not afraid. While a Mother played a part in creating me, and I have a strong mental connection to both the Mothers and the Hungerers, I'm not reliant on the gas to live; I breathe oxygen.

If you have already read through the chronicles of the others, then you know I do not sleep. You also know that I only eat meat and that as a child I had nearly adult-sized teeth suited to those of an exclusive carnivore.

I still have the teeth, but only their sharpness stands out today as my body has grown. I have also since gained control over how I hear, feel and communicate with the Mothers and Hungerers, which was something I was forced to learn at age three.

I do not know if my lifespan will be significantly shorter than that of my human counterparts. I understand that I'm unusual in the world of humans.

I'm turning fifteen in approximately nine months from now. I'm 6'-2". I have long, wavy blond hair that falls to my waist. I have a photographic memory every bit as good or better than that of Nelson Moore, and I've read every volume of a 2012 Encyclopedia Britannica we found in a local library.

Flex and Gem Sheridan told me I wouldn't be able to understand the world in which we now live without knowing what it was like before.

The violence, despite the zombie situation, seems reduced.

I did not return the books, but I did not need them after the first reading.

Max Chatsworth is a thirteen-year-old boy very much like me and created in the same way. His mother, Charlie, was near giving birth to him when she was exposed to a large amount of the red-eye vapor. Nobody expected that he would metamorphose so quickly.

He is a Transceiver, like me. Also known as a Hybrid.

My mother was exposed to the vapor weeks – not hours – before I was born. Because Charlie's water had already broken and she was a few hours from giving birth to Max, it was everyone's hope and prayer that the vapor would have little effect on him. Even his father, Hemp, was certain the vapor would require far more time to genetically alter the makeup of a human fetus – but he and everybody else had been wrong.

Max carries some of my most important attributes, as well as those that just seem strange to the casual observer. He also does not sleep, but he can and will eat things other than meat, though he does prefer animal protein. Our eyes have a constant red glow that can be disconcerting to those unfamiliar with the condition. This has caused many a child in our community to run away frightened, and for this reason we have taken to wearing sunglasses, particularly at night.

He can call the Mothers like me, but neither of us has been able to draw the Hungerers. The Mothers naturally utilize them as their army of sorts, so always gather them as they move. As I had attained the ability to do a year earlier, Max can use his connection like a divining rod, guiding him to our intended prey, rather than drawing them to us and our loved ones. This ability, which came to both of us at around age twelve, is paramount to the survival of all those in our community.

To explain further, I was a child who experienced a condition known as precocious puberty. That is to say it is the medical term for a normal eight-year-old girl who begins to grow breasts and sprout pubic hair as I did, while normal puberty occurs anywhere from age 9 to age 14.

Hemp explained that because I had developed language and brain skills at such a young age and had grown at a much faster rate than a normal child, the only way to know if my precocious puberty was normal is when another of me comes along.

Along came Max. His puberty began at age 9, which settled the question of what was normal for Hybrids like us.

My point is, as I reached puberty, I found that not only could I block the involuntary siren call to the Mothers, I found that my connection with the Mothers – and by association, the Hungerers – changed. While I could not feel them individually, I could almost estimate the numbers of the advancing horde by a sense of their total mass. I could estimate with fair accuracy how many were making their way toward us at any given time.

That knowledge helped us determine a strategy for their annihilation, which varied depending on their numbers.

Max can now do this, too. They are drawn to both of us for the same reason; we, as infants, unknowingly beckoned them. Once they became aware of us, they sought us out, believing we were their unborn children. The reality is that their living dead babies remain squirming inside their wombs, never to be born. This hasn't changed.

Now we have the ability to determine their direction and either call them or go to them, keeping the shades pulled as we do so. We can only estimate how far away they are and we've been off by as much as sixty miles, but our sense of direction means we'll get to them eventually.

With our beacons switched off, we can take them by surprise and rid the world of them.

We have to do this; we are best equipped for it. We still have our parents to convince, though.

There has been something else leading up to this. Now, in our community, there are over 600 survivors. Many of these are pregnant women. We've had a bit of a baby boom in Kingman, Kansas.

Max and I believe we need more of us. People like me and Max, that is. Perhaps hundreds more. We understand this will pose ethical questions for the others in our community.

To Max and me there is no question. We cannot do this alone.

*****

CHAPTER ONE

Kingman, Kansas – Spring 2027

The city of Kingman in the state of Kansas was selected by Isis and Max as our home in what might as well have been a secret meeting. At the time, she was six years old and Max was just about to turn five.

Isis had read the most recent encyclopedias and knew the previous population and border dimensions of the town, so determined that it would be of a size that could ultimately be fully fenced and protected, and one that was also centrally located within the United States.

Nobody knew why that was important but Isis – and perhaps Max – and she did not reveal all of her reasons for choosing it until much later.

When they had arrived it was more a ghost town than anything else. It seemed the abnormals had taken Kingman by storm, and it took over a year and a half to eradicate the indigenous rotters. Stragglers came in on occasion from Wichita, which was about a forty-five minute drive to the east, which is why the fencing work began along that side of the town.

There was no more screwing around when they'd arrived. The presence of Max and Isis and the powers they possessed helped greatly during the process of building the fence around the entire populated area of Kingman, and when it was done folks were as proud as if they had just built the Great Wall of China.

It was for the same purpose, essentially. To repel the enemy – of which there were only a few types – all without heartbeats.

Some farmers remained, and along with Hemp and others, they created a water supply system designed after the system used at the Jack Daniel's Whiskey facility in Lynchburg, Tennessee. They tapped into a decent river on the south side of town and diverted water through a trough, even dumping it from the trough to an enclosed pipe when necessary to move it under a roadway.

More primitive but effective methods of filtration, such as gravel and some charcoal, were utilized in a world with limited power, so the water was safe enough to drink. A second stream of water was provided shortly after, primarily for washing and other purposes. Nobody had gotten sick from it, so their methods were eventually proven, despite their inexperience in such technology.

It helped to have Isis who had read and remembered the Encyclopedia Britannica and who could recite what components were required for proper filtration. She was often Hemp's reference guide.

Everyone chipped in. The gender breakdown was off-kilter, though. It was clear upon their arrival in Kingman that more men than women had survived the initial zombie outbreak, and that seemed to never quite equalize. Of the roughly six hundred occupants of the town, 44% were women and girls, and the remainder were men and boys.

If they could maintain the world they had restored, that gender imbalance would correct itself. Hemp said so, so everyone believed it to be true. Not only because women lived longer than men, but because little boys *and* little girls were being raised with intense weapons training and fighting skills, which meant that there were no victims in this new society. No bullies.

Nelson Moore made sure of that. His Subdudo classes were well-attended, and he had, in his infinite wisdom, added a more lethal set of moves – to be used by choice and when necessary.

Bunsen passed away in 2018, and her boy, Slider, died in 2023. Both passed from natural causes, but that did not make it any easier for those who loved them.

Charlie had found herself a litter of Golden Retriever mixes and had taken a runt female for herself, naming it Baby. The rest were claimed quickly by other townsfolk. Before you knew it, Baby was retrieving Charlie's crossbow bolts from targets – and from dead zombies.

There were several hotels in town, which surprised Flex, Gem, and the others at first. It just wasn't clear what people would come to Kingman to do, and with 29 motels and hotels, it seemed like overkill.

Much of the city near the riverside was industrial, which provided a plethora of materials both for building and otherwise, and while there were homes near downtown, much was commercial. The hotels were excellent for those who wanted to be close to their neighbors – which was the majority of the population.

The Hampton Inn was among the largest and first to fill up. Next, the Best Western, followed by the Quality Inn and last, the Motel 6. These inhabitants of Kingman were among the happiest, though. They had achieved what they may not have had even in the pre-zombie world; a community of people who looked out for one another.

The fence is what made everything else possible. It was not some flimsy chain link barrier; it was solid and strong. It was constructed with every type of treated wood and steel upright they could get their hands on, and when that wasn't available, they used composite materials. The Great Wall of Kingman – which is what people began calling it upon its completion – stood seven feet tall – though not exactly, because it was about function, not esthetics – and it ran all the way around the city for a total length of six miles. The barbed wire that snaked along the top wasn't much, but it was the razor variety that could slice through flesh easily, be it living or dead.

Kingman's wall was a bit shy of the 5,500 miles of the Great Wall of China, but was an accomplishment nonetheless. They had to make several dangerous runs into Wichita to get enough material to finish it, and it took them almost eight years before they were able to put in the last section.

It was a celebration that day. One that Flex would never forget. Watching Gem's face when she realized what they had achieved after so many years of fighting and running. They had cried as they held each other that day.

Solar power made sense, and thanks to Flex's electrical abilities, along with other men and women with electrical expertise who found Kingman along the way, they were able to raid a solar panel manufacturing facility and use the panels to keep an enormous bank of batteries fully charged, providing limited power to the citizens of Kingman.

They were always expanding it – because the population wasn't static by any means – and when they tied their makeshift power plant into the town's main power grid, another great cheer erupted in the community. Once it was dialed in and adjusted, people in various sections of Kingman were given specific times to use power and limited to no more than two hours per day, not consecutive.

As for gasoline, logic would dictate that it had all gone bad and that driving or running generators was a thing of the past. Perhaps so for other communities, but not for Kingman.

Hemp had long insisted that gasoline always has the same amount of energy in it, no matter its condition. What it loses is its ability to vaporize, which is what it has to do within the carburetion system of an engine.

What did Hemp do? Obviously, utilizing his brilliant mind, he developed highly advanced methods of storing mass quantities of gasoline in underground, aluminum tanks. They installed tank filtration and water separation systems to prevent the intrusion of moisture, and a certain amount of empty space was left in each tank to allow for expansion and contraction.

Sometimes – on rare occasions – they required a starter fluid, such as ether, to fire the engine, but after that the gasoline would vaporize flawlessly.

So it was life, sort of. Worse than in 2010, but shitloads better than in 2012.

Flex sat in what people had begun to call his office in the old Kingman City Hall building. Gem and Hemp sat across from him.

Gem took a last toke from the roach in her fingers and held it out for Flex, who let her drop it in his open hand. He pinched it between his fingers and got another hit off it before snuffing it out between his thumb and index finger and dropping it into the wastebasket.

Clearly, they had not outlawed pot in their new world. To Flex, it was one of the best parts of calling the shots. If you didn't like it, don't move to Kingman – or move here and shut the fuck up about it. There was plenty to be thankful for, after all.

Almost all of the core group that had tried to give Concord, New Hampshire a go were now in Kingman, including Kevin Reeves, the three sisters, Kimberly, Vikki and Victoria (formerly Jasmine) and the former kids of Concord.

Not that you would recognize any of them anymore. It was, after all, thirteen post-apocalyptic years since Hurricane George struck and wiped out their former home. Hard labor, such as it took to survive in a world like this, could age a person.

It was during that horrible storm and the Diphtheria outbreak of 2014 that Tony Mallette was lost, and Flex thought about him often. He would've been a great citizen of Kingman.

Flex Sheridan barely recognized himself when he looked in the mirror, but he was in pretty good shape for an old man.

Flex wasn't the mayor of the town; they'd let Kevin Reeves take that job again because he had already garnered the respect of many from the days in Concord. There were a couple of cops, too, and a judge. Kingman also had a jail in which nobody had ever yet been incarcerated.

Life in Kingman in 2027 was about as close to normal life as Flex and anyone else had seen since that fateful day he made the phone call to his kid sister, Jamie.

Flex was 58 years old and Gem was 47. Flex thought about that sometimes, remembering how he thought he'd never make it to 46 or 47 after the world took such a strange turn.

Charlie, who had been a mere 26 when they found her hiding in that hospital closet, was turning 40. Hemp just had his 46th birthday.

Of all of this, the most rewarding thing beyond still being alive and in relatively good shape, was that his little

Trina, the foul-mouthed girl who gave them so many laughs in a world that desperately needed them, was 21, and her pseudo-sister, Taylor, was 22.

Oh, and were they formidable. Flex often called them the Gem and Charlie of Generation Z.

Charlie didn't mind the comparison, but she was quick to remind Flex that she wasn't over the hill just yet. If it was possible, the woman had increased her crossbow skills. She also taught her son Max how to use the weapon, and the kid – who wasn't so much a kid as everyone had expected he would be at age 13 – had now exceeded her abilities.

Charlie, Taylor and Trina were out picking up supplies in a fast-dwindling neighboring town, and Flex was about to be off the clock, so to speak.

"You know what they wanna talk about?" Flex asked. He wore boots that were currently propped up on the desk in front of him. He didn't actually have a job in the building, but he'd agreed to station himself there for two hours a day, at least six days a week, in case new arrivals came in or folks had questions about how things worked in Kingman.

"No clue," said Gem. "I get kind of a bad feeling, though."

"I believe I know," said Hemp. "Max hasn't come right out and said anything, but I know him. He's got a lot on his mind."

"Is it about leaving?" asked Gem. "I know they're antsy. They think just repelling them or waiting for them to show up isn't enough. They want to go to where they are and kill them."

Hemp nodded. "Yes, I know. They think it's their duty," he said. "I know Max believes they were created for that purpose."

"Think they were?" asked Flex.

Hemp looked at Gem, who had recently cut her hair to shoulder length, her big brown eyes smiling back at him. "Well?" she asked, letting her mouth in on the smile.

Hemp shrugged. "Perhaps, if you're of the mind that everything happens for a reason."

"I am," said Gem.

"I have to agree," said Flex. "We've been through some pretty shitty stuff and look where we are now. For fuck's sake, people are talking about the spring planting season, Hemp."

"No argument here," he said. "And I appreciate their sense of responsibility, but I can't help but feel that even with their abilities, the task is too large."

"You got a solar calculator there, babe?" asked Gem, swiping her hair over her left ear as she leaned forward. Flex smiled as she did this because he found it sexy, even with the wisps of grey that now resided among her still mostly dark locks.

"Hell yes," he said. "Made in fucking China and still workin'. What you lookin' at?"

"Give it," she said.

He pushed it to her and Gem slid it in front of her. "Okay. It's 2027, right? This shit started in … what, 2011?"

"It began in June of 2011," said Hemp.

"Okay, so … that's 27 minus 11 …"

"Sixteen," said Hemp.

"Okay," said Gem. "Multiply that times 365 days, and we've got … 5,840." She looked up at Hemp. "Not so fucking fast on the big numbers are you, Einstein?"

Hemp smiled, shook his head and put up his middle finger.

"Now, now kids," said Flex. "What are you up to, Gem?"

18

"Figuring out how many rotters we've killed," she said. "Let's use a nice round number of thirty a day, every day since this thing started. Sound like too many or too few?"

"To account for the days when we killed hundreds, just use a figure of fifty per day."

"Fine," said Gem. "Fifty kills per day, including red-eyes and regular zombies –"

"Mothers and Hungerers, according to Max and Isis," said Flex.

"They all stink the same," said Gem. She punched the numbers into the calculator. When she was finished, she held it up.

"292,000," she said. "But that's not the most important number."

"And what is the most important number, sweetheart?" asked Flex, his eyes bloodshot and narrow, but still attentive.

Hemp said, "So if we started with approximately 279,000,000 infecteds and we've only killed, on the outside, 292,000 of them, what you're saying is –"

"What I'm saying is there is a shit-ton of zombies left to kill and what we've done is like nothing."

"Others have killed them," said Flex. "We know that."

"Not enough," said Gem.

"Never enough," said Hemp. "We can't truly experience a normal world until the gas flow ceases. There's a chance that mankind will simply have to await that and not rely on Max and Isis – or us."

The door opened and Max stepped in, a crossbow over his shoulder, partially obscuring an Ozzy Osbourne *Blizzard of Oz* concert tee shirt.

Like mother like son, thought Flex, smiling.

Behind him, Isis stepped in. Both of them smiled briefly, removed their sunglasses, and nodded hello. Their red eyes were intense and through them, the seriousness of their purpose was still evident.

Max waved his hand in the air, fanning it. "Jeez, guys. If you're gonna smoke weed in the city seat of government, you should really open a window."

"Government's closed, buddy," said Flex, smiling. "Thanks for getting here before I got off my shift."

"Our pleasure," said Isis, smiling.

She carried weapons infrequently; only when she headed directly into a confrontation with an extraordinary number of rotters. She knew how to use all weapons with precision, and she was an expert with everything they had in decent supply, but her natural abilities often negated the need for traditional defenses.

Her favorite weapon was her mind, and she continued to hone her skills in that regard.

"Hello, son," said Hemp. "How are you, Isis?"

"I'm fine, Uncle Hemp," she said. "Hi, Flex, Gem."

Flex wasn't sure why she called Hemp uncle, but not him and Gem. He never asked her, but attributed it to the fact that growing up so close in age to one another, Max was like a brother or cousin to her, and she saw Hemp as an uncle.

Isis could only be described in one way. She was gorgeous. As a child, she had never wanted her hair cut, so over her fourteen years, it had become a wavy, platinum blond waterfall down to her hips. She often twisted it and put it on her head, but today she let it hang down, with just a rubber band on its tip.

Isis had grown to a height of 6'-2", and while she was technically a teenager if judged only by her years and human societal terms, she was not that at all. Isis had been

20

nothing less than a mature woman from age twelve and by then had been menstruating since her eighth year.

Max had developed similarly. He looked like the spitting image of Hemp with regard to his facial shape and his nose, but he had Charlie's eyes and mouth. He was around 6'-1", but at age thirteen, he was not yet done growing. He had a full beard, which was something even Hemp could not pull off.

"Hey, pops," said Max, leaning down to kiss his old man on the cheek. Flex thought it was cool. The kid never acted embarrassed to show affection to his father. "Hey, Uncle Flex, Aunt Gem," he said.

Flex and Gem both smiled at him. "Hey," they said together.

"We're glad you're all here," said Isis. "My father is at home, but I didn't want him here for this anyway. Where's Aunt Charlie?"

"She's with Tay and Trina," said Max. "Remember? They left this morning to go hunting."

"Yes," said Isis. "I thought they might be back. I'm sorry she's not here, but you can fill her in later."

"Pull up a chair, kids," said Flex, pointing to the corners of the room. They did, and sat down.

Max looked at Isis. She met the eyes of Flex, then Gem, then Hemp. She spoke:

"Max and I have reached a decision that we feel is crucial, but that may have ethical considerations when considered by you and others."

Gem turned her head. "Like what kind of ethical considerations?"

"First we have to examine the scope of the task before us," said Isis.

"Too late," said Gem, holding up the calculator. "There aren't enough zeroes on this Chinese piece of shit to

21

actually show you the whole number, but there are roughly 278,708,000 Mothers and Hungerers left in the United States alone. Right?"

"Precisely," said Isis. "So you have considered it.

"My shift is almost over, kids," said Flex. What's your proposal, 'cause I can sense we're gettin' to one."

"Max and I have enhanced our skills over the years," said Isis. "Some through maturity and some through training, but it's pretty easy to conclude that we're far more useful and dangerous to the Mothers and Hungerers than we were as younger children."

"No argument there," said Hemp. "How does that relate to the numbers of infecteds?"

Isis seemed reluctant to go on. Max reached out and took her by the hand and gave it a squeeze. She looked at him and smiled. Then she nodded.

"Dad, what Isis is trying to say is that we don't feel different," said Max. "We were born like this and we don't feel like outcasts and we don't feel like ... I dunno, freaks."

Hemp's eyes grew concerned. "That's because anyone who enters this community is immediately told about you and of your value to this community and keeping everyone safe. They learn about you at the same time they're told about urushiol and WAT-5. You are not only wonderful, loving children and citizens of Kingman, Kansas, you are an important part of everyone's survival."

"He can't fish," said Flex, winking.

"What?" asked Hemp, missing the wink.

"Kid can't fish for shit," said Flex. "I say we boot him to the curb."

"Could be my teacher, Uncle Flex," said Max.

Flex laughed and shook his head.

"The bottom line," said Isis, "is that it's because of our abilities and our willingness –"

Isis paused and bit her lip briefly before going on. Flex watched her face, and even in the interior of the building with only a propane lantern lighting the room, her skin was the consistency of cream, her features so goddess-like that she appeared to be more than merely human – which of course, she was.

"Not willingness," she said. "That was the wrong word. *Eagerness.* We're eager to use our abilities because through them we see hope for the restoration of the world. Eventually, anyway."

Gem sat forward in her chair and brushed Isis' hair away from her face, her smile gone for the moment. "Okay, then. It's time to tell us. We got that you're okay in your skin."

"We need more of us," said Isis, all hesitation gone. "Many more. They have to be created, not only here, but across the country."

Gem's face went white. Flex stared at Max and Isis. Hemp nodded.

"I understand," he said. "Furthermore, I agree with you and I've thought about it myself."

"You never said anything to me, buddy," said Flex.

"Me either," said Gem. "Guys, do you really think people will agree to it?"

Max was more animated now, and Flex wondered if he would like nothing more than to be one of many instead of one of only two.

"I believe with some counseling, the pregnant women out there will agree to it," said Isis. "Some of them, anyway. Maybe more than we think."

"You said across the country," said Hemp.

"Pops, I'd be leaving," said Max. "We would both go."

"Max," said Hemp, calmly. "You're only thirteen."

"You know that's not really true," said Max, putting a hand on his father's shoulder. "I never really was thirteen. Or twelve. Or eleven."

"You were never really three," said Hemp, his shoulders drooping, his eyes falling to the floor. "I realize that."

Max knelt down and rested his hand on Hemp's arm. "Pops, you're all set up here. We wouldn't suggest this if we didn't know you'd be safe without us."

"Are you going alone?" asked Gem. "You'll need more than just the two of you, right?"

Max took a slow, deep breath. "Yeah, that's the other part."

"What?" asked Gem, getting on her feet now. She moved to sit on the corner of the desk, her jeans with holes in the knees and her beige, peasant blouse oversized for comfort.

"Trina and Tay want to go with us," said Isis, her face unreadable.

Gem slid off the corner of the desk, caught herself, and steadied a hand on the corner. Flex noticed her visibly gulp, and a second later she dropped back into the leather chair opposite him, her face pale.

Isis slid out of her chair and knelt in front of Gem, grasping her hands and squeezing them.

"Gem," she said. "There's another reason we need to go, and soon."

Gem looked up. Flex and Hemp stared at Isis, too. "Spit it out, Isis," said Flex.

"We've just gotten back from the pit," she said. "We've been calling the Mothers for two days, and they're not coming."

Gem, Hemp and Flex all looked at one another. Max picked it up.

"Guys, we gave it everything. We know they're out there, but they're not coming and we don't know why."

"How do you know?" asked Flex.

"We can feel them," said Isis. "With the Hungerers, there are hundreds. Maybe more."

It was Gem's turn to look even more worried. "I know you can call them and I know you can find them, but you never said you can estimate their numbers," she said.

"It's like a resistance," said Max. "Isis and I talked about it. We call them, but these aren't responding. Instead, it feels as though we sense each and every individual who won't succumb to our call."

"Do you have any idea why?" asked Hemp. "Anything in that head of yours churning?"

Isis and Max both shook their heads. That made Flex more nervous about it. These particular teenagers were rarely dumbfounded.

"So, anyway," said Max. "We have to go after them. If the Mothers and Hungerers can resist us, they may be able to overpower us face to face. That's what Isis thinks, anyway. That they've evolved even further somehow."

"Possibly into something we're no longer equipped to face," said Isis.

"So you believe they're aware we're here," said Hemp.

Flex's mind went back to the last time they thought life was going to be a breeze, and he was pretty sure Hemp's did, too.

"It makes sense," Isis said. "We know from past experience that they are aware of Kingman and of the gathering of humanity here. Max and I both read your chronicles, and we're well aware of what happened in Concord."

"They came for us," said Gem.

25

"They did. In numbers," said Max.

"Fucknuts," said Gem.

"Second that," said Flex.

*****

Flex figured that Max and Isis had sensed the three needed to have a conversation, so they left.

"They're not equipped for that yet," said Gem. "Trini's just 21 years old."

"She's tougher than you were at that age," said Flex.

Gem stared at him. "You really believe I can stand behind that fence and watch them leave?"

Flex shook his head. "Hemp, what do you think, man?"

"Try and stop them is what I think," said Hemp. "Compared to us, she is a goddess and he is a god, guys. We must defer to them, despite their tender years."

The door came open and Charlie came striding in with several mesh bags in her hands. She placed them on the floor and ran to Hemp, plopping down on his lap. He winced and groaned, but she kissed him before he could complain.

"Who's a goddess? You talking about me again?" she asked, looking at Gem.

"You know it, sweetie," said Gem. "Get what you went out for?"

"Rabbits," said Charlie. "Love beef, but it's a nice change."

"Trina and Tay got them?" asked Gem.

"I got two, they got six between them."

"You've taught them well, master," said Flex.

"Uh, that would be mistress, but it carries too many other connotations."

26

Gem's face turned serious. "Did the girls share anything with you?" she asked.

Charlie's face scrunched. "No. Like what?"

"Holy shit, here it comes," said Flex.

They told her what Max and Isis were planning to do and she dropped into the chair beside Gem, her mouth hanging open.

"They've been calling them to the pit for two days and they didn't get a single one?" she asked.

"That's what they said," answered Hemp. "Never happened before."

The pit was Hemp's design, but Max and Isis contributed greatly to the functionality. It took two years to build, but when completed, was the greatest mass zombie killing system anybody had ever seen.

The pit was a hundred and twenty feet in diameter; a perfect circle. It was only five feet deep, but a five-foot chain link fence encircled it. When you stood inside the pit – which was a risky place to stand – the fence was essentially ten feet, so it was enough.

More chain link fencing covered the top of the pit, making it essentially a cage, and winding through this fencing, in approximate one-foot rows, was heavy plastic tubing with fine spray water nozzles spaced every twenty inches, connected to large tanks of the deadly urushiol blend.

This took care of the Hungerers, as Max and Isis – and now, many of the citizens of Kingman – called the creatures.

To this liquid blend, Hemp had added the necessary ratio of estrogen blocking agent to neutralize and kill the Mothers as well.

Two large storage tanks were mounted on welded steel towers eight feet tall. These were sealed, stainless steel tanks, and were pressurized by solar panel-charged batteries and two twelve-volt compressors.

The pressure was constant and one-way valves prevented the leakage when the system's motors were not running, maintaining pressure. When a sensor detected it had dropped below a designated threshold, the motors would come on and recharge the system where it needed to be.

No zombie-killing pit would be complete without a backup system. Buried in the floor of the pit were over a thousand fully sealed hydraulic cylinders with 48" stainless steel, sharpened shafts that shot out of the ground at strategically calculated angles.

All of this ran off a small diesel generator powering a hydraulic pump and motor combo.

If the zombies were on their feet when the shafts extended, it would break their legs or knock them over. After the rotters were down, the second shaft extension usually rammed straight through their skulls, killing them.

The most they ever needed – during quality testing – was four shaft extensions to kill all the occupants of the pit.

Afterward, they would burn them in place using an accelerant, and roll the bulldozer in to clean out the remains.

The pit was strategically located and three fully cleared entry paths led from the main highway directly to the pit. The gates leading into the pit were spring loaded so that only one, skinny rotter could lean on it and it would swing inward, but once in, it would spring closed, trapping them.

It was an old idea, but it worked well. Zombies didn't get the whole *pull, don't push* thing very well – even the red-eyes.

Because Max and Isis could draw the rotters to a very specific location, it was their idea to construct a catwalk over the pit's cage where two chairs were placed.

Not thrones, or anything so dramatic. Just two, stackable, resin chairs.

Despite being a mere infant at the time, Isis had very clear memories of dangling below the helicopter with Rachel at the controls. She also remembered how the zombies were mindlessly drawn to her even then.

The kids could sense when the rotters were near, so when it was almost time, they would access the catwalk via an attached, exterior ladder and take their seats.

Once inside the pit, the area of the cage directly below Max and Isis was as close as they could get to the two.

In they pushed, their emaciated bodies adorned in filthy, bloody clothing, their skin pocked and shredded, their eyes red or pink. Their never-ending hunger drew them forward, unable to resist.

They pushed toward the center of the pit to be close to their children, Max and Isis.

Charlie stood and folded her arms. "Details," she said.

"I might as well cut to the chase," said Gem. "They're taking Trina and Taylor."

"My fuckin' ass they are," said Charlie. "Not Max, not Trina and Taylor, and not without me."

Flex, Gem and Hemp stared at Charlie. Her response could have been scripted, and she played the part perfectly.

"Well, sister," said Gem. "When I get Flexy squared away, I'm booking my tickets, too."

"You mean our son, right?" asked Flex. "Because there's no way I'm letting you go without me."

Hemp stood, shaking his head. "Guys, there's no way they'll allow it. If you tell them you intend to go, they'll slip away in the night. I think we know them that well."

"Then we don't tell them," said Charlie. "We just follow them."

"I swore I'd never say this," said Flex, "but I'm gettin' too old for this shit."

"Yeah," said Gem. "Like ten years ago."

"Let's get home," said Flex. "We need to start acting like this is okay with us if we're going. Plus we need to pack our shit in secret."

Gem smiled. "I'm kind of excited. We've been living the domestic life for a while now."

As they all headed for the door, Hemp added, "We're all probably a bit rusty. That said, I'm kind of looking forward to spending some time on the road, just the four of us again."

*****

CHAPTER TWO

The sun sank below the horizon and shadows fell over the kitchen and family room of the small house in which Flex, Gem, Trina, and Flex Jr. lived.

Flex opened the back door and gave the magnetic motor a spin, closing the magnets around it. It silently wound up to speed.

Flex had coupled the electricity-free motor to a small generator, the wires from which were channeled into the house, to a portable electrical outlet. Into this, they had plugged a lamp.

Back inside, Flex turned the switch and the table lamp illuminated the room. It didn't burn at full wattage, but it was light. He and Hemp were hoping to build one large enough to power the equipment at the pit. Fuel was becoming more and more unreliable, no matter their efforts.

Flex Sheridan Jr. sat at the glass top table and worked on a pencil sketch by the meager light.

"Let me see that," said Gem, sliding her chair closer to his.

"It's not done yet," objected her son. "Later. Maybe."

"Maybe? I'll have you know you got all your artistic skill from these loins," she said. "That guy over there can't draw stick people."

"I get that," said Flex Jr., smiling.

"If I had a leg to stand on I'd argue just on principal," said Flex. "Talkin' about me like I'm not here." He pretend pouted.

"We really never mentioned you," said Gem.

"Insult by omission," he said. "Even worse."

How's the math coming?" asked Gem, sitting back.

"Already done and it was a breeze," said Flex Jr. "Uncle Hemp helped me a couple of weeks ago. I shoulda asked him sooner."

"He's got a way of explaining things," said Gem, rubbing his arm. "Way more patient than me."

The thirteen-year-old smiled and shook his head. "Yeah. They'd put me on the short bus if I counted on your math skills."

Gem slapped him playfully in the back of the head. "You don't even know what that means," she said, smiling.

"Ha!" said Flex, a big smile on his face. "Shit comes back pretty fast, doesn't it mama?"

"Don't be a dick," she said, reaching out and snatching Flex Jr.'s sketch pad and flipping the cover over. She raised her eyebrows. "Is that … Isis?" she asked.

"Give it back, mom," he said, his face blushing red.

"She's a bit your senior," said Flex. "And while I think you'll get taller yet, she might have an inch or two to go yet, too."

"I'm good with tall chicks," he shot back. "And she likes me. I mean, what's not to like?"

Flex looked at his son. He was pretty tall for his age at 5'8", and Flex was pretty sure he'd top 6' one way or the other. Maybe more. He had dark brown hair and brown eyes, Gem's Latin heritage taking over there.

"The sketch is awesome, kiddo," said Gem. "I mean … really good." She held it up for Flex to see. "Hey," she said, getting his attention.

Flex turned to look, but his son grabbed it and put it back on the table. "When it's done you can frame the damned thing," he said, smiling. Then: "Mom, when can we go out on a run? It's been like a month."

A run is what Flex Jr. called a zombie hunt. He hadn't had any close calls since he was around eight years old and he often went out on killing runs with other boys and girls in the community, but Gem was always nervous about it, and he had to get permission. She hadn't given it in a long time.

"Soon," she said. "You done with your homework, then? We need to talk."

He rolled his eyes. "What the hell did I do now?"

Flex leaned against the counter and laughed. "You remind me of me," he said. "Jesus, Flexy. Fuckin' uncanny."

"I know," said Gem. "He's like a miniature version of you when I first started dating you. Single-minded."

"Oh, yeah?" asked Flex Jr. "What was his obsession?"

"Me, of course," said Gem.

"Still is, as far as I can tell," said their son, smiling. "So I'll let it go for now but I wanna go out. I'm gonna lose my knife skills."

Against Gem's better judgment, Flex Jr. had become enthralled by Lola's abilities with knives. She seemed to enjoy using them as her primary weapons when trouble – zombie trouble – presented itself.

Nelson acquired some throwing knives, and when Flex Jr. put all that together in his head, he became a lean, mean, zombie-killing machine. He wore a narrow nylon belt with pockets all the way around. It held thirty throwing knives, all 9" long and made of stainless steel.

"Like I said, Flexy," said Gem. "We'll get you out there before too much longer. Let's let Max and Isis get them closer and you can put together a welcoming party."

"Sweet," he said. "What do you want to talk about?" With one hand he tucked his hair, which he had chosen to grow long from age ten, behind his right ear. It was as straight as that of any red-eye, and down to his shoulder blades.

Flex came in and sat down. "It's about your sister."

"Trini? What's up with her?"

"It also involves Max and Isis," said Gem.

Now suddenly, Flex Jr. looked concerned. "What?"

Gem looked at Flex, who gave her a quick nod. She went on: "They said they need to go," she said. "Maybe head something off at the pass."

"What do you mean by that?" asked Flex Jr.

"They're sensing something strange out there," said Flex. "Big numbers of infecteds that don't come when they're called."

"How far away?"

"I think they know direction but not necessarily distance," said Gem. "But they also have a proposal to make. I think I'll let you hear that from them. And no, it doesn't involve taking you with."

"Shit," said Flex Jr. "How long are they gonna be gone?" he asked.

"Let's see if they even leave," said Gem. "Maybe something will change before then. We're not even sure of their timeline."

"They acted like it was pretty dire," said Flex. "And to be honest, I'd rather not take chances. If there's something brewing out there, better we get ahead of it."

"We?" asked Flex Jr. "What, you're going?"

This time Flex looked at Gem and she shrugged.

"Your mom won't let Trina go alone," she said.

"So you're both going," said Flex Jr.

He was pissed and Flex knew it. Like father, like son. "Buddy, you know we can't sit back and –"

Flex Jr. suddenly stood and went to the sofa, retrieving his crossbow. Walking toward them and loading a bolt at the same time, he turned and fired into the door. The bolt embedded itself just above the peephole. In four seconds he had another bolt loaded and fired, and this one embedded just below the peephole. The next two shots fired took care of both sides. Perfect formation.

Flex Jr. looked at them. "Sorry about the door, but you guys know I'm easily as good as either of you. And I can outrun you both."

"You're gonna need those fuckin' skills for trashing the door," said Flex, pushing off the counter and going after his son.

"Good luck!" shouted Flex Jr., barely dodging Flex's outstretched arm.

He was at the door and twisting out two of the bolts before Flex got to him. He ducked out of the way and was back at the table before his dad could make the turn.

"If you're going, I'm going," he said. "We'll call it a family outing."

Gem looked at Flex. There was a bemused smile on her face. "What the fuck's with this kid, anyway?" she said, shaking her head. "Babe, we really have to rethink our parenting skills."

"No shit," he laughed. "Kid's outta control."

Flex Jr. was smiling, too, staring at his out-of-breath father.

Flex leaned on a chair and looked at his son. He attempted his angriest face but knew he wasn't quite pulling it off. "Fix that damned door. Wood putty, sandpaper. a coat of paint – you're an artist – figure it out. Then I'll think about it."

"Cool, I'm goin'," said Flex Jr. "Thanks mom. Thanks, dad. This is gonna be fun."

*****

The three sisters, Vikki, Victoria and Kimberly sat in the front row of the town square meeting area, and at present Hemp, Isis, and Max stood on the stage, waiting for the crowd to settle in.

There was a posting area in the square telling people what was going on, and people usually checked it a couple of times a day.

Word spread fast and most everyone was there. There wasn't any sort of roll call taken, but it didn't matter. If someone missed a meeting, word of mouth filled them in shortly after.

About a year after clearing Kingman, it became clear that with the growing numbers of uninfecteds coming to town, all with various skills, that a centrally located meeting place was necessary. The town square of Kingman was perfect; nobody really drove around town, choosing bicycles and motorcycles instead of cars, so it wasn't a problem blocking the roadway.

They built a small, three-foot high stage and a series of simple, straight benches. There were only twenty rows, forty feet long, which would accommodate a little over 500 people comfortably.

There was room for more, and judging by the number of residents standing up, it was time to get them built.

Hemp turned on an amplifier connected to a power inverter mounted on a rolling cart with several batteries.

Flex and Gem sat beside the sisters, and Flex Jr. was on his other side with Trina and Taylor. Beside Taylor was Charlie, who wore a shirt that said, "God Bless America. Except California. Fuck California."

On her other side was Dave and Serena Gammon and Doctor Jim Scofield.

"Thank you for coming today," said Hemp. "Nice day, right?"

The crowd seemed to agree and murmured in the affirmative.

"I'll just let you hear the subject of this meeting from Max and Isis. For those of you who have only been here a short time, Max is my son, and he is unique in that he and Isis both had an identical experience before they were born that made them a bit … let's say, special." He gave his microphone to Max and nodded. Isis already held hers. Hemp climbed down the steps and took his seat.

Isis stepped forward. "Hello, everyone."

More murmurs followed. Friendly and jovial.

"What I have to speak with you about might be controversial. It involves volunteers, but these will be extraordinary people. Not to say that you aren't all extraordinary, but this could be considered a sacrifice to some. At least until we explain it."

Max stepped forward. "I'm Max Chatsworth," he said. "And most of you know that Isis and I share some abilities that make us different. What makes us different also keeps all of us safer than we would be otherwise."

The crowd was not called upon to agree or disagree, but most of them nodded in agreement.

37

"I'd like to ask that all of our pregnant women stand up," said Isis.

In the crowd of what Flex estimated to be over five hundred people, around 18 women stood.

Flex looked back and smiled. It was what he had hoped for; he and Gem and everyone, for that matter. A safe place where the cycle of life did not begin again when you died, and where actual babies replaced those who did pass away.

"Okay," said Max. "You are the reason for this meeting, but obviously you all have families who must give you their thoughts, which means they must also know what the situation is."

The crowd began shifting nervously, and Flex wished he was close enough to say, "Okay, tell 'em already."

"You all know who we are," said Isis. "And most of you, I believe, know how we became this way."

Max joined in and it was like a perfect partnership. "My mother, Charlie Chatsworth, was exposed to a red-eye's vapor," he said. "I was literally hours from being born when it happened, and it changed me. Instantly. When I was born, I had these red eyes. I began to talk at a very young age, and I remember experiences from when I was a month old."

"He actually began learning to talk and understand words while still in Charlie's womb," said Isis. "I know, because I was there and I could sense him and his thoughts."

The murmur grew, but it was pleasant. Max and Isis were favorites among everyone.

"Allow me to cut to the chase," said Isis. "We need more of us. People like Max and me. We live in Kingman and we're not going anywhere; our families are here. We can venture out for a few hundred miles and come back, but ultimately, if we ever hope to rid North America of the threat of the Hungerers and Mothers, we need more like us."

Max stepped forward. "The only way to accomplish this is to purposely expose pregnant women to the eye vapor of one of the Mothers, what you call the red-eyes."

A woman stood in the third row. Her belly was very large; a woman due to give birth any day. "I'll volunteer," she said.

A man beside her stood quickly and pulled her back down into her seat. She brushed his hand from her arm and stood again, shooting him a dirty look.

"I said I'll volunteer."

Isis smiled. "You're Jill Richman, aren't you?" she asked.

The woman nodded. "Yes."

"Before you commit to this, I want to explain something to you and everyone else. Max and I were born this way. Because of the state of the world, I wasn't around many other children as I grew up. Flex Sheridan Jr. is one, and Trina and Taylor were only seven and eight years old."

"Woo hoo!" yelled Trina from her seat, giving Isis a thumbs up.

Isis smiled back at her, and it seemed to break the tension. The crowd before Isis laughed, along with Flex and Gem.

"In short, they didn't make fun of us or try to make us feel as though we didn't belong," said Isis. "We've never been made to feel like freaks from any of you, either. It's important that you know that what happened in 2011, while it was devastating, it also did its part in eliminating negativity and distrust among the survivors. We all stand shoulder to shoulder, and when necessary, back to back, watching out for one another."

"There are pros and cons to being who and what we are," added Max. "With our abilities, we're called upon to use them to protect our friends, family and neighbors. It's not a burden; Isis and I both feel it's part of the reason we're here. We were the next logical step in the evolution of mankind to combat the threat of the moment. The living dead."

"We don't feel imposed upon," said Isis. "Our parents love us as yours love or once loved you. When we have to repel or call the Mothers and Hungerers, it is second nature to us. It's a part of our day, if you want to put it that way."

Jill had not yet returned to her seat. "I want to do this," she said. "I would be honored to have my son or daughter join you in protecting all of us."

A woman stood in the sixth row. It was Teressa Ainsley. "I might be willing," she said. "Do we have to get close to the … red-eyes?"

Hemp stood and went to the stage again. He did not get on, but Max handed him down the microphone.

"We've not used any artificial methods of transferring their eye vapor to a pregnant woman," he said. "The two times it's been done it was not intentional, obviously."

"So, the answer is yes?" Teressa said.

"To be sure the vapor's properties are adequately introduced into your system, I would say it is important that it be a direct transference," said Hemp.

"You can always wear a mask during the process," said Isis. "They'll be strapped down so you don't have any worries there, but that way you don't have to see what's going on."

"I'll do it too," said Teressa.

"Some of you may be called upon to leave here and venture out into another place to begin building there," said Isis.

Teressa and Jill looked at one another, then back at Isis. "Do we have to leave?" Jill asked.

"No, no," said Hemp, still holding the microphone. "We're still trying to operate under a constitutional republic. It will be your choice, but I want you to understand that when your child grows up – and that happens faster than with an ordinary child, as you can see – they will know what must be done, just as Max and Isis do. We want you to be prepared for the day your child tells you they're leaving, or that they want you to come with them."

"Do you feel like you have to kill them?" asked Teressa.

Max looked at her. "Kinda."

Isis said nothing.

"Can you elaborate?" asked Teressa.

"Like a gun is made to shoot, and a car is made to drive, I guess we were made for a purpose," said Max. "So the answer is yes. We're compelled to kill them and when we do, it feels like it's what we're supposed to be doing. It may sound weird to you, but it feels pretty good, but maybe in a different way than when you kill them."

He looked at Isis for a moment before continuing. "When they die, I don't know about Isis, but I get a feeling like a great big door is closing just a bit more." Max pantomimed this with his arms and clapped his hands together as the imaginary door closed.

Everybody smiled and Max smiled back.

Max paced to the opposite side of the stage and Flex saw Hemp watching him, smiling. He turned to see Charlie smiling as well. They were so proud of their kid. So was Flex.

"I think," said Max, "that when you kill them, there's a feeling of relief; that you killed them before they killed you. The feeling I get when I kill them is less emotional than that, maybe because I've grown up without ever knowing anything different. Those things have been the enemy since I was born, and since I was literally a baby, I realized I had the advantage over them. For that reason, I was never really that scared of them."

Five more women stood up. All pregnant.

Flex was surprised, but then it was logical. Seems mothers don't want their children to be afraid, and if making them like Max and Isis achieved that, maybe it was a gift.

Overall, fourteen women volunteered, and some were ready to give birth any time. The work would begin soon.

*****

"When were you going to tell us?" asked Gem.

Flex, Hemp and Charlie were in the room along with Trina, Taylor and Flex Jr.

"Mom, it's not that I was keeping it a secret," she said. "I hadn't decided for sure yet."

"Do you know where they're going?" asked Hemp.

"They don't even know yet, but they're gonna need us," said Taylor. "I think you know we're equipped to do this."

"That's not the point," said Gem. "I don't even know the point except I can't stand you going. Shit. You're my girls." Her eyes watered and she stood and went to the sink, pulling a paper towel off the roll and dabbing her eyes.

Trina got up and went to her. They were the same height now, only Trina was the spitting image of Flex's sister Jamie, which made him happy. Sometimes, when they lay in bed late at night, he would tell Gem that looking at Trina was like seeing his late sister again – before she changed into a horror.

"I know, mom. But I'll be careful. You've taught me how, you know."

Gem looked at her and took her face in her hands. "Urushiol and estrogen blend, WAT-6 and your Uzi," she said. "And a couple of drop-holstered Glocks."

"I'd venture out into the world with nothing less, mom. You know me."

"Flex, I blame you for this," said Gem.

"Me?" asked Flex Jr.

"No, your fucking dad."

"Now, now," said Flex. "We trained 'em, I guess we can take the blame."

"Wouldn't you rather a couple of capable, willing, brave huntresses than a couple of idiots who only thought they could handle it?"

"Don't bring the neighbor kids into this," said Trina, nudging Taylor with a smile.

"I know," said Taylor. "Our parents kick ass. Most of my friends can't hit the side of a barn with a shotgun."

"So ... three days? Is that the plan?" asked Flex.

"According to Isis, yes," said Trina. "And you're really not going to try to stop us?"

"Nope," said Gem.

"I might," said Charlie, who had been looking from Taylor to Trina, her eyes moist. "You two are like a part of me."

"And we'll be back, mom," said Taylor. She went to Charlie, who stood and pulled her into her arms.

"Take care of your brother," she said.

"If it's not the other way around," said Taylor. "Max is a force to be reckoned with."

"So are you, sweetie," said Charlie. "You too, Trini."

"I'm going to set your packs up," said Hemp. "I want you to be packed with at least enough food, water and

43

ammo to get you through a week. After that, you know how to find what you need."

"I'd prefer you just turn around and head back when your pack gets light," said Charlie. "If it feels right."

In the end, the decision had been made. Flex, Hemp, Gem and Charlie had to begin packing for their own, covert journey.

*****

Of the eighteen volunteers, five of them were due to give birth within a week, give or take another few days. For this reason, Hemp decided he could not wait until their return. If they were to follow Max and Isis, the babies might be born before their return, which would result in a missed opportunity.

"We've got to go out and capture a red-eye," said Hemp.

"Shouldn't be too hard," said Flex. "Ask Isis to point the way and I'll go with you."

"I did. She said the only direction she feels them is among those who refused to come. That in itself is unusual; she used to feel them in all directions."

Flex was inside the pit. All the hydraulics were fully extended, and he went from shaft to shaft, making sure there were no ridges on them that might cause a leak at the hydraulic seal. When he found one, he would take a piece of steel wool to it, followed by a clean swipe with a towel.

"Got it," he said. Hemp pushed a button and they all retracted, providing Flex with a clear, unobstructed path to reach the spring-loaded gate. As he approached it, Hemp called out, "Heads up, buddy."

Flex looked up and saw what Hemp's warning was about. Two rotters – standard issue – were staggering up the path from the highway, heading into the chute. They were about twenty yards up the trail and in under a minute, they would reach the gate.

"Don't use the hydraulics," said Flex. "I don't feel like a big cleanup."

"Your call," said Hemp. "Just be ready."

"Born ready, buddy," said Flex. "Just like John Wayne."

"Nothing changes," said Hemp, smiling. Then: "Okay, Flex."

The zombies got to the gate and Flex stood around ten feet behind it, facing them. When they touched the gate, Flex said, "Welcome to Kingman, Kansas. The local time is 2:35 PM Central, and the air temperature is 65 degrees. Your stay with us will be brief but painless."

With that, Flex walked toward a man in torn, bloodied bun-huggers and a flannel shirt and unsheathed his knife. A ragged pair of Nike tennis shoes remained on the thing's feet, and as it neared Flex, it's black teeth oozed something he could not identify.

Flex suddenly wished his knife was longer. He put it back in and withdrew his Glock from his right drop holster. He raised the gun and fired into its forehead, blowing blackish spray in a wide pattern behind the creature.

"So much for minimizing cleanup. Might as well put the system to a test, Flex," said Hemp. "Skirt around that chap and come out."

"Fine," said Flex. He straight-armed the other zombie, this one only wearing jeans. No shoes, no shirt. The dude would not get into Three Sister's Bar – the new one in Kingman – dressed like that. Victoria was the strict one.

Flex jogged up beside Hemp. "Go."

Hemp pushed one of the smaller buttons. The floor was divided into quadrants. If you had a full pit, you would hit the main button and all of the makeshift spears would protrude at once. If you had a couple of rotters in the same area, you could activate the appropriate quarter, sparing the remainder of the system the wear and tear.

The sharpened, stainless steel stake shot up through the creature's right foot, through his calf and came out just above his right knee. This impact spun his emaciated body around and he plunged face first onto another of the spikes. In mere seconds he hung there, pinned and dead, the sharpened rod protruding from the back of his skull.

"Notice any sticking?" asked Flex.

"Nope," said Hemp. "Perfect working order."

He retracted the shafts and the zombie's body seemed to remain suspended in the air for a moment before slapping the pit's dirt floor with a wet thud.

"We need to hit the road and find a red-eye like today. Wanna make a run in the Crown Vic?"

Hemp nodded. "Yes, but let's talk to Max or Isis beforehand. Perhaps we can narrow the hunting grounds."

*****

"Yeah, there are others," said Max. "We've been closing off the call lately though. Isis is uncomfortable about broadcasting right now. It was fine until they didn't respond. Now she's worried about them knowing where we are."

"I don't get it," said Charlie. Flex Jr. sat beside her, his eyes intense as he stared from one of them to the other. "What about the pit?"

"I think she's pretty sure there's more than will fit into the pit," said Max. "I get that feeling, too. When I try to sense them individually, I get overwhelmed," he said.

46

"Like instead of one or ten or a hundred, there's an entire wall of them with one blending into the next."

"Otherwise, does it feel normal, Max?"

"No," he said. "It feels as though they want to come but are confined in some way. I suppose they could be trapped somehow or other – something like our pit that someone else built – but their desire to submit to our call is being neutralized by something."

"So there's a chance that all you really need to do is go and kill them where they are," said Flex. "If they're being blocked."

"I don't want to throw water on that theory," said Gem, "but that would be ideal. They get there, a thousand zombies are trapped behind a fence, and they just shower them with our urushiol-estrogen blocking agent and come on back home."

"In our dreams," said Charlie.

"Exactly, said Gem. "The hands we're dealt are never ideal, and I doubt this is any exception. Max, can you point these guys to a nearby red-eye?"

"Hate to send you to Wichita again," he said. "But that's where you'll find them."

"How did I know that was coming?" asked Flex.

"And the Wichita lineman ..." sang Gem.

"... is still on the line," sang Flex, smiling as he finished the verse, his pitch wavering in and out of tune.

"Well," said Hemp. "We might as well get it out of the way now. Perhaps Flex can coax a red-eye to us with his soothing singing voice."

"We'd have better luck trying to immobilize them with cans of Silly String," said Gem. "Just sayin'."

"That's because fuck you," said Flex, with a wink. "Who's in?"

"I am," said Flex Jr.

"I remember the door episode," said Gem. "You'll just shoot her in the head. We need this one alive."

"I've been wanting to try something," he said. "Now I gotta go."

"Crown Vic. Ten minutes," said Gem.

*****

CHAPTER THREE

The fortified 2012 Crown Victoria, complete with ballistic steel exterior, a pivoting AK-47 on top, and a heavy-duty cowcatcher mounted on front was in great condition, even after all it had been through. While Gem drove it like a rental car, it was built for worse than she could give it, and there were a couple of excellent automotive technicians in town for when it did need attention.

One of them was Luke McCabe, whose family once owned an auto repair business in southern California. Luke seemed to like working on Gem's car, and Flex was pretty sure it was because he had the hots for Gem.

A good mechanic was even harder to find these days, so Flex never messed with him about it. Of course, the kid would fantasize about Gem. She was lean, toned and bronze-skinned, not to mention confident. There wasn't much else a man could want, but if there was, Gem had that, too.

For Hemp's part, he had some lab preparation to do to get ready for the new red-eye and the vapor transference procedure, and he wanted to sit for a while with the women who had volunteered, just to talk and make sure they were solid with their decision and not waffling. There was no going back once the exposure took place, so it was crucial.

Gem drove. Flex rode shotgun, Flex Jr. was in the back seat, and Charlie and Nelson tucked in beside him.

"I can use my original Subdudo if you need me to," said Nelson. "If you want one unhurt."

"We'll play it by ear," said Flex. "Depends on the situation."

"Luke asked me if we could stop by the bicycle shop on Trafalgar Street and grab him a mountain bike," said Flex Jr.

"My mechanic?" asked Gem.

"He does work for other people," said Flex.

"Somebody's jealous," said Gem, smiling. "He thinks Luke would rotate my tires anytime for free."

"Don't even start, you two," said Flex Jr. "It's disgusting."

They drove into Wichita and the difference between Kingman and the larger city to the east was instantly apparent.

"Look at 'em all," said Flex Jr., smiling.

"Exactly," said Charlie. "You can sure tell Max and Isis keep their shades drawn."

In the streets, wandering without purpose or focus, were abnormals by the score. Clearly the red-eyes in the city were not taking control of these inferior creatures, for they sensed no pull from Max and Isis toward Kingman. The gifted kids had once described what they did in their minds to stop the siren call to the zombies as drawing the shades. It was some sort of mental gate that they could close off, preventing the red-eyes from knowing where they were. It was a process they were incapable of as infants, which is why their very existence was so dangerous to their parents and guardians in those early months.

If the pregnant volunteers went through with their commitment, Flex wondered how they would deal with it again. It was similar to having full-grown kids attending college, then having brand new babies all over again. Only worse. Way worse.

All of the issues that hadn't been dealt with in so many years would be back in the forefront. The difference being, it was far more serious and the potential for disaster was monumentally greater with the number of residents in Kingman.

On the plus side, this time they would have Max and Isis, who would be pulling and pushing the Mothers and Hungerers as they willed. This time, it would not just be a bunch of newbie uninfecteds trying to figure out why there were hundreds of zombies at the door, as Bug had experienced in his fortified bunker.

Flex Jr. leaned toward his side window, scanning the street for their target. "Just a buncha pink eyes, damnit!" he said, frustrated.

"It's not like they just step out and say hey," said Gem. "Unless they've got a goal, they stay out of sight for the most part."

"Checking buildings would take too long," said Flex. "We might have to wait until dark. They can't hide their shining eyes."

"You can't hide, your shining eyes," sang Gem, to the tune of the Eagles' Lyin' Eyes.

As she cruised down the street, easing the car into the oncoming lanes to skirt around vehicles, Flex picked it up.

"And your silky straight hair is a thin disguise," he sang.

"Seems by now," sang Flex Jr., "your rotten brain would realize."

"I think Red Angel Dragnet is a better song to parody," said Charlie. "The Clash."

Nelson spoke up. "We are kinda setting up a dragnet, huh? But still, there ain't no way to hide your stonedy red eyes," finished Nelson.

Gem laughed. "Stonedy? We makin' up words now, are we Nel?"

"Ha ha, Gem. I make lots of stuff up, right?" said Nelson. "Subdudo, stuff like that. I suppose I coulda just said stony, but they look stoned, right? So they're stonedy lookin'."

Flex had a smile on his face that he could not wipe out, but a second later, it disappeared on its own. "Hey, Gem. Stop the car."

She applied the brakes and the Ford rolled to a stop.

"See? On the corner up ahead there. Against that low wall."

They all craned their necks to see. "I don't see what you're talking about, babe."

"I do," said Nelson. "Look lower. She's sitting down."

"I see her now," said Gem and Flex Jr. at the same time.

The creature sat, her straight, brown hair falling over her face, obscuring her features, including her eyes. In the daylight, it was not possible to see whether they were red, but if she were alive, the Hungerers on the street would be piled on top of her, tearing at her flesh.

This was no live girl.

"Did she move?" asked Gem.

"I thought I saw her head move," said Flex. "Just slightly."

"Look," said Charlie. "Look at them."

As the group looked on, the tattered rotters once scattered around the streets began moving toward the seated girl. Initially, it was imperceptible, but as they drew closer to her, it was clear what was happening.

They were moving in – likely at her call – to shield her.

"How many?" asked Flex Jr. "If we hurry we can take them."

"There's more than ... fifteen, I'd say," said Gem. "But we don't know how many are just around that corner behind her, either."

"We're on WAT-5, guys," said Charlie. "Let's move before it's too late."

"Plow through 'em, mom," said Flex Jr.

"What?" she asked, looking at her son.

"You've got the cowcatcher, mom! Floor it and clear them out. We'll chase her down."

Gem didn't wait for consensus. She put her foot to the floor and everyone held on.

The Crown Vic's engine roared as the tires spun, then gained traction. The Ford shot forward, closing the gap between the group of rotters, their controlling Mother, and the fortified vehicle.

Suddenly the ragtag cluster of walking dead rotters tightened and began moving away from the street. Before the Crown Vic reached the group, they had moved several feet to the west, showing that the piece of sidewalk where they first spotted the Mother was now vacant.

She was in their midst; being protected by her decaying puppets as they clustered around her.

"Jump the curb!" shouted Nelson. "Gem, it's the only way you'll stop them!"

"Jesus Christ," she muttered. "If I fuck the rims, we're done!"

53

"There!" shouted Flex, pointing. "There's a handicap ramp cut in. Aim for that!"

Gem readjusted and hit the gas again. Now just thirty yards from the tattered group, the Crown Vic hit the ramp and drove up onto the narrow sidewalk, barely missing a traffic signal stanchion.

Flex saw the side of the building just inches from his door and slid down the window, pulling the side mirror in. The window went up just as the cowcatcher slammed into the first several of the many bodies.

The angled, steel grid caught five abnormals and threw them hard into the wall of the building, their bodies tearing in two at the waist as they were twisted apart like human-sized Twizzlers, leaving black-red spatter smears behind as they flopped to the ground, their faces still hungry; mouths still gnashing.

Gem spun the wheel to the left and tried to take out another seven rotters, now rounding the corner, clearly following their mistress.

The Ford caught three of them, but at thirty miles per hour, Gem was unable to crank the wheel right, and the rest of the group slid around the corner as she jumped the far curb. Straight ahead of her was a crashed Smart Car that the Crown Victoria hit head on, the cowcatcher lifting the small car's front end up and flipping it over. When it landed, it spun like a giant, metal dreidel.

Gem cranked right and the Crown Vic's rear end slammed into the spinning Smart Car again, doubling its speed.

"Notes to self, dude!" shouted Nelson. "Don't buy a Smart Car, and don't ride with Gem anymore!"

"Don't be a pussy, Nelson!" shouted Gem, flooring the Ford. The rotters ahead pushed into a shattered set of double glass doors, and Gem reached it and slammed on her brakes, throwing the car in park.

"Whoa, mom!" shouted Flex Jr., a huge smile on his face. "Wow!"

Gem looked back and gave him a quick smile. "I can only do this because of the ballistic steel," she said. "Don't get any ideas or I'll cut you off before you ever get your license. Grab your crossbow."

"Fuckin' A!" he said, checking his watch. "We got like four and a half more hours of WAT-5. We should stick around here and put it to use."

"First off, remember it doesn't work perfectly on the red-eyes, buddy,' said Flex. "If you act differently than the regular horde, she's gonna figure you out."

"And don't let her see your weapon," said Charlie. "She'll recognize it and by association, she'll know you're not one of them."

"Got the eye drops, Gem?" asked Flex.

Gem reached into a vest pocket. She withdrew a small, plastic tube and pinched it hard between her fingers. It cracked, and she shook it.

She then unscrewed the cap, tilted her head back and applied one drop of the glowing, pink liquid to each eye.

She kept her eyes closed for a moment, and when she opened them, her eyes were luminescent pink.

"I'm a zombie," she said. "Want your brains."

"Freaky," said Flex. "Never get used to that."

Two years after they moved to Kingman, Hemp figured out that part of the recognition factor for the red-eyes was the fact that the eyes of the uninfecteds did not glow. It was, to the smarter females, as obvious as if you were missing your entire head. It was far more difficult for them to identify you as human if you had the same glowing pink eyes as the masses.

Hemp experimented with various components until he came up with the right color with a chemiluminescence that would work for around an hour.

Everyone else doctored their eyes and Gem tossed the container into the street, a tiny trail of glowing pink streaking behind it.

The container it came in had two small compartments, and just like a glow stick, it lasted as long as it lasted and the container could not be re-sealed. After the first use, you just tossed it.

Gem pulled Queenie, her Uzi, from the car and slung it on her back. She kept a Ruger .380 in her hand, and the gun was almost small enough that it couldn't be seen from just a few feet away.

"Keep that crossbow down, Flexy," she said. "Until you see a clear shot where she's not looking at you, I want that behind your back. All these precautions won't mean shit if she sees your weapon."

"You know I know all this, mom, right?"

"Repetition, kid," said Charlie. "*Right*? What do I always tell you? We gotta drill this shit into your head while you still think you know everything. I guess maybe we figure if you hear it enough, you'll begin to think it's your idea and you'll actually do it."

"Ha ha," he said. "Your psychology won't work on me."

"Meanwhile, the crossbow's on your back, so whatever," said Charlie, smiling. "Use a knife anyway. Got that, everyone?"

"She's right," said Gem. "Bring your guns but have knives ready. Red-eye hears a shot and you can kiss her goodbye."

"Blah," said Flex Jr. "Nelson can kiss her."

"Stars for me, bra," said Nelson, ignoring the remark.

"Me and Nelson in front," said Flex. "Then Flex Jr., then you guys," he said, indicating to Gem and Charlie.

"It's a trade off," said Charlie. "Next time I lead in."

"No argument," said Flex. "Now zip it, everyone." He moved through the door. The room was only lit by ambient daylight streaming through the shattered glass doors, and there were tons of dark shadows just beyond where the light reached.

The room just inside appeared to be vacant, so the red-eye had clearly led her minions deeper into the building. From the outside it appeared to be a single story, but could have a low-ceilinged storage area above.

Flex instinctively knew they had brought too many people with them; they only needed him and either Gem or Nelson, but much of the reason he'd agreed to the large party was in deference to the need to get the hell out of Kingman once in a while, even if it was dangerous elsewhere.

It was easy to get lackadaisical after surviving a world occupied by the walking dead for nearly fifteen years, but it only took one dumb move to end your life. He and Gem had already made those moves and survived – not in any small part due to Hemp – but Flex didn't like risking his son. He was as adept at killing zombies as a 2011 kid his age was at working their way through Mortal Kombat, but the stakes were so much higher here.

They moved in and came across a large, curved reception desk. On the front it said, "Preston Manufacturing," with a drawing of what looked like a rake.

Flex knew the name. They made gardening tools, both hand and machine. The buildings were all connected on the street, so you could not really judge the size of a building or company until you got inside.

He waved them forward, leaning to look over the counter. A fully decomposed body lay on the floor behind the desk, the clothing torn to shreds all around it, and Flex instantly knew the woman to whom the sling back high heels belonged did not die of natural causes.

His Bowie knife in his right hand, Flex moved toward a door on the right behind the desk. He motioned Flex Jr. to stay with him and the girls to approach an identical door on the same wall but twenty feet to his left.

The light was fading more as they moved deeper inside. He could still see Gem's glowing eyes, and he knew she could see his, so he nodded and pushed the door. It swung in, and he saw that Gem and Charlie's did, too.

As they entered what was a large factory floor, Flex could see rows of equipment. The ceiling of the room was dotted with filthy skylights that still allowed enough filtered sunlight in to make the room visible.

Flex recognized the two machines nearest to him as wood lathes, and because a shovel handle was still mounted in the machine, he knew it was for their manufacture.

His eyes fell to the wall where there were rows of bins containing stacks of shovels and rakes, hoes and edgers, post-hole diggers, spades and every other wood or fiberglass-handled gardening tool you could ask for.

"Stop and listen," whispered Flex. "These things aren't good at being quiet."

They stood for nearly a full minute before the first sound came. Everyone's head jerked toward the far left rear of the room as they faced it. Now Gem led the way, right down the middle. She instinctively ducked alongside the machines as she walked.

When she tripped and staggered forward hard, her right leg bent at an awkward angle, Flex was sure she was going to face plant.

Somehow, Gem threw her left leg beneath her and stopped the inevitable fall. She looked back and everyone saw what she'd tripped on.

A bag of bones with a bashed in skull.

Despite this, the room did not smell of decay; it smelled instead of dust and old grease.

Flex came up beside Gem and now Nelson, Charlie and Flex Jr. followed behind. Each held their blades and Nelson had his stars.

As they reached the back of the building, the rotters stood nearly motionless. Instinctively, the five visitors began a slow, shuffling walk. It was how they completed the masquerade. WAT-5 and pink eyes, with a bit of shambling to top off the ruse.

Flex turned and waved everyone close to him. They complied and he whispered, "Just push your way into the crowd, nice and easy. She's in there somewhere. Just gotta get through the bodyguards." He looked at his son and whispered, "You sure you're ready for this, buddy? You're more of a long-distance zombie killer, right?"

"I can do it, dad."

"Remember," said Flex. "Knife under the chin and deep into the temporal lobe, or in the soft spot at the base of the back of their skulls, straight into the cerebellum. One by one we'll drop them until she's exposed." He looked at Gem, Charlie and Nelson. "Clear?"

They all nodded, and Nelson said, "Dude, you've been brushing up on your brain parts. Very good."

"Thanks, Nel," said Flex. "Gem, you got the cuffs?"

"The fur-lined or the others?" she asked, holding them up.

"Very funny," said Flex. "I hope we're approaching this with the seriousness it deserves."

"Holy fuck," said Charlie. "Flex, you know we never approach anything with the seriousness it deserves. And yet … here we are."

"Touché," he said. "Let's get this done."

They moved in to execute their plan.

*****

They spread out enough to each have their own working area. Now there were no fewer than twenty rotters between where they believed the red-eye to be and where they stood.

Flex moved in, pulled the shoulder of a female backward and slid his long, curved blade into her brain. He was shocked how easily it went in, and poked through the top of her head. She slumped to the ground.

As he approached another, he saw Gem take her first. They had seen it a number of times and it was heartbreaking. The boy could have been no more than thirteen; about their son's age. His hair was wispy and as thin as a duckling's feathers.

The former boy's nose was missing, as was his left ear, the rotting canal exposed. Gem made quick work of him, sliding the knife beneath his chin and lowering him to the floor slowly by holding onto his deteriorating shirt as he fell.

A heart the size of Texas beat inside that woman, and Flex remembered again how much he loved her.

Nelson used two quick Subdudo moves on another male and as his legs buckled, his head fell onto Nelson's blade, which he held straight up at his waist.

Flex Jr. was focused. He had already taken out a petite female in a gore-stained bathrobe, only he jammed his knife straight through the back of her skull and into what Flex figured was the parietal lobe.

To each his own. If he was comfortable with that method, Flex was good with it.

Meanwhile, Charlie was about to take down her fourth. She was no-nonsense about it, approaching, jamming, twisting and extracting. She also gave them a little toss behind her when she was done so they wouldn't clog up her forward movement.

Flex dropped down into a crouch and started pushing through the abnormals toward the wall, turning his shoulders to maintain as narrow a mass as possible. He wanted to get eyes on her.

Sensing the wall was nearing, he pushed to the front and saw her legs. Gray but smooth, less pocked and trashed than the others. She stood perfectly still while the rest pushed against one another, unable to simply stand immobile, something within them forcing them to be moving, always moving, like a shark seeking prey in the ocean's depths.

The bodies pressed in on him and Flex felt a sort of panic washing over him. It took him by surprise.

A premonition? No matter, he needed relief. Flex found he could hardly breathe in the dense crowd, and he raised his knife, sliding it easily into the skulls of the three closest to him. They collapsed to the floor and he turned back to his prey.

She was gone. His eyes searched, but only legs covered in tattered clothing shuffled around him.

A sense of panic overtook him. *Where was she?*

He heard running. Feet slamming pavement. Shoed feet. Not her. The others didn't run, so who was it?

"She's gone!" he shouted, now pushing himself back through the dispersing infecteds. They were moving off to the sides now as though without direction. Flex leapt over one body and tripped on the next, dropping him to the ground hard.

"Flex!" It was Gem. The breath had gotten knocked out of him and he couldn't answer, but she didn't wait. "Where's Flexy? Where is he?"

"I'm here, mom!" shouted their son, and hearing his voice, Flex could not have been happier. He pushed himself back to his feet, felt a sharp pain in his sciatica, and straightened up slowly. When he did, he saw his son standing atop a table saw twenty feet behind them.

Nelson ran up beside Flex. "Dude, you okay?"

"I'm good, man. But –"

Nelson didn't wait to hear the rest. He interrupted Flex and yelled, "Flexy, bro! Get over here! You know never to leave the group, kid!"

Gem was deep in the group, still taking them out, but seconds later she emerged. "Now, Flex Sheridan Jr.! Hurry!" she shouted.

He wasn't looking at his mother or his father. He pointed. "I saw her over there! The one from outside!"

"Fuck this," said Flex, running toward him. Gem, Charlie and Nelson followed. When he was just ten feet away, Flex saw his son raise the crossbow, his eyes wide. He was aiming low. Way too low.

He fired, but the creature was in mid air and landed on top of him, knocking him backward flat on the piece of machinery.

Things moved into slow motion for Flex. He now felt like he was running through molasses, unable to get to his boy. The creature's silken hair floated down over her face as she buried her mouth into his son's neck.

"Aghhhhhhhhhh!" shouted Flex, on her before he even realized he'd reached them, and with both arms he tore her away from his son and threw her emaciated body into a large drill press next to the table saw.

Flex no longer saw or heard anything that went on. He looked at his bloodied, teenaged son, just about to turn fourteen years old, and realized the worst.

Gem's cries brought Flex out of his dumb stupor, as she dropped down atop him and tried to lift his shoulders. His eyes were open, staring into hers, and Flex crawled up to be beside her.

Flex Jr.'s neck was ripped open, and blood gushed from his jugular vein. Flex instinctively slapped his hand over it, stopping the flow.

"Mom ..." his voice bubbled from his mouth. "Dad," he managed. "I'm . . . I'm sorry ... I fucked up."

Flex pulled a bottle of urushiol blend from his jacket pocket and poured it over the boy's neck and his hand, and said, "Hang on, son. Hold on, kid. We'll get you to the car and back to Hemp and Doc Scofield. Just hold on, Flex."

"I didn't want ... to kill her," he said, barely understandable now. "In her legs ..."

His voice drifted into silence.

Flex shook his shoulders even as he eyed the mortal injury. "Flex, son. Hang on for us, buddy."

Gem whispered, "Oh, Flex," and dropped her head onto her son's chest, crying. "Look ... beneath him."

Flex leaned over to look under his son's body. The sixteen-inch circular table saw blade was embedded in Flex Jr.'s back.

"God! Oh, God!" cried Gem, and this time Charlie came running from across the warehouse. She climbed up beside them and screamed. Her scream became one long shriek, and the shriek turned into sobs.

"Oh, my God, Gem, Flex," she managed. "Oh, my God, not our Flexy." Her face contorted as she stared at the boy Flex knew she loved like her own son.

He was gone. His eyes remained wide open, revealing the brown eyes Gem had given him. His pupils were saucers, and Gem's body heaved with shuddering sobs as she seemed to lose all strength.

She let go of her son and her body slid down the dead boy's legs, off the machine and to the floor.

"I want to kill her," said Nelson, from behind them.

Flex looked over to see the red-eye in cuffs, Nelson holding her by the back of her neck, his eyes pouring tears as he stared at Flex Sheridan Jr., dead on the machine.

Flex looked at her legs. Flexy had done what he tried to do, only it was too late by the time he fired.

His intention had been to fire a single bolt through both of her legs so that she could no longer walk. Now, as Flex looked at the creature that had ended his son's life, the broken arrow jutted from both legs, just above the knee.

His aim had been true. His last shot was on target.

Too late to save his life.

*****

Flex had no idea how long they sat there in silence. The captive red-eye was still alive only because Gem had withdrawn into herself and wasn't really there at that moment. Flex had removed their son from the saw blade and rested him in her lap, and she cradled the dead boy, her tears of pain and sorrow running nonstop.

Flex felt dead inside. As dead and useless as any of the creatures they hunted every day. Nelson and Charlie had taken out their aggressions by killing every remaining

64

rotter in the building, and now the rancid, stinking bodies lay strewn all around them.

Nelson had cuffed the red-eye to one of the machines. Once in a while, Gem's eyes would focus on her and a look of malice would emerge through her tremendous sadness.

Then it would be gone, Flex thought, possibly with the realization that *they* had come hunting for *her*, as a matter of fact.

Flex knew the reason they took all the precautions they did – the WAT-5, the urushiol, the other weapons – was because this was a potentially deadly mission; capturing red-eyes.

They had lost others since coming to Kingman. Flex never imagined losing his son, or what it would feel like, except in the most abstract terms, and only briefly.

Flex's mind flashed back, as he had at least once every two minutes, to what had happened, second-by-second. Why had he ducked into the crowd? Why had he gotten suddenly claustrophobic and taken his eyes off her?

He knew in his heart it was his fault, but if he told Gem that, she would not forgive him.

He pushed himself to his feet, walked over to Gem and bent down to scoop his dead son into his arms.

He started walking toward the door. Without looking back, he said, "It's gonna be dark soon. Let's get this bitch back to Kingman."

"She rides in the trunk or I'll kill her," said Gem, her face a mask of death.

Nobody answered her.

*****

Charlie drove the Crown Vic back to Kingman. Nelson rode up front with her, and Flex sat in the back seat

65

with Gem and the body of their son, whom she cradled in her arms. Flex found himself stroking his cold hand.

At one point, about two miles from the gates of town, Gem leaned over and rested her head on Flex's shoulder. Her tears came again and he found his matched those of the woman he loved more than any before her.

Flex silently gave thanks that Gem still wanted to touch him at all.

Flex looked up as the guards rolled open the gate and waved them in, and their faces turned somber when they looked into the car and saw the sadness in his and Gem's eyes, and their mortally wounded son in their laps.

"Pull it as close to the house as you can," said Flex, as they neared home.

"I will," said Charlie.

As the car came to a stop, Flex felt something move. His son's hand. It twitched.

His heart raced. "Flexy? Flexy, are you … son!"

Flex threw open the door and looked up to see the hope in Gem's eyes, and he reached in and pulled his son into his arms, got him out, and rested him on the ground on his back.

Now all of his limbs were moving. Flex put his hands on his boy's face as Gem dropped down beside him, and with his thumbs, he raised Flex Jr.'s eyelids.

Pinkish white nothingness stared back.

The boy growled.

"Oh, God, no!" screamed Gem. "We let this happen, Flex! Oh, my God! We let this happen to him! Stop it! Stop it!"

She stood and ran toward the house. She reached the door and struggled with the knob, finally getting it, and charging inside, letting it slam against the wall.

Flex looked down in horror at his reanimated son, his teeth gnashing, his throat gurgling.

Nelson dropped down and pushed Flex away, his strength surprising Flex. Flex fell back and pressed his fists to his temples and stared at the sky. A scream erupted from him, and he let it come. He was screaming at the world, at the red-eyes, at God, at anyone who would listen.

The next thing Flex felt were Nelson's hands on his shoulders, pulling him up off the ground. He swiped at his eyes and looked at his son's body, lying supine.

A narrow, black-red wound adorned Flex Jr.'s forehead just at the hairline. He lay still; at peace.

The worst day of Flex Sheridan's life had arrived.

He got off the ground and dragged himself into the house with no idea how he would continue on.

*****

CHAPTER FOUR

Gem was in their bedroom lying down. When Flex walked up and stood in the doorway, watching her, he heard her sobs grow more pronounced.

"Flex," her weak voice came. "Tell me it was a bad dream. Please tell me it didn't really happen."

Flex broke down, his eyes flooding with tears, and he staggered to the bed and sat on the edge. His body shuddered with grief, and Gem's cries were masked by his own.

He didn't know how much time had passed; whether it was ten minutes or two hours, but eventually he felt a hand on his back. He started, then turned to see Gem sitting up behind him.

His eyes met hers, and her sadness at first consumed him. For a brief, fleeting moment, Flex felt as though he could remember every detail of every second they had ever spent together.

Each second was important, not to be forgotten. Seeing her there at Jamie's house when the world seemed to have gone haywire. Embracing her after burying little Jesse. The two of them, finding Hemp in that jail cell, and again, Flex and Gem, the indomitable pair, finding Charlie in that hospital storage closet.

Making love, conceiving Flex Jr. Watching her give birth to him and later, dancing with him in her arms to Elton John's Can You Feel the Love Tonight.

He leaned back and rested his head in her lap, and she leaned forward and put her cheek to his, her hair draping down over his face; the two of them hiding away from the rest of the world.

Exhaustion must have taken them both, for when Flex awoke, it was three hours later. Gem still slept, and he touched her gently, wanting to let her sleep, but needing to have her with him.

She did not awaken and he saw her cheeks were wet. She had not forgotten her sorrow in her dreams; still, she cried. Flex eased himself off the bed, unfolded a light blanket, and covered his wife.

He left the room.

Hemp and Charlie awaited him in the living room. When he walked in, Hemp stood and hurried to him, hugging him.

"I'm so, so sorry, Flex." It was all he could get out before he, too, broke down. Still, through his unabashed tears, he managed, "I couldn't have asked for a more loving Godson, Flex. I loved him as my own."

Flex held onto Hemp, hugging him tightly. This was his best friend in the world besides Gem, and their shared sorrow seemed to drain some of his away.

"I can't believe it, Hemp," he said. "I saw him there, and then she was there, and it was –"

"It was nobody's fault," said Hemp, interrupting him. "Please don't carry this on your shoulders."

"God, Hemp!" he said. "How can I not carry it? I was there! He wasn't even fourteen! I'm his father and I should have kept my eye on him!"

Hemp took him by the shoulders and Flex's tears erupted again. "And he knew how to use that crossbow, and he was expert with a blade, too," said Hemp. "Flexy was an excellent fighter and he gave you no reason to believe he couldn't defend himself, Flex. You and Gem taught him well, and he had been doing it for years, Flex. For years he has defended not only himself, but many, many others in Kingman."

Flex nodded and said nothing. He looked up from the floor and swiped his eyes, and noticed Charlie standing beside them, her eyes red and swollen.

"You told him you loved him every day, Flex," she said. "I know, because I heard you say it. Gem, too. He grew up and had more love in his life and in his heart than any fourteen-year-old, or twenty-year-old, or even any sixty-year-old. You let him know what love was, and he shared that with all of us."

Hemp slipped away and Charlie embraced Flex. He realized his tears had stopped. He took a deep breath and exhaled, managing a very weak, insincere smile.

"Where's Trina?" he asked. "And Tay and Max. I have to tell 'em before it gets to them some other way. Did you put his body somewhere?"

"He's in my lab," said Hemp. "Nel wrapped him and drove him over in the car. Nobody saw."

His face was strange, though. Flex saw something behind his eyes.

"What is it?" he asked, looking at Charlie, who held the same expression as her husband.

"Flex," Charlie said. "I don't know how to tell you this."

Flex shook his head. "There's nothing you can tell me that's any worse than what I've just been through, so just say it."

"Trina's gone," said Charlie. "She went with Max, Isis and Taylor."

It seemed as if every ounce of blood in Flex's body rushed to his face, and he felt the pressure and the redness all at once. It was like his head was on the brink of exploding.

"When? Where did they go?" he asked.

"They didn't tell anyone, Flex. They –"

"They what? Did they go on a supply run or did they … did they … did they go to find the ones they've been calling?"

Charlie nodded. "We left here and searched for them in town, but when we couldn't find them, we came back here and checked her room."

"We found this note on the dresser, Flex," said Hemp, pulling a piece of paper from his pocket. "You'd have been in no condition to deal with it then, and I'm not sure you are now."

"Give it to me," said Flex.

Hemp did, and Flex wiped at his blurred eyes, blinked them twice to clear his vision, and looked at it.

The note was in Trina's bad cursive writing. It read:

Mom and Dad,

We left while you were away because we didn't want you to change your mind and tell us no. Max and Isis said this is important. We'll be safe. I love you both. Love, Trini.

Flex paced back and forth, staring at them. "Hemp, where were you? Who else knew about this? Jesus, what time did they go, does anybody know?"

"I was at my lab preparing for the red-eye you were going to bring back, and I haven't seen Trina all day, so I have no idea when they left."

"What vehicle did they take?"

"Isis' H3 is missing," said Charlie.

"Goddamnit!" shouted Flex, slamming his fists down on a table.

Isis, while only 14 years of age, did not look so. She was over six feet tall and usually kept her hair pulled back in a long, blonde ponytail. She was as developed as any 28-year-old, revealing to all that it was not only her mind that had been affected by the red-eye vapor.

All of this hadn't been easy on Bug. He was constantly trying to push young men away from Isis, but there wasn't an issue there; Isis could handle herself.

"Flex, we've readied Gem's car," said Hemp. "It's got a trunk full of ammo, and by that, I'm sure you know I mean all types."

Charlie jumped in. "Nelson, Dave and Punch want to go with us, so they got Punch's car loaded up."

"What about Serena?" asked Hemp.

"She's staying here with Ben," said Charlie. "I don't blame her. If Max and Tay were here, I wouldn't be going anywhere either, and I'd do what I could to make Gem stay."

Ben was Dave and Serena's son, who was just about to turn 13 years old. He was a nice, quiet kid who had known the difference between an abnormal and a living human being since he was a year old. Flex could not help but think of his son when he thought of Ben; even though Ben was a bit younger than Flexy, he had been the best friend to Flex and Gem's son that Max could not be.

The thought made Flex consider, for the first time, the downside to creating more humans like Max and Isis; Max had matured so fast that while it was clear he was fond of Flex Jr., their interests could not have been more different. While Flexy was asking his dad if they could pick up some comic books at a drug store, Max exercised his telepathic abilities in order to annihilate more of the walking dead.

Isis and Max's lives would always be more serious; more purposeful, in a way. There had been no time or desire for typical childhood interests like puzzles, dodge ball and hopscotch.

"Doc Scofield wanted to go as well," said Hemp, snapping Flex out of his deep thoughts. "But I convinced him to stay here and handle the transference procedure with the red-eye's vapor and our volunteers. That can't wait, because we don't know how long we'll be gone."

Flex felt the change within him. If he thought about his son he knew he would cry again, but there was nothing anyone could do about that. Trina and Taylor, not to mention Max and Isis, were out there, and whether they knew it or not, they were getting backup.

"I need to go wake Gem," he said.

"It's dark out, Flex," said Charlie. "And you know I'd never suggest it ordinarily, but Max and Isis are not your typical kids. They *will* be okay, and they'll take care of Trini and Tay."

"What she's saying is maybe we should wait until daylight," said Hemp. "We know approximately where they're going anyway."

Flex shook his head. "Here's the deal," he said. "We saw that it only takes a split second for something to go really wrong. The reason we're not leaving tomorrow is because our mission, as I see it, is to get to where Max and Isis are a split second before they need us rather than a split second after it's too late."

"Fair enough,' said Charlie.

Flex wasn't done. "The minute I tell Gem about this, she's going on a rampage, and you know I'm not guessing when I tell you that. You're lucky the car's packed, because she's going to be in it and her foot to the floor the minute she knows, and I won't blame her."

"I'll leave it to you, then, said Hemp. "I'll radio Punch and tell him to be ready to roll."

Flex nodded. He took a deep breath. What he was about to do was the second worst thing he would do all day.

*****

Gem sat in the passenger seat of the Crown Victoria, staring through the window. Flex drove, which was the first sign that everything was topsy-turvy.

Gem never let anyone else drive her baby if she was inside.

Flex eased the Crown Vic through the gate and watched in his rear view as Punch guided his purple GTO through and the men closed it behind them. He looked over at his wife.

Her eyes were dry and clear. She had her Uzi across her lap and a bottle of water between her legs, but she had not taken a drink. She couldn't be far from dehydration after her hours of crying.

"Drink that, babe," said Flex.

She looked at Flex, her face expressionless now, and then down at the bottle. She pulled it out, unscrewed the cap, and tilted it up to her lips.

She drained the bottle and threw it on the floor.

Flex nodded, satisfied, and said nothing.

He drove slowly enough to be careful, but not so slowly that Gem would freak out and insist on driving herself. He had a vague idea of where to go. Max and Isis had told him which direction they were being pulled, and not by mere pointing. They specifically stated that it was due northwest of Kingman.

How far was the part of the equation to which they were not privy. As the two had grown older and more powerful, they could feel the presence of the other zombies for months before their siren call would pull them to Kingman and into the pit. They could be a hundred miles or a thousand miles away.

Grass had begun to grow through the cracks in almost all the highways over the last decade and a half. That made it more difficult to see obstructions in the roadway, but this early section of the highway was frequented by many from Kingman, so was not as bad. The farther away they drove, the more intense the challenge would be not to crash into some unseen obstacle.

Flex eased off the gas slightly and drove on through the night.

*****

"Stop the car," said Gem, leaning forward in her seat.

Flex looked out the window and saw nothing. "What's up?"

"Stop the car!" she shouted. "Flex! Now!"

Flex hit the brake hard, and Gem flung the door open, grabbed her Uzi and jumped out, immediately breaking into a run.

Punch's GTO slid up and stopped about ten yards behind them.

"What the fuck?" asked Flex, reaching down for his Daewoo and flying out of the car.

Nelson called, "Dude, where's she going?"

"I don't know what she saw," said Flex. "Gem!" he screamed, scanning the packed, Kia car dealership parking lot.

"Where the hell did she go?" he asked. "By the time I got out I lost her. Did she run into the lot?"

"She did!" shouted Dave, scooping up his weapon from the GTO.

Machine gun fire erupted and they all charged toward the parking lot.

"Gem!" Flex shouted again, but she did not come and she did not answer. The lot was packed full and Gem had disappeared among the small SUVs. Flex scanned each row as he ran along and did not see her.

"You guys break off to the left!" he shouted to Dave, Punch and Nelson. "Hemp, Charlie! Work these aisles!"

"This sucks!" shouted Charlie. "We're not even on WAT-5!"

"Let's all keep that in mind," said Hemp. "Charlie, keep your distance if you see any."

"Gem saw some biters or she wouldn't have done this," said Charlie, hefting her crossbow and cutting down an aisle between the Sorrentos and the Sportages, both taller cars behind which anything could hide.

"Everyone, be vocal so we keep track of one another!" shouted Hemp.

Gunfire sounded again and Flex saw sparks flying off a car about a hundred yards ahead. He broke into a full run and soon heard other footfalls behind him as Hemp and Charlie pursued.

Off to his left he caught sight of the other three men, zigzagging through the lot in the same general direction as them, but closer to the front of the large, glass showroom.

When they drew to within fifty yards of the showroom, Flex saw Gem standing there, her Uzi on the ground beside her and her 9mm in her hand, firing on an empty chamber.

The creatures moved toward her. There must have been a sales meeting inside that dealership showroom back on that fateful Sunday in 2011, for around twelve of the most business casual zombies Flex had ever seen were closing in on her, shambling over the shattered glass of the showroom window, their faint, pink eyes focused on their prey.

"Gem! Run!" shouted Flex, unable to run any faster. He would not get to her before the infecteds did.

Gem did not acknowledge his call; she just held her expended Glock out, pulling the trigger over and over, the moans and snarls of the creatures drowning out the useless clicking of her empty firearm.

Two rotters were within five feet of Gem – and closing. Flex raised his Daewoo, but an arrow pierced the eye of a man in a red Fucillo Kia shirt, dropping him in a heap.

Gem stared at the thing blankly. Flex finally reached her and grabbed her by the shoulder, pulling her backward. Gem fell to the ground and he immediately felt bad, but there was more to worry about.

Another explosion sounded off to their left, and out of the corner of his eye, Flex saw the entire front wall of the showroom explode, raining down flat-square chunks of tempered glass like crystalline hail, shimmering under the moonlight like a million egg-laying grunion on a southern California beach.

They saw Punch, Nelson and Dave charge inside, their weapons blazing, thinning the predators at their source.

Hemp and Charlie had now reached the horde that had already left the building and focused on Gem, and Charlie fired several perfectly aimed bolts, taking another four down. Flex sprayed his K-7 along the crowd, blasting crowns off brittle skulls, tossing several of them back toward the showroom.

Hemp did his part, too, using the Heckler & Koch for all it was worth before lowering it and scanning the lot.

It appeared that the *Kia Super Sunday Sale Event* was over and there was no more staff left to handle any new patrons.

Flex turned and held his breath. Gem was on her knees, straddling one of the creatures lying on its back with an arrow protruding from its cheek. Her arm raised and lowered over and over, stabbing the flesh-eating humanoid in the chest, face and neck.

Just behind Gem a large male with half a leg crawled toward her, and he was directly between Charlie and Flex. If he fired, he could kill Charlie and vice-versa.

"Charlie, down! Now!"

Charlie dropped flat on the ground and Flex swung the Daewoo around and opened up the chamber.

The rounds were not enough to push the creature backward, but as it collapsed onto Gem, shocking her out of her stupor, its bullet-riddled body was of no danger to his distraught wife.

As it landed on Gem's back, she was smashed down onto the dead rotter she had been punishing, their faces practically cheek to cheek. Flex ran over, dropped his gun and reached down to pull the now lifeless corpse off her and roll it aside.

To his surprise, Gem sat up, gripped the knife sticking out of the dead zombie's head beneath her, and stabbed him again … and again … and again.

Flex moved toward her and caught her wrist, mid plunge. With his other hand, he peeled the knife from her fingers and threw it aside. He grunted as he dropped down beside her and gripped her hands in his, trying to make eye contact.

"Gemina Cardoza Sheridan," he said. "Are you in there, sweetheart?"

Hemp and Charlie stood nearby, breathing hard. Flex saw they scanned the parking lot, so he knew he had cover and time, both of which he needed right now to reach his wife.

"Babe," he said, pulling her to him and putting his arms around her. "We got 'em. All of 'em."

"We cleared out the showroom, Gem," said Nelson, appearing between Punch and Dave. "They're all dead – and I mean really dead – now."

Her breathing was steady, but deep. When she released her breath, it came out in a shudder. Her face was soaked with tears of grief.

Flex saw that pain and it bubbled up in him again, and this time he pulled her so tight to him it felt like he might break her. In his heart, Flex knew Gem was already broken, just as he was.

"Oh, Flex!" she cried, looking up at him, her face smeared with chunks of gore and blood. "I miss him so much! I can't believe we'll never see him again!"

Hearing the truth spoken aloud by the woman and mother he loved more than he had ever loved anyone before, shattered him all over again. Flex fell into her and broke into heaving sobs.

Flex wasn't sure how long the others let them stay there like that, but to his surprise, it was Gem who finally called an end to it.

Her arms slid off Flex and she took a deep breath, looking up at the sky. The moon was bright and had served as their lighting to take on this horde of living dead, and its brightness washed out the stars.

"Charlie," she said. "Help me up, would you?"

"Sure," said Charlie. She slung her crossbow over her shoulder and held her hands out. Gem reached over, grabbed the empty 9mm and tucked it into the back of her pants, then reached out and took Charlie's hands.

Charlie pulled her up and then put her arms around Gem, holding her. They embraced for a long time.

Dave came to give Flex a hand up, and he stood. Gem and Charlie held one another until Flex touched Charlie on the shoulder and they both pulled apart and looked at him.

Flex nodded at Gem, and she gave him a weak smile. "Thank you," she said, looking at Punch, Nelson, Dave and Hemp. "I know we've had a credo for a long time, but I'd like to reinforce it right here. Right now."

"What's that, Gem?" asked Punch.

"None of them alive," she said. "Not a single one. From here on out, if we see them – I don't give a shit if they're half a mile away – we go get them and rid the world of them."

"Fair enough," said Punch. "It's how any war should be fought."

"Yep," said Flex. "And this is a war, Gem, but we can start that later. Right now, let's go get our kids."

Gem did not move. Instead, she stared at Flex and said, "By doing what we said we'd do over a decade ago, we make sure that when we find our kids, the world is a few dead fucks safer."

Flex nodded and held a hand out to her. Gem nodded at him and took it. They walked back to the car.

*****

"Looks like due northwest will take us straight to either Great Bend, Kansas, or Casper, Wyoming," said Charlie, the map open on her lap. "I sure hope they're headed to Great Bend, 'cause even though Casper is more dead-on northwest, it's also almost 800 miles away."

"They don't sleep," said Gem.

"What?" asked Hemp.

"We can't stop because Isis and Max don't sleep, and they'll drive straight through," said Gem, her voice flat. "We can't stop."

"We can switch off driving, but if we get there and we're exhausted, it's not going to help us help them," said Hemp. "I suggest we drive until we find a place to rest, then stop for the night."

"Just so long as that place to rest is Great Bend, I'm cool with that," said Gem. "That way if they're not there, we know we have to go on to Wyoming."

"If they're even in a larger city," said Flex. "We might be making assumptions. Which means we could miss them entirely, because we can't drive there as the crow flies."

"Let's get to Great Bend and take it from there," said Hemp. "I'll get on the radio and let the guys know."

"God, I pray they're in Great Bend," said Gem. "I feel like I'm in a movie where every scene is a cliffhanger."

"Somebody yell cut, please," said Charlie. "End scene. That would be nice."

Flex thought about that. It could happen. He could wake up any moment and just marvel at the realism of the

81

nightmare he'd just had, and he could decide whether or not to share it with Gem before it was whisked away, obliterated by time.

He blinked his eyes, coating them with fluid, and drove. The moon fell behind clouds as he passed a sign that said: GREAT BEND   62 mi.

*****

Even when America was bustling, Flex could tell Highway 281 wasn't a major travel route. The traffic between Kingman and Great Bend was pretty much exclusive, and it did not appear that anyone from Kingman was fleeing toward Great Bend or vice-versa at the onset of the highly anticipated but never expected zombie apocalypse.

Sure, there were broken down cars here and there, but nothing was so jammed up that they couldn't snake through. They only had to use the winch once.

Gem finally told Flex to pull over about ten miles outside of Great Bend. He did, and she said she would drive. Flex didn't argue the point. If it helped her feel more normal and helped her work her way back to Gem, that was cool.

He wasn't fooling himself; Flex Sheridan knew that neither he nor Gem would ever be the same again. Their son was gone forever, and it was a hole in their lives they would simply have to get used to.

As Flex sat there, the tears came again. This time he looked out the window, trying to blink them away. Of course Gem knew he was sad, but there was no reason for him to rub that in over and over, especially when it was only her sheer willpower that prevented her from breaking down.

82

"Looks like we're getting real close," said Dave on the radio. "Start looking for a place to hole up for the night."

Flex pulled the binoculars from the glove box and looked down the dark highway. Nothing. A world without lights was something they'd gotten used to, but it was still a bizarre experience. Especially since they'd gotten Kingman pretty lit up compared to most parts of the country.

"I think up here on the right," said Gem, putting on her high beams. She turned the steering wheel and drove into a long driveway and stopped. The GTO followed behind.

"Hard to see them because of the tall grass, but it looks like there are two decent sized houses there," said Gem.

"They'll do," said Flex," scanning the area around the brick houses for movement.

"I've been looking," said Hemp. "Nothing out there so far."

"Everyone got their headlamps on?" asked Charlie. "Punch can do his thing and we can get this place cleared. Then we can get settled and run the radio around all the channels to see if Max did what I told him and kept his ears on."

"Charlie," said Hemp. "How did you learn to talk like a truck driver?"

"First off, it's trucker, and fuckin'-A, Mr. Chatsworth, you know I've talked like a trucker since I came out of the closet."

"In all fairness, your first sentence you spoke out of the closet did not contain any swear words," said Hemp. "I've heard the story."

"Yeah, but they don't know what I was thinkin'."

She opened her door and everyone else followed suit. Dave, Punch and Nelson walked up to the door.

Nelson still hadn't cut his hair, though he had gotten rid of the dreadlocks. It was now down to his ass. When he and Dave were together, they looked like part of early REO Speedwagon.

Punch was a former United States Marine and he had his ways of approaching things. He liked to lead and nobody got in his way. He had a pair of night vision goggles that he carried everywhere, and he put them on now. It wasn't pitch black, but Punch would be clearing the rooms, so Flex was glad he had them.

He was also glad he'd found Punch on that anti-toxin run so many years ago. Punch had been a hell of an asset since that day, particularly in the clearing and taming of Kingman, Kansas.

"This house looks a little bigger," said Punch. "So I'll clear it first in case it's enough for all of us. "You guys work the outside of both and check some windows with your headlamps. Hemp, help me get inside, would you?"

"I'm right behind you guys," said Nelson. "Dude, this stuff is still exciting even after all this time. Kinda makes me realize what a bunch of nothing I did before this all happened."

"Exciting or not, Nel," said Gem. "It's dangerous. Be careful."

"Oh, I will, dude. I don't plan to give you any more fuel for your sadness today, Gem. Promise."

Flex cringed at Nelson's reference, but in the shadowy, gray night, he saw Gem nod with a sad smile on her face. She loved and understood Nelson, and knew that he would die for her without giving it a second thought. He was that kind of friend.

Flex hoped it would never come to that.

He and Gem stayed in front while Charlie and Dave took off around the left side.

Hemp, Nelson and Punch moved toward the house. Punch reached the front door and tried the knob.

"Locked," he said. "That's a good sign. All the front windows are intact, too."

"Could mean supplies," said Nelson. "Maybe even some cookies."

"Even loaded up with preservatives, you'll be lucky to find anything edible," said Hemp.

"I'll take stale cookies over zombies like 80% of the time," said Nelson.

Flex silently wondered about that other 20% and just what situation would cause Nelson to choose zombies over stale cookies.

Hemp slid up beside Punch and slipped his lock picking kit from his jacket pocket.

"Keeping an eye out there, guys?" he asked.

Gem and I faced the street and tried to differentiate between the blowing 3' tall grass and the sometimes very sneaky walking dead.

So far it was just grass.

Flex turned back to see Hemp leaned forward, his headlight aimed dead on. The click was audible as Hemp straightened up and said, "That's the tough one."

In another ten seconds he had the doorknob unlocked and the door swung in on its hinges.

"You guys wait out here," said Punch. "I'll do this fast." He carried an M27 like the one he carried in the Corps. He still had his tactical shotgun and he always packed it for trips into the badlands – complete with estrogen blocker flechette rounds – now so common everyone called them EBFRs.

The Badlands were now what everyone called everywhere but Kingman.

As Punch and Nelson stepped inside, Charlie and Dave reappeared around the far corner of the house, having completed their sweep of the perimeter.

"Nothing out there?" asked Flex, stepping up onto the porch.

"Nada," said Dave. "Kinda sketchy with the tall grass, but nothing jumped out at us."

"I just want to get inside," said Gem. "This fucking day is catching up with me."

Charlie said nothing; she just walked over and took Gem's hand.

Suddenly gunfire erupted from the house. Three short bursts, a brief pause, another series, then silence.

Everyone flinched, eyeing the house, but Flex knew it was mainly an instinctive reaction to the possibility of flying lead; Punch had no doubt fired the shots, though, and he would never fire in the direction of the living – unless the living is who he wanted to kill.

"Sounds pretty minimal," said Charlie, walking inside with her crossbow up, and Flex and Gem on her heels.

Nelson ran to the door and said, "Gem … I mean … just hold on for a minute, okay? Just a sec."

"What's up, Nel?" asked Gem. "I don't need to be babied."

"It's … nothing, really," said Nelson. "Flex, maybe we can use your help."

"What the hell is it Nelson?" asked Charlie.

"It's … well, just take my word for it and stay out there for a minute. The house is good, but this made kind of a mess."

"I was doing relatively okay most of the trip," said Gem. "Now that I feel like collapsing we have a holdup."

Flex said, "I'll help. This'll be fast. Kick your feet up on this bench, Gem." He patted the rusty, wrought iron bench on the front porch and reached in his pocket. "Have a stale smoke." He dropped the pack of Marlboros on the bench with the pack of matches. They had taken to storing the old cartons of smokes in a humidor they took from a smoke shop, but no matter how they tried, the fifteen year old cigarettes were still pretty raspy.

Flex flipped on his headlamp and walked inside. The house was nice. Hardwood floors throughout with nice, albeit a bit dusty, area rugs. There was a stack of firewood waiting by a stone hearth fireplace, too. Cobwebs covered the logs but they were dry and the fireplace looked like it could handle a blazing big fire.

"Back here, Flex," said Nelson.

Dave stood behind Flex. "What is it?" he asked.

"Not sure yet," said Flex. "We're about to find out."

As they rounded the corner, two pairs of legs jutted out from what appeared to be a coat closet. Flex and Dave drew closer and Nelson stood aside.

"Fuck, am I seein' double?" asked Flex.

"I guess they were twins," said Punch. "Now they got twin bullet holes."

"I get it," said Flex. He stared at the boys, who could be no older than their Flexy had been. Gem didn't need to see this, and Flex understood why they told her to wait.

A smear of black goo and bullet holes adorned the back of the coat closet where they had been standing, but now the boys sat on the floor at the base of the wall, their dead eyes staring sightless. Their hair was an identical, wispy red, and the only thing that could have told anyone which was which was their clothes. The one on the left wore a Sum 41 tee shirt, and the dead kid on the right wore a collared, button-down shirt. Both wore jeans.

"Let's take 'em outside," said Flex. "Out back."

87

"I'll get the door," said Nelson. "You guys are better equipped to haul 'em." He ran out.

Besides the blue jeans, the only other matching article of clothing the twins wore were high-top, canvas sneakers, the kind that Isis liked to wear. Vans, Flex recalled.

Punch leaned over and pulled the torso of the one boy forward, got on his knees, and threw the corpse over his shoulder. Flex and Dave gave him room as he grunted to his feet.

Flex looked at the other body and shook his head. He was 58 years old and his back hurt. He stared at the boy, then back at Dave. "I need your help, buddy," he said.

"We got it," said Dave. "You're gettin' too old for this shit, right?"

"I only wish that was a joke," he said. "C'mon, I'll get his right side and you get his left."

Together, they knelt down and took an arm and a leg. Neither one lifted yet.

"Fucker stinks," said Dave. "But he looks pretty light."

They shifted the boy to center the weight.

"No food in what … fourteen years?" said Flex.

"Guess they were hiding in the closet together?" asked Dave.

"I'm sure that neither of them expected to turn," said Flex. "Same DNA, same metabolism. Must have happened at exactly the same time or one of them would've had some interesting injuries."

"Ready?" asked Dave.

"Go," said Flex. They started the lift and Flex got one knee beneath him and pushed up. His grunt was more pronounced than Punch's had been, but at least the kid was off the floor.

They turned toward the door to the living room, where they had to go to get to the kitchen. As they stepped out of the hall, Gem was there. Her headlamp shone right on the boy's face and she stared at the bullet holes dotting the middle of his forehead.

"Gem, you weren't sup –"

"Too late," she said, staring at the dead thing. "Don't worry, babe. That thing is not our son. Flex Sheridan Junior is back in Kingman, waiting for us to bring his sister home so we can bury him."

Flex said nothing. He nodded and looked at Dave. Together they carried the dead young rotter out the back door.

Gem never needed to know about the twin.

*****

CHAPTER FIVE

Flex couldn't sleep. He got up and walked into the living room where an enormous fire still burned in the fireplace. They'd had to check the flue before starting it, because there was no telling what might have crawled up or down the chimney over the last decade and a half.

It was clear, but the flue was closed. Nobody enjoyed the fire very long, for they were exhausted. When Flex sat on the sofa, he was surprised to hear Hemp speak.

"You too, eh?" he said, sitting up. "I don't blame you, Flex."

"Jesus, man. Didn't see you there. Mind if I smoke in here?"

"I wish I smoked," he said. "I could use a little nicotine now and then."

Flex lit a stale Marlboro and braced himself against the first hit. It was always the harshest until he got used to it. He exhaled, blowing a few smoke rings as he did so; an old habit he couldn't break.

"Flex, we haven't had any time alone, but I just want to let you know that I'm barely holding it together. I loved your boy like my own. Every minute I spent with him was like knowing you when you were a boy, I imagine. Smart, inquisitive, and a little damned John Wayne if I've ever met one … and I have."

Flex stared at the fire that was half the size it was when everyone went to bed. The feeling of crying came over him, but the tears had dried up.

"I'm just so sorry, friend," added Hemp.

"Thank you buddy," he said. "I've been thinkin' … but it's … it's crazy. The minute I lost him I couldn't stand the thought of never hugging him again, to never be able to just sit around and talk about what was goin' on with him." Flex looked at Hemp, and like a good friend, he just nodded.

"Hemp, I realize it just happened a few hours ago, and my head is no doubt *really* fucked up, but I can't stop thinking that Gem could …" Flex stopped and shook his head and this time the tears did come again. "Fuck it," he finished. "I'm an idiot and I'm just talkin' crazy."

Hemp swung his feet off the couch and looked at Flex. "Flex, yes, you're in tremendous mourning and it is too soon to being considering it without having a conversation with Gem, but it's *not* crazy. You and Gem can have another baby. She's not the oldest woman to have a healthy baby, and at almost 47, she's nearing the cutoff, but she's not there."

"Jeez, man, how'd you know?"

"I was afraid to say anything because of course your son cannot be replaced; you wouldn't want that anyway. But I've also got another idea that could speed the process."

Flex looked at him in the firelight. "9 months is 9 months, buddy, plus the time it's gonna take for a couple of old farts like us to get it done. I have no idea if I'm shootin' blanks at this age."

"Chances are, you've still got some swimmers."

Flex nodded and stared at the fire for a full minute. He looked at Hemp, who was already looking at him. "So," said Flex, "Go ahead and tell me what you mean by speeding the process."

"Well," said Hemp. "As you know, I've had years to consider this and calculate things based on Max and Isis' development from childhood to adulthood."

"Yeah, sure," said Flex. "It's what you do. Analyze shit."

"How would you feel about exposing Gem to the red-eye vapor the moment she conceives?"

Flex turned his face slowly toward Hemp, and he was not smiling.

"Buddy, to be honest, I wanna kill every red-eye I see. I fucking literally hate 'em. I never felt that way about the others; the dumb ones. They run on instinct and orders from the red-eyes. Nothin' else. The red-eyes, well, they're somehow more than that. I almost feel hatred from them. Vengeance. Like they're keeping score and getting even with us."

"Their actions and reactions are as much instinct as the others, Flex," said Hemp.

"Anyway. How do you think that would make a difference? Exposing her early, I mean."

Hemp leaned forward and interlocked his fingers. "Once born, they develop much faster than unaffected children," he said. "Their brains, their bodies, even their emotional maturity. I believe the gestation period may be cut to as much as one third of the normal time. Perhaps more."

"Are you shittin' me?" asked Flex.

"I am not shitting on you," said Hemp.

Flex laughed for the first time since his son died. He felt instantly guilty.

92

"It would do something else, Flex," said Hemp.

"What's that?"

Hemp was about to answer, but Flex held up his hand. "Nope, nope. I got it. And you're right. If Gem and I have a baby, it's gonna have some abilities that can keep it safe."

Hemp pointed at him. "Exactly. And others. Like Isis and Max."

"Hemp," said Flex, "be honest with me."

"Always, brother," said Hemp.

"What's it been like having Max? Like he is, I mean."

"As a scientist, it's been fascinating," he said. "As a father, it's been extraordinary. Flex, I was playing chess – and losing to him – since he was two years old. He's never cried because he can tell us what he wants. Now he's an asset to the community, and he's every bit a son to me as Trina is a daughter to you, the only difference being that he's my direct blood."

"Am I wrong to have some hope here?" asked Flex.

"In this world, my friend, hope is a guiding light. It makes us push on to that next adventure. To open another door. Have hope, Flex. Make your own hope. Talk to Gem about it."

Flex felt some butterflies in his stomach, but their fluttering also chased away a bit of his sadness.

"I just gotta make sure this isn't like getting a new puppy when your dog passes on," said Flex. "Our reasons have to be right."

"I have a reason for you, Flex," said Hemp.

"What's that, man?" asked Flex.

"This world without a human being borne of Flex and Gem Sheridan is not as good a world. I've no doubt that Flexy would have done great things on the shoulders of parents who fight and protect and love harder than any people I've ever met."

93

Hemp stopped for a moment, wiping his own tears away. "So please, Flex. Talk to Gem. Do the world a favor. Have your special child. We need that child to be born."

Flex stood. "Get up, man."

Hemp stood, and Flex gave him a hug. A long, tight hug. He pulled away and kept his hands on Hemp's shoulders. "I feel that way about Max," he said. "Just knowing he's a bit of you and Charlie made me love the kid from the first time I laid eyes on him."

"He loves you both," said Hemp. "I think the only one he loves more is Isis."

"He does have a thing for her, doesn't he?" said Flex.

"Anyway," said Hemp. "Down to brass tacks. I went outside for a look around earlier, and I have a feeling this is a ghost town."

"Why?" asked Flex.

"Just intuition, that's all," said Hemp. "Like I said, I went outside for a few minutes before you came out. I found a ladder leaning against that other house, so I used it to get on the roof. I looked toward town and saw nothing even remotely like a light or a fire."

"Shit, Hemp," said Flex. "Why would you do that?"

"You know at night you can always see something out there. Some survivor or other making do."

"There was nothing?" asked Flex.

"An enormous lot of it," said Hemp.

Flex looked at his watch. "It's three in the morning," he said. "Sure the world's just not asleep?"

Hemp sighed. "I could be wrong. We obviously don't have line-of-sight to the entire town, plus people are more cautious about light. I'll withhold final judgment until we drive in tomorrow."

Flex lit another smoke. "Last one," he said. "Then I'm gonna lie in bed thinkin' about what you told me. Then I'm gonna figure out a way to tell Gem what I want to do."

"Good luck," said Hemp. "But you might find it's a few days too soon. Play that one by ear."

"I'll see if I can't plant some seeds," said Flex.

"Are we talking tearing a condom?" asked Hemp, smiling.

"Not *those* kinda seeds, man," laughed Flex. "Not yet. Plus, she's on the pill, for what those expired things are worth," said Flex. "No latex bullshit shall come between me and my woman."

"Night, Flex. Get some sleep. See you in three hours or so."

"Night, Hemp. Thanks for being my best friend."

"It's my pleasure, Flex. And I mean that."

*****

When Flex finally awoke, he was surprised to see it was 7:30 AM. Gem was not in the bed beside him, so he walked down the hall and pushed another door open. Dave and Nelson were there, lying on their backs in a king sized bed, but Dave obviously slept light because as the door swung inward, he dropped his left hand and snatched his gun. His eyes were still glued shut, though.

With that, Nelson sat up, his hand coming up from beneath his pillow with a Ninja star.

"Whoa, the fuck!" said Flex, ducking. "Don't shoot and don't throw!"

"Nah, dude," said Nelson. "I gotcha, bro. Sensed it was you. Not going to take you out."

Dave looked at his watch. "Jesus!" he said. "Wow, I musta been wiped."

"I think we all were," said Flex. "Sorry you didn't bring Serena?" he asked.

"I miss her," said Dave. "But Nel didn't bring Rachel, so all's fair."

"She's takin' care of our rug rat," said Nelson.

"If you can call a ten-year-old a rug rat," said Flex.

"Good point," said Nelson.

Nelson and Rachel named their little girl Lita. She came out as skinny as a rail and still was. Nelson went out every day and found the most beautiful wildflower he could and brought it back to put in her hair. During the winter when flowers were not around, Nelson had a collection of silk flowers from which to choose.

"See you boys out there. I think Gem's gonna want to get an early start."

"Too late for that, but we'll manage," said Dave.

Flex left the door open and went into the living room. Gem had gotten the Coleman stove out of the trunk, along with eggs from the ice chest. The house smelled good and Flex found he was ravenous.

The seven of them had breakfast. When they were done, everyone helped load the stuff in the cars and before they left, they found another five-gallon can of propane, along with six small bottles, not to mention three 1-gallon jugs of purified water.

Hemp opened each one and added a drop of bleach, then closed and shook them. Backup.

Once again, Gem drove the Crown Vic. Flex was glad to see it. She even smiled at him on occasion.

*****

"Wow," said Gem, slowing the Ford as she worked her way up Main Street. "What happened here?"

"Stop the car," said Hemp.

"We're stopping," said Charlie into the radio.

"Why, what's up?" asked Nelson from behind them.

"You'll see," said Charlie.

Everyone got out. They stood and turned in all directions. They had reached the town square. Bodies lay scattered everywhere, some piled on top of one another, others face down, alone.

Hemp, hefting his H&K, walked toward one of them and knelt down. He touched the fabric of the clothing.

"What are you checking for?" asked Flex, who had come up behind him.

"Age," he said. "This person did not turn at the onset," said Hemp. "Maybe not at all." Hemp reached into his pocket and withdrew a pair of blue nitrile gloves.

"Always prepared, huh?" said Nelson, now standing beside Flex.

"Old habits," he said, as Charlie approached.

"Good habits," she said. "Keeps the muck off you."

Hemp reached down and lifted the arm of one of the corpses. He pinched the shriveled skin between his fingers and it did not crack or tear.

"I'd say this happened a couple of weeks ago at the latest," he said. "What's more, I believe ... well, wait a moment. Flex, may I use your knife?"

Flex pulled his Bowie knife from its sheath and held it out. "Here you go, bud."

"The squeamish should turn away," he said.

Nelson took Hemp up on it, saying, "I just had breakfast, dude."

Hemp pulled the hair back on the man's body and set the blade at the hairline. He then hammered on the handle with his fist, and the blade sank in to the hilt. Getting up on his knees, he pressed the blade down hard to the right, and

97

the sound of cracking skull could be heard above the silence of the dead square.

"I heard that," said Nelson.

"Sorry," said Hemp. "Here's another." He removed the blade and reversed it, then forced it down through the left side of the skull.

"Perfect," he said, giving the knife back to Flex, who wiped it on the pant leg of another body and sheathed it.

He then gripped in the cut and pulled the crown of the skull off, snapping it in back. His gloves on, he reached inside, grabbed something and gave it a twist-pull.

Even Flex was having trouble keeping his breakfast down. He turned away and smiled at Gem, who did not get out of the Ford. She was facing him, but did not respond.

She was in one of her far away moments. Flex understood. When he turned back, Hemp held up a hard chunk of something, about the size of a tangerine. He studied it.

"It's got a hole in it," he said. "Whoever did this used permakill tactics."

Permakill is a name Punch came up with for the type of death an ordinary person would have to experience in order to remain dead. It was essentially a death that included brain trauma.

Hemp looked at Flex and Nelson, who had turned around, but did not look at what he held in his hand. "This one was quite alive," he said. "Not one of them." He looked around the square. "I'll check more, but I believe we've got our answer. This was a massacre."

Dave Gammon stood beside Punch, who had been walking around the square scavenging any weapons worth keeping. He held three handguns of various brands and calibers and had a rifle of some kind strapped over his shoulder.

"Who would do this?" asked Dave. "None of them look eaten."

"Oh, yeah they do," said Punch. "Found a whole mound of bodies over there that were just ripped apart and shredded. Basically little chunks of meat left on the bones."

"Were their skulls intact?" asked Hemp, looking up.

"Some, yeah," said Punch. "But all punctured, like somebody was making sure of something. I think we can all guess what."

"Show me," said Hemp, standing.

"I'll hang with Gem," said Charlie, sliding into the back seat of the Crown Vic. Flex saw her close the door and lean forward to squeeze Gem's shoulders.

Flex turned and something in his peripheral vision caught his eye. Movement, on the other side of the square.

Hemp and Punch, with Dave and Nelson in tow, were halfway across the square, so Flex pulled out his suppressed Walther PPK and went to investigate.

He saw Gem notice he didn't follow the other guys. She did not get out of the car.

As he neared the corner, a walking corpse so destroyed it was almost unrecognizable, staggered out from behind a brick storefront, tripping over a fly-ridden pile of human remains, and tumbling to the ground, landing hard atop another half-eaten dead body.

Flex was about ten feet away when it appeared, but still he stopped dead in his tracks and took two steps back. He resumed forward movement, his pace slowed.

As he drew to within five feet, he could see the thing's hands were intact, but the skin was missing down to the second knuckle on all of its fingers. It struggled back to its bare feet, the rotted skin peeling off them in bloody flaps.

When it stood, Flex's mouth fell open. He stepped to the side. Its eyes were missing, likely eaten. It had no ears.

The fleshy cheeks, where either a man's or woman's breasts would have once been, were mere ragged holes … but there was more.

Several bite marks adorned the body where it was possible to see them, and small, yellow chunks of something were embedded into the raw meat where there was no skin. Flex could no longer tell whether this had been a man or a woman, for there was no remaining clothing, and if it once had a penis, it was also gone. The skin on the chest appeared to have been gnawed away as if by a pack of rats.

Flex had never before seen something so lacking in mass or musculature that could still move, not even in the crazy world of the living dead. He approached the thing.

The group had all taken WAT-5 just an hour before, so Flex didn't worry about being attacked. And while he did want to show this thing to Hemp and the others, he didn't want to touch it.

When on WAT-5, the creatures could basically be "walked" where they wanted, but they did tend to be gooey, and if you didn't want slime on your hands, a tool or gloves were necessary.

Suddenly, he heard, "Flex!"

He jumped at Nelson's voice and laughed at himself for a second. He had been out of their line-of-sight behind a crashed school bus.

"I'm fine! Coming to you now!"

He looked on the ground and saw a tattered umbrella. He bent down and grabbed it, shoving the Walther back into his pants. He used the old parasol as a poker, pushing the creature toward his friends.

"Whoa, buddy!" shouted Nel, as Flex nudged the walking corpse closer. When he was within five feet, he stopped and tossed the umbrella aside.

Hemp turned away from his analysis of the dead bodies and said, "A live one," his eyebrows raised.

"If only the fucker could talk," said Flex.

"So what the hell do you think happened here?" asked Dave.

Hemp stood directly in front of the zombie and put a hand on its shoulder. It did not seem to notice. It just teetered in front of him.

He stared at it, long and hard. "Whoever did this missed this one," he said, turning it. "No trauma to the skull – except the missing eyes, nose and ears, anyway."

"Why do it?" asked Dave. "Only half of them eaten, the others just killed. That doesn't sound logical at all."

"Yeah, right, dudes," said Nelson. "With all this food around, why kill 'em and leave 'em? We know these things can paralyze you and save you for later."

"That is an excellent point, Nel," said Hemp. "Back in the beginning, the creatures would simply stockpile those of us they caught. Preserve us for later consumption."

"Maybe it was a skill they stopped using as we edibles became more and more sparse," said Dave. "Maybe they lost that particular tool."

Hemp shook his head. "No. That's the thing about instincts, isn't it? They are instinctive. Natural."

"Okay, then," said Flex. "I'm stumped. Hey, what the hell are those yellow things?"

"Where?" asked Hemp.

"On that fuckin' zombie. Right where the bite marks are."

Hemp leaned forward and it raised its arm, its ragged fingers nearly clawing Hemp's cheek. He let go and jumped back.

Flex said, "You really need to look at it some more?" He pulled out his Walther.

"I'd like to, yes," said Hemp.

"Then hold his left wrist and pull his arm out."

Hemp did as he was told.

Flex went behind him, holstered the PPK and pulled out his Bowie knife. "Raise it up more."

Hemp did. It looked like a scarecrow pointing east.

Flex brought the heavy, sharp blade down and chopped its arm off at the shoulder. Hemp realized what he'd done and let go of its wrist.

"Nice," he said.

"One more," said Flex. "You're the only guy with gloves on, so do the honors."

"I'm not worried –"

"Well," interrupted Flex, "I'm worried for you. Arm."

Hemp shook his head and held out the other arm. Flex raised his Bowie knife and with one clean, downward swipe, hacked it off.

Hemp let that one drop to the pavered brick roadway, too.

"Okay, let's see what these are now." He plucked one out and held it up.

"A tooth," said Nelson.

"Exactly. Look at them all," said Hemp, picking one broken tooth after the other out of the raw meat that comprised this particular rotter. "There were a number of them eating this fellow when he was alive."

"Glad you said that, professor," said Nelson. "I was wondering what the hell ate zombies. Talk about a worrisome threat."

"This one was devoured by multiple abnormals, Nelson. There are enough bodies here that there should have been quite enough food for all of them to have their own uninfected to feast on, and yet … half were consumed and half were just killed."

"Zombies don't fucking do head shots," said Dave. "Living people killed these folks."

Hemp shook his head and looked at the others. "There are no errant shots," said Hemp. "We can look again, but did you see any bullet holes in all those others over there? The intact bodies?"

"Nope," said Flex. "Just the brain trauma."

"Exactly," said Hemp. "Which is good enough to kill an ordinary person, but also works to prevent it from coming back. As Punch said, these were all permakills."

"So," said Punch. "Where does that leave us?"

"It leaves me worried about Max and Isis," said Hemp. "They would not have done anything like this, so the question now is did they come through here and did they see this?"

"I'd hope if they did they'd come back for some backup," said Dave.

"Fuck that," said Flex. "Maturity or not, those two have powers beyond what any of us have, and they have the feeling of immortality that all teenagers have. That's a hell of a combo. I can guarantee they went on."

"No doubt seeing a clearer mission," said Hemp. "Particularly if somehow, instinctively *they* knew what happened here."

"Let's get the hell going then," said Dave.

"Wait just a moment," said Hemp. "Before we get back to the car, I have to make sure you know what I'm thinking here."

"Buddy, let me give it a shot," said Nelson.

Hemp nodded. "My confidence is high."

"Good, because what happened here was not done by just living humans and it wasn't done by just zombies, bros. This massacre was done by a combination of the two."

"Very good," said Hemp.

103

"No," said Nelson. "Not good at all. Your next question, and mine too, is this: Were the humans and zombies here at the same time doing this shit, and if so, whoa, dudes."

"Wow," said Punch. "Hemp?"

"It nags," said Hemp. "Someone was taking orders from someone, or for the first time in post-apocalyptic history, the abnormals and uninfecteds have teamed up."

"I reiterate, whoa, dudes," said Nelson.

He suddenly went into a tornado of Subdudo moves, taking the armless zombie down to the ground with his series of lightning fast hand and leg swipes. When it was down, he said, "Flex, knife please."

Flex went to grab his knife when a voice came from behind them. They all turned at once.

"No," said Gem, staring at the half-dead thing on the ground, her eyes moving to its severed arms, then back to the creature. "I got it."

She did not move closer; as she lowered the barrel of Queenie, her Uzi, toward the thing, everyone stepped back to avoid spatter.

She held down the trigger on full auto mode, emptying the magazine and detaching its head from its pustuled body.

Everyone watched until her gun fell silent. Flex stepped over the mess and put his arm around her, turning her back toward the truck.

"You need to tell me what happened here," she said.

"We'll do a bit of brainstorming in the car," said Flex. "Right now it's a mystery."

*****

"Don't leave town just yet," said Hemp.

Gem, who had insisted on driving again, said, "Why?"

"As Flex has alluded to, we have a mystery here in Great Bend, Kansas," said Hemp. "We have piles and piles of bodies that have clearly been consumed by infecteds, and were subjected to brain trauma afterward."

"Doesn't sound like zombies at work," said Charlie.

"No," said Hemp. "We've never seen them use a tool other than their hands and teeth, so it couldn't have been them. Furthermore, we have many others who were administered a permadeath, but not eaten. Now why would that be?"

"They were full?" suggested Charlie.

"I've never seen that, but Hemp, is it possible?" asked Gem. "Plus, with their vapor and their ability to stockpile bodies, why wouldn't they just do that? Save them for later."

Hemp said, "There was a point in this post-apocalyptic history of ours when the surviving human race was so scattered and spread out that stockpiling us just didn't happen because the creatures couldn't find us in significant enough numbers for that to be necessary."

"You mean they didn't need to stockpile because they never had an overabundance of food ... or us," said Nelson, from the GTO behind them.

They had developed a system whereby two sets of radios would be in use. In the lead car, Charlie would hold down the transmit button on one radio on channel 16, and in the trailing car, the matched radio on channel 16 would be open to listen. In turn, Nelson would hold down the transmit button on a radio tuned to channel 19, allowing the radio in the lead car to listen on their paired radio. This essentially provided a speakerphone of sorts.

"Exactly Nel," said Hemp. "In the beginning, when this was all starting and people were taken by surprise, there were enough unsuspecting people that they had entire housefuls stocked away, like the one in which Flex and Gem found Taylor."

Flex shook his head. "Yeah, but now we're like fourteen years into this thing, Hemp. We know from the Ham radio that other survivors are establishing sanctuaries around the country, so the ghouls could get back to their stockpiling food model, right?"

"Which begs the question," said Dave, "Why hit the jackpot of vulnerable people they clearly had the upper hand on, and just sacrifice them all when they could've paralyzed them and eaten them later?"

"They don't appear to be here," said Punch. "I know this might sound dumb, but maybe they were traveling light?"

"Nah," said Nelson. "Zombies don't have appointments to keep, and as far as I know, the only thing on their schedules is eating people. No sense in moving on unless everything here is eaten."

"Which wasn't the case here," said Flex.

"I go back to my suspicion that there are regular people involved in this somehow," said Nelson. "If they're not partnering up with the zombies, how the hell do we have devoured corpses stacked all over the square with brain trauma, and other, uneaten humans with the same kind of trauma?"

"To get back to my point," said Hemp, "We need to determine what kind of town Great Bend was. The only way to do that is to search for where they might have set up their city government."

"We always picked the most obvious places," said Gem. "City Hall, stuff like that."

"Which is right behind us," said Nelson. "Got my Rand McNally out."

"What we need to do is get to Max and Isis," said Charlie. "They could be in trouble."

"Charlie," said Hemp. "You see all these bodies out here. This was a town, not unlike Kingman. They clearly did not take the time to protect their borders as we have done, but then again, we do not know how long they've been established here. Perhaps they only just relocated here a month or two ago and didn't have time to fortify it yet. We need to know this."

"How does it help us?" asked Gem. "Charlie's right, Hemp. We need to get to Isis and your son."

Hemp took a long, slow breath. "By finding their government seat, we might find documents to tell us what this town square meeting was about," he said. "We need to know whether it was an internal thing, or if someone from outside communicated with them and asked that the occupants of the town be gathered."

"Like ... to be slaughtered?" asked Nelson. "But these had to be seasoned survivors after all these years. How could they be ... I dunno, tricked?"

"Look," Hemp said. "I've been trying to avoid going here, but I'm worried about Kingman. We're not exactly a secret. We didn't know about this group in Great Bend, but maybe they didn't have anyone knowledgeable in amateur radio and maybe they never heard our broadcasts. The other option is what I said earlier. Perhaps they just arrived here recently and hadn't really established yet."

"You think whoever – or whatever – did this," said Flex, "might hit Kingman next?"

"Flex, your guess is as good as mine," he said. "Now, if you'll pardon me, we're all on WAT-5. Let's put in the eye drops and get this done. The sooner it's over with, the sooner we can try to find the kids."

Eric A. Shelman

*****

CHAPTER SIX

After duplicating the glowing, pink eyes of the standard rotters, Gem, Flex and Punch headed out to investigate any nearby homes that appeared to have been recently occupied, or that appeared to be fortified in some way. Hemp, Charlie, Dave and Nelson headed off to City Hall.

Both groups had two radios, this time all set to channel 12.

Gem stopped the Ford in front of a yellow house. The grass was shorter than the other homes, and there was an old manual push mower tucked against the front porch. There were boards on the windows with what appeared to be view holes drilled every few feet.

"Good a start as any," said Flex. "But pull over to the side. If anyone's inside, they could take pot shots at us."

"Our eyes are bound to freak anyone out if they run into us in a dark hallway," said Punch.

"We'll make sure we're announced," said Gem. "Let's go. I'd like to get this over with as soon as we can and get back on the road. I still think this is a waste of time."

"Hemp usually knows his shit, woman," said Flex. "Maybe we should withhold judgment."

Gem pulled the car to the side of the house where there were no windows. Everyone got out.

With Queenie in fire position, Gem led. Punch chose his tactical shotgun for this outing. Flex had his Daewoo, which he had replaced three times since the beginning of the infection, and it was by far his comfort weapon.

"If you don't mind, Gem, I'll lead the way," said Punch, his voice a whisper. She allowed him to move in front of her. "Let's head to the back of the house. Too much cover in front."

They worked their way to the rear. No walkers came out of the nearby yards to get to them, and nothing at all moved in the distance, though they were alert and constantly scanned the streets, sidewalks, and other areas.

Punch stepped onto the porch, his boot not making a sound. He waved Flex and Gem up behind him. He reached a sliding door and hooked his fingers around the handle, giving it a pull.

Turning to look at them, he said, "It's locked, but hold on."

Flex and Gem nodded together as Punch leaned his gun against the deck railing. The vertical blinds were fully closed, so he put his palms flat on the glass and pushed upward.

The locked audibly popped, and Punch slid the door open.

Suddenly a blast sounded from inside the house and the entire glass shattered, peppering all of them in the face and knocking the three of them off the porch, with Punch coming to land on his back on top of Flex, who had just missed landing on Gem.

Gem was on her feet first, her Uzi pointed at the shattered door.

Flex and Punch were up next, brushing glass from their clothing and staring at the darkness beyond the fluttering blinds.

"Hello!" shouted Punch. "We're not here to harm anyone!"

"We saw the town square," said Gem. "All of your friends and neighbors killed. We're trying to find out what happened."

Another shot rang out, this time breaking the window of the house directly behind them.

"Knock that shit off!" yelled Flex. "We'll help you if we can!"

"Fuck this," whispered Punch. You guys stay here and keep talking, distracting them. I'll go around to the side and look for another way in."

"Better get the fuck in there before I kill them," said Flex.

"If you hear me kick in a door, that might be a good time to charge inside," said Punch. "Whoever's in there is going to be instantly focused on that noise. Just get low when you do."

Punch disappeared around the corner. It did not take very long for Flex and Gem to hear the noise. It sounded as though Punch had a battering ram.

"Go!" shouted Flex, spreading apart the blinds and diving into the bedroom that lay beyond. Gem came in right behind him, diving to the floor beside Flex, her Uzi in front of her.

The gun went off again and the round whizzed overhead. Punch had been right to tell them to get low.

"Stop shooting!" shouted Flex.

Another shot sounded, but this time it was directed away from them.

Flex nudged Gem and nodded. "Let's get up a bit and see if we can get a feel for the room."

When they had charged through the verticals, several had broken off, so a decent amount of sunlight now filtered into the room.

They raised their heads to peer over a double bed between them and the source of the flying rounds.

On the bed in front of them, lying on its back, was a shriveled corpse. Dark stains, clearly spatter, dotted the pillow beneath its head, and wisps of gray hair stuck out from its dried skull.

"Holy shit," said Gem. "Scared me."

Flex looked over to see the room was now empty. Whomever had been shooting at them had slipped away.

A thump came from outside the room, accompanied by a squeal and a cry. "I'm sorry, Ma'am," came Punch's voice. "Stop struggling, please. I'm not here to hurt you."

"You okay in there, Punch?" asked Flex.

"I am," he said, and as Gem and Flex got to their feet, Punch appeared in the doorway with an old woman in front of him. She stared at the corpse on the bed and then at Flex and Gem. Then she slapped at Punch's arms, tears flowing down her face.

Gem did not hesitate. She walked around the bed and put her weapon on the dresser. She approached the woman and took her hands, though the elderly woman tried to pull away. "Hi, sweetie," she said. "I'm Gem Sheridan. Behind me is my husband, Flex, and the man holding you is a former Marine named Punch. We're not here to harm you."

"Let me go!" she shouted.

"Her rifle's empty," said Punch, nodding toward a bolt-action rifle lying on the floor by the door.

The old man on the bed had to have been her husband. Flex went to the corpse and looked it over.

The blood spatter was from a head shot, administered right in the center of the forehead.

"They killed Henry!" she cried. "Came in here and saw him in the bed and shot him right there!" she screamed.

"I'm so, so sorry," said Gem, not letting go of her hands. "We're here to find out who these people were," she added.

"They were murderers!" said the woman, who appeared to be in her late seventies or early eighties. Her white hair was dirty and the creases on her face told the story of each year she had struggled through since 2011 and the start of the apocalypse that now spanned a decade and a half.

"I ... I crawled from under my bed to beneath the sink in the bathroom," she said. "I tucked in there and slid over as far as I could to the corner. They opened it and took a first aid kit from in front, but they didn't see me, I was so far back."

"Was that after they shot your husband?"

"Henry wasn't my husband. He was my brother," she said. "My husband died years ago – before the monsters came. Henry had a stroke a couple months ago, right after he got here from Arizona. I hadn't heard from him in so long I thought he was already dead, but there he was on my doorstep, delivered by some good people."

"What's your name, sweetie?" asked Gem, releasing her hands. Punch let go of her shoulders, and she shuffled to the bed and sat on the corner, by her dead brother's feet.

"I'm Irene Danner," she said. "Henry was my older brother."

"So you were alone before he got here?" asked Punch.

113

"I still haven't forgiven you, young man," said Irene, looking at Punch.

"You were shooting that rifle, ma'am," he said. "I had to come at you from the rear. It's my training. I'm sorry."

She shook her head and looked from one to the other of them, her intense, green eyes checking for signs of deceit.

"Irene," said Gem. "My Godson and another young girl came through Great Bend within the last day, we're pretty sure. We only need to get an idea what happened so we can figure out what conclusions they might have reached. They're pretty special kids, and we know they didn't turn back."

"I couldn't make it to the square for the meeting," said Irene. "I know it's just a walk from here, but Henry here was bedridden, and he's been having bladder issues. I had to stay to tend to him."

"What did you hear, ma'am?" asked Punch.

"It was terrible," she said, her eyes darting between them and her brother's body on the bed. "Can we go into the other room?"

Flex noticed what had distracted her and said, "Sorry, ma'am. Yeah, let's go in the other room."

The four walked into the living room where Irene Danner sat on the end of a threadbare sofa. The interior of the house appeared to have been from the 1980s, with wood paneling and green shag carpeting.

"When I heard you at the back door, I thought someone came back to kill me," she said. "They left ten, twelve days ago I think. I mark my calendar every day and I haven't really counted them up. It's on the fridge."

Punch got up and went into the kitchen, returning a moment later with something in his hand. "Exactly two weeks," he said. "Good guess by Hemp on that."

"Who was here, Irene?" asked Gem.

"They were young men," she said. "I could tell from their voices."

"Good move getting under the bathroom sink. I wouldn't look for anyone in there." asked Gem.

"If I didn't, I'd be dead now," she said. "I was under the bed when they shot Henry, and when they left the room for a few minutes it didn't seem safe enough, so I hurried myself up and moved. I had my gun with me, but all my bullets were in a box under my mattress, so a lot of good it did me."

"At least they didn't find it," said Punch. "Have you needed it since they left?"

She shook her head. "No, but I did see a few of those things outside. Zombies, people were calling them. I didn't shoot at them because I'm just not that good a shot. If I missed they'd come over and try to get in."

"Smart move," said Flex. "Anyway, Irene, do you know what the meeting in the square was about?"

"I thought I had the flyer here somewhere," she said. "I might've burned it for heat. It was an organization meeting. There were some folks up in Hoisington who wanted to join with us. A nothin' little town, even worse than this one. I've been there a lot of times over the years."

Punch looked at Flex. "I wonder if Max and Isis found one of the flyers," he said.

"Irene, have you heard from anyone else since that happened?" asked Flex. "Any survivors?"

She shook her head again. "Not a peep. Just those things in the street, the zombies. And not many of them. I had enough water, but I'm runnin' out of food. They just built a big greenhouse for the town where we were going to grow our own food and we had a line on some cattle, too. There was a large herd roaming wild a couple of miles west of us that they were gonna go try to round up the day after the meeting. I bet we could have had it better than a lot of folks if all this hadn't happened."

"How many people lived here before the massacre?" asked Gem.

"The number 345 rings a bell," she said. "It was always big news when we hit another ten, you know, like 320, 330, 340, and so on. Felt like we were creatin' a real community again."

"Where did you live before this all happened?" asked Punch. "I ask because my grandma was a sweetheart just like you and this house reminds me of her old place."

"That's because this old lady's son built this place a long time ago, mister, and I decorated it myself. I was born and raised in another tiny house on the other side of town. My place is close to the town square and I can tell you I'm glad I was here. I'd have died a few times over if it wasn't for them using my garage for storing supplies."

"Who is them?" asked Punch.

"My nephew and a friend or two that I had left would go out on supply runs and they'd just bring everything here. One day they quit comin' and I never heard of 'em again. But I had all the food and water, I sure did."

Flex did not need to ask what she thought happened to them. If you went out regularly enough, your ticket would eventually get punched. Their son's fate proved that with a vengeance.

Irene continued: "Place was pretty overrun with the monsters until Colin and his group came into town."

"Colin?" asked Gem.

"Colin Weller," said Irene. "He showed up one day with over a hundred or so people, which brought us up over three hundred, and they just started wiping the things out."

"How did they kill them?"

116

"Hell, I don't know," she said. "Guns mostly. Knives and swords, though I have no idea where they got the damned swords."

"Did they kill anyone else – like the other folks did Henry?" asked Punch.

"No, no," she said. "Colin was a good young man. His group came from Garden City and Dodge City, they said. Got as many survivors as they could and came here."

"Why?"

"How do I know? Maybe it was worse there. The younger people brought me food and water on a regular basis, so I just bided my time with Henry, hoping it would end and we could get back to normal life again. They even brought me firewood in the winter. It was better than what I'd been going through before they showed up."

The radio on Gem's belt clicked, and Nelson's voice came on. "Dudes, you read?"

Gem pushed the button. "Nel, we're with a resident named Irene Danner. She said there was a meeting called. Two weeks ago."

"Yeah, Gem, that's what we found. The announcement sheet says they were supposed to get together to discuss creating a cooperative between two towns. Great Bend and Hoisington."

"Where's Hoisington?" asked Punch.

"Where's Hoisington?" asked Gem.

"Dude, I looked it up on my map like right away. So the good news is we don't have to drive like seven hundred miles to Casper Wyoming."

"Yeah, but the bad news is we have some murderous A-holes to deal with," came Dave's voice over the radio.

"I wonder if this is connected to the red-eyes not coming when Isis and Max call them," said Gem, her eyes meeting Flex's.

117

"Might be," he said. He turned to Irene. "Irene, we'd like you to come with us. We have a community of over 600 people just a bit south of here, and it's secure and safe. But we can't take you right this minute. We'll go ahead and get Henry's body out of here and you can just stay put. We'll come back for you after we see what we have to deal with in Hoisington."

"I don't want to see those people again," she said. "They brought those things inside."

"What?" asked Gem.

"The monsters," she said. "I saw their feet when they were in the room. Their darned moaning and snarling just scares the bejesus out of me. I almost peed myself when I was under the bed."

"You were very lucky, ma'am," said Punch. "That was some fast thinking, and it's the only reason you're alive now. Let us come back for you, okay? Stay out of sight until we do?"

She nodded. "There's really nothing left out there?" she asked, her eyes tearing up.

Gem went to her and put her arms around the old woman who had spent her entire life in Great Bend, Kansas. "No, sweetie," she said. "It's not the place you remember anymore. But we've made a pretty nice place, and it's still in your home state."

Her frail shoulders almost appeared to melt into the cushions of the sofa itself, they were so slight and defeated. "I'll wait. I'll miss Henry."

"Okay," said Gem. "We'll go now, but before we head out we'll drop you more water and some canned goods. We're glad you're alive."

"Not as glad as I am," she said. "And I'm glad I didn't shoot you."

"Not as glad as we are," said Flex. He knelt down in front of her on the sofa and leaned in to kiss her on the cheek. "You remind me of my grandma, but I was a little kid when she died," he said. "I'd love to have you with us in Kingman."

*****

They rolled Henry's decomposing body in a rug they found in the garage, and carried it into the neighboring yard so it would not be visible from her window.

Flex, Gem and Punch didn't bother searching any more houses. Irene hadn't gone to the meeting, but she did know the basics of who attended and how they were invited. It was enough information with what Nelson had found.

As the Crown Victoria pulled up to the city hall building of Great Bend, Kansas, Nelson sat on the front porch, a map book on his lap. He looked up as we trotted up the stairs. "Hey!"

"Hey, Nel," said Flex. "Hoisington, did you say?"

"Yeah, man. Small, like Kingman, I think. Still northwest of us, too, which fits with what Max and Isis said about the direction of the stagnant Mothers and Hungerers."

"How far?' asked Gem. "I want to be there like now."

"It's only like ten miles north of here," said Nelson. "And since we're still standing around this place, that's too close for comfort."

"Why do you say that?" asked Flex.

"Because, dude," said Nelson. "If they did this to these folks, they're evil. And if they're evil, then 10 miles is within striking distance, so they could be anywhere between here and there, including in this place, hiding somewhere."

"Yeah," said Gem. "I guess they could be camped out on the other side of town. Wish Isis and Max could sense us."

"Me, too," said Punch. "They'd find a way to give us a heads up on what they know."

"We'll get near the town limits and see if we can scare 'em up on the radio," said Flex.

Hemp, Charlie and Dave Gammon came out of the building and trotted down the steps. Their shadows were right underneath them now, with the sun directly overhead. Right around noon.

"Any word on who requested the meeting?" asked Gem.

"It just says A. Almaraz on the bulletin," said Hemp. "I wonder where the intended cooperation between these two communities deteriorated, or if it was a ruse on the part of this Almaraz the entire time."

"We found an elderly woman we're coming back to get on the way home," said Punch. "Irene Danner. She said they came into her house couple of weeks ago. Rotters and humans. Together. Killed her invalid brother with a head shot. We told her we'd bring her some more food and water before we leave."

Everyone looked at everyone else, but only Gem spoke. "We need Max and Isis, and we need them like yesterday," she said.

"I have a question before we leave," said Flex. He looked at Hemp, deep in thought.

"What is it, Flex?" asked Hemp.

"I'm no mathematician," he said. "But Miss Irene told us they had around 340 people in town before that meeting. I'm pretty certain there weren't that many bodies in the town square."

Both he and Hemp turned their heads toward the center of town, the distant, stacked bodies readily visible from the City Hall building.

"As you know, I'm a statistician to a degree," said Hemp. "My informal count of bodies is around two hundred. Just more than half were consumed, either wholly or in part – save for the bones – and the rest were just killed."

So that leaves around 140 people unaccounted for," said Flex. "Anything unusual about the ones left behind?"

"While we've still got daylight, let's take a closer look," said Hemp. "Now you've piqued my curiosity. Why all the questions, Flex?"

Flex shook his head. "Just tryin' to figure out why they'd kill a couple hundred folks and take over a hundred with 'em. Makes no sense."

"Unless someone's building an army."

"Killin' people's friends and family is no way to ingratiate yourself to strangers," said Flex.

"Let's go," said Hemp, starting to walk. "We'll just be a minute. If you'd like to stay here, feel free. It is ripe down there. When we're finished we'll just whistle, and you can bring the cars down and retrieve us."

Only Flex, Gem, and Hemp ended up going back into the town square. As they walked, Hemp said, "You may be onto something, Flex."

"I'm thinkin' I might be." He took Gem's hand as they walked and she let him. She said nothing, but she squeezed it and looked at him.

When they got back down to the square, Hemp reached into his pack and pulled out three packets containing surgical masks. "Here," he said, holding them out. "Put these on. Don't do a bloody lot, but they will make you feel better about breathing."

Flex and Gem put the masks on.

Hemp knelt down next to four bodies stacked in the area of those who were not eaten, only killed. He rolled the first body over.

The bullet hole was cleanly in the center of the forehead. There was a larger circle around the hole itself.

"See this?" asked Hemp.

"Yes," said Gem. "What is it?"

"That's where the barrel was pressed against the skin when the gun was fired. There are no defensive wounds, no other sign of trauma to the body. I would say this man might have been unconscious when killed."

"He's older," said Gem. "Gray hair."

"Clothing is consistent with an older man," said Hemp. He looked up. "Hey. Look at this one."

Hemp moved to another body and rolled it over. This one had a cameo broach on her blouse. The hair was wispy, thin and gray.

"Another senior citizen," he said, looking around.

"And there," he said, standing and walking toward another group of bodies. These were all small.

He got there, snapped on a quick pair of nitrile gloves from his pack, and rolled the smaller body over onto its back.

Gem gasped. "Oh, my God," she whispered. "The face ... it's so tiny."

"A damned kid," said Flex. "What, Hemp? Maybe five, six years old?"

Flex thought back to Trina when he'd found her hiding in her bedroom. She had been that exact age then.

"There are more," said Hemp. "Many more, but it seems mostly the elderly."

"Just like the fuckin' Nazis," said Flex. "Kill all the prisoners too young or too old to pitch in."

Gem stood up and said, "Either they're building an army or collecting slave labor. From what I see here, they're not looking for the very old and very young, which means they're looking for muscle mass."

Hemp looked at Gem. "That is who I would choose for my army."

"Can we go now?" asked Gem.

*****

Before heading out of town they huddled for a moment between the vehicles.

"Wonder if there are any side roads," said Punch. "Ruthless bastards like that are likely to protect the main access road."

"Maybe there are some farming roads," said Nelson. We might just have to walk the last mile or so if they peter out."

Gem tapped the hood of the Crown Vic, impatient. "Let's go, everyone," she said. "We can figure that out on the fly. I want to get this over and done and get back home."

Flex listened to her words that sounded so simple. *Over. Done. Home.* He wondered if it would be as easy as that. If he were a gambling man – and he was – he'd bet against it.

*****

After dropping the supplies to Irene Danner, the caravan of two cars drove north through town.

"Slow down," said Hemp, rolling down his window. "Darling, you've got three on that side as well."

"I got it," she said, lowering her window. "Stop for a sec, would ya, Gem?"

"Sure, babe," said Gem, easing the Ford to a stop.

Charlie opened the door and got out, looked at the Taurus 9mm in her hand and said, "Fuck it. Pop the trunk, Gem. I need a bow fix."

Flex knew what she meant, and he smiled. Gem looked at him as she stopped the car and put it in park. Charlie was good with a gun – damned good – but if she didn't use her crossbow for a few kills, she got absolutely depressed.

"Make it snappy, please," said Flex.

Punch, in his cautious way, had stopped perhaps a hundred yards back. Because of his military training, he never liked it when two vehicles were right on top of one another, for they would too easily be taken out by a single IED or mortar shell – not that anyone had been utilizing weapons like those in the last decade or so – but old training was hard to shake.

Just ask Punch.

They were only two miles out of the square, but straggler walkers were clearly making their way into the undefended town of Great Bend, and they needed killing like all the rest.

"May I, brother?" asked Hemp, who had opted to stay in the car.

"Absolutely," said Flex, passing Hemp the suppressed Walther PPK.

"Want me to get those rotters, guys?" asked Nelson, the radio crackling to life.

Flex grabbed it. "Hemp's got these guys, and I think you can see Charlie's got the others."

"Cool," said Nelson. "Guys need a bowl?"

Nelson was a man who enjoyed his marijuana, but since the birth of his son, he'd cut back a bit. Now he only smoked when he either really needed to focus or he really needed to relax. As for supply, he had gathered up some of the wild pot that grew along the highways in Kansas, and over the years, had manipulated it into some fine weed that even Flex, Gem and Charlie indulged in with relative regularity.

Hemp sat in occasionally, and it was always hilarious to mimic his British accent when they were wasted. Flex smiled at the thought.

Gem took the radio. "Not now, Nel," she said. "Save me some. That really sounds good."

Flex didn't need to ask why. He could use a little out-of-his-head time, too.

There were now two rotters on Hemp's side, and he merely held his arm out the open window and waited until they drew within five feet. Then he put clean holes between their eyes, the hollow points blasting the back of their skulls wide open. *Pop! Pop!* One down ... then the other.

"Bloody hell," said Hemp. "See that spray? Lucky the breeze wasn't coming at us."

With the right side of the car clear, everyone turned to watch Charlie. They'd missed the first shot.

After fourteen years, the rotter population hadn't seemed to thin very much, unless of course you were talking in the literal sense. Their skin rotted if without fresh meat for too long, and there were plenty of creatures around that fell into that category.

The skin wrinkled like old leather and shrunk tightly over their skeletons. Hemp had explained that it was no longer the presence of tendons and muscles that allowed them to move. It was, as he had discovered some years before, individual cells that clustered, disbursed, regathered, and manipulated the body to move in a certain direction, or to stop altogether.

No, it didn't make any sense. The old, human ways of doing things, where the brain sent a signal through the nervous system and a muscle responded, were now joined on the other side by these things that did not need all that complexity to get from point A to point B. Hunger drove each cell within them and seemed to do so very effectively.

Charlie was not in any danger as she skirted around another of the ragged abnormals and retrieved her arrow from the downed creature's head. She mounted it back in the crossbow and ran about thirty yards toward Punch and the others waiting in the grape GTO.

Flex saw Dave wave to her as she ran by his car, and she waved back. Flex smiled. Ever since they had stolen away in the night to find the kidnapped Hemp – in Gem's stolen car, mind you – they had developed a special bond. Hemp did not mind, because he wasn't jealous. Charlie loved Dave and so did Hemp.

Charlie caught the female rotter's attention, and with no scent coming from her because of the WAT-5, it was clear the zombie was drawn solely by her movement. The jerky corpse turned and shambled unsteadily toward Charlie's location, even as the crossbow ace raised her weapon, ready to let a bolt fly.

Something distracted Charlie, and she glanced to her left. A second later, she lowered her crossbow and squinted at something.

"What the hell is she lookin' at?" asked Flex.

"Whatever it is, it's between those buildings," said Gem. "I can't see down that alley from here."

The female rotter continued to advance toward Charlie, but still she stared into the alley. She turned and took three slow steps, her eyes still narrowed.

"Jesus Christ," said Flex. "Hemp, if the girl needs glasses, you should just tell her."

"Her vision is spot on, but I agree, Flex. She should kill it *now*," said Hemp. "The other one is right behind it."

"Guys, what the hell is she doing?" asked Punch.

Gem threw the car in park as she and Flex unbuckled their seatbelts at the same time. They both flung the car doors open together, as if choreographed. Gem's ballistic steel door and bulletproof glass smacked the advancing she-rotter hard in the face. It crumpled backward, landing so awkwardly that its right arm snapped, now caught behind the thing's back. It had been a very solid impact, and Flex figured if they *could* be stunned, that one definitely was.

"Charlie!" yelled Gem. Charlie looked as though she were about to say something, but stopped and just nodded at Gem. Gem jabbed her finger toward the remaining zombie struggling to get back to its feet just three feet in front of her.

She held up one finger as she stood aside and closed the Crown Vic's door. She stepped around the Ford and returned Charlie's nod.

As the rotter got back to her feet, the severed arm held there only by the shriveled skin, she resumed her forward movement. Charlie finally focused on the kill at hand and brought the crossbow up to her eye. She fired from ten yards distant, hitting the creature squarely in the dark spot its nose had once occupied.

The abnormal dropped to her knees and collapsed forward, face down, hammering the arrow clean through her skull as she smacked the cracked asphalt hard.

"Nice shot, darling, but don't cut it so close next time," called Hemp.

"Guys!" Charlie called, pointing. "If that is not Isis' Hummer in that alley, then I'm going crazy."

They all ran. Gem passed both men, her feet laced into a pair of new Nike running shoes. The leather on the millions of pairs of shoes that could be found in any number of shoe stores was still in good shape, but the glue on all of the aged Chinese footwear had dried and cracked.

Hemp fixed that by formulating a strong, pliable glue that he gave over to the only cobbler in Kingman, a thin, jovial man who had changed his name to Daryl Shoemaker. Nobody was sure what he went by before, and it didn't matter.

Gem looked down the alley as Flex and Hemp reached them and said, "If the roof-mount machine gun wasn't your first clue, I don't know what was, kiddo."

Charlie remembered the last rotter, which had been behind the one she'd just taken out. "Hold on," she said, mounting an arrow, raising her bow and firing it unceremoniously. The bolt tore through the eye socket and the zombie's head flipped backward before it dropped like a stone.

"How we doing on our current dose of WAT-5?" asked Charlie, looking at Hemp.

"We've got a couple of hours of protection remaining."

"If they were in the vehicle they'd have seen us and let us know they did, so let's go see what we're up against."

*****

Punch, Dave, and Nelson joined them, but not before Nelson pulled Gem's car into the alley right behind Punch's GTO.

Good thinking, Flex thought. There was no sense in leaving vehicles as unusual as the Ford and the Pontiac in

128

obvious places in case the perpetrators of the slaughter returned to Great Bend.

As they approached the black H^3, they could see it appeared normal. No blood sprays on the glass, nothing shattered. It had clearly been parked there, tucked beside the building.

Nelson approached it and peered through the passenger side window, his hands cupped around his face. "There's a note on the seat," he said, turning toward the others.

Charlie was there before he could move out of the way. "Excuse me, Nel," she said, pulling the door open.

She retrieved the note and read it aloud:

We left without telling you because Max and I felt a sense of urgency. We knew you had enough experience that you did not need us along on your run to Wichita.

We rested in this warehouse for the night, so if you stopped as well, you will not be far behind us. There was no planning to do because it is unclear what we will face once there.

We thought it best to stash the car here and hike the rest of the way. We found some flyers in the City Hall building that said the meeting in the middle of town was with people from Hoisington, about seven or so miles north of here. As you no doubt saw, the intent of their guests does not appear to have been what the people of Great Bend expected.

Max and I are not sure what it is, but we feel something. There's the constant push and pull of the

Mothers and Hungerers, but there's something else. It is at once familiar and strange and something that feels dark. I mean that in the evil sense, not the opposite of light.

We are not going into Hoisington today; rather we are waiting at the edge of town until nightfall. We intend to stop once we see lights from the town.

It feels as though that will be the better plan. If you make it here today, we will be walking north on the road you were just on.

We will wait until an hour after dark. We should be in radio contact when you are two or three miles out. Use channel 12. Safe travels. We love you.

Isis, Max, Trina & Taylor

Charlie looked up. "Backpacks. Guns, crossbow, ammo, lots of it. Now I'm glad we've got so many pack mules."

"Is that what we are to you, Charlie?" asked Punch. "You got a ball buster there, Hemp, old buddy."

"She's been busting balls since the day I met her," he said. "What should change after a dozen years or so?"

As they walked briskly to the Crown Vic and GTO, Gem hit the remote, popping the trunk latch. She got to it, reached in, and pulled out her backpack.

The high-quality pack had been custom sewn to handle every weapon any of them could ever need. It had two separate slots for high-end water guns filled with urushiol blend, a lined, waterproof zipper pouch for WAT-5 wafers, and another compartment for sealed canisters of pure urushiol oil. This was enough to make gallons of the blended mix. There were other compartments for loaded ammo magazines and two for 50-round boxes.

Her Uzi was secured to the side, almost in firing position, with a rear bungee holding the butt and a quick-pull Velcro strap to free the barrel. She had it down so that she could go from empty hands to up and firing in under three seconds.

Nelson, as usual, configured his pack differently, as his weapons of choice were unique, and of course, he had to have a little compartment for weed. And a lighter, which they all carried.

Most of the Bics had leaked out all the butane, but some of them still held it. They now resorted to Zippos and Ronson lighter fluid refill cans.

In ten hurried minutes, they were on the road, walking north at a good clip.

Gem tried the radio far too soon. There was no answer, and all it served to do was make her anxious. Flex walked beside her and held her hand, and she let him. Nobody spoke, but Flex knew that all seven sets of eyes were on the road ahead, hoping to be the first to spot their loved ones.

*****

They had no idea how far they had walked, but after entering and leaving an industrial area, where Hemp pointed out several tanker trucks that appeared to have propane symbols on them, the buildings became fewer and farther between.

Hemp passed around what was the equivalent of an energy bar, developed by him and Charlie. They actually

131

tasted good, but unlike the old pre-packaged type loaded with preservatives, these never quite dried enough not to be sticky as hell. They had used honey for a sweetener and they filled you up fast, providing the necessary energy.

Flex said, "Is that them?"

As they watched, what appeared to be just a light pink spot in the distance rose from ground level to a few feet off the street ahead. It was a person, to be sure, and judging from the color, it was a girl.

Three more figures entered the roadway from the east, and all four began waving their arms.

"There's no need to run," said Flex, but before the words were out of his mouth, Gem and Charlie started running as fast as their tired legs could carry them.

"Aw, shit no," said Flex, shifting his pack on his back.

"This is why I didn't bring Serena," said Dave. "What is it with women and their emotion-induced desire to run to people?"

"Can't fight City Hall," said Nelson, breaking into a jog and laughing as he passed them. The others followed him.

Nelson turned back, smiling. "Just be glad you didn't bring Lola, Punch. That chick can run."

"Wasn't easy to chase her down that first time," he said.

"As I recall it, she chased you down, buddy," said Flex. It was true. Lola had been drawn to Punch the first time they laid eyes on one another. They had gotten married six years ago, but both had decided they did not want to bring children into a world mostly populated with zombies.

Flex wasn't sure about that. By the time the world was clear of them, Punch and Lola would probably be dead.

Maybe they feared it would happen by other than old age and they would leave their children without parents.

Flex's mind returned to his son, but by the time that happened, they had reached the girls and he thought about how they would break the news to them about what had happened to Flexy.

By the time Flex and the others reached them, Gem was in tears again, her arms wrapped around a sobbing Trina. Gem must have blurted out the horrible news the moment she reached her daughter.

*****

CHAPTER SEVEN

Gem cried as though she had just received the news of her son's death for the first time. Her tremendous sadness ripped Flex's heart apart, but she had to let it come. Coupled with his own, he wondered how they would bear it.

Now, with no rotters nearby, was as good a time as any to feel the pain and let it come. Shared grief healed broken people more quickly – at least that's what Flex had always believed.

Taylor and Charlie were in an embrace so tight Flex could not imagine either of them could breathe. Taylor had loved Flex Sheridan Jr. like a kid brother, and she taught him how to play *Fuck Off* – the renamed card game, *Go Fish* – as soon as he could hold five cards in his little hands and say the words.

After Hemp released him from a relieved hug, Flex, Nelson, and Punch greeted Max Chatsworth, who, like Isis, had not a tear in his eyes. While clearly devastated, neither he nor Isis *could* cry. It was not a part of their physiological makeup; just another thing that made them unique from unaffected humans. Hemp said it was because of the compound leaking from their tear ducts that caused their eyes to appear red. The ducts had clearly been repurposed in the womb.

Flex knew from watching both of them grow up that they felt the pain of loss very deeply, perhaps more deeply than anyone else did.

Their grief was a heavy burden on their shoulders, with no way to express it.

Flex finally got his arms around Max and hugged his Godson long and hard. He pulled back and put his hand on Max's cheek. "I'm glad you're okay, kid," he said. "Thanks for taking care of our girls."

"You know they don't need much taking care of," said Max. "We haven't run into much trouble – Great Bend aside – but when we did they were on top of it."

Max looked so much like Hemp that to Flex, it was like going back in a time machine. He did have a bit of Charlie, particularly in his nose and cheekbones, but his hair, eyes and chin – even under that beard – were all Hemp.

Dave and Isis, who had been very close since the day he arrived to rescue them from that underground bunker, held one another in silence. She was his cousin, and family meant more than ever on a post-apocalyptic planet Earth.

They had found Max, Isis, Trina and Taylor well before nightfall, so they had time to sit and grieve together. It was necessary, though it would never be enough time, Flex knew.

*****

"I don't know if I can do this now," said Trina, wiping her eyes in a fruitless effort to dry them. Her tears continued to come, and occasionally, the 21-year-old would revert to sobs again.

135

Eric A. Shelman

Isis put a hand on Trina's shoulder. "What's happened is more serious than we sensed from Kingman, Trina," she said. "Now that we're so close, we have to learn the motives behind the inhabitants of Hoisington."

"She's right," said Max. "We need your skills, Trina, every bit as much as we need everyone else. I'm glad you all came."

Charlie said, "Did you come up with a plan?"

"A few options are on the table," said Isis.

"Now would be a good time to talk about it," said Gem. "The sun's starting to set."

"Agreed," said Isis. "Before you arrived, Max and I were talking about what we feel from the town."

"How do you feel a town?" asked Nelson. His hand subconsciously moved to his pocket and he withdrew a glass pipe and a Zippo.

"It's what's in the town, Nel," said Isis. "As you know, since I was around a year old, I haven't been without Max. I recall feeling his presence then, the moment he was born and took his first breath. There was a kind of connection, a sense of light and presence."

"And I've never known a world without Isis' energy," said Max. "But since we started feeling the Mothers and Hungerers in the northwest, there's been something darker. We didn't say anything to you because we knew we had to come and we didn't want to worry you."

"Color me worried," said Flex. "But I'm glad we're here, too."

"You brought WAT-5?" asked Isis.

"Does the pope shit in the woods?" asked Punch.

"I imagine he does if he's on a camping trip," said Nelson. "That's what I do."

"Yeah, we brought it. Lots of it. Why?"

"Isis and I need to go out for a few," said Max.

136

"Out, like unconscious?" asked Dave. "Why?"

Isis looked toward Hoisington and got on her feet. Flex followed suit, standing beside her.

The sun had now dropped below the horizon and now, faint glows had appeared in the town.

"Okay, so that's where they are," she said. "I thought there might be a chance they came from somewhere else and wiped out the people in Hoisington, too."

"I hadn't thought of that," said Gem. "So why do you need to go out?"

"They want to see what it feels like without the other," said Trina, sniffling. "Right now, the darkness they sense is masked by the goodness of Max. If he's out, she won't sense him."

"We did that in Bug's bunker," said Dave. "Gave you some WAT-5 dust we had left in the corner of a baggie, and you were out like a light."

"It's the only blacked out spot in my history," she said, "which is how it sits in my memory. I remember, in vivid detail, every other second of my life. All but that one."

"When you were out, the red-eye didn't pay any attention to you," said Dave.

"Exactly," said Isis. "Give Max a WAT-5, please."

"Are you guys on it now?" asked Nel, looking at Trina and Taylor.

Neither answered, but they looked guilty and a bit embarrassed.

"Trina, Tay?" asked Gem.

They shook their heads.

"Seriously?" said Gem.

"Then it's nap time," said Flex. "Max, take the whole thing. You might close that fuckin' mental gate of yours, but let's call this backup."

As they did when they were kids, Trina and Taylor sat cross-legged, back to back. When they took their doses, Nelson went over and steadied them so they didn't topple over sideways. Everyone else took theirs, too, but all were already on it so they did not sleep.

Isis took none for the moment, and Max was ready to pop the wafer into his mouth.

"Okay," said Isis.

Max lay on his back in the grass beside the roadway and took the wafer. Two chews and a swallow, and his eyes rolled back, his eyelids fluttered.

Isis gasped. She sat, cross-legged, staring straight ahead; not at anyone or anything. In the waning evening light, her eyes appeared glossy.

Gem scooted to her and Dave moved to her other side. They held her hands and she slowly closed them, squeezing their fingers in hers. She stared into an abyss that none of the others could see, but all could feel.

"Isis," said Dave. "Tell us what … what do you feel?"

"Terror," she murmured. "And … anger. Power and evil."

"It's me," she said. "But not me. It's pain and fear and … anger. The fear rises above all."

Isis stood slowly and turned again toward the distant town of Hoisington. Nelson woke up the girls, and Trina said, "What's wrong with Isis?"

"Shh," said Punch, his finger to his lips. "She might be figuring things out."

"If anything, I am more confused," she said. "I feel as though something that had the potential to be very good has turned very bad. Not one, but many. Wake Max, please. It's enough."

"Are you sure you can't –"

"Now, please!" shouted Isis.

138

It was rare. Isis never raised her voice; never became agitated. Never.

Flex felt the hair on the back of his neck rise to attention. Whatever they faced was even more serious and frightening than a town full of corpses could convey.

Trina hurried over and shook Max awake. The moment he sat up, it was as though Isis had been freed from a prison cell. She dropped to the ground and said, "Max, I don't know if you should feel what I just did."

"I don't have a choice," he said. "You know it's true."

Isis nodded. She held out her hand and Gem put a wafer into it.

Before she took it, she whispered, "I'm sorry, Max."

*****

The moment Isis' eyes rolled back in her head and closed, Max's face turned frightened.

"Oh … my God," he said. His hands shook so badly that Flex noticed him interlace his fingers together to keep them still.

"What do you feel, Max?" asked Charlie in her most soothing voice.

Max did not answer immediately. He slowly stood and turned toward the town, rotating his head to the right as if to position one ear to listen to whatever sounds he heard in his mind.

"There's anguish," he said. "Not from the Hungerers, but from the Mothers."

"Are the Hungerers capable of anguish? Of feelings?" asked Taylor.

Max moved his head side to side very slowly. "No," he said. "They hunger and do the bidding of the Mothers. None can obey now."

139

"Obey who?" asked Taylor, her eyes fixed upon the transfixed boy who did not look like a boy.

"Mothers, Hungerers. None have freewill," said Max.

Flex looked at the others. "Hemp? Go ahead."

"Max, do you feel the same darkness that Isis felt?" he asked.

He turned to look at his father, as though the voice that had soothed him while he lay awake in his crib so many long hours brought him out of his trance. He nodded. "I do, dad. Not from the Mothers, and not from the Hungerers. I hear it from …"

He trailed off. Flex wanted to discuss his current mental state with Hemp, but he did not want to talk about him as if he was not there.

Max certainly heard or felt something they could not, and Flex wasn't sure he wanted to know what it was. Still, if they were to go into Hoisington, they had to know.

"From what, son?" asked Hemp.

"I … I feel as if it's just out of my reach," said Max. "I feel Isis … but not like her at all. Threatening."

Nelson walked up and touched Max's arm, and the boy jerked away as though receiving an electrical shock. He spun away from Nelson so fast that it caused the ninja star expert to stagger backward for a moment before catching his balance.

"Whoa, dude, I'm sorry," said Nelson. "I thought a human touch might calm you down, bro."

"There are others like me. Others like Isis," said Max. "They do not have freewill, and I … I …"

This time Charlie stood again and moved beside Max. She took his hand in hers very gently and he turned to look down at her face. "Mom," he said. "They feel us too."

"Lower your shade, Max," said Hemp. "Now."

'Yeah, right," he said, closing his eyes for a long moment. "It's done."

"Do you feel them sensing you now?" asked Hemp.

"Confusion," he said. "We shouldn't call. They might understand what we are." He looked at Dave, his eyes suddenly clear. "Wake Isis, please Dave?"

"You got it," said Dave, and knelt down beside Isis. He shook her shoulder and her eyelids fluttered open. She sat, then stood.

"Max," she said. "Did you feel it?"

"The darkness," said Max. "The confusion at us ... the feeling it *was* us."

Isis said, "Max, I think we both know the truth now. They stared at one another for a long moment, then each of them nodded.

"No closed door meetings, you little shits," said Gem.

Flex realized they had been using their telepathic communication, which was something nobody could believe when they were infants.

When they played one another at chess, it was impossible to determine who would win. Each player anticipated the other's moves right through the very end of the game. Ultimately, one of them always had to make a move they knew would be their demise. As adults, they had taken to blocking one another to make for a fair game, but there were many intense, mental battles when they were young, to be sure.

Both had explained that they were aware of the perceived pointlessness of playing one another back then, but they used it intentionally to sharpen their abilities.

"There are more there like us," said Isis. "My gender allows me more connection with them, but they are like us only in how they were created."

"What do you mean by that?" asked Hemp.

"They don't have any self-purpose," said Isis. "They're slaves."

"Who the fuck's slaves are they?" asked Trina, dropping her crossbow down into her hand, her eyes flashing anger.

That little girl who used to charge us a quarter for a curse word would be dead broke if abiding by her own rules.

"I heard a name," said Max. "I'm not sure it's anything to do with it, but it kept floating into my mind while you were sleeping, Isis."

"What's the name?" asked Punch.

"Maestro," said Isis.

"Master," said Dave. "In Spanish."

"Anything else?" asked Flex. "Angus maybe?"

"No," said Isis. "The only name I associated fear with was Maestro."

"I don't like the sound of that," said Nelson, reaching for his pipe.

"Is this a good idea?" asked Dave. "Going in there? I mean, has anyone ever heard of letting sleeping dogs lie?"

Isis looked back toward the town of Great Bend, where Irene Danner waited for her salvation, hiding in her home in a town occupied only by her, some wayward zombies, and stacks and stacks of dead bodies. She turned back to Dave.

"Clearly the dogs around here aren't sleeping," said Isis. "What happens if we don't act? They can just as easily venture south until they hit Kingman. There's dark power amassing here, and it has to be stopped now."

Hemp looked at the sky, now dark, moonless and starting to fill in with a billion flickering stars.

He looked at the others. "It's impossible to make a plan until we reach the city proper and have a look around,"

142

he said. "We've got the night-vision goggles in the Crown Victoria. Bring binoculars and all of our radios. Most importantly – Max and Isis, I hope you are listening – we stay together. If you need to separate from us, then please explain your plan beforehand."

They both nodded.

"Let's load up," said Gem. "And if we can finish this tonight, that's what I'd like to do."

Flex looked at Gem, her eyes tired, her shoulders slumped. In short, she looked defeated, but he wasn't fooled.

Gem Cardoza Sheridan was never defeated. Ever. When the time came to put her fierce intensity to the test, Gem would dazzle.

As always.

*****

The group of eleven walked along the edge of the road toward Hoisington. It increased the risk of being observed, but after a short time trying to approach on smaller, overgrown paths that ran parallel to the road, it was necessary. Without a lead team with sickles, or machetes, or a John Deere tractor, it was too arduous a process.

"Doesn't take long for nature to wipe out every trace of mankind, does it?" asked Flex, to nobody in particular.

"In another twenty years, unless something changes, most of this planet will be primitive once again," said Hemp. "We're well on our way there, save for places like Kingman."

"We'll see what there is to offer in Hoisington," said Punch. "I might suggest we stick to quiet methods of taking out the deadheads or anyone else who needs it. Knives, and in Nel's case, the stars."

143

"Agreed," said Hemp. "Use the estrogen blocker-tipped knives, too. Cover all bases. That way if you encounter a red-eye you don't have to penetrate very far with the blade. Just a poke will do."

Hemp had created knife sheaths with plastic ends approximately an inch deep. This last section was filled with the estrogen-blocking agent in an oil base, so clung to the blades as they came out. It did not take much to do the necessary damage to an aggressive red-eye.

A noise came in the night. Everyone stopped.

"Shh," said Taylor. "Look!" She pointed ahead.

A small light bounced up and down, floating just a few feet from the ground. It was clearly moving toward them, and the sound was now louder.

"That's a two-stroke engine," said Punch. "Sounds like a little bike."

"Everyone off the road," said Flex.

They split up and moved to both sides of the street. Flex lay beside Gem in the tall grass on the east side of the two-lane road.

The light bounced toward them, moving fairly slow. Every once in a while another light would come on and shine on both sides of the road, then go out again.

"99.9% chance they're armed," said Punch. "Be smart and quiet, people."

Everyone shut up. The whining motor approached, and as the bike whizzed by us without using its search beams, Flex saw there were two riders. Just after passing them, the passenger, who held a flashlight in one hand and a rifle in the other, flicked on the light again and shone it on both sides of the road before clicking it off.

Everyone watched it recede into the gray-black distance and moved back into the road.

"Wonder where they're headed," said Trina, watching the last vestiges of the bobbing light. "Maybe on some kind of supply run?"

"There's no resistance in Great Bend anymore," said Hemp. "Perhaps they cleaned it out to use it for resources and they're going on a supply run."

"Not enough room on that mini bike for that," said Punch. "That right there's a perimeter check."

"Let's get a move on," said Charlie. "Max, be sure to let us know if at any time you think we should turn around and head back to Kingman."

"If you want to go," said Isis, "then you should. Some of us may die here."

"Isis!" said Dave. "Seriously?"

She stopped walking and turned to face the others. "I love all of you," she said. "I've always been honest with you for that very reason; it keeps you safe."

"We know that, Isis," said Nelson.

"But you don't know what I feel right now. You would call them *alarm bells* going off in your head. I feel the danger of this journey in every nerve ending in my body, and I know that's difficult to understand, but it's more intense than anything I've ever felt before."

"It's the same for me," said Max. "Mom, when Isis was out for that brief time, it was as though all goodness in the world was quieted, and only the darkness could reach me. I don't know if I hid it very well, but I was scared as hell."

Charlie put her arm around her son. "I saw it. I'm sorry."

"It's okay, mom. But that's why we can't turn back. What we're feeling here can't be content to stay put. Eventually they'll come to us where we live."

145

Isis continued. "There's a darkness in that town, and perhaps other towns like it. It's why we told you there had to be more of us created."

"But don't you have second thoughts now?" asked Taylor. "I mean ... you said you sense others like you are there, and I can only presume that they're not ... I don't know ... *good* like you?"

"I don't know that they are inherently cruel and evil," said Isis, "but they appear to be under the control of, and alive at the behest of, someone who refers to himself as Maestro."

Max squeezed Charlie's hand and looked at her in the gloom. "Mom, there's nothing about this that feels like it's going to be easy, and I know the years haven't been easy on –"

"If you even go there I'll kick your ass, mister," interrupted Charlie. "I'm only 39 years old you little shit, and I've still got a crapload of kickass left in my tank."

"God, I've known you all my life," said Max. "You'd think I'd know when to shut the hell up."

"And yet you don't," said Hemp, smiling. "But Max and Isis are absolutely right about one thing. If any one of you is not up to whatever might be waiting up ahead, you should go back to Kingman now. Without delay."

"Don't look at me, dude," said Nelson. "I went to California with Davy, and I didn't even have a good reason for that. This sounds like a pretty good reason to be here."

Nobody else left, either. They passed a street called Sheridan Avenue and Flex was tempted to steal the sign – a tribute to his days as a teenager.

It would keep for when they were on the way home. They would be coming home. All of them.

If Flex had anything to say about it.

146

*****

They reached a place with a sign in front that said, *Springer's Used Cars*, and the lot brimmed with very old vehicles barely visible behind the brown weeds that had overtaken the lot.

"Damned sign should say Springer's Very Used Cars," said Punch. "What's that, a fucking Cutlass?"

"Looks like it, but we're getting close now. Good time to duck back here and strategize."

Everyone moved off the road again and zigzagged through the weeds and cars until they were behind a corrugated steel building.

On the road there had been more lights ahead, albeit dim, likely candles or some sort of lanterns.

"It doesn't appear that they've gotten any significant power up in town," said Hemp.

"It's quiet, too," said Gem. "I don't hear any generators running at all."

"Good," said Punch. "Means we'll hear the two-stroke if it comes back." He was always looking at every situation from a Marine's perspective. Logistics.

Max and Isis were quietly staring into one another's eyes, so everyone just allowed them to finish whatever it was they were communicating. Finally, Isis turned to us. "We feel them very close now," she said. "Hundreds, we believe. Mothers, Hungerers and others like us."

Trina said, "Isis, do you know how many? Could you and Max be overpowered?"

Isis shook her head. "We just don't know, Trina. We've never faced others like us, much less with a malevolent intent."

"Fuckin' bugs are eating me alive," said Charlie. "Can we do something?"

147

"We must defer to Max and Isis," said Hemp, turning to the pair. "What would your plan have been if we weren't here?"

"To leave Trina and Taylor here with radios and we would have gone into town to investigate," said Max.

"And is that still viable?" asked Hemp. "Preferred?"

"Actually, yes," said Isis. "We'll bring conventional weapons, too. But we should go in alone."

"Fuck," said Charlie.

"I know," said Hemp.

"We'll be safe, mom and dad," said Max.

"Just go. Hurry back." Charlie threw her arms around Max's neck. "Hit that radio and we'll come. Use the tap method unless you need to tell us something."

"I will, mom." He let go of her and looked at Isis. "Ready?"

"Yes," she said. "Give us an hour. We'll be in touch. Sync the radios to frequency hopping so nobody can listen in."

The radios were turned on and synced. With the frequency hopping setting, the radios changed channels constantly, hopping from frequency to frequency in microsecond bursts, allowing them to always be synced, but anyone listening in on a single frequency would hear such a short blip of sound they would likely not recognize it as a human voice.

Max and Isis set out. Everyone sat down for a good rest.

In twenty minutes, they heard the sound of the motorcycle engine off in the distance.

*****

CHAPTER EIGHT

Flex unclipped the radio, paired with the one that Isis and Max had with them, and pushed the transmit button. "Max, come in."

Immediately came, "We hear it." It was Max.

"Okay," said Flex. "You in a safe place?"

"Yes, for now," said Max. "There's an odd series of fences here."

"Odd?" asked Flex. The motorcycle passed him and he got low with the others and remained silent for a moment.

"Yes, but we're not sure what the design is yet."

"Okay, they just passed us," warned Flex. "Should be to you soon. Get out of sight."

"Roger," said Max.

It was quiet for a few minutes. Then he came back on and said, "It's like a maze."

"A maze?" asked Flex. "How do you know?"

"We saw the motorcycle go through, but we couldn't tell how. We were hiding."

Flex turned to Hemp. "Looks like there may be a maze at the entrance to Hoisington."

Hemp stared back at him. "I'm sorry, did you say a *maze*?"

"That's what he said. Flex pushed the button. "Max, come in."

"Here, Flex."

"What is the maze made of? Hedges?"

"No, no. It's some sort of custom-built, steel fencing. Tall, like eight or nine feet, and it has barbed wire on top."

"Can you tell its purpose?" asked Flex.

Isis came on. "Flex, it appears at this point they've sealed off any southern access points into the town except for this maze entrance. There are two doors side-by-side, and I assume one of them will not get you in at all, while the other may be challenging. We've only ventured in a short distance. Because of our memory abilities, we will remember it when we get through it once."

"Good," said Flex. "Isis, are you guys gonna be exposed when you go through?"

"If anyone's watching us from a remote, elevated post, yes," she said. "There's no moon, but the stars are bright. We'll keep an eye out, but it's a distinct possibility."

"No way around that entrance?" asked Flex.

Another pause. "The fence runs east and west as far as we can see in this light," said Isis.

"You guys comfortable going in?"

"I can tell you we're more comfortable with the two of us rather than eleven," she said.

"Okay, but just for a quick reconnaissance mission. We didn't follow you up here so we could sit back like lumps while you get killed, so be careful and stay in communication when you can," said Flex.

"Roger that," said Max, who had apparently resumed communication duties.

"We wait," said Flex, to the others, putting the radio down. "Oh, fuckin' joy."

*****

Thirty minutes had passed. "Dudes, this is driving me nuts!" said Nelson. "I wonder if they got caught or something."

"Don't even say that, Nel," said Gem.

Flex caught Gem throwing quick glances at Trina and Taylor, and he knew she was grateful they were there with them.

It was 8:45 PM when they heard Max's voice say in a whisper, "Okay, we're through."

"What's the story?" asked Flex.

"It is elaborate," said Max. "And we noticed there are wheels on the bottom of some sections of fencing, but they're locked in place by padlocks."

"Does it look like it can be opened and just made into a big walkway?"

"No," said Max. "Several of the pieces have the wheels. Isis thinks it's so the maze can be reconfigured if someone figures it out."

"That's stupid," said Flex. "Why the hell build an elaborate maze when you could just post guards? How long did it take you guys to get through?"

"The fence has some areas where it might be possible to see into it while people are coming through, but now we're in, we don't see any towers or anything," said Max. "Just in case, we crouched down low while we went through. Having to figure it out and backtrack a bunch of times, it still only took about twenty-five minutes. Coming home it should be a straight run, so maybe five minutes to get back through."

151

"As long as they don't discover you and reconfigure it," said Flex. "Or they could have a regular schedule for reconfiguration that inhabitants of Hoisington know."

"Let's hope not," said Max. "Flex, we're continuing north. We'll be in touch."

*****

"How many people do you think were involved in the Great Bend attack?" asked Nelson.

Hemp shook his head. "It's impossible to say, Nel. If it's as we suspect and there were Mothers, Hungerers and Hybrids like Max and Isis involved, the number of humans would only be significant to how easy or difficult it will be for us to maneuver within Hoisington."

"What do you mean?" asked Trina.

"To answer that, we must review the chain of command, as it were. If there are Hybrids here, as Max and Isis stated they feel, then they control the Mothers to a degree, and in turn, the Hungerers. If the Hybrids do not have freewill, then we can assume that means they are under this Maestro's control."

"So, long story short?" said Punch.

"Long story short," said Hemp, "We know that well-seasoned Hybrids can handle the Mothers and Hungerers. Minimal human involvement is necessary."

Punch stood up and stared toward the town. "I say we recon the place and see if there's another way in besides the damned maze."

"It's not a bad idea," said Gem. "If they discover the kids, they'll zero in on them fast. If there are three groups, they'd have a harder time of it."

"Let's give them another half hour," said Dave. "Then I'm game for whatever."

*****

Gem kept checking the radio to make sure it was working. Isis' voice came on at twenty-nine minutes, just one minute until the end of their self-imposed deadline.

"Okay, guys, we've found them," she said. "Now I know why there weren't sentries."

"Why's that?" asked Gem, who had been clutching the radio like it was a stress reliever.

"Everyone in this place is a prisoner," she said. "At least that's what it looks like."

"Where are you?" asked Gem.

"At the high school," she said. "It's dark and we're still outside the main school grounds, so we can't see a whole lot, but we can feel hundreds of them here. Maybe thousands."

"Should you get out?" asked Gem, her face worried as she stared at Flex.

"No," said Isis. "We need to be positioned inside before daylight, so you guys need to get through the maze."

"Seriously?" asked Gem.

"If we're going to take out this threat here, then yes," she said. "We can guide you through. In fact, we can do it now if you can write down the turns."

"I have a pencil and paper in my pack," said Hemp. He grabbed it and rummaged around, withdrawing them. He gave them over to Gem.

"Okay," she said. "Ready, Isis."

As Flex and the others looked on, Gem wrote down a series of numbers, associated with either an S, L or R. When she was done, she repeated the sequence of what were apparently turns, back to Isis.

"That's correct," she said. "If you look overhead, you'll see that some clouds appear to be moving in, so if you wait perhaps another fifteen minutes, I believe you'll have better cover. Once you're through the maze, get out of sight and radio me again."

"Done," said Gem. She turned the volume down and looked at everyone. "Get your game faces on, everyone. I have a feeling this is going to get serious."

Flex watched Gem's face. She hadn't cried in a while, and she had been avoiding eye contact with him, probably for that very reason. He knew that if she looked at him she would think of the son they had lost, and that would be the trigger for Niagara Falls. It was better she remain focused on whatever task lay ahead.

*****

Flex and Gem approached the maze entry first. They stood and looked east and west, confirming what Max and Isis had said. The fence extended in both directions as far as the eye could see.

"Which door?" asked Taylor, who stood beside the left one.

"Other one," said Gem. "I've got the direction key so I'll lead. Let's go single file and be as quiet as possible."

Flex followed her, his Daewoo out just for good measure. He had quick access to his knife, but in the confines of the maze it did not appear he would need one.

Gem reached the first turn and said, "Left." She checked off the first L on her paper and kept walking. She reached another left right choice and said, Right."

She turned and stifled a scream. In front of her was perhaps the tallest, palest zombie Flex had ever seen. His arms extended, the fingers of his left hand got entangled in

154

Gem's wild hair, so when she dropped down quickly to avoid his mouth, his caught hand followed. Now on the ground, she seized the wrist of the creature with both hands and twisted it.

The large zombie's body turned in the direction of Gem's assault as Flex withdrew his knife from its sheath and thrust it quickly underneath the monster's chin. The long blade poked through the rotting flap of neck skin and plunged deep into the rotter's gray matter, dripping black-red lifeblood from the creature onto Gem as she hid her face from the oozing muck.

The monster's knees buckled forward and he dropped to his back beside Gem and lay still. She stared down at the corpse and held out her hand. Flex helped her up with a quick pull.

"You okay, babe?" asked Flex.

"Yeah," said Gem. "Startled me is all. Won't happen again."

"It's not a crime," he said, turning to Hemp.

"Hemp," whispered Flex. "I've noticed when I stab 'em under the chin their knees tend to buckle. Is there some sort of connector between those places?"

"I'm not an acupuncturist Flex, but I promise to look into it if you remind me later."

Flex shrugged. "Not important, pal. Old habits from the early days is all."

"You sure you're okay, mom?" asked Trina.

"Yeah, sweetie," she answered, trying to wipe some of the muck from her hair. "Not sure why but I didn't expect them in here. Guess they make their way in now and then."

"Or it's part of the obstacle," said Punch.

"Just keep an eye out, mom," said Trina.

"I will, Trini," said Gem, resuming. She turned left, then right, then right, then passed a left and a right and

155

made a second left, which she had marked as a 2L. It took them a full seven minutes to get through, but eventually a doorway revealing the town of Hoisington emerged.

"I have the night vision goggles," said Punch, activating them. "Let me slide through and take a look."

He stood at the door and scanned from left to right. A strange noise came from somewhere, but it was distant. There was nobody near the maze entrance.

"Looks clear," he said. "Hey. There's an auto supply store over there. Let's get away from this maze and under cover."

"I could use a crowbar," said Dave. "Wonder how the stock is."

*****

"Max, Isis, come in," said Flex, into the radio.

A few seconds passed and Isis came on. "Are you in?"

"We are," said Flex. "We're inside this picked through Auto Parts store by the maze."

"We're at Hoisington High School. We've accessed a small building at the end of the football field," said Isis. "I believe it was a concession stand, judging from the equipment inside. There are some holes in the front that we can see through."

"Why did you set up there?" asked Flex.

"Because this is where they're amassed," said Isis. "Red mist coats the entire field. It's thick and stationary, as though contained on its own. It doesn't drift upward, nor does it seep through the fencing. It just … *it stays*. It defies logic when you think about the typical properties of a vapor."

156

Flex looked at the others. The radio was very low to keep it from being overheard by anyone outside, but it was enough that everyone huddled around could hear it.

"So it's like the auction house Hemp and I found in Concord," said Flex. "Underneath that vapor are hundreds of zombies."

"That's the process by which the red-eyes advance their connection with the Hungerers," said Hemp. "Flex, please. The radio."

He held out his hand and Flex handed him the walkie-talkie.

"Max, Isis," he began. "Have you seen any other movement? Lights, activity of any kind?"

"Max and I feel the focus is on this football field," she said. "Coming through town we saw two or three Hungerers, but we're on WAT-5, so they paid us no mind."

"Isn't the football field all overgrown?" asked Hemp.

"Hey, Dad, it's me," said Max. "Isis is checking something out. Anyway, for the Mothers to be using the football field for their conditioning sessions, someone is definitely cutting the grass. Otherwise, it would be tall enough to see above the vapor and it would be nearly impossible to lie down in it."

The connection with the red-eyes seemed to have resulted in Isis and Max gleaning more detailed information than what could be gathered by an unaffected human from simply observing them. While Max had explained it one night as not being information intentionally shared, it was as though when in close proximity to them, an understanding of their actions was attained, almost by osmosis.

"So we have no idea where this Maestro is," said Flex.

Hemp shook his head, then pushed the button. "It makes sense that we must cut off the proverbial head of the snake," he said. "But first we've got to find it."

"Hold on for a second dad," said Max.

Everyone just stared at one another in silence until Max came back on. "Okay. I know we didn't want to have to do this, but it's time to put on your zombie outfits."

"Everything?" asked Hemp.

"Eye drops, too."

Flex shook his head. "Hemp, tell me you brought that nose shit with you."

"Flex," he said, "Whenever I anticipate needing to disguise myself as a zombie, I always bring it."

There was a time that Hemp invented something called a BSN, or a Brain Scent Neutralizer. It was a helmet that when worn, sniffed the odor coming from a human head – such as the brain – and reversed and neutralized that odor. It was essentially the first attempt at being invisible to the abnormals, and it did work, though crudely. The WAT-5 negated the need for the outdated device.

In the meantime, after finding the need to "fit in" with the zombies now and again, Hemp was tired of gagging from the necessary muck and biological matter he had to smear on himself.

Necessity being the mother of invention, Hemp created something he called OSN. Olfactory Sense Neutralizer. It was used like a nasal mist and consisted of all natural ingredients. When applied, it eliminated a person's sense of smell for up to two hours at a time.

"Thank God," said Flex. "If I can't smell it, I'm less likely to puke on someone."

"Once you're in character, remember to walk the part," said Max. "Find a safe place to stash your stuff and use the sewn-in pockets to carry your weapons and spare rounds. Remember your knives, too."

"Okay, Max," said Hemp. "You'll see us coming when we're ready. I think we'll wander over a few at a time so we don't look out of place if anyone is watching."

Hemp put down the radio and said, "Let's suit up."

With a universal groan, everyone unzipped the special compartments in their backpacks. These had been incorporated into everyone's gear all over Kingman. It started with a plastic-lined pocket large enough to hold clothing that had been pilfered from the actual Hungerers themselves.

To avoid actual infection from the nasty, biological matter the creatures leaked onto their garments, they took digital photographs of the clothes from all angles once they were removed from their previous owners. Afterward, they washed them thoroughly. Most did not come very clean, but it didn't matter. Once dry, the staining and markings they had washed out were reapplied using paints and stains. The result was uncanny. Perfect, in fact.

Everyone also carried a bag of what Hemp called the most benign biological matter he could come up with, though he would not say what exactly it was. It was used to smear over one's exposed body parts, face included.

This costume muck was what triggered the gag reflex and required the OSN. Once they were dressed and their hair teased into 80's hairstyles, along with a few twigs and leaves for good measure, the slime was applied.

It was the finishing touch. When they were done, Flex would have put a bullet into the skulls of any one of his companions if they approached him out of the blue.

Except Gem. He'd know her anywhere. Hell, he'd slept with her.

"Time to roll?" he asked. "See what this is all about?"

"Let's do this, bro," said Nelson.

"It's that awkward moment when you're dressed like a zombie but you're not sure if the gig you're going to is a costume party," said Dave.

"If Max and Isis said it is, then it is," said Trina.

"Roger that," said Dave.

"Okay, look the part, guys," said Gem. "More moaning, less gum flapping."

"Alright everyone," said Flex. "Eye drops."

The eye drops Hemp pulled out were pink, not red, because to masquerade as a Mother would not be wise; if Isis and Max could sense one another, there was a chance that the Mothers could, too. To disguise oneself as one of the powerful abnormals and come face-to-face with them might result in disaster.

They all applied the glowing, pink drops to their eyes and Flex tossed the bottle. Hemp had more, which was a good thing because it lasted about as long as the OSN so might have to be refreshed.

The disguise was complete.

"Hey, Hemp, why don't you, Charlie, Dave and Taylor head out," said Flex. "Spread all over the street, though. Don't stay together."

"I was going to suggest that to all of you," said Hemp. "We'll see you there. Don't take too long."

They left. Flex and the others watched them go, shambling down the street, slowly drifting apart as they moved north toward the high school. They looked perfect, in Flex's humble opinion.

"Punch, Nel, you guys bring up the rear. Me, Trina and Gem will go."

"I'm gonna tuck these night vision goggles in my pants," said Punch. "Might come in handy."

"Everyone got the EB sheaths on?" asked Dave.

It stood for estrogen blocker. With a town chock with Mothers, it would be perhaps the most crucial weapon, Flex knew.

"If you don't, get 'em on now," said Flex. "Trini, Gem, you good?"

Gem looked at him and nodded. Her hair was festooned with twigs, leaves and dirt, and her face smeared with zombie blood. She managed a closed-mouth smile. Flex wanted to kiss her, but his sense of taste was intact, and he knew he would get some of that rank concoction in his mouth. So he nodded instead, returning her smile.

"This is exciting," said Trina.

"It's dangerous," Nelson reminded her. "We don't know who this dude is."

"I get that," she said. "but this shit gets my adrenaline pumping." She looked at Flex and Gem. "Let's get going already."

They set out. Walking like a zombie was necessary, but it wasn't easy. Dragging a leg or hunching over while you tried to maintain forward momentum could be taxing over a half-mile or so.

The radio under Flex's rancid shirt crackled to life. "Flex, come in."

Flex moved to the side of the road as though staggering. Gem and Trina took the cue also stopping in inconspicuous locations.

Flex pushed the button, eyeing the streets around him. "Yeah, Isis," he whispered. "We're all on the way there."

"I need to make you aware," she said. "People are coming from the west side of town. There are probably fifteen men with guns and one man without. There are women, too, but none of them have guns."

"Maestro?" asked Flex. "The guy without a gun?"

"That was my first thought," said Isis. "He is essentially surrounded. They're going to the football field."

"If they've got a handle on this shit, why do they need all the guns?"

"Maybe just to be ready in case people like us come to see what kind of society is being created in Hoisington, Kansas," said Isis.

"And by whom," said Flex. "Can you recommend a safe place?"

"It appears they are headed to the stone building beneath the bleachers," she said. "But I'm not radioing you with instructions to abort. I want you to re-double your commitment."

"How so?" asked Flex.

"You need to slip beneath the vapor and join the others on the field.

A chill ran down Flex's back. It was one thing looking like them. It was another thing entirely to lay side-by-side with them beneath a red-eye vapor that after fifteen years, they still did not entirely understand.

"Isis, what about the vapor?"

"The men do not have to worry about being affected," she said. "Have all the women take the red-eye wafers you brought with you. That way, even if affected, it will allow them to sense their intentions, which may be enough to assist us."

Gem wandered over and slipped into the shadows behind him. Trina saw and did the same thing.

"What's the hold up?" she asked.

"She wants us to lay under the vapor," said Flex.

"Why?" asked Gem. The question was not unexpected by Flex.

He shrugged and pushed the button. "Why, Isis?"

"Because this Maestro, if that is who this man is, is not here to simply observe. I kind of get the sense he's here to collect them. You need to be with them when that happens."

"What about you?"

"We've both changed, too, and I used the red eye drops. Max, the pink."

"Masquerading as a Mother?" asked Flex. "Have you done that before?"

"There's never been a situation that called for it," she said. "But I want to be in a position to see and hear what happens … when it happens."

"One more question," said Flex.

"What is it, Flex?" asked Isis.

"How did you get so smart at age fourteen?"

Isis smiled, but said nothing in response. She understood humor, and some things struck her funny, but overall, she was a serious girl with enormous responsibilities that she seemed to relish most of the time.

"Okay," Flex said. "Fair enough. Be sure to muss up Max's hair. You, my dear are fine leaving yours straight."

"We'll watch for you," she said. "Be careful and don't get caught. Hurry, Flex. I have a feeling that whatever is happening is going to happen soon."

Flex tucked the radio away. "Guys, come here, would you?"

Gem and Trina moved in close. He saw Nelson and Punch coming, glanced to the north to make sure the street was clear, then stepped into the roadway and waved to them.

They came over. "Hey," said Flex. "New instructions from Isis. We all need to get to the football field and slide

163

underneath the vapor with the other freaks. I know, don't even say it."

"Fuck," said Punch.

"Dude, serious?" said Nelson. He reached into a dirty pocket and withdrew his pipe. Sliding into a small entrance alcove of the building, Flex heard the Zippo wheel striking on flint.

"I don't think Hemp has his radio on right now, so if you're feeling energetic, I need someone to run up there and let them know. They're only about three minutes ahead."

"I'll go," said Punch. He turned back to the street and looked in all directions. He shuffled across the street until the low buildings shadowed him, and put his feet into high gear.

"Okay, let's move," Flex said. "Let's follow Punch's lead. C'mon, Nel."

Nelson stepped out of the alcove and exhaled a mouthful of smoke. "Right behind you, bro," he said.

They all moved to the other side of the street, slow-shuffling together, which wasn't altogether unusual for the walking dead. Now if the whole batch of them were running, that might draw some attention.

Flex got a stitch in his right ribcage and put one hand on it to push away the pain. It didn't work. He pushed through and felt his sciatica screaming.

Getting old ain't for pussies, he thought. He'd thought it before and he'd think it a thousand times before he died. Despite his fifty-eight years, he was in perhaps the best condition of his life. Still, the curses of age sought him out.

Hell, at least he still had all his hair, and he didn't need to tap into the Viagra supplies left on the pharmacy shelves in quantity.

They ran until they saw deeper shadows off to the right. A zombie stepped out and waved. It was Gammon.

They all tucked in. "I've got my wire cutters," said Hemp. "The field is on the other side of this building. Flex, radio Max and Isis and see if they can guide us to a good place to slip in undetected."

After a brief, quiet conversation, they moved south, crouched low along a path worn into fields of six-foot-tall grass, and followed the same path north.

Flex and Hemp stood briefly to get a bearing on their location.

"Let's position ourselves about ten feet back from the north fence," said Hemp. "We slip in behind the stored football sleds. See them there?"

"Got it," said Punch.

"Everyone?"

"Are we staying together now?" asked Trina.

"Yes, but we mustn't speak from here on out," said Hemp. "I don't care what happens. Keep quiet and if there's a point where we can slip away for a quick strategy meeting, then so be it. If not, we must simply move with the crowd and blend in."

"Everyone has a radio," said Flex. "Gem, write this down. Nelson is one click. Charlie's two. I'm three and Gem's four. Punch is five, Hemp's six, Dave's seven, Taylor's eight, Trina's nine, and Max and Isis are ten and eleven. You read that, Isis? Everyone has to remember their numbers."

"Yes," she said. "I'm eleven and Max is ten."

"And what's the purpose?" asked Taylor.

"If we get separated, we meet up at the parts store by the maze," said Flex. "Get there somehow. It's unlocked, we know that, and it's unoccupied."

"Okay, but what are the clicks for?"

"Everyone take out your radios now. Put them on the channel of the number I gave you. That is your channel. If

165

we're all together and you get separated, you'd better be on your channel. We'll all turn our radios to the missing person's channel, that way if you click in some pattern – you know, like you'd do a secret knock on a door – we'll know it's you."

"Yes, then we'll know it's not random," said Hemp. "If you see one of us at a distance and you wish to let us know, turn your radio to that person's channel and click your specific number. That way they will know to look for you."

"Understood," said Nelson. "So we have no idea what's about to happen here?"

"None. Now hurry," said Hemp. "Everyone take these red-eye wafers. Men and women alike. I don't know that they'll do the men any good but they can't hurt, and we can't afford to take any chances with this level of immersion into their vapor."

They all choked them down and chased it with bottled water.

Hemp led the way through the grass to the fence and clipped through it.

Trina and Taylor were the first to slip into the red mist.

Everyone else followed. Flex brought up the rear, his eyes on the concession stand. Just as he crouched to make his move, he saw Isis and Max slip out of the east side door and make their way into the grass.

The plan was in motion.

The question was whether it was a plan or a suicide mission.

It was a question Flex could not shake as he lay beneath the eerie, red vapor, feeling the flaking skin of monsters just inches away.

Dead Hunger VII: The Reign Of Isis

*****

CHAPTER NINE

"We need to go back," said Isis, nodding toward the concession stand.

"We just left," said Max.

"Max, I'll explain in a second," said Isis.

They crouched low and ducked back into the concession stand's rear access door.

"Aren't we going in?" asked Max, his voice low and his eyes on the wispy vapor licking the air above the football field.

"I changed my mind," said Isis. "We don't know what's about to happen, but we can observe better from here than anywhere else. The others are committed and surrounded, so we shouldn't put ourselves at risk … yet."

"Yeah, but that's the point, Isis," pleaded Max. "My parents are under that stuff and we *don't* know what's going to happen. They could be killed."

Isis shook her head and looked at Max. "I don't think that's part of Maestro's plan," she said. "If Great Bend is any indicator, this man is about power. To destroy them would be to destroy his army."

As Isis and Max looked on, dark sunglasses covering their glowing, red eyes, an unheard command appeared to have been issued. Fifty yards away on the sideline in front of the stone building on the south side of the field, the group of men and women with guns began to disburse.

Behind them emerged what appeared to be twelve women; all of them wearing shackles and wrist irons, one linked to the other in two groups of six. Their eyes were red points.

Isis stared at them. She felt them in her mind, but they were not probing or inquiring. She merely felt their presence, for their shades were drawn; no commands were being issued.

These women were Hybrids; Isis could see it clearly from her distant location. It was because of another of Isis' powers.

Isis had discovered many things about herself over the years that had at once surprised her and answered many questions she had been accumulating since childhood. She often thought of the age-old question of humankind, *Why are we here?*

She had never gained any knowledge that equipped her to answer that question, but she often wondered if her special abilities were given to her by a supreme being that recognized that without her and others like her, this human experiment would end in short order.

Max's powers, while often formidable, were not as diverse as her own; she had always assumed it was due to his gender.

There were other things, too. As an eight and nine-year-old at the gun range in Kingman, Isis had often wondered why she was such a better shot than anybody else, no matter which weapon she used.

She appealed to Hemp, who took her to the only ophthalmologist in town, Ken Applebaum. He quickly discovered something about her, and immediately brought Max in for testing, too.

Her eyesight was closer to that of an eagle than a human. Max's eyesight was the same. Beyond that, their eye-hand coordination was off the charts.

It was just one more thing that made them different from everybody else. They possessed advanced size, strength, no need for sleep and they were highly intelligent. Just when you thought all the differences were named, it was like a late-night infomercial: *But WAIT! There's more! Now with Eaglevision!*

Yes, at times the jealousy from others their age in Kingman could be difficult. Isis' physical appearance also caused problems, but mostly from those who did not know her from infancy. Older men approached her and flirted. They had no way of knowing she was so young, but that was another point of confusion and struggle for her.

She was not young and she knew it. While she realized that it was difficult for people she had known all her life to think of her as more than a fourteen-year-old girl, inside she knew what was really happening to her and Max.

They were aging at a rate perhaps twice that of regular human beings. She was fourteen actual years old, but appeared closer to twenty-eight. More than mere numbers, she *felt* like an adult; not a child.

While Max Chatsworth had experienced an accelerated growth rate too, he still had a boyish face that made him look younger. He did not appear thirteen by any stretch of the imagination, but nor did he look twenty-six. He came somewhere in the middle, around twenty-one or so. The full beard had a lot to do with it, too.

The internal struggles she and Max experienced accounted for her hesitation to advise the elders of Kingman of the need to create more Hybrids. Of course it was a sacrifice for the parents and the children to be born, but having read the entire encyclopedia, Isis knew well that throughout the world's history, men and women had made sacrifices for the lives of others.

Now, as Max and Isis stared across the field, she said, "Their eyes, Max."

"Yeah," said Max. "They're Hybrids like us."

"Still not sure I like that term," said Isis.

"We're a blend, Isis," said Max. "I don't know what else works."

"I know," she said. Then: "Look. Something's happening."

As they looked on, the gun-wielding men and women broke into two groups and headed east and west, following the field's edge. They walked along the outside of the perimeter fence, their guns slung over their shoulders. These were machine guns, similar to those carried by Flex, Hemp and many others in Kingman – but not unless going on a supply run.

While there were centralized stashes of available community weapons in Kingman in case of emergency, there was no need to carry them while going about one's daily routine. The only open paths into the town led directly into the pit, and from there, no exit was possible.

"Max," said Isis. "If they notice where your dad cut the fence, they could be in trouble."

"Shit," said Max. "I didn't think about that."

They watched in silence as the armed patrol passed in front of the concession stand. They were nearly all the way around now, and were approaching the stack of football sleds.

Isis held her breath. It was something she could do for up to ten minutes; another of her self-discoveries.

"They're staring at the benches," said Isis. "Good."

171

The eyes of the men and women were, without exception, fixed on the man standing in the center of the sideline area near the team benches, the bleachers stretching high above their heads.

The thrum from the field, like an enormous, low-toned tuning fork, vibrated the very walls of the concession building, and at first, Isis wondered if the mortar would begin to dissolve from the reverberation.

A thought occurred to her. She whispered, "Max, on three, I want you to command the Mothers to stop the vibration."

"Will they know where we are?" he asked, looking at her in the darkness of the structure's interior. They could see one another clearly despite the gloom; it went along with the excellent vision. Night vision goggles would be wasted on either of them.

"They won't be able to locate us. Quickly, Max. Now."

The word that Isis and Max projected into the minds of the Mothers that emitted the vapor floating above the field was *silence*.

Silence ... silence ... silence.

Isis' command combined with Max's as they projected it outward, their two, individual thoughts fusing together as one to create a powerful directive.

Instantly the vibration ceased. It did not taper off or slowly dissipate; it stopped as if an organist removed his finger from the low G key.

"Okay," said Isis. "Release."

The pulsation rose in volume again, but not before everyone standing around the field looked at one another in apparent confusion.

"At least we can still control them when these Hybrids aren't," whispered Isis. "That's good."

172

"Shh," said Max. "I'm not sure if we're in the clear yet."

The man stepped forward and stood almost at the fence, the gunmen on either side of him. His hair was dark and wild and his face appeared to be white and sunken, an eerie impression of a skull.

He wore a pair of blue jeans and a brown pullover shirt. He also wore a pair of drop holsters, each with a pearl-handled gun tucked inside.

The man reached behind his head and pulled the shirt off. Something – a tattoo of some kind – emblazoned his chest, abdomen and arms. Isis could see, but not clearly enough to identify the exact image inked there, but as she looked, it appeared he was wearing a tuxedo of some kind.

Maestro raised his arms and in his right hand was a long whip. He snapped it in the air over the chained women and girls; in response, they moved forward to stand beside him, stretched out to the length of their chains.

Their eyes grew more intense. The red practically pulsated in their pupils like the droning that came from the Mothers.

"Max," said Isis. "Look. The vapor."

Slowly, inch-by-inch, the red, almost solid-looking fog that had coated the field began to dissolve. It sank lower and lower to the field until the many bodies beneath it came into view.

"My God," whispered Max. "Isis. There are … well over a thousand here. Maybe double that."

"Indeed, there are," she said. "He did not need all of them in Great Bend."

"Half could have wiped out that town," said Max. "I can't believe Irene Danner survived."

"Had a Mother been in that house, she would be dead," said Isis. "Shh. Watch."

173

The remaining red mist sank into the brown grass as water might drain into a sinkhole. It was just gone.

Isis' eyes moved to her family. All of them had worked their way into spots very near one another, having slid into the mix after the fact. She located all of them except for Nelson.

Their eyes went back to the row of Hybrids beside the man who called himself Maestro. Again, the man held out his arms and made an upward gesture with just his fingertips.

Inexplicably, music began to play.

Isis had never heard the piece, but she placed the notes and knew without a moment's hesitation that the piece was O Fortuna. It was a dark, Medieval Latin Goliardic poem put to music by German composer, Carl Orff in the mid-1930s.

Rising up slightly higher, she saw the vehicle from whose speakers the music blared. The pickup truck had a metal cage surrounding the bed. It reversed to where Maestro stood, pulling to within three feet of him before stopping. A man got out of the passenger side, opened the rear gate and placed a compact stairway behind Maestro. He turned and mounted the steps into the truck.

He then turned to face the crowd of Mothers and Hungerers. He raised his arms and Isis knew immediately what the artwork on his front side was.

It was a demonic orchestra conductor, the man similar in appearance to Maestro, but wearing a tuxedo and more evil looking than any man could be without extensive plastic surgery designed for that sole purpose.

"Magas, all present!" he called, his hands holding invisible batons as he conducted his symphony of the undead.

"Return these Mothers and Hungerers, now replenished, to their enclosure! There they will feed!"

The truck pulled smoothly away, driving very slowly. The Magas walked behind, all of them single file, all staring upward at Maestro.

Isis was certain that if they did not keep their eyes on him, he would make them pay.

Suddenly the truck stopped and the music increased in volume. The captive Magas behind the vehicle rotated again so that they were facing the field before turning their heads from side-to-side, their eyes burning like tiny, red planets within their sockets. With their arms thrust straight down and their hands clenched into fists, they clearly issued the instructed command.

All of the figures that had been lying on the field got to their feet as one.

Flex, Gem and the others, while not in absolute lockstep, were smooth enough that the fact they were mimicking the others should not be readily observable by any of Maestro's people.

Still, Isis only took her eyes from them when she felt it was important to observe either Maestro or the Mothers.

*****

Flex stood when he felt the others around him shifting into position. Somehow, even with a gunman just ten feet to his right, he was able to keep his composure.

The music was clear and intense. A man in the back of a pickup was orchestrating everything.

Gem was just in front of him. He could no more speak to her here than he could call a strategy meeting. For that reason, he hoped Isis had some idea of what she was doing.

175

Just a plan. Not too much to ask. Of course, even without a plan, Isis was one of the best improvisers he had ever known. She had been instrumental in the design of the pit, and it worked flawlessly.

They were now on their feet, facing north. As if they were one organism, the tightly packed bodies on the field turned counter-clockwise and now stood facing west. For the first sustained amount of time, the crowd in front of him shifted so that he could see the shadowy figure of Maestro, his arms moving with precision in time with the symphony. Flex recognized it, but did not know the name.

He thought it was what the Anaheim Ducks hockey team played when their mascot, Wild Wing, flew into the arena at the beginning of each game.

Flex could not see his face from this distance, and the pink eye drops did not lend to better vision at all. It did, in fact, cloud it somewhat.

Maestro's gun-toting guards pulled open a gate directly ahead of the horde and the truck rolled through, maintaining a steady speed that could be matched by the shambling creatures. The hundreds and hundreds of reanimated corpses moved toward it like an avalanche flowing down a mountainside. Flex and the others matched steps as everyone shuffled toward the exit.

Gem slid in beside him as he walked, jostled by the undead creatures around them, the crowd so tight he could hardly get a breath.

He wanted to soothe Gem, but despite the cover of the loud music, he dared not speak. He saw Trina off to his right, and Taylor was just behind her. Gammon and Punch were off to his left, and Hemp and Charlie were right behind him.

Nelson was nowhere in sight. *Where the hell was he?*

Then Flex realized that Max and Isis were not there, either. They surely would have been close to the rest of the group. Flex had neither seen nor heard any commotion, so it was not likely they'd been caught. Maybe they had come up with some other plan.

Flex was halfway across the field with the others and found himself hoping that their ability to think and strategize would be enough to get them out of whatever it was they had voluntarily gotten themselves into. Time would tell.

He felt Gem's hand brush his, and he fought the urge to squeeze it and hold onto her as they approached the opening in the fence.

He and Gem slid through the gate opening, and he felt the eyes of the armed men on either side of him. They did not look twice at him, and he moved through, unmolested.

He made some observations as he walked; these creatures were intact. None was missing limbs or eyes, and the emaciated, tattered diggers were completely missing from the equation. It *was* unusual. The diggers were always there in smaller numbers than the ones who had changed while alive, but there nonetheless.

Not here. Not one that Flex could see. It was actually a good thing. Flex was well fed, as were most others in Kingman. They worked hard in this post-apocalyptic world, so burned off many calories, but aside from their elaborate disguises, the red-eye drops and the WAT-5, physically they did not draw attention, particularly through the loose, rancid clothing.

While the diggers were non-existent, Flex had spotted six red-eyes in close proximity to him, which meant that there were a lot more. The field had been full in his estimation, which meant that if he saw six just around them, there had to be hundreds of the powerful, pregnant females here.

They now moved into the street, the crowd of dead people spreading out to fill the available space. On the outside of the group walked the armed men and women. They did not appear frightened in any way.

Flex wondered at this arrangement. How the Hybrids controlled the Mothers and Hungerers, if that is what was going on here.

The main question pounded his brain again: *Where the hell were Max and Isis?*

He suddenly wished none of them had come here. It all seemed like a huge mistake. Thoughts of his dead son flooded back to him, and now he wondered if he had not just sacrificed the people he loved most in the world in a display of overconfidence.

As these thoughts filled his mind, he felt Gem's hand touch, then grip and squeeze his fingers. She released them quickly, but he glanced over at her and met her eyes. The briefest of glimpses allowed her reassuring look and slight smile to calm him some.

Flex shook off the doubt. Nobody got Gem – or anybody else he knew for that matter – *into* situations. None of his friends and family was without great intelligence and the ability to decide if they wanted to do something or not. Nobody else called the shots for them.

It was called freedom and freewill; something that perhaps only one person in Hoisington had: Maestro. *The Master*.

Considering the group of brave men and women around him, Flex decided that among this giant crowd of bodies moving through the town of Hoisington, Kansas, he and the ten or so others with him were the force to be reckoned with.

They were the threat.

The walk took them two blocks and into an industrial area on the north side of town. Flex found himself walking through another set of gates, passing a sign that said Martinez Lumber. This time the steel fence, identical to the material the maze was made of, looked to be no less than eighteen feet tall. It was topped with angled bars that attached a rat's nest of twisted, barbed wire that ran up another three feet.

This must have been the yard that once held the stacks and stacks of lumber, but it had long since been depleted. Now it was just an expansive prison yard. There was no shade and obviously no bathroom facilities.

Some of the folks in this lockup might have an issue in an hour or two.

Hell, Flex had to pee already.

*****

Isis recalled the map of the town in her mind, and knew that while the handlers, if that's what they could be called, were guiding the horde along 8th Street, 9th Street, which ran the same direction a block north, was the safer route to follow. She and Max could stay out of sight until they determined their destination.

After the ever-conducting Maestro, his chain gang of captive Hybrids, and the horde of Mothers and Hungerers passed, they again slipped out of the small, cinderblock building and took a path through the grass behind the bleachers toward 9th Street. They crouched on the corner until they saw the last of the group; Maestro and the others.

"So, we just follow them?" asked Max.

"No," said Isis. "Max, did you ever see Nelson? Even once after our people moved to the field?"

Max shook his head.

Isis removed the radio from her belt and turned it over to channel six, which she remembered was Nelson's channel. Isis then hit the transmit button eleven times.

She waited five minutes and when no response came, she clicked eleven times again.

"Let's start walking. I'd just tell him the hell to answer, but if he's being held captive, it'll tip them off he's not alone."

"Wouldn't the radio itself do that?" asked Max.

"Good point, but he could always say he monitors it just in case he finds people. The clicks could be anything."

Isis always used very specific timing between clicks so it sounded almost machine-driven.

"Okay," said Isis. "They're probably far enough ahead now. Let's go."

The street they walked was besieged by weeds, growing up through every crack and pothole in the asphalt. At one point, they came across a sinkhole that was perhaps eighty feet around. Several of the buildings around it had fallen victim, sliding into the bottomless pit, the earth reclaiming its own.

Max had read the encyclopedia as well, so he knew instantly what it was. "Sinkhole," he said. "Wow. First one I've seen."

"Not surprising, since you've only been to Wichita and Kingman."

"Yeah," said Max, smiling. "I gotta travel more."

They walked north, finding they had to get on the sidewalk to avoid being too close to the ledge, and still uncomfortable that near. They could not see down inside in the gloom, but dirt slid into it even as they walked alongside it, so it was still doing its thing.

Once past it, Max stopped. "Wait, Isis," he said. "Hear that?"

Isis stopped and listened. "It's them," she said. "The horde."

"What's our plan?" asked Max. "I'm beginning to believe having them get under that mist was not the best idea."

Isis sighed. She respected Max, but his abilities were no match for hers – at least not in attack strategy. She had also read the book, The Art Of War, by Sun Tzu, many times. Not so much for the psychological aspects of warfare, but to learn strategy. Not everything came naturally to her.

Hungerers were the most instinctual of all opponents. They had only one desire and one focus. Eat flesh and blood. Go to where it is. They were predictable and easy to kill.

The Mothers were a different story. They did have some ability to strategize, even if in the most basic sense. They also had an army of followers in the Hungerers, whom they could command. For this reason, Sun Tzu's text was helpful; part of it, anyway. In a world of dark threats, having too much knowledge was impossible.

She not only had the benefit of being a female – and the Mothers were among the most powerful of the transformed, dead creatures – estrogen charged every cell of her body when she *became*.

It was how she thought of the process that occurred in the womb; *becoming*. It seemed to describe the process well.

She finally addressed Max's statement. "Your parents and the others were not harmed by the vapor," said Isis. "They are now among the horde *and* in disguise. What isn't working out like you thought it would?"

"Wait," said Max. He reached beneath his ragged coat and unhooked the small crossbow he carried. His mother had taught him how to shoot it like a pro, and he could beat Isis in a contest. He had done so many times, in fact.

In a fluid motion, he had it in his hand and turned to his right. He raised it to his eye and loosed an arrow. It buzzed through the air like a sonic fly, and a shadowy figure, its pink eyes glowing in the gray distance, stopped in its tracks and fell over sideways.

Isis held her breath as she watched the eyes, their pink glow as clear as if right in front of them.

The pink slowly faded to black. She released her breath.

"Max," she said, feeling her own powerful heart pounding in her chest. "I know you think I constantly ride you, but it's because we are all we have. We are all Kingman has, at least for now, as far as I know. I'm going to say this one time, and I know I won't have to say it again."

He hung his head. "Don't," he said. "I know. It struck me the second that bolt left my bow. That could have been Nel. I'm sorry, Isis."

"Impulse is a hard thing to fight," she said. "But Max, you're too good a shot with that bow to be impulsive, at least while Nel's unaccounted for. Now go get your arrow."

Max did.

They walked until the noise became quite palpable. It was just off to the south, and it was loud enough that Isis became immediately concerned about what it meant for their fellow travelers.

They turned left onto Court Street and stayed in the shadows of some residential homes there. When they came around the corner of 9th and Court, at first they weren't sure what they were looking at.

A swath had been taken out of the town. Piles of rubble stood seven and eight feet high all around a steel fence that appeared to be of similar construction to the maze.

"Unless the destruction came by way of bulldozer, a tornado did this," she said.

"I can hear them," said Max. "They're behind that fence."

"Agreed," said Isis. "Now let's go find your parents."

*****

Flex accounted for everyone for the twenty-second time. Worried about Nelson, Max and Isis, and fearful of someone else disappearing, his eyes darted back and forth, taking in his family and friends.

There were eight of them.

It was an oddly disturbing scene, and a situation in which none of them had been before. The horde of Hungerers moved constantly, like sharks swimming in their hunting grounds. The red-eyed Mothers sat, some on their haunches, others on their rear ends. They stared straight ahead, like robots awaiting execution of their next program command. The fenced area was huge, but it was packed with the walking dead nonetheless.

Flex leaned in toward Gem, making sure no Mothers were near them. The coast was clear.

"To the fence," he whispered, nodding. "Over there."

She nodded. She, in turn, nudged Trina and tipped her head toward the fence. Trina got it and nudged Taylor. Before long, everyone was moving toward the far fence.

A noise came from behind them. It was the sound of a bell's peal. At once, the Mothers stood and turned, not toward the source of the sound, but toward another part of the fence.

Flex looked, but he could not see what was happening. He whispered to Gem, "I have to go see why they're moving. Go to the fence with the others. To the corner. Stay low, out of sight. If anyone notices you're not moving with the rest, it might spell trouble."

"The fuck I'll let you go alone," she said.

She fell in beside Flex. Trina came up to her and said, "I thought we were going to the fence."

"Go, Trini," said Gem. "Make sure everyone's there, and stay as low as you can. We'll be just a minute." Gem's tone conveyed that there was to be no argument.

That applied to Flex, too, and he knew it.

They followed behind the Mothers, staying clear of them. Flex began moving toward the east as the crowd pushed inward.

"What is it?" whispered Gem over the din of the snarling abnormals.

Flex did not need to answer, for as the last word left her lips a fence rolled open and the screaming began.

At first, Flex did not realize what was happening. There was an influx of new bodies flooding in, but they were running and screaming.

Hemp was suddenly beside him. "Flex, these people are alive," he said. "And something else is wrong."

"What?" asked Flex.

"The Mothers," said Hemp. "There are far too many of them. Their numbers are completely out of ratio."

"What does that mean?" asked Flex, wishing he were one quarter as smart or observant as Hemp.

"I may have figured it out already," said Hemp. "Look at their necks."

184

Flex looked around, trying to spot one of the Mothers. It did not take long. Keeping his voice down to a whisper, he said, "The ... what is that? A bite wound on her neck?"

Hemp nodded. "Yes, and I believe it's relevant. Now find another."

Flex scanned the crowd of voracious rotters that grew more animated as the screaming people intermingled with them.

An old man came face-to-face with a completely nude male zombie. The senior citizen was feisty, screaming at the top of his lungs as he pistoned both frail arms outward, trying to knock the creature off balance. It did not work. The naked rotter spun slightly to the left and leaned in, sinking its teeth into the old man's left cheek, its gnarled fingers seizing his gray hair and jerking it back.

By the time it got its arm around the old man's waist, he was down on his back and four other Hungerers fell upon him and began consuming him.

Flex's eyes went back to the cage door. It had rolled open, but Flex wasn't sure why the prisoners would leave it and run inside where these monsters waited.

Their faces were etched with pure terror as they realized what was to be their fate. Among them, dozens and dozens of elderly men and women, all screaming or crying. Once inside, most ran to the best of their ability, but the majority tripped and tumbled to the ground when either their bodies or their spirit gave way to the reality of their fate.

"Hemp, what can we do?" asked Gem, her eyes darting back and forth, her hand planted firmly on the barrel of her pistol. Flex could not see this, but he knew where her drop holster fell and her hand was beneath her ragged clothing and prepared to pull it out.

"Nothing, Gem," said the professor. "Absolutely nothing. If you give us away, we're all dead."

Flex looked around and his eyes fell on another nearby Mother. On the right side of her neck, centered on her jugular vein, was a large, oval bite mark. Where the individual teeth had torn through the skin was obvious; centered within the ragged, oozing black wound was raw, rotted flesh. His eyes then found yet another. She had the same bite wound, and judging by her stomach, she had been in the early stages of pregnancy when her transformation had occurred.

"So it is the neck wound," he said. "Is this Maestro … creating Red-Eyes?"

Hemp nodded but didn't answer. Charlie's voice rose above their thoughts.

"Oh, my God," said Charlie. "Oh, my God." Her eyes were fixed on the cage. All of the elderly were now inside the large pen.

"Shh, Charlie," said Hemp. "Please keep your voice down. We cannot help these people."

"Then what good are we?" she asked. "Can we help the people of Kingman?"

The screaming intensified, and everyone turned toward the flood of humanity pouring into the yard filled with the walking dead. The holding area where they had been was getting smaller.

"They're being pushed out," said Hemp, pointing toward the pen. "That rear wall is moving."

As Hemp had pointed out, the rear fence was set on roller wheels identical to those within the maze. A chain gear turned, mounted to the top of the fence. The long chain disappeared beyond where they could see, and as the gears spun, the back wall of the pen moved farther and farther forward, shrinking the holding area.

186

It was now around half the size it had originally been, pushing the living human beings toward the single door that led into the cage filled with the hungry dead.

As the last of the old men and women entered their living Hell, the sounds of the screams changed. Now boys and girls staggered inside, ranging in age from six to around twelve years old, all screaming and crying. As they tried to stop or cling to the side fences, the moving fence behind them crashed into their backs, forcing them forward into a living dead horror from which there was no retreat.

Something happened then. The horde around them settled as suddenly as if a switch had flipped, and stopped attacking. The feeding Hungerers fell still, most of them on their hands and knees, formerly consuming the flesh of the elderly men and women. For the moment, none of the children had been attacked.

"Hemp," he whispered. "Why not the kids? How can they tell the difference?"

Hemp did not answer. He shook his head and stared. Between the many crouched and formerly feeding Hungerers, the Mothers moved through the crowd as though floating on a thin layer of air. It almost seemed they were positioning themselves.

Flex crouched low and pulled Gem down beside him. Together, they peered through the legs of the dead and saw the Mothers stop.

The children, many of them at least, cried out in sheer terror as they continued to push deeper through the throng of zombies, as if they would ultimately reach a clearing where they could run to freedom, escaping the nightmare.

The Hungerers remained motionless for the moment; crouched over ripped-open bodies in a partially eaten state, their faces staring down, awaiting some expected command to resume feeding.

Flex saw that many of their eviscerated victims were nowhere near dead as their quivering flesh was being consumed. Their agonized moans filled the still air as the masses around them waited, deaf to their agony.

Suddenly the Mothers moved. If one had been hovering overhead and looking down, it would have appeared to be a coordinated action. All at once, as though by silent command, each Mother moved at lightning speed toward a young, terrified child near them.

Flex wished he could gouge his own eyes out, but instead he watched as a red-haired Mother to his right rocketed toward what might have been a six-year-old girl in her Sunday best. Her dress was dirty, but had once been a bright Easter yellow and still held some of its former gaiety.

The little, brown-haired, nameless six-year-old had been born into this world long after the apocalypse had wiped out most of her ancestors. She was a child of this apocalypse.

No more. The Mother snatched her from the ground and lifted her body as though she weighed nothing. The jagged fingernails of the Mother tore into the young girl's flesh as she brought the child's neck to her mouth, opened wide, and tore her open.

Gem started to get to her feet and Flex grabbed her with all his strength and threw his hand over her mouth. She struggled, but Flex could not look at her. His eyes were transfixed on the Mother who now tore the child's head open with one strong pull and reached in to the skull cavity to tear out the brain in one chunk.

She put it to her mouth and in two bites, consumed it.

She dropped the body onto the ground and fell to her knees, tearing open the now blood-soaked yellow dress.

All of the Mothers were down now, and as they buried their heads into the young, human meat, it was again as though a silent command was issued.

All the Hungerers around them resumed killing and eating the residents of Great Bend, Kansas.

Flex knew now what had happened.

The bodies they had found in Great Bend were either very, very old or very, very young. They would not have made even a 10-mile walk to Hoisington.

They would not serve as food for Maestro's army.

Flex tugged on Gem's shirt. She met his eyes and he nodded toward a nearby corpse, one with only two of the Hungerers consuming it.

They were too close to the front not to appear to be feeding. Flex was afraid that right now they stood out like a sore thumb.

"No," she whispered, barely moving her lips. Her red eyes told the story.

Flex crawled to the corpse, pushed one of the other Hungerers aside, and made room for Gem.

Kneeling side-by-side, they lowered their heads just inches from the warm, steaming human carcass.

Flex and Gem cried there, as they grieved the lives of the hundred or so men, women and children that had died around them. They steeled their nerves and waited until it was safe to make their way back to the others.

*****

CHAPTER TEN

Isis and Max crouched just outside the fence. The design made it difficult, but not impossible, to see through. You had to get close and peer between the uprights.

"Start at the south corner," said Max. "I'll start at the north corner, and we can work our way toward one another."

"Good," Isis said, ducking down in the weeds, making her way to the southern edge of the corral.

Both put their eyes to the steel slats and looked through. Isis saw a mass of moving bodies in front of the spot she had chosen, and moved five more uprights north.

She looked through. The thing that immediately caught her eye and repulsed her was a young boy, his dead face staring skyward, his eyes open wide. A mother had cracked open his skull and now busily consumed his brain, the gray matter squishing through her fingers as she shoved it into her mouth. When it was gone, she turned and melted back into the crowd.

A Hungerer moved in following her departure, tearing into the boy's neck. Another two of them buried their faces into his midsection, having their fill.

Isis felt rage in the form of pressure building up inside of her, and she stared intently at the Hungerer at the boy's neck.

As she focused her mind power, the creature stopped eating the boy, raised its head and turned to look toward the fence behind which she stood. Isis raised her right hand and formed the fingers like a claw, and the creature's hand lifted too.

Its fingers plunged into its own pink eyes, and pushed in all the way to the third knuckle. Isis closed the claw into a tight fist, pulling her own hand hard backward, watching as the zombie just feet away from her tore its eye sockets and nasal cavity away with a brittle-sounding crack, now a dark access hole.

She then pushed her hand forward, watching as the creature reached inside its own head. With one more motion, she snapped her hand closed again and pulled backward.

The creature ripped whatever remained of its brain out of its dead body.

Like a rag doll, it collapsed to the concrete atop the two other Hungerers who continued to eat, oblivious.

Isis felt the rage inside of her subside. She still had enough fury left to want to destroy the entire horde of flesh-eaters, but instead, backed away from the fence. She knew it was their nature, and that being the case, they did not have a choice in what they did, what they ate or who they killed.

Something caught her eye and she looked toward Max, who was waving his arms and motioning her to come to him.

She ducked back through the weeds and moved as silently as possible.

*****

191

"Max!" said Charlie, pressing her face against the fence, an inch from his. "Baby, I was worried. Are you okay?"

"Mom, I'm fine," said Max. "So far it's all according to plan."

"And what exactly is the plan?" asked Taylor. "I think being in here, we should probably be in on it."

Flex shuffled around and moved Taylor away from the fence with a nudge. She glared at him, but her face softened a moment later.

"Sorry, Uncle Flex," she said. "I don't like it here. It's fucking horrible."

"It is, sweetheart," he said. "We might have to wait until morning. Just mentally prepare yourself."

"While it's night, we should try to get out," she whispered. "It's going to be a lot harder in daylight, plus these fucks will have a better look at us."

Flex whispered, "Please keep your voice down, Tay. If the Mothers hear you they may put those brains to work and figure out we don't belong here."

"We don't belong here," she whispered. "Plus, didn't we come here to kill that Maestro guy?"

"Give us some more time to figure this out. When we followed along, we didn't know we were gonna be put in a pen. Isis might have some ideas."

Flex turned his attention to Gem, who was at the fence talking to Isis. She whispered, "They released like a hundred or so people in here. The elderly and very young boys and girls."

"They're feeding them the people they can't use for anything else and the children they desire most," said Isis. "Logic dictates that their reasons are twofold; they need to keep the Mothers fed and able to generate their vapor. In turn, they can continue to immerse the Hungerers in it, enhancing their telepathic control over them."

"Plus, it seems to maintain the Hungerers' ability to generate their knockout vapor and also minimizes their deterioration," said Hemp.

"I don't want to be in here when they feed again," said Charlie. "Look at this," she said. Her eyes moved briefly to what now amounted to meat clinging to the recognizable skeletal remains that lay all around them.

"So I'm guessing all those folks that got let in here were from Great Bend. Brought here for one purpose. Zombie food."

"That does explain a few things," said Hemp. "I couldn't figure out why some of the dead were consumed and others weren't. I'm guessing the abnormals there simply could not eat them all in the time allowed, and Maestro refused to leave those incapable of walking ten miles alive. Perhaps for fear they might make their way to neighboring settlements and alert others."

"Like the people of Kingman?" asked Trina.

"Exactly," said Punch.

"Any sign of Nel, you guys?"

Max shook his head. "We were hoping he was in here with you, but we didn't see him either. We were watching you from the concession stand while you were on the field."

"Why didn't you guys come in?" asked Dave Gammon. "I thought you were."

They could not crouch down to carry on a substantial conversation. If anyone was watching, the unnatural position would draw suspicion, so all of them simply walked slowly back and forth, mimicking the constantly moving Hungerers, speaking as they turned their heads away from the crowd behind them.

"After seeing Maestro come in with his captive Hybrids, I felt it was best that we remain on the outside," said Isis. "Do you feel you're in danger?"

"No," said Hemp. "Not as long as the Mothers don't get wise to us. I have a good supply of the eye drops and everyone has plenty of WAT-5. We can reapply our makeup by swiping some from the ghouls around us, though it might smell a bit worse than the concoction I use."

"So he's conditioning the Hungerers," said Max. "I don't know how often he does it, but we absolutely know the Mothers' control over them increases with each immersion in their vapor emissions."

"So this Maestro knows the ins and outs of what creates an obedient zombie," said Flex. "There's something I didn't think about, though."

"What is that, Flex?" asked Isis.

"Us," he said. "We're not zombies, so we won't be able to stay upright for too long before we get exhausted. Eventually we'll be dead on our feet, if you'll pardon the expression."

"Good point," said Hemp. "Isis? Any ideas?"

Isis shook her head. "Just lean against the fence when you can. Try to be inconspicuous about it. And stay clear of the Mothers. Even with your eye trick, they could get onto you. We're all due for more WAT-5, too. I suggest you take yours now."

"I hope Nel isn't in trouble," said Trina, turning toward the fence as she withdrew a plastic container from a pocket. She removed one WAT-5 and popped it in her mouth. She grimaced as she swallowed it.

"Wafer face," said Taylor. "You made the wafer face."

They had, since they were little girls, challenged one another not to make the wafer face, but no matter how used to the WAT-5 they got, the bitter taste always elicited the dreaded look.

"Yeah, eat yours, Tay," said Trina, smiling. "I'll be looking." She looked at Flex. "I wish I didn't come in here either. I'd go find Nelson."

Flex saw Gem's hand reach for Trina's, and she held onto it for a moment before releasing it. "He's smart, Trini," she said. "And he can get back through that maze as easily as Max and Isis here."

"If they don't slide the gates around," said Trina. "So what's next? I really don't want to wait until the morning. Can't you get us out of here?"

"My wire cutters will be useless to cut through this fence, I'm afraid," said Hemp. "Whether we can escape from here or not, some of us should make our way toward the gates where we entered and see if there are any guards posted there. If this Maestro is certain enough of the integrity of the enclosure, perhaps he doesn't feel there's a need."

"I'll go," said Punch. "Dave, wanna join me?"

Dave swallowed his WAT-5 and wiped his mouth with a filthy sleeve. "Sure," he said.

"Careful, guys," said Flex. "Blend in."

*****

"While they do that, we're going to try to find the Hybrids," said Isis. "They are the key to everything. Without them, Maestro could not control the Mothers, and in turn, the Hungerers."

"Okay," said Flex, watching as Dave and Punch left, moving through the crowd, their arms hanging limp and their legs moving in listless jerks as the pack closed behind them. "If you find 'em, what's your plan from there?"

"Isis," said Hemp. "They are enslaved, and we know they are intelligent, like you. If you can find some way to appeal to their desire for freedom, perhaps that can help you devise a plan of which they are a part."

"They are all my age or younger," said Isis. "Some looked far younger, but our knowledge tells us that while they appear fourteen or fifteen, they are likely only seven or eight years old."

"How does that matter?" asked Gem.

"Because Gem," said Isis, "No matter a person's intelligence, they can still only know as much as they are allowed to learn. The young ones are capable of knowing as much as Max and I do, but it is not likely."

"Because they were raised by a man who calls himself The Master," said Gem.

"Correct," said Isis. "A man such as that will demand 100% compliance and submission; he would not allow these Hybrids to know anything other than what he feels they need to know. In other words, they likely have no sense of what freedom is, versus captivity."

"So your work will be cut out for you if you're able to get near enough to them to communicate."

"I'll attempt a telepathic method at a distance," she said. "I may be able to soften them before we get to that point."

"But you're dressed like a fucking zombie," said Trina.

"They're smart enough to understand why," said Isis. "If they're open to listening to me at all, that can be explained."

Flex shook his head and glanced behind them. The shamblers continued their slow walk around the cage, paying them no mind. "How do you explain freedom to one who's never had it?" he asked.

"You paint a picture," said Isis. "You describe a world that is far different; far better than their own. Depending on how we find them, it should be possible to create a contrast."

"Okay," said Max. "Mom, we're going now. Are you going to be okay?"

"I'll be okay if you are," said Charlie. She put her fingers though the uprights and Max touched them.

"Love you, mom," he said.

"Love you more," said Charlie.

"Good bye, son," said Hemp. "Goodbye, Isis. Be careful, and take care of this chap for us."

"I count on him as much as he counts on me," she said. With that, they turned away and disappeared into the tall, brown grass.

Flex watched them go. He decided he would walk the perimeter to get a feel for any weaknesses of their confines.

Gem and Trina went with him, while Charlie, Hemp and Taylor stayed put to be there when Dave and Punch returned.

*****

Isis and Max reached the south end of the field next to the fence. They had worn their dark sunglasses up until then, but if they were to play the part of the walking dead, they would need to come off.

Not many zombies still had their sunglasses sixteen years after the apocalypse. Into their pockets they went.

As they parted the tall grass in front of them, a street came into view. It was 8th Street, where the Hybrids had led the horde to their pen.

Eric A. Shelman

They stepped onto the asphalt, both scanning the ribbon of dark highway. Only a distant rotter moved, picked up over half a mile away by Max.

Isis swiped her hair behind her right ear and remained very still, listening.

Max waited.

"I hear them," she said. "To the west."

"Let's cross then, and stay on the smaller streets," said Max.

She nodded, and they began their slow trek across the asphalt roadway. The constant moans and snarls of the captive creatures diminished until they could not be heard at all and Max and Isis walked south down Principia Drive, turning right onto Lakeland.

"I feel them ahead," she said.

They remained close to the buildings, but kept up the zombie walk ruse. Even in shadows it was possible for someone to figure out you had more in your noggin than a petrified chunk of gray matter.

"I feel them too, now," said Max. "Very close. Very strong. Wish I had your senses, though."

"We're different," said Isis. "Physiology determined how we developed, nothing else."

"Still," said Max. "Hey, look." A round sign mounted in front of a low, brick building with glass entry doors read, *Hoisington Police Headquarters.*

Isis looked at Max. "The ultimate captivity. He keeps them in jail?"

"At least it's a small town," said Max. "It'll be easier to get to them here than in a prison."

Isis looked alongside the building. "We can go between these two buildings and around to the back. If we can't figure it out from there, we're going to have to go right in the front door."

198

"Then we need to be prepared to kill some people," said Max. He slid his bow out from under his thin jacket.

Isis withdrew her silenced Walther and fell in behind Max, who stepped into the shadows between the brick structures.

From off to their right, a rotter staggered toward them. Max raised the crossbow and put the bolt between its eyes, even in the semi-darkness.

"Nice," said Isis. "Looks like I might make it back with a full magazine."

Max knelt down, his boot on the face of the rotter. He withdrew the bolt and checked the tip before re-mounting it in his crossbow. He carried a Cobra 80-pound bow. It had a pistol grip design; it was small and easily concealable. The bolts were only 6-1/2", but still flew with deadly accuracy at a blinding 160 feet per second.

Most importantly, it provided for a silent kill.

They moved around the rear of the building and saw two men in the distance. They were too far away to get a good look at them, but they were talking aloud as if they belonged here.

Max and Isis stopped in the shadows and waited for them to move out of sight.

*****

Nelson reached the maze. He was certain he would remember every turn and there were no obvious signs that it had been rearranged since they had come through almost two hours before. He scanned the area nearby and made a break for the entrance to the man-made labyrinth of twists and turns.

He did not make a fast break. A slow, shambling break. Now he was just a wayward Hungerer; a roaming inhabitant of Hoisington, Kansas.

Nelson stayed south of the huge horde of walkers that had been guided down 8th Street into a large, fenced facility. For a while, he had been able to keep his eye on Flex because of his height, but as the crowd moved and he found it necessary to duck temporarily into deeper shadows, by the time he got back into position, he could no longer find them.

He dared not click them or speak to them on the radio.

Nelson found himself too exposed on the south side and never checked out the east side of the pen. Instead, he kept his eyes peeled and remained concealed until he got to the west side fence. He remained crouched down and out of sight.

Nelson watched the crowd carefully, evaluating the make up of it and attempting to gather as much information as he could. Anything he could remember to tell Lola and Rachel might be of some help.

He randomly counted the Mothers to see what they were up against. When he got to forty-eight, he stopped. There were a lot of them, and the numbers did not make any sense. To reach that kind of number in an organic situation, it would take a crowd of around 1,600. There were perhaps a thousand, maybe as many as twelve hundred rotters here, but nowhere near as many as would be required to result in that many Mothers.

When the living humans were forced into the cage, Nelson had to choke back tears and vomit. It was horrid. It was also when he realized his friends needed to escape and he could not do it alone.

Kingman was 96 miles away. If he jogged back to the Crown Vic, he could get in and be back in Kingman by 11:30 or midnight.

Maximum half hour there. And while Punch might not like it, he was bringing Lola back with him. Rachel too, if she was willing. He would let Sabrina know that Dave was fine and that she didn't need to come, but he knew she would.

Lola still had a strong connection to the Red-Eyes, so she might pick things up and give them some sort of advantage. It didn't hurt that her knife skills were off the charts.

*****

Punch and Dave returned to the northeast corner of the cage where Flex and the others waited.

"There's four men at the front," said Punch. "They're not elevated, so can't see into the cage for any distance. We glanced and kept our heads down, so we're cool."

"If we stay back in that northeast corner we'll essentially be out of sight," said Dave. "When I was trying to check out the guards I ran right into a damned Mother. Scared the shit out of me."

"What did she do?" asked Taylor.

"I didn't wait to see," said Dave. "I backed the hell away from her and staggered my way into the crowd."

"I followed him," said Punch. "Bitches scare me, too, and I'm not afraid of much."

"Do you believe you compromised yourself in any way?" asked Hemp.

"I don't ... oh, shit," said Dave, staring past Hemp.

Hemp looked confused. "What is it?" He turned.

201

Behind him were two Mothers, fifteen feet away. Both stared toward the group, their red eyes intense and unwavering.

"This might not be good," said Gem.

"It's definitely not," said Flex. "Everybody needs to get in tight now. Let's cluster, backs in, facing out."

In the crowd, Flex watched as more Mothers worked their way to where the others stood. Soon there were a dozen or more, their straight hair blowing slightly in the breeze that whispered through the enclosure.

Everyone moved into position in a circle, their shoulders touching.

"I'm not feeling this," said Taylor. Flex looked down and saw her gun in her hand. For now she kept the barrel lowered to the ground.

"Everyone get ready," said Punch. "I don't see how this ends without a fight."

"All accounted for?" asked Hemp, who faced away from the gathering Mothers on the opposite side of the circle from Flex.

"I'm here," said Charlie, who loved to wear shirts that turned heads. Even her tattered zombie disguise shirt read, "I put the lotion in the basket on the first date."

"It's fucking urushiol time," said Trina. "Get your EB-tipped knives ready, too. Move aside your shirts so the sheaths are exposed for quick access."

"Good call," said Flex, noticing that now there had to be twenty or more Mothers within striking distance.

"Fuck this," said Gem. "Flex, keep an eye out, okay?"

"What's up?"

"We've got nothing to lose." She crouched down, surrounded by her family. Flex moved in tighter when she withdrew the radio.

She turned to channel 11 and pressed her button. "Isis. We need you here, now. There are a couple of dozen Mothers ready to pounce. We don't have a shitload of time, so if you hear me, please come now. Find a way to break this fence if you can't kill them all. I'll say it again. *Now* would be really good."

When she stood up, a red-eyed Mother stood a foot in front of Flex, staring him in the eyes.

He felt Gem's eyes on him and whispered, "Knife her, Gem. Go down, come in low."

In a smooth motion, Gem crouched again, withdrawing the knife from the Estrogen Blocker sheath. She reached between Flex and Punch's legs and poked the Mother in the ankle.

She stood up fast and moved back into the circle, her knife still in her hand.

As they watched the Mother, her face changed. Veins appeared, roadmap-like on her face. The skin transformed from icy smooth to desert parched. Cracks formed like a spider break on a windshield and traversed every exposed part of her body. Her head fell to almost a ninety-degree angle against her shoulder, snapped off with a wet sound and dropped to the concrete. The remainder of her body sucked in on itself and shimmered in a bubbling pile before melting further to become what looked like a puddle of mud and clay, intermingled with a long-faded maternity blouse.

As Flex looked up again, a second Mother stood there, her red eyes blazing. If they had the capacity to express anger, it could be seen there.

Her arm shot toward him and her fingers seized his throat, lifting him off his feet.

With blistering speed, Gem drew back her arm and plunged her knife, the blade tip dripping with estrogen blocker, deep into the creature's forehead. Her head

203

literally exploded on her shoulders, splattering everyone within ten feet with her pungent brain matter.

Her hand released Flex whose feet were not properly beneath him when he fell to the ground. His ankle twisted and he felt something pop.

He tried to get to his feet, but the ankle folded. When he looked up, he saw a wall of red-eyed Mothers moving toward them.

"Fuck stealth!" he said. "Punch, give me a hand up, man!"

Punch practically pulled his left arm out of its socket as he yanked him back to his feet, but not before he snatched Gem's knife from the bloody scum puddle that was once his red-eyed attacker.

There was no more need for stealth. There was no time for it.

Flex turned and eyed the fence. It was nearly solid steel with such narrow gaps between. One could see through it but could not insert fingers through to gain purchase. They could not climb it to get out of their reach. He worried most for Gem and Trina, but everyone was on his mind. All of his family.

Fight or flight. There was no flight. There were too many of them. It could only be fight. The ruse could not be re-established now. Too many Mothers had seen.

"On my go, everybody get their backs against the north fence and get the urushiol and EB-tipped knives ready," said Flex. "Don't stop, don't get bitten. Fight until we're finished."

"Trini, Tay, if you get tired get behind me," said Gem. "I'll eat those motherfuckers myself before I'll let them get to you."

"Ready?" asked Flex, feeling every muscle in his body twitching.

Murmurs of acknowledgement came from behind him.
"Okay, on five."
In his heart, Flex believed they were all about to die.

*****

After the men disappeared from view, Max and Isis moved along the back wall of the police station. As they reached the northwest corner, a fence jutted off to the west and stretched to the north the depth of the building. Inside the fence, the painted stripes on the concrete had long faded, now only barely visible.

In what appeared to be a temporary shelter on one side of the fenced area, there were several beds lined up beside one another. They appeared to have been taken from some sort of shelter, as all were identical, folding type beds with thin mattresses.

"Is that a basketball court?" asked Max.

"Were the nets your first clue?" asked Isis.

"Very funny," said Max. "I think we've found the Hybrids."

"Where they are kept, anyway," said Isis. "It appears there are six here now, but these are not the ones that were at the football field tonight."

"No," said Max. "None of them looks familiar."

"That may be to our advantage," said Isis. "I'll try to connect with them."

"Just you?" asked Max.

Isis nodded, and she instantly felt bad for Max. While she had some instinctive knowledge of her own abilities, and had initially assumed that Max had his own, it had become clear over the years that while they may possess almost the same abilities, he was not aware of some things of which he was capable.

205

When Gem revealed to them what the Mother had done to her son Flexy in Wichita, Isis had almost unleashed her anger, directing it against any Hungerer or Mother within a hundred miles. She loved the younger Flex Sheridan; he had possessed the strong, handsome looks of his father and he had been raised to ask questions and consider all angles to a situation prior to taking action.

Had she not been twice his age psychologically, she would have pursued him when he came of age. What had happened to him was unlikely and predictable at the same time; unlikely because of his own skills and who he was with at the time. It was predictable because the Mothers were extremely skillful at pursuing the weak and those separated from their companions.

Isis smiled at Max before closing her eyes. She lifted her mental shade, but did not call to the Mothers or let them in. Rather, she announced herself to the Hybrids.

There was a sense of confusion at first contact. Isis felt them there, stirring in their cheap beds, and as she and Max watched, one-by-one, they swung their legs to the edge and sat up, many of them rubbing their eyes. They did not sleep, but they could and often did rest.

Isis wondered what criteria caused Maestro to choose one over the other for his purposes, whatever they may be. No matter; these were not chosen for the task that had earlier been at hand.

The immersion.

"I hear them, Isis. You should go to the fence," said Max.

For the moment, they were still standing out of sight of the basketball court on the north wall of the police station.

"They're confused," said Max. "If they see you it might calm them."

Isis considered it only briefly and said, "You're right. The grass is high on the west side. I'll walk north until I can pass around those trees and cut in that direction. Stay here?"

"I'll watch and cover," he said, his loaded crossbow in his hand. "Hurry. Since there are so many of us here, turn your radio up just a bit. I'll let you know the old fashioned way if anything changes."

Max could "listen" to any of Isis' communications, and his suggestions were often helpful to her. She knew he had felt their confusion and discomfort, as did she.

The act of communicating with other Hybrids was not so much using words; it was more a sense of well-being and good intentions she and Max conveyed, which broke the ice, so to speak. These silent communications could also announce arrival. The announcement would convey without any ambivalence whatsoever, "We are here, we are strangers, and we mean you no harm."

Max and Isis had practiced it their entire lives. There was never a time Max was coming to see Isis that she was not aware of it by way of his announcement, and it was true the other way around as well.

These were the first Hybrids they had encountered other than each other, but as far as Isis could tell, the differences were minimal. There was only one way to create a Hybrid, after all.

But there were a lot of them. The intentional creation of Hybrids was apparently not a unique idea. Isis wondered, as she ran through the grass, what intention lay behind the act.

She reached the point where she would turn west and work her way back, under cover of the brush. The overgrowth of the world's foliage was sometimes inconvenient, but more often than not, it provided excellent camouflage when necessary.

She pushed her thoughts out in advance of her arrival, letting them know she would come to the northwest corner of the fence line.

The radio came alive. "Isis," said Max. "Three of them are moving toward the west fence."

"Good," she said. "I see them."

Isis drew to within eight or nine feet of the fence, still hidden by the brush. She peered through and saw three females dressed in what appeared to be prison clothes. They wore orange jumpsuits. None of the Mothers and Hungerers wore these.

The Hybrids at the football field had them on. She did not put it together until seeing the number on the right chest and the DOC PRISONER words stenciled on the back.

As the women awaited her, she stepped into the open.

The three took a step back and their faces changed. They were attempting to control her; they thought she was a Mother.

"I'm not one of them, so you won't be able to command me," she said. "This is a disguise to allow me to blend in among the Mothers and Hungerers."

The three women appeared to be of Hispanic heritage. It had not struck Isis before; there had been no reason to consider it. They looked confused. Isis tried again.

"My name is Isis," she said. "I'm like you. My mother was exposed to the vapor of the Mothers when I was in her womb."

"What is Isis?" one of them asked. She was tall, perhaps approaching six feet, but not quite. She moved closer to the fence. The others stayed back.

"I was named after an ancient Egyptian Goddess of motherhood, nature and magic," said Isis, her voice soft and soothing. "Now please listen to me because I don't know how much time I have."

The women nodded.

"I came here to help you," said Isis. "We live in a town to the south of here. Please, tell me what you know of the world and why you're kept here."

"We obey," she said. "We are clothed and fed and we follow Maestro."

"Or we die," said another, now emboldened to step forward.

As she drew closer, Isis could see her red eyes more clearly. Despite the mist over them, her emotion was strong. She was rebellious. Isis knew the feeling. This one would be the one to listen. She would be the connection Isis needed to nurture.

"I'm sorry your lives are threatened," she said. "Please, tell me your names."

"I am Alpha and she is Omega," said the first young woman who had come over. She indicated to a second woman standing just a little farther back, who looked similar to her, both in her eyes and the shape of her face. She appeared to be approximately the same age as well.

"The rest are all called Maga," she added.

A third girl, clearly younger than Alpha and Omega, approached. "I am Maga 7. All of us are named the same, but identified with numbers."

"Maga means magician," said Isis. "Why?"

"Maestro says we are his magic," said Maga 7.

Isis looked at Omega. She also had dark hair, brown skin and brown eyes, like Maga 7. "Omega is a word that means 'the last'," said Isis. "It is also not appropriate for a young woman. I would like to call you Megan."

Omega nodded. "Megan," she repeated.

"And Alpha?" she said, looking at the other, older woman.

"Yes?"

"With your permission, you will be Alyssa. It is a very pretty name."

"Alyssa," she said. Isis almost believed she saw a smile touch the girl's lips.

The third came forward. "Who am I?" she asked.

Instead of answering, Isis pushed the word forth in her mind: *Beauty.*

And she was. Her face was filthy, and she was perhaps 5'10" tall, her long, dark, nearly black hair hanging down to the middle of her back, as straight as that of a Mother. Her inquisitive eyes were not brown, but instead were a deep green. Again, something about all of these women appeared the same.

"How old are you?" asked Isis. "I am fourteen years old."

"Years?" asked Beauty. "This is a word we have heard but have no concept of."

"It is a measure of time," she answered. "From sunrise to sunrise is one day. A year is 365 of these periods."

"I have counted each sunrise," said Megan. "There have been 3,655 of them. This means I am ten of your years."

"They're not my years," said Isis. "They simply are. They are something Maestro has determined you need no knowledge of."

Isis knew she had to broach the subject of why she had come to them. "Please," she said. "You said you obey Maestro. I need to know why he created you. I can only assume Maestro has made you for a reason. There are too many of you all together to have been unintentional."

"We beckon Mothers to come, who bring the Hungerers," said Beauty. "Once they are here, Maestro holds them, and commands us. We repeat his commands to the Mothers, who then command the Hungerers."

"What do you know of the Mothers?" asked Isis.

"They are Goddesses," said Alyssa. "Like you."

Isis shook her head. "No, they're not, and neither am I. I was named after a mythical Goddess, but I am *not* a Goddess. The Mothers and Hungerers aren't Gods, nor are they Goddesses. They're abominations of nature."

The three women stepped back as though struck by a blow.

"Please," said Isis. "Try to understand what I'm saying. I was created by the actions of a Mother. Before becoming a Mother, she was just a regular human being who was pregnant with a child. The elevated chemicals in her body, naturally augmented to assist with her baby's development, made her change into a far more powerful creature than the Hungerers."

The three stepped forward again. Megan asked, "They are not Goddesses?"

"No," said Isis. "They're humans who died and who should have dissolved into dust years ago. They sustain themselves by consuming those of us who are immune to the thing that changed them."

To call them Mothers and Hungerers in the first place told Isis more than young Megan realized. It meant that much of what they knew was instinctual. Maestro could not have known what they were, or what word fit them. From infancy, Isis thought of them as the Mothers. Now she knew it was true.

To her surprise, Max popped out behind her and said, "Hey."

211

The three within the cage blanched, and Max held up his hands. "I'm good, guys," he said. "I'm with Isis. We grew up together."

"It's true," she said. "He is also a Hybrid. Max, this is Alyssa, Meg and Beauty."

Max gave an open palm, sideways swipe in the air, waving to them with a smile.

"Hybrid is a combination of multiple things," said Beauty.

"Yes, exactly," said Isis. "We are essentially mutated humans, nothing more. Maestro is human, and so are all of you."

"We command the Mothers," said Megan. "We tell them to command the Hungerers when to feed and where to go."

"But you're instructed by Maestro?" asked Isis.

"Yes," the three answered in unison.

"Did you go to Great Bend?" asked Max.

"I have seen signs that say the words Great Bend. If this is a place, we have been there."

Max looked at Isis. "He keeps 'em in the dark, right?"

"He can't teach them or they'll outgrow his control," said Isis. She turned back to them. "There was a massive slaughter of human beings in Great Bend," she said.

"The Hungerers and the Mothers must eat," said Megan."

"I'm going to explain something to you and I pray that you listen and understand," said Isis. "The Mothers and Hungerers are dead. They should not exist. Without them I would still exist, but I wouldn't be like you."

Alyssa's expression illustrated her confusion.

Isis said, "Put your fingers to the sides of your necks, please." As she said the words, Isis did it. So did Max.

The three inside followed suit. The others in the cage began to make their way over. Isis issued a silent order to stop. They heeded her command.

"Why mustn't they come?" asked Beauty.

"Because it will draw attention should someone see from a distance," said Isis. "Listen to me. You feel that pulsation against your fingertips?"

The three nodded.

"That's your heartbeat," she said. "It is an organ within you that pumps your lifeblood throughout your body and keeps you alive. It enables everything else. If feeds your brain and makes you vital."

Megan lowered her hand. "We knew they were not like us," she said. "You said they are dead."

"They are," said Isis. "A disease has taken over the planet upon which we live and killed 90% of us. Other factors have come into play that allow us to exist."

"And the dead ones, too," said Max. "But you've got it wrong if you think your purpose is to help them. As far as Isis and I know, we're here to rid the world of them."

"Have you been caged from birth?" asked Isis.

"Confined?" asked Alyssa.

"Yes, confined."

Alyssa nodded. "This is our home now, but it is the same as in the past."

"This is no home," said Isis. "Alyssa, Megan, Beauty," she said. "Where we came from, people speak in soft tones to one another. They take care of each other and they love their neighbors. They build things and create things; they plant gardens and grow food. Nobody is killed unless they come with the intention of killing us. We live in peace."

"Peace," repeated Megan, as if the word held no meaning. "Why have you come?"

213

"Our reasons have changed," said Max. "Now that we've discovered you."

Isis looked at Max and smiled. It was something none of the three had yet done. Isis wondered if any of them had the capacity for a smile. Even babies knew how to smile; it was a natural response to joy.

Isis considered if they had ever known joy. Something struck her. "Megan, Alyssa and Beauty," she said, "You said the signs said Great Bend. So you know how to read."

The three nodded. "The great matriarchs shared their knowledge."

"The great matriarchs?"

"They were Maria and Sofia. They are no more."

"Did Maestro kill them?"

The three nodded. "It was a terrible moment of pain for all of us."

Isis looked at Max. "I know what we need to do." She looked back at the three special girls. "If I bring you a document, will you promise to read it?"

"If we can do so without being observed," she said.

"It will not take you long," said Isis.

A loud crash came from the north. The three Hybrids in the enclosure turned and bolted back to the east side of the cage, never once looking back.

Max and Isis ran into the night, the tall brush whipping at their arms and faces as they sped toward the holding pen where the blaring emotions of the Mothers and Hungerers drowned out their very thoughts.

*****

CHAPTER ELEVEN

The moment the first Mother went down, Flex had known there would be no other option than to eradicate as many of them as possible in order to save themselves.

Even then, it was hopeless.

After killing the first two Mothers, they had done what Gem had suggested. The eight of them, their backs to the fence, used their guns sparingly, for almost none of them were suppressed, and each shot was another invitation to the party.

Maestro was likely on his way there now.

Three came at Trina and Taylor, and they quickly evaluated their enemy. All Hungerers. Quick shots of urushiol and they were hissing, melting piles of bloody goo.

The Mothers were fast, though, and when they came in, it was nearly impossible to react quickly enough with the muck building at their feet. It was quickly becoming as slippery as an ice rink, and there were so many heading toward them from all points within the cage that it was all they could do to intercept each one.

Taylor was a machine, her urushiol bottle in her left hand and her knife, which she kept re-dipping into the sheath as they all did, flew with expert precision. She had worked with Lola extensively, and she was the best among them with a blade.

Trina held her own, but Gem kept her eye out for her. Flex had seen Gem take out at least three that Trina had never seen coming.

Flex had counted his shots; he was down to one round left and in the melee they were in the middle of, he could not occupy both hands long enough to lift his tattered shirt and unzip the pouch holding his other ammo.

They were not minutes from dead; they were seconds away.

An engine noise sounded in the distance. It emerged like a guttural growl, and it grew louder as the seconds passed. Flex fought the urge to turn and look, but instead he kept on fighting, hoping the sound he heard was Max or Isis, coming to work their magic on the crew of rotters and Mothers.

The roar then became so loud that Flex had to look. When he glanced over his left shoulder to see where the noise originated, he still had no clue. An eight foot swath of grass was bending forward as though it were being blown flat by a great wind, but the air was still.

As the bright red Jeep rocketed out of the tall weeds and smashed headlong into the fence, they all watched in awe as the Cherokee, all four tires spinning, crashed through the fence, plowing over dozens of the zombies before turning hard right and making a deadly U-turn.

The front bumper was forged of massive, black steel tubes, and as it met the fragile bodies of the Hungerers, their brittle bones crushed and their heads popped like gore-filled water balloons, stilling them for the last time.

Then Flex looked up to see the driver's face. Nelson Moore's eyes shone wide as he headed back, honking his horn and flashing his lights. He held something in his hand

and the next thing they knew, his amplified voice boomed out over the walking dead crowd.

"Dudes, get through the hole in the fence, now! Run!"

With that, Nelson cranked the wheel again, driving parallel to Flex and his family, the knobby tires plowing through the emaciated bodies of the Hungerers and Mothers, his tires alternately gaining and losing purchase with the concrete through the massive bloodletting.

When the Jeep reached the north fence, the engine accelerated again and Nelson drove without letting up. The upright fence posts dislodged, throwing the fence down flat into the weeds beyond.

"C'mon, everyone!" screamed Gem, and Flex struggled to hop toward the first hole Nelson had poked through the east fence. As he reached down to straighten his foot enough to take another step, he felt himself being lifted off his feet.

To his shock and surprise, he was over Punch's shoulder; the former U.S. Marine grunted as he ran toward the hole while Flex pushed up to maintain his view of the oncoming horde.

Flex had his knife in his hand and jabbed at two Mothers closing in on them from the west. He slashed the blade horizontally across both of their eerily calm faces and the effect was immediate; the facial features melted into one another, the formerly vibrant, pregnant women, long since dead and now appearing like wax figures that had been moved too close to a fireplace.

As Flex watched them fall, he saw the edge of the fence pass his eyes. Once through, Punch kept running.

A cacophony of gunshots erupted from the south, and Punch dove to the ground, covered by the tall grass.

"Down! Down!" yelled Punch, and Flex knew why. The gunfire was from automatics, and there were a shitload of them.

"Is everyone here?" asked Flex. "Punch, man, you gotta find them. Do you see them?"

Flex saw Punch stand up for a moment. Another barrage of gunfire sounded and he dropped back down. "They're not in the pen, brother. They're out. I'm not sure where."

Flex heard the sound of the Jeep's engine winding out, and said, "What is that? Is Nelson in trouble?"

"I can't lift my head right now, Flex," he said, breathing hard. "I need to keep it."

"Fuck!" yelled Flex. He sat up in the grass and pulled off his shirt, popping the buttons that flew away and disappeared around him.

He quickly tore the ragged shirt in two and positioned his foot on the ground. Getting to one knee, he put some weight on the foot and grimaced. Once in position, he reached down and began wrapping his ankle as tightly as he could.

"Punch, man," he said. "I need you to pull on this as tight as you can and knot it. Can you do that?"

"Sure, buddy, but those freaks are coming through the fence. I need to …"

He stopped talking. "Wait," he said. "What the fuck?"

"What is it?" asked Flex, holding the two ends of the shirt taut.

"They stopped," he said. "They're just standing there now.

"Hurry, Punch," said Flex. "My ankle, man."

Punch reached down and pulled the ends tight. He looked at Flex. "Good?"

Flex nodded quickly.

Punch tied it off. The minute it was done, Flex stood in a crouch, testing it with weight.

"Think it's a sprain," he said. "Fuckin' numb."

"That's called radiculopathy," said Hemp, who poked his face through the brush, just two feet away from where Punch and Flex sat. "You okay, old man?" he asked.

"Where is everyone else?" asked Flex, his face panicked. He did not need a mirror to see this. He felt it in every muscle. These people were his entire reason for living.

"Right behind me," said Hemp. "We're all safe."

Flex realized the Jeep's engine had fallen silent.

"Where's Nel?" he asked.

The answer came very quickly.

"Stand up!" came a voice. "Stand up and drop your weapons. Otherwise, I'll kill this fool and then I'll kill all of you anyway."

Punch peered through the brush and dropped back down. "Oh, fuck," he breathed. "He's got Nel."

*****

Isis and Max waited across the street out of view. They had arrived in time to see the Jeep crash through the fence and begin to plow down the Mothers and Hungerers.

The throes of death, when experienced by the undead, was an extraordinary sound. The shrieks were not of terror but of pure pain, not experienced in an oral sense.

It was not pain in the traditional sense; the Mothers and Hungerers projected their dying agony as frustration for no longer being able to consume flesh and satisfy their insatiable appetites. They did not know that beyond this supernatural life they lived was peace, silence and pure darkness.

They also did not know that finally, their red and pink eyes would fade and silence would overtake them, allowing their bodies to dissolve to dust as they should have done so long ago.

Soon it was over and Isis knew the creatures in the cage had fallen back under the control of the Hybrids and Mothers. A man, pulling Nelson by the length of his hair balled in his fist, a large caliber handgun to his head, stood among the remaining Mothers and Hungerers. There were still well over a thousand of them left alive, as far as Isis could tell.

"Isis," said Max. "Should we intervene?"

"There are two many of them," she said, indicating toward the Hybrids.

Max turned his head and saw them there. They had moved into the street, now standing against the south fence by the original entry gate, staring into the cage.

These were not the Hybrids Max and Isis had met; they still wore their orange jumpsuits with the DOC stenciling on the backs, and each was still chained to the other, as they likely always were.

Their words were clear in the heads of Max and Isis. Calm. Stay. Remain still.

Words for us; abstract, decipherable commands for the walking dead.

Still, the command issued by the captive Hybrids was as clear to Isis as it was to them. She may as well have issued it herself.

"Come out now," shouted Maestro again. "I'll count to three. Surely you know how fast that goes."

He did not wait. "One!" he called. "Two!"

He drew back the hammer and smiled.

"Wait!" shouted Hemp, rising from the weeds to the right of the destroyed pen.

"Ah, there you are. Where are the rest of you?"

"C'mon guys," said Hemp. "We've nowhere to go. Flex can't run on that ankle. We'd best surrender."

"You're a smart man," said Maestro. "Hurry and get into the street. All of you."

The man was of medium height and was again shirtless. The demonic facial ink, which may or may not have been a tattoo, made him appear to be more of a Joker from a deck of cards, but it was clear his intention had been to make his face appear as a skull. From a distance, he had achieved that effect.

The tuxedo drawn or tattooed on him gave him the appearance of an evil symphony conductor; it adorned his entire abdomen, the character's sleeves extending all the way to Maestro's wrists.

Appearing from the tall grass of the field, Gem stepped into the street first, grass and weeds sticking from her hair, her undead makeup now mussed and running. She wore no backpack.

Gem stopped and reached her hand behind her, and Trina clasped it, emerging with Taylor stepping out behind her. Next came Dave, Hemp, Flex and Punch. All without backpacks. Isis breathed a sigh of relief.

Acknowledging it, Max said, "Me, too. If they're alive, we *can* save them."

"Wait," said Isis. "Where is Charlie?"

They watched the field. Hemp's eyes remained there, too. His expression was one of anguish as he waited, but she did not appear. He suddenly averted his gaze from the weeds and looked again at the line of gunmen facing them. Isis knew immediately why. He did not want to draw their attention to the fact that one or more of their group might be missing.

"How many of there were you?" asked one of the men wielding the guns. He was short; maybe just over five and a half feet tall. He wore a baseball cap low over his eyes and wore camouflage pants of some kind.

"Eight," answered Hemp, louder than necessary. "There are eight of us."

"He's protecting Charlie," said Max. "We need to find her, Isis. Like quick. Are you sure we can't do something? Get everyone out of here?"

Isis shook her head. "We proved that if not fighting these other Hybrids we can control this number of Mothers, but we'll never be able to wrest control from them. Too many of them and I'm not sure we're strong enough for that."

"Bullshit," said Max. "My dad's over there and my mom's missing. That makes me feel pretty goddamned strong."

Isis only nodded. It was true. Being Hybrids and wanting to learn more about their abilities, she and Max had often slipped away to privately experiment with several variables. Often, without advance warning, they would lead one another to believe the other was in mortal danger. This could only be achieved by closing their mental shade and involving a third person to convey the situation to the other, at which time a certain adrenaline kicked in, but ultimately, it was far more powerful than adrenaline.

It was adrenaline on steroids.

Everything increased. Distance of telepathic control; detail of control. Perhaps most important of their discoveries was an ability, when under tremendous tension and stress, to take distant, physical control over not only animate objects, but inanimate objects.

They had not perfected this with any consistency, though. There had only been a couple of times when Max had thoroughly and completely convinced Isis he was about to die, and what happened next was something they both swore to secrecy.

They feared it would be too much for the people of Kingman. They could be ostracized, and they loved their home far too much for that.

Maestro walked nonchalantly through the idle zombies, toward the fence, which his guards had now rolled open. He carefully stepped over the carcasses of the elderly and juvenile bodies that lay strewn all around, and he was sure to keep his hand firmly looped around Nelson's hair, his gun pointed at the blonde man's thin abdomen.

Isis wondered if Nelson would Subdudo him.

It would be a mistake. She wished she could reach him.

When the shirtless man reached the street, he walked casually toward the group of strangers, pulling Nelson along behind him.

Isis watched intently. Her eye was on the gun barrel. When he reached them, he stopped five feet back and jerked Nelson forward, essentially tossing him back to his own.

Max quickly withdrew his crossbow and raised it to his eye.

At that moment, Maestro thrust his arm forward and snatched Trina by the wrist, yanking her toward him. She let loose a scream, then anger flooded over her face and she said, "I'll kill you, you smelly fuck."

"Not right now, you won't," he said, his arm hooked around her neck and his breath in her face.

Isis fought the urge to unleash everything she had, but it was just too risky with the powers of the other Hybrids unfamiliar to her.

Eric A. Shelman

Flex, his face red with anger, tried to make a move forward, but his ankle gave way and he fell to one knee, grunting in frustration.

He looked up, his nostrils flaring as he stared at the man holding the niece he had raised like a daughter. "You fucking hurt that girl and I'll cut you into a goddamned thousand pieces," he growled.

"And if there's anything still big enough left," said Gem, "I'll slice it in half again."

The man laughed and said, "Oh, I see! You're a couple of badasses, huh?" He pointed directly at Gem. "You clearly don't know me very well. One more word and I'll slice off her head while you watch."

He withdrew a knife with a long, curved blade.

Isis saw Gem's eyes soften before she lowered them and choked back her anger for Trina's sake.

Maestro then reached in and snatched Taylor's arm, pulling them both in tight to him, one arm wrapped around both their necks now, his large pistol in position to kill one or both of them.

"This is in case you have anyone else waiting to shoot me from a distance."

"We don't," snarled Gem. "But don't worry about that. You've got enough trouble right here."

"Gem," said Flex. "It's okay."

Max lowered his crossbow. Isis nodded. "Our time will come," she said.

Maestro said, "You are a definite interruption to my regular routine, but you're pretty interesting, dressed like my Hungerers." He laughed aloud and added, "Let's get somewhere more comfortable, then we'll find out where you're from. It might be a place I'd like to visit someday."

He turned and addressed his men. "Get the crew over here and tell them I want this fence fixed within three hours.

All of it, and like it was before. Get the other ladies from the police pen, too. We need to rotate the Mistresses."

Isis turned to Max. "We need to get to them before they do that. Tuck everything in and get ready to run."

*****

Flex and Gem stayed in front and Hemp came in behind them. Maestro had handcuffed Trina and Taylor and made them walk on either side of him, gunmen outside of the young women.

Flex whispered, "Good thing we dropped our stash bags in the field. Good idea, Hemp."

From behind him, Hemp said, "It wouldn't do to get caught with urushiol, the estrogen blocker, and WAT-5. That's far too much intelligence to lose to a man like this."

Flex stared at Maestro for several minutes, focusing on his strangely altered face. His eyes were close-set, staring out from the black ink, and his brows blended with it, making them almost nonexistent. His mouth was large and his jaw square. The bones in his neck had been tattooed on to complete the appearance of an exposed skeleton.

His eyes were sharp and intense; the eyes of someone who had observed much in his life. From the evidence staring at them now, Flex assumed that whatever this man had seen, either as a boy or a man, had changed him into a lunatic. All evidence suggested he was quick to threaten; a hair-trigger reactionary.

"Almost there," said the inked man. "Just another 1/8th mile or so."

"Hemp, did you see Charlie?" whispered Gem. "Did she tell you she was staying?"

"No, Gem. I was very surprised when she didn't come out, but in retrospect, I'm not sure why I was. It *is* Charlie, after all."

"We've still got Isis and Max out there, too," said Nelson, who was beside Hemp.

Punch and Dave walked behind the rest of them with guards at their backs. They said nothing. Flex assumed it was for fear of being heard.

"Do we have any plan?" asked Gem.

"Yeah," said Flex. "For now, we play it by ear and hope Charlie, Isis and Max come through."

"At least we have them," said Hemp. "I like our chances."

They said nothing more until they reached an Applebee's Restaurant. The guards opened the door and held it. Maestro pushed Taylor and Trina through and walked inside before turning and waving the rest of them in.

Once inside, he motioned to the many tables and booths. "Go ahead and sit down. We can move tables together to accommodate the size of your party."

Flex wasn't in the mood for the cute jokes. He limped to a large, round table and pulled out a chair for Gem, who dropped down into it. Flex did not sit. Instead, he leaned on the back of a chair and stared at Maestro.

A distant engine spun to life, and in seconds, the hanging lamps over the tables lit up. Now illuminated, Flex could see the bare-chested man clearly. What had appeared to be odd facial and body paint was clearly not that at all.

It was meant to be a transformation of Maestro himself, from a mere mortal man to a demon. His muscles rippled beneath the ink, and Flex wondered just how far the tattoo extended beyond what was visible.

"Ah, I see you've noticed my ink." With that, he removed his whip from a pouch on his waistband, raised his arms as a music conductor might raise them to lead a symphony, and snapped it in the air, inches from Flex.

Flex tried to study his face beneath the skull-like shading, but it was near impossible to separate the horrid mask from the features beneath. It was good work. The image was shaded and done with great care. It must have taken many sessions to complete.

As Maestro held out his arms, he moved them in and out as the whip snapped air, its three worn tails blistering nothing – for now.

This guy's a crazy, sadistic son of a bitch, thought Flex. He sat down and turned away from the freak.

They were pretty much fucked for the moment. He sent out good thoughts to Charlie, Isis and Max, hoping the former was okay and the latter two could feel them there.

*****

Isis and Max reached the basketball court cage in minutes. Nobody had yet arrived to retrieve the remaining Hybrids.

Isis projected to them prior to their arrival, and by the time they reached the fence, Alyssa, Megan and Beauty were there, but now they were joined by the rest, as Isis had suggested. The others stayed back several feet.

"Our friends are in trouble," said Isis. "The man you call Maestro has captured them, and we need your help."

The look on their faces changed, all echoing the same fear and confusion. This man frightened them; he was their keeper and no doubt, their torturer.

Beauty's eyes shifted upward for a moment before returning to meet those of Max and Isis. "I do not think we can help you," she said, her voice less confident than when they had spoken with her earlier.

Isis said, "Why? You are prisoners, can't you see that?"

Now Megan's eyes shifted upward, and Max said, "What the hell are you looking at?"

The basketball backboard and net faced the other direction, and neither of them could see it from their vantage point. Max said, "I'll be right back."

He ran around the north side of the fence, no longer trying to stay in the cover of the brush and weeds.

Isis watched him. He was perhaps no more than ten feet along the north fence when he looked up and stopped.

Even in the darkness, Isis could see the expression on his face droop, understanding replacing his frustration.

Come here, came Max's silent call.

Isis stared into the eyes of Megan, Alyssa and Beauty for a few moments before walking around the corner of their prison to stand beside Max.

Positioned on the basket and spiked to the backboard, was a body, nude and shriveled. The long hair told them it was likely that of a woman.

Its head drooped to the left side, but it was clear that half its skull had been bashed open. It was impossible to say whether a baseball bat or high-caliber round had done the damage, but the message was very clear:

Cross Maestro and die. Disobey Maestro and die. This was their constant reminder to conform.

No words were necessary between Max and Isis. They returned to the west side of the fence.

"Was that one of your sisters?" asked Isis.

The three nodded and said nothing. They had a clear view of the threatening corpse from their positions inside the fence, and once more, their eyes shifted upward before returning to Max and Isis.

"They're going to be back for you," said Isis. "Please, please do not tell them of our presence. There's nothing more in this world I would like to do but save our friends and take all of you away with us to a place where you will be free to build your own lives and have friends and begin to have hope."

"What must become of Maestro?" asked Megan, her intense brown eyes penetrating.

"The guy's a monster," said Max. "He told you to have the Mothers kill everyone in Great Bend."

"The Mothers and Hungerers must eat," said Beauty, just as Megan had said before.

"You must understand that you are not one of them," said Isis. "You have no obligation to them, for you live and they do not. This is a concept you must understand, because if that does not happen, your lives will always be as they are today." Isis spoke in a more formal way, avoiding contractions with which they may be unfamiliar.

"And what are they?" asked Megan.

Max looked at Isis, then back at them. "What are what?"

"Our lives?"

"Right now?" asked Max. "Right now your lives are pointless to everyone but this Maestro, and from the looks of that poor girl up there," he said pointing, "you're mostly pointless to him, too. We can help you to a life of happiness that right now you have no concept of."

"They're coming now to take you to the containment area of the Mothers and Hungerers," said Isis. "We'll meet you over there. Do you think you can speak with some of the others and convince them to help?"

"Screw that," said Max, before any of them could answer. "Are *you* going to help us?"

229

Isis felt the deep confusion and conflict in their hearts and minds. She silently connected with them and projected:

Your lives at this moment are meaningless. Whether you live or die does not matter. If you come with us – if you help us – your lives will then have purpose, for you will aid humankind and rescue this world from a darkness it has never known before. In that function, you will come to know great joy.

Beauty stepped forward with one more glance up at the basketball net. She stared into Isis' eyes.

"What will become of Maestro?" she asked, as Megan had done before.

"He has to die, Beauty," said Isis.

Suddenly, the other Hybrids, who had not come as close as the three they had met earlier, staggered backward, as though an earthquake had made them stumble to keep their balance.

The three captive Hybrids standing before them all reached out and clasped one another's hands, their eyes not wavering from Isis and Max.

"What is it?" asked Max. "We told you the truth. The evil and darkness that exists within the man who caged you and killed that woman up there can't be reversed. From history we know people like that don't change."

"This may be true," said Alyssa. "But what you say must be done is more difficult than you know."

"Why?" asked Max.

Beauty looked up again at the shriveled corpse nailed to the backboard above their heads. "Because she was our sister," she said. "And Maestro is our father."

Max's jaw dropped as he stared at them. Now the resemblance to one another was clear.

Isis now knew it was not only the constant reminder and threat of death that held them back; it was the idea of killing the person who had created them.

Beauty let go of Alyssa's hand and pressed both of her hands to her stomach.

It was then that Isis noticed the slight bulge there.

She stepped closer to the fence, her eyes intent on Beauty. "Beauty, are you ... pregnant?"

She nodded.

Isis' mind spun. She looked again into the girls' green eyes. "Is Maestro the father?"

"He is," she said.

Aside from the incestuous component of what was happening, a larger, more pressing question came to Isis.

"Has he exposed you to the eye vapor of one of the Mothers?" asked Isis."

Beauty's expression grew confused. "Yes," she said. "How did you know?"

"Do you hear the commands of the Mothers?" Isis asked. "To help them?"

"We hear them," said Beauty, "but unlike our great matriarchs, Maria and Sofia, we are not compelled to follow them."

Isis looked at Max. The implications of what these special women had revealed were enormous.

If they did not rescue these women before this third generation Hybrid was born, that potentially powerful child would also fall under Maestro's control.

What would they be? Isis knew of her own power, even that which she did not share with others. What possible enhancements might exist from a third-generation Hybrid? Could they have twice the abilities? Would their power increase a tenfold? Perhaps a hundredfold?

"Beauty," said Isis. "I want your baby to be born into freedom. She will be an amazing child."

She. Isis could feel her. Because it was a girl, her potential power was immeasurable, which made the threat of her falling under Maestro's control even more dire.

The sound of people approaching from the east interrupted Isis' thoughts.

As Max and Isis backed into the brush, she whispered, "Please help us, and yourselves. Now go back. Hurry."

The three turned and separated as Max and Isis disappeared into the field beyond.

*****

CHAPTER TWELVE
Laredo, Texas
1984

The house on San Jorge Street was set deep within the spreading oak trees, almost invisible from the road. When it rained, the drops rattled against the tin roof and often kept Angus Almaraz awake through the night.

It wasn't so bad. It was peaceful in the early morning hours when his mother and sister were asleep and all the customers were gone. His only peace.

Inside, curled up in the corner of his cage he lay, listening to the wind driven rain. He could not tell time, but at five years old, he had lain awake enough nights to know that morning would be there soon.

Morning finally came and the rain subsided. His mother plodded into the living room wearing a sheer lace cover-up over her nakedness, bumping his cage with her left thigh as she passed. She did not say anything to him, but there was nothing odd about that.

Angus allowed only his eyes to follow her as she passed the metal cage and entered the kitchen of the old house, for Nancy Almaraz did not like her son staring at her.

With the men who frequented their home, she did not mind at all. She wanted their attention. It had been clear to Angus since he had been three that they were of greater importance.

His mother put on a teapot, using a match to light the gas burner on the old stove. She then removed a jar of instant coffee from the cupboard, unscrewed the lid and put it on the counter beside a dirty teaspoon. Taking a cup from the sink, she rinsed it and dipped the spoon into the jar, dropping a heaping teaspoon of freeze-dried coffee into the mug.

Angus had never had coffee, but his mother would eat soon. His stomach growled.

Another pair of legs passed by his cage, and Angus looked up to see his nude sister walk into the kitchen and open the cupboard to remove another cup. She then opened a pantry and pulled down a box of Frosted Flakes.

Now his stomach was flip-flopping inside of him. He shifted to reposition himself without appearing too obvious. If they noticed him, they may feed him.

He let loose a small sound to see if it might remind them he was there. He had to pee, too.

The mason jar in the corner was nearly full, and he wasn't sure he could manage filling it the rest of the way without spilling it.

Angus held it, saying nothing.

"Why you gotta eat breakfast with your tits hangin' out?" asked his mother.

"Tits out, tits in. They're not in your cereal bowl, so why do you give a shit?"

"Smartass."

"When's the first one gonna get here?" asked his 16-year-old sister, Jane.

"Frank'll be here in an hour."

234

Angus cringed. He knew that name well. Frank touched him and hurt him. Involuntary tears leaked from Angus' eyes and he buried his face in the threadbare towels bunched up on the bottom of his wire-walled prison.

Jane pulled a rag off the knob of the cabinet beneath the sink and turned on the water in the kitchen sink. She wet the filthy rag and squeezed it out only slightly. She carried it to Angus' cage and stuffed it between the upright rails, saying, "Wipe yourself down. You can't be stinkin' when Frank gets here."

"My jar's full," he said. "And I'm hungry."

"Do what your sister said!" his mother shouted, her eyes flashing anger. "You make sure Frank's happy and maybe you'll get lunch. If you don't clean up with that rag right now, we'll take you outside and you'll get the hose."

Angus didn't like the hose. It was cold and everything in his cage got soaked. He recalled many a night when he would shiver for hours with no hope of relief.

He picked up the wet towel and wiped himself in preparation for Frank.

He hoped Frank would die before he arrived.

*****

Frank, the first trick of the day, was a Saturday regular. He would come anywhere between eleven and one o'clock, and after Angus' sister took his cock in her mouth for a while, he would begin staring toward Angus' cage.

Angus never looked over. He would do his best to cover himself with the meager towels and pillow he was given, but it never mattered.

Today was no different, but instead of sucking him off, Jane sat atop Frank on the broken down, worn out sofa. He lay on his back, a fat man with a rough beard and thick,

235

curly hair all over his body. She moved up and down as he put his cock inside her, all the while staring at Angus' cage.

"That's good," he said.

Angus shuddered. Those words meant he was about to shift his attention.

"Pay up front, Frankie," said his mother, who sat on the other ragged sofa smoking a cigarette.

"Fuck you, you don't trust me after all these years?"

"Business is business," said Nancy. "You wanna play you gotta pay in advance."

Frank scooped up his pants from the floor and pulled out his wallet. He removed a ten dollar bill, wadded it and threw it across the room where Angus' mother caught it and tucked it between her breasts.

She waved a hand toward Angus' cage. "Be my guest."

Frank wasn't the only trick to pay for Angus. He was the largest and the one that Angus hated the most besides his mother and sister.

Frank did not seem to care that Angus was crying while he did his business.

In fact, he did not seem to notice at all.

*****

Laredo, Texas
Nine Years Later - 1993

The storm raged outside, and the only light Angus could see by came from the frequent lightning strikes that flashed daylight through the room and lit the interior of his cage.

236

He was now fourteen years old, though he was not aware of that fact. The naked boy lay curled in a fetal position, his fingers busily working with the latch on the padlocked, oversized dog cage in which he had lived since he was an infant.

Two nights earlier, he had noticed that a crack had formed on the lock hasp of the old, rusted pen. It was in the weld that connected the hasp to the metal bars. Wiggling it back and forth, back and forth, he had soon cracked another weld. Now only one more held it in place.

The little hand of the Sunbeam clock on the wall was on the four when he finally heard the little snap!, telling him it was time.

He pushed on the door. It swung outward, the padlock still latched, but now useless.

Angus crawled out of the cage door and stood, careful to extend his body and muscles slowly; he had not been allowed out of the cage for six days, and it was far smaller now than it had been when he was a child.

His young, malnourished bones and muscles screamed as he reached his full height of just five feet, two inches. Angus stretched his arms high over his head, shaking them out until the numbness went away. Walking quietly around the room, he spied the handle of a baseball bat sticking out from behind the sofa.

His mother kept it there in case she and Jane ran into a trick who needed to learn a lesson. He had seen her raise it to threaten, though Nancy Almaraz never had to use it.

He walked to the bat, bent down and slid it out from behind the couch. It was solid and heavy in his hands, and he let it swing from side to side in one hand.

He looked toward the kitchen. Angus was hungry; starving, actually. He opened the refrigerator and saw the paper carton of milk. He pulled it out, opened the carton and drank it all.

Putting it on the counter, he opened the cupboard and found a loaf of bread. He held the bat between his knees and tore open the plastic loaf. He pulled out piece after piece, stuffing them into his mouth and repeating it until the bag was empty.

Angus felt good. He felt strong. He walked into the living room and stood beside his cage. He held his penis and urinated into the cage, soaking the putrid towels and old, torn sheets that served as his bedding.

He would not be going back in there, he decided.

Not ever.

He took the bat in both hands and slammed it into the floor, then the walls, before moving to the side of the hallway, the bat raised over his head.

His mother's voice sounded clear in the night, even above the noise of the storm, and Angus waited patiently, tapping twice more on the wall with the Louisville Slugger.

His mother stepped out of the hallway, her voice angry.

"Who the fuck is out here –"

Angus swung the bat toward his mother, the blow connecting at the bridge of her nose, cutting her words off and erupting in a spray of blood mist.

Angus said nothing. As her body fell straight back into the hallway and she began to roll onto her right side as she moaned in agony, he brought the solid wood bat down again and again, hammering her face flat until her brains leaked into a sticky puddle and her head looked like a mass of blood, bone and hair.

Her body twitched as he administered another blow, seeing something from the corner of his eye. He looked up.

His sister stared at him as a bolt of lightning struck nearby, and he saw Jane's horrified eyes on her mother's body.

Jane screamed and ran into her room.

Angus stepped over his mother's corpse and walked calmly down the hallway. He had never run, so did not know the movement was even possible.

He reached the room, which was unfamiliar to him, and saw his sister holding the telephone.

He knew what that was for. Her finger had spun the dial around, but before it could spin back to its starting point, Angus drew back the bat and swung with all his might.

His sister's head smashed into the window, shattering it. Now the tattered curtains blew outward, sucked away by the wind, and Angus stood over Jane and beat her until he was exhausted.

As he became too tired to continue, the storm passed. The curtains settled on the rod, drifting down and coming to rest.

The morning light filtered in before long, and Angus returned to the living room and to the couch. He leaned the bat against the sofa and crawled onto it.

His head sank into the soft cushion, and his eyes went to the clock on the wall.

He was sure it was Saturday. This meant his old friend Frank would be coming, as he did every week since Angus was a young child.

This time Angus would be there to greet him.

He smiled for the first time in a long, long time as he stared at his mother's body, lying supine in the hallway.

He was free.

*****

Mexico-Texas Border
June, 2011

The tanker truck looked like any other. Bright, gleaming chrome, polished as brightly as any mirror, so that occupants of trailing cars could marvel at their own fisheye reflection as they rolled down the highway.

While it was meant to appear to be identical to any other tanker truck on the roadways, this one was different.

Inside, a narrow center walkway allowed handlers to access two rows of cages on either side. Each cage was narrow and tall, running from floor to ceiling. There were twenty-four cages in all, each with an upward-sliding hatch to gain entry. The tank side of the cages were covered with thick padding to prevent their captives from banging on the stainless steel walls and drawing outsider attention.

At the lowest possible point, a flat floor had been welded to the stainless steel floor so that the occupants of the cages did not constantly slide toward the center of the truck. The interior was cooled by a narrow cavity that encompassed the entire outer shell of the truck where cooling fluids ran, fed through hoses leading from the Freightliner's engine compartment.

In fact, the interior of the tank could get as cool as 50 degrees, and there was no valve to control it. Angus did not mind, though. The occupants were rarely encased in the truck for more than two hundred miles once they crossed into the United States.

The exterior of the cab and the tank itself were emblazoned with the Pemex logo, Mexico's state gasoline company. A dummy corporation, AmeriMex, had been created to certify the frequent trips across both borders by

240

way of a joint partnership of both countries, and Angus had made sure the forged paperwork would verify and pass any inspection.

There had been some failures early on, but they were dry runs. He was now in his fourteenth year of trafficking young women, and he had never even had a close call.

The road leading to the U.S. border was more congested than usual. It was a Sunday, and that could make a difference, for people did like to venture into Laredo to buy food and gifts for family in Mexico.

The current haul was a full load. Each narrow cage held one girl. Angus had long ago developed a relationship with the Fuentes Cartel, with a heavy focus on human trafficking. They made their way through several small towns and villages, snatching girls from their homes and holding them in captivity until Angus' next run.

Among his current haul were seven pregnant girls, ranging in age from seventeen to twenty-three. They were a two-for-one deal for Angus, and he always demanded a minimum of five pregnant girls per transaction. The farther along the better. Angus did not like to hold his stock for long before moving them, but it was more profitable to wait until the children were born so that they could be sold off separately.

Angus slowed, now just five cars from the border crossing. As he sat there staring at the guards, with whom he was familiar, a car blew through the border gate coming into Mexico, angling directly toward Angus' tanker.

He saw the driver through the glare of the glass; he looked insane. His hands were not on the steering wheel, rather it appeared he was attacking the woman in his passenger seat.

Angus saw all of this just seconds before the green hatchback careened hard left and smashed into the concrete

241

barrier just a foot to the left of his combo's wheels, flipping over and spinning on its roof.

Traffic was still stopped in front of Angus, so he watched in amazement as the driver of the vehicle crawled out of the wrecked car and staggered around to the passenger side, reaching in and dragging the woman out. He walked strangely; no coordination. Angus could not see his pupils from his location, but had seen enough people on PCP to know that was likely what was going on.

The man lifted the woman and bit into her face. He tore at her hair as though he wanted to rip it clean away, and he chewed on her face even as she screamed at the top of her lungs and beat at him with her flailing arms and hands.

Four border patrol agents charged toward them with their guns drawn, but the man paid them no attention. He threw the woman down on the concrete, her head slamming hard against the pavement, knocking her into blissful unconsciousness. The insane man fell on top of her, ripping the front of her Sunday dress open and sinking his face into her abdomen, even as his fingers clawed at whatever exposed skin they could sink into.

The border agents reached him and pointed their guns downward, but none of them fired, for the woman was beneath him. One tried to pull him off, but when the man lifted his face, the woman's entrails hung bloody and dripping from his teeth.

His eyes were mad. Angus watched, fascinated. The traffic in front of him moved, but he was reluctant to drive away. It was mesmerizing, watching this woman being eaten by another human.

My mother should have died the same way. She got off easy, he thought. *Jane, too.*

One of the border agents was looking straight at him and waving him on, ordering him to go. He did not,

242

temporarily forgetting about his highly-illegal cargo in the face of this strangely fascinating display of cannibalism.

As the man stood up and moved toward the border agents surrounding him on four sides, two of them shot him. The explosions rang out as the rounds blew out his chest and right ribcage.

The man spun to his right as the first shot found its mark, and the chest shot sent him flying backward, slamming into the rear bumper of the overturned Toyota he had been driving.

Angus could not leave. The man got up, a huge hole in his chest, a chunk out of his side. The four then started firing with reckless abandon, and the man's body danced as it still moved toward them.

Finally one of the officers blew out his knees and he fell to the ground, still growling and looking absolutely mad. Instead of dying, the man clawed at the pavement until he had again reached the dead woman's body. He sank his teeth in and once more began to feed.

The men unloaded their weapons then. The woman was clearly dead and they were obviously freaked out. The rounds struck him in the head, neck, back, buttocks and legs.

He finally lay still atop the dead woman. Angus let out the breath he'd been unaware he was holding and realized he had an erection.

He reached up to the sun visor and pulled down a pack of Winstons. He lit one and accelerated to the border gate. All the vehicles in front of him had already gone through.

He passed without incident, as usual. It was perhaps even easier that day because of the horrific attack that had just occurred. The agents were more interested in looking into the strange, rabid man who had just killed a woman by eating her alive.

243

*****

The next 200 miles were far from uneventful. In several places, stopped cars blocked the roadway, and people staggered around, many of them approaching his rig, staring up at him as though he were of great interest to them.

Whatever was going on, it wasn't just in Mexico. At his first opportunity, Angus turned off the road to take smaller side roads. Every cop car he'd seen had its lights and siren on and were headed toward something very important, so it did not seem he would need to worry about taking his tanker down a road where such vehicles were prohibited.

He knew all the best, least-used shortcuts anyway.

Rock Springs was mostly an industrial town, but he owned an isolated ranch on the southwest side. There were four gravel roads one had to navigate to reach it, and none featured signage. This was where he lived; he had long ago constructed a barn that would accommodate up to eighty girls at a time. Among these women he created trustees, of a sort.

They were not actually trustees because Angus trusted no women; but they were as close as he would get. The small nursery, designed to accommodate up to eight babies, was contained in a 10' x 10' cell. The two adult beds in here were more comfortable than the meager mattresses on which his other captives rested. There had to be some reward for the infants caretakers other than being allowed to live.

Perception was everything.

Angus slowed at the gate and pressed the remote control. The large gates swung inward, and he drove into the yard and pulled the tanker alongside the barn. It was time to unload and have a shower and dinner.

From beneath the trailer, he withdrew a four-foot long steel bar with a star socket on the end. He inserted this into a hole on the rear of the tanker truck. From a compartment at the rear of the tank, he removed a two-foot long rod with a center slot. This piece fit on top of the other, creating a T-handle with which he could loosen the bolts holding the tank hatch closed.

Removing a ladder from a narrow but deep slot in the back, he leaned it against the rear of the trailer so that he could reach the rest of the bolts.

When he had removed all them, Angus repositioned the ladder and pulled open the rear cap, which he swung out to the left, like a massive, pivoting wall mirror. A strange, reddish mist kissed the air as soon as he cracked the hatch.

Angus stepped back and stared. Could it have been some sort of contamination? He sniffed at the air, but did not smell anything. His relationship with the Fuentes Cartel told him never to take chances. To rush could mean to die.

Angus returned to the cab of his truck and unlatched the driver's seat of the Freightliner cab, flipping it forward. Behind the seat was a 12" x 12" hinged box. He removed it, pushed the seat back into position and placed the box on the seat.

He opened it and withdrew a gas mask and a small tank of oxygen. He kept them because he had seen the cartels in action before, and they had been known to use gas to exact their carnage. He wouldn't be falling victim to that.

He adjusted the straps. In a situation where the toxicity level was unknown and the particulate size in question, only this type of device would do. He cracked the oxygen cylinder and quickly pulled the mask over his face.

He returned to the truck, pulled out the sliding steps and climbed up.

In the darkness of the tank's interior, pairs of reddish dots floated in the air, running from front to rear. Strange growls and shrieks were coming from all around him.

Angus' hand went for the light switch.

When the bright light bathed the interior of the transport, Angus nearly staggered backward so far he barely escaped toppling out the back. He steadied himself.

The occupants of almost every cage had thrown themselves forward into the heavy wire, clearly unconcerned with their own well-being. They smashed the front of their cages relentlessly, tearing and clawing at the wire as though believing they could work their way through it. Angus stood back and stared in amazement and horror.

What the hell happened here?

The frenzy was happening further back, though. He looked into the cage just in front of him along the right wall. This cage contained a pregnant girl that his coded paperwork listed as seventeen years old.

There was a distinct lack of aggression on her part. Her face was still, but as she turned her eyes toward him, they blazed a piercing red. She sat inside her small cage, her knees drawn up to her chest in order to allow her to position herself that way in such a small space.

Her hair, which Angus had remembered to be long and wavy, now appeared straight, as though flattened with a hot iron.

Something lay by her feet.

He knelt down and she snarled, causing him to move away slightly. He squinted at the thing on the floor and realized it was a severed hand – or to be more precise, now mostly the bones of a hand. Skin and meat still clung to it, but not very much.

246

"What the hell did you do?" he asked her, his eyes moving to the cage beside hers.

The moment he did so, the woman in the next cage slammed the steel bars, snarling and biting the air as she pressed her face against the cage's interior. While the bars on the sides of the adjoining cages were far enough apart that it was possible for small hands to reach into another cage, the front was made of a thick steel mesh, preventing any reaching or clawing into the narrow aisle.

The whores had badly scratched Angus in the past, so he had learned his lesson. It would not happen again.

The snarling girl-thing's eyes were pinpoints; black dots beneath a wispy reddish mist. Her skin was a roadmap of blue-black veins. Angus noticed that several front upper and lower teeth that had been intact at the trip's outset were now missing. Blood stained her face, but he was not certain how it had gotten that way.

The caged thing attempted to claw at the mesh with both hands, but now only her right one remained. The left hand was lying, mostly eaten, at the bottom of the first cage, leaving only a tattered stump at the end of her left wrist, nerve endings and shriveled tendons dangling.

Angus' eyes dropped again to the devoured hand on the floor of the next cage, and to the very calm woman-thing staring at him from within, her red eyes penetrating his as though wishing to command him in some way.

He looked again at the shrieking thing's stump, from which no blood at all leaked. Angus' eyes fell to the thing's feet. The pan at the bottom of her cage was half-full of a dark, thick liquid. He had installed the pans to contain urine and feces in case the women could not hold it for the duration of their transport.

It was not bloody urine, for there was far too much of it. It could only be her blood. No other options remained.

Any ordinary person would be dead.

Angus staggered back from the cage again at the realization. His eyes remained fixed on her. Even as she snarled and clawed, her flat eyes had never wavered from his. The look fixed there was as emotionless as that of a reptile.

If the expressionless eyes held any sign of emotion, it was of hunger. Insatiable hunger.

Maybe she is dead, thought Angus. If she was, her body was not, for it still moved as if she would never tire.

Angus stepped back from her and stared down the rows of cages. What growled and clawed within many of them were not what the Mexican handlers had put there. This entire load had been one of the best he had seen; very attractive girls and young women who would have fetched him top dollar. Looking around the interior, Angus had no idea what had happened.

"Goddamnit!" shouted Angus. "What the hell is going on! My whole damned load is fucked!"

"Get us out of here, please," said a woman's voice.

Reluctant, but without a choice, Angus turned sideways and side-stepped down to the front end of the tanker, the frenzied creatures slamming the cages each time he passed in front of them.

Acting afraid was a sure way to lose respect, especially in front of a woman. No woman could or ever would scare him. Even a diseased one.

He was wearing a gas mask. Untouchable.

He reached the prisoner who had spoken. She sat, her legs drawn up with her head as low as she could manage. She stared downward so that Angus could not see her eyes.

"Why are you on the floor?" asked Angus. "Stand up."

248

"I can't," she said. "The one beside me sprayed me, and I got a headache."

"Sprayed you with what?"

"The red mist from her eyes," said the girl. "Please," she whispered. "Let me out of here." She looked up finally, and Angus saw her eyes were a deep red, almost with their own illumination.

She finally stood, but pressed herself into the side of her cage opposite the next cage over.

"What happened in here?" asked Angus, relieved she spoke English. He spoke broken Spanish – enough to communicate with his cartel connections. Many of them spoke decent English, so he never had the need to learn. He was often surprised at how much English the girls they got him knew. Likely because many of them came from border towns and villages, and it helped to have some English skills.

"I could not see," she said. "I am pregnant. Please, let me out of here, away from these ... these things!"

"Why are your eyes red?" he asked.

"Are they?" she said. "I do not know. I felt dizzy a few hours ago after I was sprayed by her, but I do not know why. Please, I hear things within my head. I must leave this place."

Beside her, another of the straight-haired creatures stood, clearly not normal, but not as ravaged as the woman in the second cage near the hatch. She appeared almost identical in condition to the woman he had found in the first cage.

"What did you hear?" asked Angus, his voice muffled through his mask.

"They complained of pains in their heads, some of them," she said. "Terrible pains."

"Down here!" shouted another woman from the rear of the tanker.

"Por favor!" shouted another voice. "Afuera, por favor! Afuera! Afuera!"

"She wants out," said the woman in the cage before Angus. "Please, before we all get … changed. Hurry."

Angus shook his head. "You sure you're not sick? Like I said, your eyes are red."

"I was dizzy before, but I'm okay. Please, senor, I am pregnant. Something could be wrong with my baby. I'm bigger than when I was put here."

Angus looked at her belly. Indeed, she did appear larger. She hardly showed when she was put in the cage, for he inspected each piece of merchandise. Now her swollen stomach appeared at least twice the size.

He removed a key from his pocket and said, "In a few moments. I have to deal with these others before I can get you girls out of here."

He walked to the rear to inspect the other two women who apparently had not changed like most of the others. These three were the only ones remaining out of his entire haul that could speak. Of these prisoners, two of them were pregnant.

Good. At least he would still have the income from the babies. The rest was a total loss. He would demand his money back from the Fuentes Cartel men who had captured them. Clearly, there had been an epidemic spreading through the villages where they snatched the girls.

The cartel had fucked him with faulty merchandise, and they had likely known what they were selling him in advance. Something this contagious could not just spring up out of nowhere.

As he moved to the rear, the creatures, without exception, slammed against their cages, and pink vapor emitted from their eyes as though pumped from a fog machine.

Suddenly, the three women who had, moments before, been speaking to him, collapsed to the bottom of their cages, unconscious.

This was a mess. They were clearly rabid, but he could not shoot them within their cages, for the rounds might penetrate and puncture the outer cooling cavity. He would need a different approach.

Angus scooted sideways back down the aisle, doing his best to ignore the snarling creatures slamming into their cages as he passed, save for a few of them.

As he passed the front cage, he saw the creature there was now standing, facing the front. Her head turned as he stepped by.

A chill ran down his spine. He was not afraid of anything, so Angus was not sure why. After what he had been through in his childhood, no woman, no matter her condition, would ever frighten him again.

He got down the steps and went into a shed beside the barn. He pulled a machete from a hook on the back wall and leaving the door open, he returned to the tanker and climbed inside.

Angus stopped to check his oxygen supply. He had another five minutes or so. That would be enough for the task at hand. His keys in one hand and the machete in the other, he again slid down the center aisle and walked to the last cage containing a hissing, clawing crazy, and unlocked the padlock. He lifted it out and triggered the mechanism that raised the sliding cage door.

He then moved backward down the aisle fast, reaching the ladder and climbing down, never allowing his eyes to leave the creature who shambled toward him.

Angus stepped back from the trailer, his machete raised. The thing reached the end of the cylinder and tumbled out of the back, her head hitting the sandy, desert floor.

She did not stay down long, and in fact, never stopped moving. She was back on her feet as Angus again stepped back, the machete high in the air.

"Alto!" he shouted, but the demented woman kept coming. No more chances. He raised the machete and brought it down on top of her head with all his might, cracking through the top of her skull and splitting her face in two, down to the middle of the nose.

Instead of a spray of red blood pumping from the enormous gash, a reddish-black muck oozed out of the wound as she dropped like a stone to the low brush and sand.

Angus stared at her for a moment. He kicked her arm. Nothing. Watching her for another few seconds before he was sure, he nodded. She was dead.

He went back into the trailer and opened another cage.

Same procedure over and over again. The process took longer than he expected, and he used up two more cylinders of oxygen before the task was complete.

Of the three survivors, the one that wasn't pregnant had perfectly normal eyes. The other two both had red eyes. Both of them swore their stomachs had grown since being placed in the cages.

It was too much to think about. All of it was too much. He'd just killed nineteen of his twenty-four girls, and it was just a matter of pure luck that two of them had been pregnant.

The barn had been empty on his most recent run. There were no babies and only his trustees remained. That is why he insisted on a full load on his most recent trip into

252

Mexico. Now another run would be required long before he had intended.

He would not be paying for most of the girls he brought back. He would photograph the condition of these girls and the cartel would see things his way or lose his future business – which was very lucrative.

When he opened the three cages containing the only viable stock, the girls awoke with just a shake. Groggily they stood and obeyed him when he ordered them to move toward the open end of the trailer, then to climb slowly down the steps.

When he got inside the barn, the stench was horrific. The same snarling he had experienced inside the tanker also echoed through the stillness of the barn, and it could only originate from one place.

The nursery.

Though he had no babies at the moment, Angus kept two trustees at all times for when babies came; he had to have women he trusted to take charge of them. A woman with her own baby would always be a slave to her maternal instinct to flee in order to protect her child.

Ordinary women, that is.

My fucking bitch of a mother would've sold me in a heartbeat at the right price, he thought, bitterly.

The nursery cell was located in the southeast corner of the barn, at the opposite end from the door. He quickly opened the three cells closest to the entrance. He did not want this merchandise close to whatever now occupied the nursery.

*****

As he walked the length of the barn toward the nursery, he held his Tisas .45 caliber in his hand. It was a

253

precision-made handgun with a Turkish walnut grip and blued steel. It fired true, and one bullet was usually enough to do what needed to be done.

For the moment, he held it down by his side as he walked, not in any hurry to reach the last cell.

Angus knew there would be no more runs to Mexico. That became clear the moment he realized something was wrong in the barn, too. No, it was not just limited to the girls he had brought from Mexico in the tanker. Whatever this disease was, it wasn't so easy now to chalk it up to careless vaccination standards and extreme poverty.

His trustees, Lissette and Estela, had been in excellent health.

As he approached the cage he felt bile and vomit coming up from his stomach, and he did not fight it. He bent forward and threw up onto the floor, wiping his mouth on his shirt sleeve.

Estela stood at the bars, shriek-screaming with gray, addled skin, the thin, black veins so tightly patterned that they seemed to obscure the very facial features beneath them.

The cell bars were wide enough here – very much like a typical prison enclosure – that her arms could easily fit between them, and she now clawed at the air as Angus moved closer. He held his gun in the firing position as he moved in, cursing his shaking hand.

At Estela's feet were human remains. The blue dress that Lissette, a young 20-year-old that Angus had enjoyed fucking at least twice a week, lay in tatters and blood-soaked on the concrete floor. Estela had strewn parts of her body everywhere, for reasons that Angus did not know.

Lissette's severed left arm and hand lay within one of the bassinettes, the interior stained with dried blood. Her right foot, almost gnawed down to bone, stuck out of the sink basin. The once pretty girl's shattered head was nearly unrecognizable as such; only the matted, long black hair identified it.

It lay smashed and broken, now just a crushed shell with a face. That face was turned toward Angus, and where the eyes had been were now black holes through which he was sure Hell could be seen if one were to peer into them deeply enough.

Angus' eyes moved past the snarling creature in front of him, scanning the floor of the cell. He thought he could identify bits of brain matter among the rest of the gore. The torso and trunk remained intact, smashed against the back corner of the cage, facing away from him.

He was glad. A dead body only amused him when he had done the killing. A murder this messy was never an option. This building was his place of business, and if a girl needed to bleed, he would take them outside and gut them in a more controlled, more easily cleanable spot, such as in the shade of his killing tree. Many had met their ends beneath the sprawling oak. It was a favorite spot.

Lissette's only dress lay in tattered shreds on the floor, each ripped piece soaked with the blood of its former wearer. Anger welled up inside him, and his eyes returned to his former trustee.

Estela stood there, her mouth and teeth gnashing together as she reached toward him, singularly focused. Angus suddenly shoved the gun into his pants and reached out, grabbing her right arm with both hands and twisting it as hard as he could, snapping the bone clean.

She did not seem to notice. She continued reaching for him with her other arm, but this time Angus pushed it hard to the left, bending it back until it was flat against the cage at full extension.

The violent crack that met his ears resulted in the bone tearing through the vein-riddled flesh, leaving her with two useless, dangling appendages.

No blood from the wound. What did leak out looked more like motor oil, and smelled like shit and vomit.

His manipulation of her arm had knocked Estela slightly backward, but the shattered humerus caught on the cell bars, leaving her hanging there, gnashing and snarling like nothing had changed.

Angus raised the gun and held it toward her, walking forward. He moved so that the end of the barrel was within six inches of the creature now pressed against the iron bars, her pink eyes staring, no semblance of life remaining in them.

Pink eyes, he thought.

He looked back down the row of cells. He could not see the women from his location, but of the three, two of them had red eyes. The other appeared perfectly normal.

Glancing back at Estela, he lowered the gun and returned to the other end of the barn. "You feel alright?" he asked.

"We are prisoners, but we are alive," said the one who had appealed for help first inside the tanker. "It's better than being in that damned metal hell."

"This is your new hell," he said. "I'm bringing the others in."

"Not them!" shouted the woman. "Please, not those things!"

"Shut the fuck up!" said Angus. "I'll put them well away from you. Keep your fuckin' mouth going and I'll put you in with one of 'em."

The two who spoke English turned away from him. The one that did not still seemed to get the point.

From the wall, he retrieved the extension pole with the slip ring on the end. He used this when his captives fought him too hard, scratching at him with their nails. It rarely happened after he got them settled and they realized they needed to be on his good side. If trouble was to be had, it was with the new purchases.

Putting his gas mask back on, Angus climbed the steps and entered the tanker.

When he approached the first strange creature, she looked at him and stood from her sitting position. Her crimson eyes stared into his, but she did not charge forward and she did not press herself into the back of the tanker.

He extended the pole and loosened the thick neck strap. Turning the strap sideways, he fed it into the cell and snapped it quickly down over her head, cinching it tight around her neck by sliding the handle toward him.

She simply stared at him, her mouth moving side-to-side. Angus pushed her backward with the pole and leaned down to slide the key into the lock. He triggered the latch, and the spring-loaded door slid upward.

"Come on out of there now," he said. He guided her toward the open gate and when she was through, he pushed her toward the rear of the trailer and pushed the end of the handle the rest of the way through the bars until it was clear of the cage.

He then walked her toward the opening, jerking the rod backward with each step he took. When he reached the end, he carefully climbed down the steps, holding on to the stick with one hand for the moment.

The red-eyed thing surprised him then; she leapt from the open trailer, right at him, her body slamming into his and driving him into the dirt. He was taken by complete surprise but was able to scramble away and get to his feet, his hand immediately pulling out the .45.

She came at him fast, her arms outstretched, and for the first time, her mouth open wide as she jerkily charged him.

He fired, the bullet blowing a black hole through her chest, and she flew backward, the neck strap and pole whipped from side to side, barely missing his eye.

She was back on her feet so fast that Angus hardly had time to raise the gun again. He got it up when she was three feet away and closing.

Boom! Boom! He fired twice more and this time the top of her head shattered and she crumpled to the ground immediately.

He watched her, hyperventilating at the adrenaline charge that rocked his metabolism. Her red eyes faded to black and all movement ceased.

Angus stared at her for a long time. He wondered if the others he had put in cells would change the same way. He wanted none of it. Not if that was how it was going to go. It was too much. Too exhausting. And pointless. Nobody would want these women. They had no monetary value with their strange, red eyes.

Maybe the babies, he thought. *I'll wait for them to be born and see what happens.*

The government would get the epidemic under control soon. It would definitely be the first order of business.

Angus was more careful with the second red-eyed girl. He used a rope along with the neck restraint and tied her off to the trailer before getting her out. When he was ready and she was down, he just used his knife to cut the rope.

As he promised, he tucked her away in the cell three down from the nursery, but a strange thing occurred when he led her inside.

She stared toward the women in their individual cages, her red eyes increasing in intensity. As she passed, the two females with the red eyes similar to hers said, "Open cage," together. In perfect unison.

The Spanish speaking girl – the one without red eyes – said nothing. She cowered in her cell facing away from the monster that Angus had decided to keep.

For the moment.

*****

Watching the evening news, it became obvious that the epidemic was everywhere. Nearly every channel showed live images of insane people who looked exactly like his former charges, attacking and biting people. These attacks were not halfhearted efforts; the aggression with which they attacked their fellow human beings was as cannibalistic as the man who had been eating the woman at the border.

That was when it struck him. It had begun earlier than he had known. The accidents and crazies he'd seen on the way home; the man killing the woman at the border.

Angus had questions. He was tired, though. They would wait until morning. He turned off the television and lowered the exterior shutters, using the single switch by the front door.

His home was an impenetrable barrier while he slept. The barn was booby-trapped with tripwires and explosives.

Everything would keep through the night.

*****

The morning came earlier than Angus had wanted. His mind rolled over and over the women and the thing that was not quite a woman out in his barn.

At just before 6:00 AM, he got out of bed and threw on a pair of jeans and a shirt. He went to the pantry to get some food.

He looked over at the book of word and shape puzzles on the table; it was how he relaxed. Not so much crosswords, but the maze puzzles. He loved them. He would begin his pencil line and draw, his eyes moving ahead to determine the path that would lead him through.

He had been very young when first introduced to the puzzles. When he was just five years old, one of the men who had come in to fuck his sister had dropped a puzzle book filled with over 500 maze puzzles. He had been pretending to be asleep as the man passed by – something he had done often – and when the book had dropped near his cage, he cracked an eye and saw immediately that nobody had noticed. He reached through the cage bars and snatched it, tucking it beneath his dirty towels.

A pencil had been closed inside the book. Angus had spent many a night on his stomach, drawing lines on the many puzzles within. It had been his escape from the monotonous horror that was his life of captivity and sexual favor.

There would be no puzzles today. He walked to the mirror and looked at himself. His eyes were fine, and he felt okay. No veins traversed his face or arms. He nodded and left the room.

He glanced at the coffee pot, but kept walking toward the front door. He checked the peephole – a habit he had adopted years ago – and saw the yard outside empty. If he were surrounded by cops or worse, he wanted to know about it before stepping into the middle of the shit.

He opened the door and walked to the barn, dialing in the combo on the six-digit padlock with a concealed hasp. No bolt cutters would allow access.

He walked in and hit the lights. The three women in the cages were in their cots topped with thin mattresses, sleeping.

That was fine. He wasn't interested in them at the moment anyway.

With intentional stealth, he eased past the first cage where the taller, prettier of the pregnant women slept.

The girl who wasn't pregnant stirred, but as he drew beside the cell containing the other pregnant woman, she said, "Free me."

Angus jumped a bit, stopping to stare at her. She was sleeping, for he could hear her steady breathing.

As he watched, her mouth moved again and she very clearly said, "Free Mother."

"Hey," he said, softly. He waited, but she did not respond. Her slow breathing continued. He looked down toward the end of the building and saw the red-eyed creature standing there, facing the front bars of her cage.

He walked down to where she stood and stayed about four feet back from the cell bars, studying her.

He smiled. "What the hell are you?" he asked. "Red eyes, hair like fine silk. Skin ain't as bad as some in my tanker had."

Her head turned to the left, and she appeared to stare toward the woman in the nearest cell. As she did so, the voice came from the distance, "Free Mother."

"Whoa, fuck!" he said, looking from the sleeping woman back to her. "Are you the fuck doing that?"

Suddenly the creature in the cage slammed her body against the bars, reaching her clawing hand as far through them as she could. While he was not close enough for her to make contact, he jumped backward anyway.

He looked down at her stomach and noticed the bulge there for the first time. "You got a goddamned baby in ya?"

he asked. He smiled and looked back up at her. She did not return his smile.

"I'll be damned," he said. "Is that what makes you different than the others that have normal hair and just seem crazy?"

Again, no answer, no smile – not even a hint that he was correct. No matter. He went down to where the other women slept and banged on the front of their cages. "Wake up, ladies!" he shouted. "Time to get the hell up and join the living!"

He looked down the row of cells and added, "Well, pretty much living, anyway."

He walked to the door and pulled a folding chair from a rack on the wall and carried it to the cell where the tall one now sat up on her bed.

"Tell me what happened to you."

"I was kidnapped and thrown into the truck outside," she said. "Now I'm here."

"No," said Angus. "Tell me what happened in the truck."

"It was dark. I have no idea what happened."

"How far along are you?"

"I'm six months," she said.

"So three to go," he said."

"That is how God arranged things, yes."

"You look bigger than six months."

"I look bigger since I went to sleep," she said, her hands on the bulge in her abdomen.

Angus leaned forward. "I need you to think about this very carefully before answering," he said. "I need to know if anything happened to you in that tanker. Even if you couldn't see it. Did you get the sense anything happened to you?"

The woman nodded. "My name is Maria," she said.

"I don't give a shit. Half you bitches are Maria," spat Angus.

"I'm telling you because I want you to know I am a human being with a mother and father and sisters and brothers."

"And apparently one of them is fucking you. How old are you?"

"I'm seventeen," said Maria.

"You're about the age my sister was when I beat her to death with a baseball bat. Answer the fucking question."

"About who is *fucking* me?"

"No, goddamnit! Tell me what happened in that goddamned cage!"

"I do not know!" she said. "I was standing there, and I was very tired. I was beginning to fall asleep on my feet, and I slid toward the next cage over. When I opened my eyes, two red dots were very near me, but then they became very fuzzy, as though clouded by fog."

"Did you feel anything?" he asked.

"Yes, I did," she said. "I grew lightheaded and dizzy. My eyes began to sting. I moved away from her and slid down to the floor."

"Did you feel anything different about your baby?"

"Did I feel differently about it?"

"No, no! Jesus, are you fucking stupid? I asked if you felt something was different about the baby!"

"Leave her alone!" said the other pregnant woman in the next cell. "And my name is not Maria. It is Sofia. And as far as what she is telling you, what happened to her is exactly what happened to me. You had us in such small boxes, of course whatever infected them would infect us! You've killed us, turned us into the insane!"

"If you weren't pregnant too, I'd take you outside to a nice shady spot under my oak tree. You might wanna watch your whore mouth."

The woman looked down, then back up. "Oh, my God," she said. Her hands rubbed her swollen belly.

Angus stood and pulled his chair to her cell. "What is it?"

But he did not need to await an answer. Sofia's stomach appeared three times the size it had been.

"How far along are you?"

"I'm seven months, but I was hardly showing before I was put in there. Everyone told me how it was a shame I did not show my motherhood more."

"Well, you're sure showin' it now. Perfect. We got no damned trustees to take care of the babies."

"We can take care of our own children," said Maria.

"Well, from the looks of it, you'll be doin' it sooner than later. I'll get you some food," said Angus.

*****

The moment the first child was born, a month later, all the demons of hell came to Rock Springs, Texas.

First off, the baby was deformed. At birth, it had teeth. The moment its eyes opened, it was as if it wore bright red contact lenses. Within another month, the teeth were almost adult sized. Worse, with all that was going on in the world, it would only eat meat.

Angus would have put the first one into a cell all its own, but it had begun crawling early, and would possibly have wormed its way through the bars.

But the freaks who arrived at his gate were the most confounding thing of all.

Dead people. He knew this because most of them wore suits or nicer dresses, all caked with mud, grass and dirt. Some were nearly skinless, but come they did, standing at the gate, pushing against the corrugated crossbeams as though they would never tire.

And they never did.

The second child was born a month later, both of the babies arriving far earlier than the due dates their mothers had expected.

After the second baby was born and the ranch was surrounded by the rotting creatures, Angus had begun to notice things about the first child. It was aware, both of itself and of everything around it.

It was a she. The second child was a girl as well. Both were identical in their abnormalities, but otherwise, seemed like normal babies.

Except for the fact that they did not sleep, nor did they ever cry. They stared at things with their strange, red eyes.

Particularly Angus.

He had a lot of food for babies, being in the business he was in, but he had run completely out of everything but vegetables. He had to figure out how to get the hell out of there and raid a grocery store. Unfortunately, now he was completely surrounded and wasn't sure what to do. Life as a human trafficker was far easier than this new one.

Of the hundreds of smelly dead people who showed up at his gate and refused to leave, a few scattered here and there were the type with the bright, red eyes and straight, corn silk hair.

If he had the energy, he captured them. Shoot all the freaks around her, open the gate and let her in.

A bullet to one leg disabled it, and from there he would drag it with a chain hooked to the back of his Ford

F150. A net over top of them, and he'd use a long pry bar to roll them up onto a large, furniture dolly.

He now had eight of them. He didn't feed them, and they didn't complain. They never died, either.

On a Friday afternoon in late September, he loaded up every long gun he had. He walked to the gate and exhausted himself while he placed round after round in the faces and skulls of the gathering creatures. Early on, he'd experimented with rounds to their chests and stomachs, but it had no effect.

They kept coming. He quickly decided not to waste any more ammo. Head shots. He started to collect the ones with straight hair, though. There was something about them. He was going to figure it out.

When no more of them moved, he drove his John Deere skiploader to the open fence and pushed the piles of bodies to the side of the drive. Once clear, he dug two trenches forty feet long by ten feet wide, and shoved the rotting corpses into them, eventually covering them over. The job didn't have to be perfect; he wouldn't be staying here long.

He just had to figure things out first. Now it was time to restock on food, fuel and supplies.

*****

CHAPTER THIRTEEN

Rock Springs, Texas
2020

Angus had raped Maria and Sofia in 2011 just to see what kind of babies would be born to them.

He had captured several men and women from the city with the promise of salvation on his sprawling ranch. By the time he got them back there, they were drugged by his bottled water and easy to get into their holding cells. The men were for nothing but feeding to the females with the red eyes.

Angus learned very quickly that if he wanted more trustees, he would have to keep them away from the ones with the red eyes. They would spray them with the strange vapor that pumped from their eyes, and they would fall under their telepathic commands.

It sounded crazy as hell, even to Angus. Soon he had begun experimenting.

After determining that Maria and Sofia were pregnant again, he immediately exposed them to the vapor from one of the females with straight hair. There was no hesitation on their part. When the women were led to their cells, the straight-haired, red-eyed things sprayed them.

Angus wasn't even sure if it was necessary to expose them to the vapor again after they had been sprayed previously, but it didn't cost him anything, so he led them there.

It was about midday when he went to the cell containing his girls. These were the first babies born into his new, growing family. The daughters of Maria and Sofia.

He had also impregnated the only normal girl who had come out of the ill-fated trailer load, whose name was Lupe. He had never exposed her to the vapor, and he gave her nearly everything she asked for. Angus needed to learn as much as he could about what made the special children with the red eyes, but he needed help that he could trust.

In Angus' experience, two things created obedience; fear and kindness. Kindness led to a greed for more; he had seen it in the tricks that had come by on a regular basis to screw his mother and sister. The kinder they treated the men, the more their customers demanded.

He beat Lupe often, but never to the point she would be seriously wounded; he had become an expert at administering pain without permanently maiming. Lupe was his trustee, and she was important to him.

The children, whom he called Alpha and Omega – the first and last – were nine years old, but appeared to be eighteen or nineteen. What was even odder was the fact that the women had their babies in four months rather than nine.

The vapor was amazing, creating accelerated growth and abilities. His problem with the advancing hordes was gone, for his new creations controlled the Mothers and they controlled the Hungerers. His problem controlling the silken-haired creatures was no more.

The girls had done it, almost as though it was second nature.

"Alpha and Omega," he said, one afternoon. "Come with me."

He watched as they pulled open the cell door, waved to Lupe, and left, easing it closed behind them.

Maria and Sofia eyed Angus as their daughters fell in behind him without hesitation. He stared back at them refusing to offer even a slight smile of reassurance.

"Yes, Maestro?" they said in unison.

"In the house. We need to talk."

The girls followed him inside.

"Sit on the couch there," he said.

They did. "I am hungry," said Alpha. She looked very much like her mother, Maria. She was on the taller side, and her facial features were long and her jaw femininely rounded.

"I intend to fuck both of you today," he said. "I have to further my experimentation and you're both crucial."

They nodded, clearly unaffected by his announcement. "May we eat?" Their English was perfect.

"Of course," he said. "Are you keeping them away?"

"As you wish," they said. "We are not calling them."

"But you will when I tell you to," said Angus.

"Yes," said Omega. "Now please, the food."

Angus sighed and got up. He had begun making his own beef jerky, because the dried meat kept longer, and the electricity had gone out long ago, making refrigeration possible, but challenging.

He had a diesel generator and mostly diesel vehicles, and he was glad his ranch featured an underground diesel tank for fueling his equipment. While he had kept a huge supply on hand to keep his transport tanker fueled up, he no longer needed the fuel for that, because his runs into Mexico were long over.

He had read in a book that old diesel could be polished – which was essentially running it through a filtering system – and used for many years. His pumping system had in-line filters that he changed often. So far, the fuel was still viable.

He returned with two handfuls of beef jerky and two bottles of water from his well. The girls took it and began eating immediately.

"You are loyal to me, right?" he asked.

Alpha looked at him. "You know we are."

The other words entered his head as Omega stared at him. *We love you, Maestro.*

"Don't do that," he said, staring at her. "Speak aloud if you want to talk to me. You know I don't like you in my head."

"I am sorry," she said. "Do you intend to impregnate us?" she asked.

"How the hell do you even know that word?" he asked.

Both looked down, not meeting his eyes.

"Anyway, yeah. I need more of you, and second generation ought to be better. You two are going to be the start of my army. You've got good control over them now, right?"

"The Mothers?" asked Alpha.

"Yeah, the Mothers," he said. "The pregnant ones with the red eyes."

"There are thirty six of them now," said Omega.

"Will you protect me?" he asked.

"With our lives, Maestro," said both of them together, again, as though one.

"Good," said Angus. He liked when they used the Spanish word for Master. He was their master; their Maestro.

"Remove your clothes," he said.

They stood and began to undress; he was not a pedophile, but these girls did not appear to be nine years old; they appeared to be twice that, and they spoke as though they were even older than eighteen.

Their condition was amazing. They were like a shield. They could not only hold off the ones they called the Mothers; they could hold off the regular hordes of walking dead, too, by ordering the Mothers to do so. They were his commanders. He was *El General.*

Both Alpha and Omega stood before him now, their clothing draped neatly over the back of the couch. He made the girls wear dresses; never pants or jeans. He liked the look of a female body, though he did not respect them.

Women were and always had been expendable, but these two were not. They would be the cornerstones of his militia. From a caged boy to the leader of a great, walking dead army.

He grew erect at the thought.

It was to be the first time he had sex with them, and it was solely to create children with one or both of these unique creatures. Offspring of whom he would be the father, and that he hoped would be gifted, not only with their amazing powers, but with more.

*****

SIX MONTHS LATER

Angus had watched the girls' stomachs grow, almost by the day. Their mothers had been furious when they

271

learned he had slept with their daughters, but there was nothing they could do about it. It was their daughters who had the powers, after all.

The gestation period for Alpha and Omega was now only three months. Twice as fast as their mothers.

Both children were female. He named them Maga 1 and Maga 2. Their development excited Angus. While Alpha and Omega had developed at approximately twice the speed of a normal human female, these two offspring grew at four times the rate.

By the time they were eight weeks old, they appeared to be six months. Angus insisted that Alpha and Omega begin training the infants immediately; he did not need them drawing every Mother and Hungerer to him as their mothers had done as babies.

But they would do it pregnant. The moment he realized the accelerated gestation period, he impregnated both of them as soon as they had healed from childbirth; something they also did more quickly than normal humans.

Alpha and Omega had called the creatures out beyond the fence Mothers and Hungerers from the time they were fourteen months old, so Angus had done the same. He had never known what they were or what to call them. Alpha and Omega seemed to have insight there.

His concerns were unfounded as well. Like their mothers, Maga 3 and 4 were able to switch off the beacon almost from the day they were born. Magas 5 through 16 all held the same powers, stronger than either of their mothers.

Angus was not finished. He impregnated Alpha and Omega over and over. They were well-trained, willing participants, and Angus was building an army, the likes of which the world had never before seen.

*****

Maga 12 had an attitude. She refused to eat to maintain her strength. Maestro constantly overheard her attempting to convince the others to let go their control of the Mothers, and in turn, the Hungerers.

Angus had enough. With two of his men at his side, he entered the barn and went directly to the cage containing Maga 12.

"Take her out."

"Who?" said Maga 12.

"You," said Maestro. "You'll accompany me to the tree."

"No, Maestro," she pleaded.

"It's too late to make requests," he said. "You know my rules."

She said no more. His men handcuffed her and Maestro dragged her out, staggering backwards, as he pulled her behind him by the chain linking the cuffs.

As they walked into the sunlight, Maestro saw she was distracted, her face turned to the sky. It was a mild day, somewhere in the high-70s, and wonderment touched her features, even as Maestro and his men dragged her to his special place.

From his killing tree hung several rusty items of torture. A fireplace poker. An old Knights of Columbus ceremonial sword that he had sharpened to a deadly edge. Now, exposed to the elements, the sword's edge was jagged and reddish-brown. Various knives and even an old Hawaiian sling spear hung there, too.

"Arrange her," he said.

His men did. They uncuffed her left wrist and drew her arms high over her head on either side of the overhead, horizontal branch. She was cuffed again, and now hung from the tree, her toes just touching the ground.

"You instigate, Maga 12."

"We are miserable," she said. "We exert all of our energy in keeping the Mothers and Hungerers calm."

"That is why you were born," said Angus.

"This place has pleasures to offer that we are not allowed to partake in," she said. "I just experienced it; the warmth and a light touch upon my skin that feels cool at the same time. I feel it now, even as I am restrained."

"These things you speak of are called the sun and the wind," said Angus. "There were many years I was caged, deprived of them. I was kept in that cage by a woman like you. Now that I am your Maestro, it is my decision that these things are only for you to enjoy in the brief moments before your death."

Maga 12 stared at him. "I will comply, Maestro."

"It's too late, Maga 12." He walked toward her and lifted the sword from its hanger. He grabbed her chin and drew the blade back.

"Maestro," she whimpered.

"Shut up," he said, fixing the point of the sword beside her mouth. He pushed it firmly until he felt it poke through her skin.

Her shriek caused gooseflesh to rise all over his body, like tiny nerve endings longing for stimulation. Blood trickled around the rusty blade as he forced it in six inches, eliciting from her another shrill howl. Ignoring it, he pressed harder and angled the blade up toward her right ear, eyeing the bump just under her skin as it separated the flesh from the meat beneath.

She clenched her teeth, tears rolling down her face as her facial muscles tensed, increasing her pain.

The blade poked out just above her ear.

At the creation of the exit wound, a flood of hot tears squirted from her red eyes and echoing though Maestro's head he heard a cry, *I love you Maestro! Please do not harm me!*

"You defy me again!" he shouted. "All your life I have told you to remain outside of my mind!"

Maga 12 sobbed. Angus jerked the rusted blade from her face and backed up five strides. He rushed toward her and stabbed her in the heart with the blade, feeling every inch as it slid through her rapidly pumping organ.

As he did so, a sound came from the distance; it was high and piercing and Angus was sure it could be heard far beyond where he stood, beside his killing tree.

He had never heard the sound before.

Maga 12 slumped forward, hanging from the branch. He walked toward her, the blade still embedded in her chest. He grabbed her hair and pulled her head back.

The red in her eyes lingered for a moment and disappeared. She was dead.

Angus turned and ran back into the field, toward the barn. His men were running toward him.

"Maestro!" one of them said. "Did you hear that? They scared the shit out of us!"

"What caused it?" asked Angus.

The men looked confused. "It was out of the blue. They were all quiet, then they all jolted all of a sudden. They settled again, then all of a sudden they all just squealed like stuck pigs!"

Stuck pigs, thought Angus.

Then he knew. They were connected. When one died, the others experienced it in some way. Their first jolt had clearly come when he had pushed the sword through Maga 12's cheek. The last shriek came at her death.

The harm and death of one of their kind physically and emotionally tortured them.

Angus honed his control over the Magas with his new knowledge. He solidified his power over them, eliminating any fear that they would ever defy him again.

Rock Springs, Texas
2026

It was almost time to take his building troops on the road. He now had the cages of his barn filled to capacity. Of these women, forty-six were second-generation versions of Alpha and Omega. He had not attempted to impregnate any of their offspring yet; they were powerful and he imagined that the gestation time would be cut in half again.

Maria and Sofia were the matriarchs, but they could not be trusted. Anytime they were given even the smallest degree of trust, the red-eyed Mothers would tell them to do things that endangered his plans, and it was as if they were unable to resist their commands. They had, at different times, attempted to release the uninfected captives. Twice they had attempted to kill Alpha and Omega, their own children.

The second-generation offspring now had a stronghold on the Mothers and Hungerers. Aside from the commands the Mothers would issue to Maria and Sofia, all were contained and Maestro was able to conduct his business without fear of surprises.

How Angus longed to show off his power. He would go north and along the way, would pick up more and more recruits to his army.

He now had ten men at his disposal who assisted him in his management of the hordes, both of the dead and living variety.

One of the men who called himself Monk was a tattoo artist. That intrigued Angus. He had been envisioning an image in his mind, and asked Monk if he could recreate it.

Monk had been more than willing; Angus went with him to raid a local tattoo shop, gathering the proper tools needed for the job. The completion of the tattoo took twelve sessions, but when it was complete, Angus felt changed; he felt complete.

He was *Maestro*. He would conduct his army of living dead and their commanders as a conductor led a symphony.

When the tattoo was complete and healed, Angus often wore no shirt; he wanted to etch his role as master into the minds of his followers.

On the day of their departure, he had his men – for there were no women other than the powerful ones – pack up all of his supplies. Not that he would need much; he intended to take what he needed from the people he encountered.

A voice came on his radio. "Maestro," it said. "I have the circus cars." It was Brian, one of his men.

"Are you kidding me?" asked Angus.

"I know better than that," Brian said. "We have six interlinking cage trailers, about fifteen feet long."

"Tell me they're yellow and red striped," said Angus. "Please."

"Some are, Maestro. Others are really decorated with gold paint and other pictures and stuff. All in excellent condition, and they were on jack stands with the tires covered when we found 'em, so when we pumped 'em up, they held air fine. In great shape."

Angus raised his hands in the air and looked down at the inked tuxedo on his chest and stomach. He wished he had a mirror. His own face aroused him. He smiled.

The Circus World Museum had been in town when the transformation of humanity took place. With them, they brought several of the old cage cars that would be pulled one after the other through town, being drawn at that time by horses, but since modified so that the Museum could drive all over the United States for their shows.

As soon as Angus made the decision to create an army of the zombie-like things, he had set his sights on those cars. They would be perfect for transporting his animals. All of his female animals, both wild and obedient.

Angus walked out and pressed the remote control, watching the gate swing outward. Brian sat behind the wheel with Curtis beside him, another of his uninfected trustees. As he pulled the several cars in, linked one after the other and rolling behind the dual-cab, Dodge diesel pickup truck, a rotter staggered toward the closing gate.

Angus quickly hit the button again, allowing him inside. Now, if straggling shamblers showed up, he would let them in. One of the many, highly sensitive Magas he had created would immediately instruct a Mother to control it as their Maestro wished, and the Hungerer would go where directed.

On the day of their departure, he had everyone put into the six rolling cages. There were no tarps on them, so his army was on display to the world that would experience them firsthand.

*****

Angus, the son of Nancy and the brother of Jane, set forth on a new path that day in 2026.

Before they departed, he had his men place a two-foot tall wooden box upside-down in the middle of his modern-day wagon train.

"Today we explore new places," he said. "We continue to grow our numbers with every town we pass; you will call to them, Magas, and they will come to us. When we are too many, we will slow to a walk to allow our army of the walking dead to stay with us, and we will ensure that you and they are fed and strong. Do you understand?"

"Yes, Maestro," they all said together.

Not all of them. His eyes had fallen on the faces of Maria and Sofia, locked in the second car and staring at him as though their hard looks could change him in some way.

They had not acknowledged him with a *Yes, Maestro*.

As Angus dismounted the box and walked toward them, he said, "Do you not wish to go?

"Of course not," spat Sofia. "You are a thug, a murderer. You are no better than the cartels."

Angus removed a small, .380 Auto Smith & Wesson from his pants, held the gun out and fired into Sofia's head. The blood spray fanned out behind her, and several of his Magas, took the spatter.

He fired once more, the hole from that round located dead center in the skull of Maria.

The shriek that filled his mind the moment the two women drew their last breaths was intense.

He clapped both his palms over his ears and begged silently for them to stop.

Eventually, they did. When they moved up to the bars to face him, their expressions filled with anguish and hatred he realized he had made a mistake; he had killed their mothers and they were now powerful *and* angry.

"Magas, you must all understand that they had become untrustworthy from the moment they were exposed to the

279

Mothers' vapor prior to your birth. Unlike you, they could not be trusted, nor could they again, ever."

"We were exposed, too!" shouted Alpha. "We have never done anything dangerous!"

"You've never followed the commands of the Mothers," said Angus. "Maria and Sofia did this. It is why they never became trustees."

Omega only stared at him.

Alpha shook her head and walked away.

Angus – Maestro – climbed up into the seat of the Freightliner and started the engine. He used his remote to open the gate, and set out on the road.

As he made his way north, it was Angus' intention to instruct all of his Magas, to call out, draw in, and control as many of the living dead creatures as possible. They would join his numbers until they had no more capacity to transport them, at which point they would slow to a march. He would capture men women and children for food and slaves as he amassed his army of the walking dead.

From his cage where men urinated on him for ten dollars, to the leader of the most powerful, indestructible army the globe had ever known.

Maestro would conquer all whom he encountered.

Similar to P.T. Barnum, Angus Almaraz was about to introduce the scariest show on earth to the masses.

*****

280

CHAPTER FOURTEEN

Charlie crouched in the field beside the breached fence, currently under repair by several men.

Crawling slowly, so as not to cause the tall grass above her to sway and reveal her presence, she searched.

Hemp had been behind her; when he had stood, revealing himself, she felt it was a mistake. She could not say anything, though. He would have revealed her and convinced her to surrender with them.

She didn't know where Max and Isis had gone, but as long as they were not caught, she knew she had a chance. She still had her radio, and it was almost time to call them.

She came upon a pack, and sighed with relief. It was Hemp's. It contained more WAT-5 than all the rest, but the more she could accumulate, the better she would feel. The pink eye drops were there, too, which could come in handy.

When she had peered through the grass to where everyone had been standing before Maestro in the street, she noticed that all of her friends had dropped their backpacks before surrendering. Perhaps it was that they hoped they would be able to escape and recover the supplies from the field later.

281

It would be a disaster for this Maestro to discover their most crucial defensive tools; while they had invited the world to learn of urushiol and WAT-5, this killer was clearly not a man who would use either for the good of humankind.

She came upon Gem's pack and smiled to herself again. Flex's was just beside it, and she found Dave and Punch's packs just a few feet away. Ten minutes later, she discovered the packs belonging to Trina and Taylor, just five or so feet east of Flex's pack. Both were beige, so had blended in with the color of the dead grass.

She did not find Nel's pack, but he wasn't wearing it when taken prisoner by Maestro's men, so she assumed he may have hidden it before making his rescue attempt.

Other than Nelson's, she had all of the packs. It was a relief.

Illuminating only the red light on her headlamp, she counted fifty-eight doses of WAT-5 in her softly-lit hands. That was 290 hours of protection for one person. Isis and Max carried only a couple of doses each, though they did not often use it.

She found 10 doses of the alternate wafers created from the Mothers' vapor, that Hemp had named REV-N. This stood for Red-Eye Vapor Neutralizer; these were only good for preventing young women of child-bearing years from falling under the control of the Mothers after being exposed to their vapor.

From experience, they knew it worked if taken quickly after the exposure – as it had on Lola – but only limited testing had been done. After the settling of Kingman, exposures such as that had simply not occurred with enough frequency to establish its effectiveness in cases of long-prior dousing.

Charlie piled the packs and stood to look at the fence. The men worked quickly. As all of the Mothers and Hungerers within the cage stood crowded in the west side of the enclosure, the men had brought in welders and generators and had repaired all but the last ten feet of fencing. They had raised and secured the north fence that Nelson had plowed over, too.

She would wait. Once they were gone, she could safely pull the many backpacks to a secure location and store them for later retrieval. She had brought her small crossbow with her, so she had the ability to kill with stealth. From Dave's pack, she took the Walther PPK with its silencer. She felt ready to mount whatever offensive she could. She would not live in a world without her husband, son and her family of friends.

Never. She would save them or die trying.

Charlie waited.

*****

Isis and Max found a nearby street with a number of small shops. Max, using the lock-picking ability taught him by his father, quickly defeated the locks of each store they wished to inspect.

Despite the several stores they entered and rummaged through, including a stationery store and a post-office annex, she could not find what she sought.

"Let's go back to the stationery store," she finally said. "We're wasting time."

As they walked, staying in the shadows, Max said, "You sure it'll have any effect?"

"It affected me when I read it for the first time," said Isis. "How did you feel?"

Max shrugged. "It was a ballsy move, I have to give it to 'em," he said. "I'd like to think it could inspire them. I felt proud, even though I didn't get to enjoy the world that resulted very much."

"They will understand it at its core," said Isis. "But since we can't find one, I'll have to write it from memory."

When they reached the stationery store and pried open the door again, they went inside. Isis took a clean piece of parchment stationery paper and found a cartridge pen set. She inserted an ink cartridge and placed the angled, ball-point against the top of the paper. Her printing was in neat block letters and was quite legible.

From memory, Isis recalled each word, understanding all too clearly their meaning. She wrote in straight, evenly spaced lines until the words filled the page.

When completed, she folded it and tucked it into her pocket. She turned to Max. "These words inspired thousands initially, and millions since then. It should have no less effect on these captives. No matter the year, the face of tyranny remains the same."

"I never would've thought of it," said Max. "Sure hope you're right."

The radio clicked. "Shh," said Isis.

"That's it?" asked Max.

"Two clicks," said Isis.

"It's my mom!" said Max, a smile spreading across his face. He grabbed the radio and pressed the button.

"Mom!" he said. "It's Max! Where are you?"

Her voice came back steady, but low, the relief in her tone clear. "Oh, my God, you guys, I'm so happy you're safe. You *are* okay, Max, right?"

"I am, Mom," he said. "Are you alright? We were across the street when Maestro took everyone."

"I'm inside a yellow house just off 9th Street," she said. "There's a detached garage and I hid everyone's pack in there. Where are you guys? Do you know where they took everyone?"

"We saw," said Isis. "We've found more Hybrids. We're trying to convince them to help us."

"Any luck?" asked Charlie.

"We're working on it," said Isis. "Many of their powers likely exceed mine," she added.

"Isis thinks making them aware of what they don't have in their present situation might sway their allegiance."

"Do you want me to come to you, or vice versa?" asked Charlie. "I have a bunch of WAT-5 and some of the other wafers, too. Lots of urushiol."

"Do you have the eye drops?" asked Isis. "Clearly for you, not us."

"I do," she said. "The pink ones. We've seen that posing as a Mother is a bad idea."

"Exactly," said Isis. "Maestro has taken them to an Applebee's Restaurant on 6th Street."

"Applebee's? Why?"

"Lots of seating, who knows?" said Max. "Mom, there's an aluminum siding shop almost directly south of the Applebee's, but two streets down. It's a beat up little building."

"Is it unlocked?" asked Charlie.

"I don't know, but there are a bunch of loose pieces of sheathing on the east side, away from the street," said Max. "Just pull one out and slip behind it. Isis and I will meet you there. Go now."

"If I can make it across 8th Street without getting caught, I'll be in the clear," said Charlie. "See you in maybe half an hour. I'll click you twice if I get into trouble."

*****

Maestro paced back and forth, occasionally eyeing Gem with contempt he did not seem to have for anyone else.

Gem didn't care; if he focused on her, he might leave Trina and Taylor alone.

Speaking of the girls, they both openly glared at him.

"So tell me why you came to my fine town of Hoisington," he said, a smile on his face.

"Just fucking passing through," said Gem. "It's time to show a little hospitality and let us go."

"Gem," said Flex, shaking his head. "She's upset," he said to Maestro. "We're not used to being held captive."

"And you would not be now had you not come here and tried to destroy my containment fencing. Now you will join us as either food or trustees or ... well, these two might work for my other purposes. The angry one is too old."

"Not too old to kick your fuckin' ass," said Gem.

Maestro laughed with a hiss, like the dry sound of leaves blowing across a sidewalk.

"I think it's time to let you know how serious this is," he said. "Brian, bring in one of the Hungerers."

Gem shot a look at Flex, who shrugged, shaking his head. "Gem, you just need to cooperate," he said.

"Ah, advice you might have offered five minutes ago," said the strange man. "Yes, yes, here they are."

Into the room, Brian, one of his men, led a ravaged rotter in on a rigid, six-foot stick with a thick, leather neck strap. This was a man, the shriveled skin of his arms black and pulled, and in his teeth, dark, stringy things dangled, looking like exactly what they most likely were; tendons and sinew from its previous meal.

286

"Stand up and move over there," said Maestro, pointing to the row of barstools.

"Fuck you," said Gem.

"Now!" shouted Maestro, pulling out his gun. This appeared to be a .44 Magnum, reminiscent of the gun used by Dirty Harry in the popular film.

He held the barrel pressed against Gem's forehead and Flex leapt to his feet and fought his restraints.

"No!" he said, desperation in his voice. "Gem, you just get your ass up and go over there. They won't hurt you and you know it."

Gem nodded quickly and Maestro pulled the weapon away.

"They won't hurt her?" asked Maestro.

Nobody answered him.

"It's what they do by the very nature of their hunger," he said. "They will of course, kill her."

Gem wasn't going to say anything. Her mind worked over what excuses she might invent. She walked over and begrudgingly sat on the barstool.

Immediately, another man came over and snapped handcuffs on her right wrist, fed the cuff chain beneath the stool, and pulled her left wrist down to secure her there. Her arms were pulled down so tightly she could not straighten her back. In seconds it was painful.

"Okay," Brian. "Lead him to her, but I would suggest you get back immediately after you do."

Gem watched Maestro as his lackey led the zombie over. All the while, the creature was snapping at Brian, trying to defeat the restraint.

Now the zombie stood right beside Gem. It kept staring at Brian.

Brian looked at Maestro for a moment, before pushing the zombie directly up against Gem's body.

Gem forced a smile and choked back her disgust, nuzzling the rotter with her cheek, saying, "Sweetheart, you look just worn out. If you're going to get some coffee, I could really use some, too."

"What the hell is going on here!" shouted Maestro, overturning an adjacent table that nearly hit one of his men. As the gunman dodged the tumbling furniture, Maestro charged up to where the rotter stood. It immediately tried to stagger toward him, and he held up the .44 and fired into the side of its skull, the black, tar-like goo splattering Gem's face, chest and shoulders.

"For fuck's sake!" shouted Gem. "Do you mind?" She spat the bitter-tasting crap from her lips and tried to wipe her mouth on her shoulder.

"Why don't they want you?" he asked. "Tell me or I'll kill you right now!"

"It's garlic," said Hemp. "Just plain garlic. We all take regular doses of garlic tablets. We've been clearing the shelves of them wherever we go, and we tell everyone to grow their own garlic. It protects us."

"Dude, we even broadcast about it like every couple of nights," said Nelson. "Just to let everyone know how to stay safe."

"I don't listen to radios," said Maestro. "I prefer the excitement of discovery and self-preservation."

"Well, should you ever wish to relax, then garlic, once built up in your system, will do the trick," said Hemp.

His tone was so sincere, Gem almost believed it herself.

The despot who called himself Maestro did not. Not yet.

"Garlic," said Maestro. "Bullshit. Show me some."

"We lost it while running from your men and fighting the ones in your cage," said Gem. "But I'm certain you have some in your stores."

Maestro looked at Brian. "Bring in another. I'm testing the rest of them."

*****

Charlie shot quick glances to the east and west before running across 8th Street. She had brought her backpack with her, leaving everyone else's safely hidden away for the moment. She brought along her small crossbow, identical to Max's, and two more Glocks, along with the noise-suppressed Walther.

While she was hesitant to do so, she carried all of their WAT-5 and two canisters of urushiol. She had stuffed her pack and pockets with as much ammo as she could carry, too.

She slid between two buildings, came upon an alley and watched.

A noise came from somewhere behind her. She ducked into the overgrown weeds, surprised by sharp burrs that clung to her ragged clothes and poked through the canvas tennis shoes she had chosen as part of her bloodied disguise. Sucking her breath between her teeth, she waited.

Moments later, two men wearing military fatigues appeared, having walked in her exact path.

"Where'd she go?" asked one of them. It was tough to see much in the dark, but the one that had spoken appeared to have a Swastika tattooed on his forearm.

"She has to be around here somewhere," said the other one. He was clearly younger than the inked man. "Boss thought there might be more of 'em."

"Where the fuck did she go?" asked Swastika.

Charlie wondered for a moment if they knew exactly where she was and this little conversation was just for show.

"She looked kinda hot," said the younger one. "Might get me a piece of it before we take her in."

Charlie could take no more. She jumped up and said, "Hey."

As they turned, she fired the small crossbow, putting the bolt right between Swastika boy's eyes.

As the other man fumbled to swing his rifle toward her, Charlie dropped her pack and the crossbow, and rushed him. Ducking behind him, she kicked the back of his leg, administered a quick, firm chop to the side of his neck as he tilted backward, and took out his other leg with a quick kick.

He was on his back looking up when she dropped down on top of him, her Walther in her hand and pressed hard against his forehead.

"That was all the piece you'll get from this girl," she said. "Yeah, I know. Thank Nel for that. He taught me. It's Subdudo."

"Sub what?" the man said.

"Tell me what goes on here and why," said Charlie.

"Patrols, for one," said the man. "You ain't got long before someone finds Billy dead there and shoots you in the head."

"In the meantime, let's chat." Charlie glanced up and down the street, pressing the barrel harder to his head while she did so. "By the way, I have nerve problems, particularly in my right index finger, which you might know as my trigger finger. Kinda twitches."

"Maestro tells us what to do and we do it," he said.

"What's your name?" asked Charlie.

"Tanner."

"Tanner, I'm Charlie. What does this Maestro tell you to do?"

"You know, like find you. Fix the fence. We do pretty much what he tells us."

"Pretty much?"

"I don't know. If you let me go I won't say anything."

"What'll you do?"

"What do you mean?"

"*If I let you go*," said Charlie, feigned frustration in her voice.

"I'll ... just be quiet."

"Will you leave town right away and never come back?"

"Sure, I guess so. If that's what you want."

"Didn't you say you were going to get a piece of me?"

"I was just kiddin', man," he said, his voice quivering.

"Have you ever gotten a piece of any of the girls he keeps captive?"

"Only when I had permission," the man said.

"Who's permission?"

"Maestro's permission." Now it was his turn to be frustrated. "He's in charge, like I said. Who else's permission would I need?"

Charlie pulled the trigger. The *thwump!* of the silenced shot contradicted the massive blood spray that fanned out behind his head.

She leaned down close to the dead man and whispered her additional explanation. "You'd need the girl's permission, Tanner. It's called consent."

She stared down at the dead man's face too long, realizing just how few living people she had ever killed. Of course, with her friends captive and these idiots working for the man that held them, she did not have a choice; she could not have locked them away someplace – there was no time

291

for that. Simply wounding them would have only given them a chance to get to this Maestro fellow and tell him about her existence.

She shook off the miniscule amount of guilt she felt for her actions and again checked both ways down the street. Charlie stood, tucking the gun away for the moment. She bent over and picked up her crossbow and pack, situating them on her back.

She took Tanner's feet and dragged his dead weight, inch by inch, into the grass where she had been hiding moments before. She did the same with Billy's body. Once there, Charlie caught her breath, keeping an eye out for more patrols.

After her heart rate settled, she checked their pockets and only found extra rounds of ammo. It was 9mm, so she took it.

With a quick glance in each direction, she ran across the street. As she ducked down another alley, she saw the dark sign of Applebee's two blocks to her west.

She ran on through the night until she spotted the metal siding shop.

*****

"Mom!" said Max, when Charlie came into the room. "Wow, it's good to see you!" He ran to her and she dropped her stuff to hug her son.

Isis watched, a smile on her face. She wondered what it was like to have a mother. Her mother had died in childbirth, and while her dad had been a loving and dedicated father, there was something she noticed in mothers that made her long for them.

Even the Mothers, with their natural, killing instincts, were drawn to her because of a preternatural, maternal pull of some kind.

Charlie finally broke free of Max and walked over to Isis, holding open her arms. Isis stepped into her embrace, and Charlie kissed her cheek. "I'm so glad you're okay, Isis. I was worried about you two."

"Thank you, Charlie," said Isis. "We've been listening. One gunshot came from the restaurant."

Charlie's eyes drew together and her brow furrowed over them. "Did you see them go in?" she asked.

"We did, but from a distance. When we noticed, we just saw Dave bringing up the rear. We know they're in there, but we don't know how many of this Maestro's men are with them."

"Or if they're gonna stay in there," added Max. "I mean, what kind of home base is that?"

"Not a very good one," agreed Charlie. "Look. I ran into a couple of Maestro's lackeys on the way over here. It's what held me up. One was a fucking skinhead and the other was a rapist. I'm not thinking this Maestro's much better."

"What did you do with them?" asked Isis.

Charlie just tilted her head and stared.

"Okay," said Isis. "I ask because it might not be long before Maestro realizes something happened to them. Once he's sure there are more of us, he may change his strategy, whatever it may be."

"Good point," said Charlie. "I checked their pockets and neither had radios. I wonder how they communicate here."

"Perhaps with runners," said Isis. "Their operations seem to be in fairly close proximity to one another."

Charlie looked at Max and smiled. "Well, now we can figure out what to do. Did you guys have a plan?"

Isis slipped the hand-written page from her pocket. "Just this," she said.

Charlie took it and opened it. She looked up at Isis, her face scrunched. "You think this Maestro guy will get sentimental about *this*?"

Isis shook her head. "Not Maestro," she said. "The Hybrids."

Charlie looked confused. "The ones at the football field? Where are they now?"

"Not all of them were there," said Max. "He either rotates which ones he uses or some have more skills for certain tasks. We're not sure about that yet. Anyway, we found some others in a fenced basketball court at the police station. Just outside the jail, probably for inmates."

"Did you talk to them?" asked Charlie.

"Yes," said Isis. They were originally Alpha, Omega and Maga 7. I told them Alpha was now Alyssa, Omega was now Megan, and Maga 7 was to be named Beauty, which she is. All of the others are called Maga, followed by a number."

"Maga?" said Charlie. "Isn't that the feminine form of magician in Spanish?"

"Good, mom!" said Max. "I didn't know you knew Spanish."

"Don't be too impressed," said Charlie. "I used to follow a punk band called Mago. I looked it up."

"Now that we're together, we should go to them," said Isis. "I need to give this to them and ask for their help. We're going to need it."

"We've dealt with lots of assholes since this crap began," said Charlie. "Why can't we just bust in there and kill this Maestro guy and get the hell home?"

"Because when he moves, he has Hybrids with him," said Isis. "Not only that, now that we're here I know the Magas are deserving of rescue."

"Not if they're fighting for the other side, Isis," said Charlie.

"She has a point, C," said Max.

"I do have a point, Isis, but that said, do you feel you've made a connection with them?"

Isis shrugged. "The beginning of one, maybe," said Isis. "Charlie, Beauty told me something. It wasn't necessarily a good thing to hear, but it's very good that she made me aware of it."

Max looked at Isis, confusion on his face. "Isis? You didn't tell me anything."

"That's because it sucks," she said. "Max, you had enough to worry about with your mom missing and your dad in that man's hands."

"Tell us," said Charlie.

Max stared at Isis.

"Charlie, you know how powerful Max and I are. You know most of the things we can do."

"Most?" asked Charlie.

Isis nodded. "We are capable of more telekinetic abilities than we let on, particularly when one of us is in danger."

"Telekinetic," said Charlie. "Like moving stuff?"

"Both inanimate and animate," said Max. "Then there's the pyrokinesis."

"Like fucking Firestarter?" asked Charlie. "Are you serious? Max, you too?"

Max shook his head. "Nah, just Isis. So far I haven't found one thing I can do that she can't, but it sure doesn't work the other way around."

"Max," said Isis. "There's a chance your abilities will just take longer to develop."

"I guess," he said.

"Now Isis, tell us what you learned," said Charlie.

"Beauty told me that their loyalty lies partially in the fact that Maestro is the father of all of the Magas. They're all half-sisters."

"Wow," said Charlie. "When did he start this? Are these girls adolescents?"

"In years, perhaps," said Isis. "In every other way, they are powerful young women. Quite possibly more powerful than Max and me."

Charlie shook her head. "Isis, no. That can't be right. If you're the same, how can they be more powerful?"

Isis sighed. She did not do it very often because she felt it was rude. "I'm sorry," she said. "What I'm trying to say is the reason lies with their mothers."

"And who were their mothers?" asked Max.

"Alyssa and Megan are like me and Max. Their mothers were accidentally exposed to the Mothers' vapor while pregnant with them. Maestro started having sex with Alyssa and Megan when they were around nine years old to create his Magas. Once they had the babies, he would impregnate them again. He did this over and over, exposing them to the Mothers' vapor each time in an effort to further enhance their abilities."

"So the Magas are all second generation Hybrids," said Charlie. "Does that make a difference?"

Isis nodded. "I feel a great power coming from them," she said. "We only discovered some of our abilities when we desperately needed them, so I'm concerned that we may learn of some of their powers when it's already too late to counter them."

"Jesus, Isis," said Max. "Now I know why you want them to work with us so much. At least we have one of them on our side, right?"

"I thought it would be clear," she said. "And yes, Beauty seems to be one of the most eager. She is the youngest, though. Whether mutated or not, the young have a taste for adventure and change."

"We definitely need them on our side," said Charlie. "And that means as quickly as possible."

Charlie returned the paper to Isis, who tucked it away and grabbed her backpack from the floor.

"Let's go then," Isis said. "Before we head that way, we'll see if we can get close enough to the restaurant to see in and confirm everyone is okay."

Charlie was already at the door. They slipped out through the loose piece of siding where Charlie had entered the building.

Isis stayed in the rear, her senses tuned to her highest capability.

*****

CHAPTER FIFTEEN

Isis used her powerful vision to analyze each street, every dark corner. Nobody was about in the town of Hoisington, Kansas.

They approached the rear of the restaurant. The night had grown darker from cloud cover, and no shadows fell beside the three.

The kitchen was in the rear, and Max approached the access door and pulled on the handle. It did not open, so he ran back to the dumpster where his mother and Isis waited.

"There's nobody outside," said Max. "The door's locked, but I have my lock pick set."

"Can you do it quietly?" asked Charlie.

"No, mom. I learned from an idiot."

Charlie smiled. She had taught her son that she found sarcasm funny, so he had used it with her since he was old enough to formulate witty comebacks.

"Okay, smart ass. Go ahead and open it, but know that I'm telling your dad what you said."

"Be very careful, Max," said Isis. "When you get it unlocked, wait for us before you go in.

Max checked his watch. "Mom, how are you on WAT-5?"

Charlie reached into her side pocket and withdrew the baggie. She took out a wafer and popped it in her mouth.

She passed out.

"Guess she was expired," said Max. "We should just let her sleep. She can get kinda crazy."

"Not a bad idea," said Isis, "but she will be angry with you, Max."

"I know, and my dad's in there," said Max. "If she can lay her eyes on him, it'll help her fighting spirit."

Isis nodded. Max was right. It was Charlie's choice – not theirs – if she accompanied them.

Max gently shook his mother's shoulder, and she came to. Her eyes focused on Max, and she said, "Damn, you look like your dad right now."

Max smiled. "Well, maybe you can see him in a minute. Just don't do anything nuts."

"That kinda depends on what they're doing to him."

"Got it. I'll get the lock," said Max.

Looking in all directions first, Max ran to the building, his lock pick set in his hand. He reached the door, and in less than a minute, he pulled it open and turned toward them with a wave.

"Guns out," said Isis. "Charlie, I recommend the crossbow for you. Do you have the suppressed Walther?"

"I do," she said, giving it to Isis. Max had his small crossbow, so they had a lot of stealth capability they might need.

Max pulled the door the rest of the way open and the three stepped inside. Isis paused there for a moment. While their enhanced vision did not require adjustment to the deeper darkness of the interior, she was aware that Charlie's did.

Max led, motioning toward a single door with a window in it. It would lead to the main restaurant. They approached the door, staying low, and when they reached it, Max rose up until he could just see through the window.

Isis did the same, just behind him. Charlie took the lower left corner of the window.

Muffled voices came from the main restaurant, but Isis could not make out the words. She sensed the presence of Hungerers, but no Mothers, and she did not sense any Hybrids.

"We're blocked by the bar," whispered Charlie. "This door swings both ways. Let's pull it open and we can slip in and get behind the bar counter."

"Charlie," said Isis. "We must get to Alyssa, Megan and Beauty."

"I still haven't heard my dad's voice," said Max. "Isis, we can't go yet. Let's just be careful."

"Have your weapons ready and do not make a sound," she said. "We just have a look to confirm everyone is okay and we go."

"Fine," said Charlie. She moved back up to look through the door again. "All clear," she whispered.

Max nodded and they moved to the side of the door as he pulled it open about fifteen inches. He fed his crossbow through first, sliding through the gap in a low squat, followed by Charlie and Isis.

They entered the bar from the rear. It was a U-shaped bar with the opening to the kitchen wall. Once inside, the voices were louder as they moved to the front of the bar and crouched there.

"So you are all invisible to them," said the man, whom Isis assumed was Maestro. "And you say it's just garlic that protects you."

"I am a scientist," said Hemp. "Because garlic has properties that repel certain pests, I felt it was a worthy experiment. It was not a quick discovery, for I did try several other known plants and drugs, such as antibiotics, to neutralize the attraction they have toward us."

"Garlic?" Max mouthed to Isis, shrugging.

Isis put a finger to her lips.

"Look, Mister," said Flex. "We don't mean you any harm here, and there's nothing sinister about the reason we're here. Since this thing started, we kill rotters. That's it, plain and simple."

"So you came to my town to kill my followers."

"Sir," said Hemp. "They cannot be your followers, because they do not follow anything except their insatiable craving for human flesh."

"Oh, they follow," said Maestro. "They followed me down to Great Bend and they'll follow me to where you're from. And you're gonna tell me where that is."

"Dude, I don't think anybody here is gonna tell you anything," said Nelson. "You've been like confrontational since we met you."

There was quiet for a moment, but if someone was moving, the carpeting masked their footsteps.

A moment later there were sounds of a scuffle, then: "Goddamnit!"

It was Maestro's voice.

"Bro, I didn't want to do that, but you just have this threatening way about you, man," said Nelson.

Max put his hand on Isis' shoulder and lifted up out of his crouch, his head rising just above the bar.

He watched for a moment before dropping back down. "Someone's on the floor beside Nel," he whispered so low that Isis could barely make out the words.

"Nel used Subdudo on Maestro?" asked Charlie.

301

Isis did not like the developments.

"Everyone else is sitting around a big, round table," said Max. "Three guys with guns are on this side, and Maestro guy's on the other side with another guy with a gun.

"You don't have to scoot away from me," said Nelson. "Just stand up. I'm not violent. I only did that because you were threatening me."

"Why aren't I hurt?" asked the man.

"Because I don't hurt breathers," said Nelson. "Let's call it passive martial arts. I created the method and it's called Subdudo. I only kill the abnormals and the Red-Eyes. And you might have my hands zipped together, but all I need is my feet, bro."

"Well, for that little stunt, we'll just let them kill you in front of your friends tomorrow. Then we'll kill your friends. I imagine that whatever makes you undesirable to my army will have worn off by then."

"Dude, I have some weed," said Nelson. "Don't hurt my friends because of what I did. I'll give you all of it. It kills aggression."

"I prefer a clear head."

"If you had a clear head you'd let us go," said Punch. "We're not here to hurt you. You stay away from us and we'll do the same. It'll be like we were never here."

"Ah, but you are here," said Maestro. "That cannot be undone."

"What is your point?" asked Trina. "Why would you fight people like us who survived this horrible thing? We're all that's left. We should work together to restore the world."

"Like most women, you're a fool," said Maestro. "You think you have some idea of what my life was like before all this happened?"

302

"I never said that," said Trina.

"Trina, don't bother," said Gem.

"Because he's human trash," said Taylor. "No better than the army of rotten flesh he controls."

"Normally I would punish you for saying such things," said Maestro, "but I'm tired now. You've wasted hours of my time already and killed a lot of my people."

"It's that awkward moment when the guy with the heartbeat forgets that in order to qualify as people, you also have to have heartbeats," said Dave.

"They are people enough for me," said Maestro. "I've just reached a decision. It's midnight now. Tomorrow at noon, we'll have another feeding. This time, all of you will be their source of nourishment."

"You are making a serious mistake sir," said Hemp. "I can show you what we've learned over the years; things that will make your life easy and render this undead army of yours pointless."

Maestro laughed. "I *am* in control and my life *is* easy," he said. "I control not only my life, but the lives of everyone I encounter. It has not always been this way, but my power grows each day, and my followers are either loyal or they will be dead. I will never regress."

"Dude, you must have had a bogus childhood," said Nelson. "You could probably use a joint – which I have, by the way."

Ignoring him, Maestro said, "Take them to the jail and lock them up for tonight. We'll have a nice, public execution by way of feeding tomorrow."

From behind the bar, they heard chairs moving. Max moved to the northeast corner of the bar and stood up slowly. Isis could see that several empty liquor bottles on the counter blocked his view. He looked for a few moments before dropping back down.

His elbow hit a bottle on the shelf beneath the bar and it tipped and started to plummet to the floor.

Max's eyes went wide, and Isis threw her hand forward, stopping the bottle in mid-fall.

Now it was Charlie's turn to become wide-eyed.

The bottle of Dewar's Gin hung in the air, a foot and a half from the floor, before slowly coming to rest atop the perforated rubber mat. It did not make a sound.

Max put his head back and knocked another liquor bottle into several others.

This time the crash was loud and obvious.

"What the hell was that?" came Maestro's voice. "You four, go now!"

"C'mon!" whispered Charlie, and pushed Max toward the back of the bar. Isis waited for them to pass her and ran behind them, still crouching. They burst through the door to the kitchen. Once Max and Charlie were almost out the rear, exterior door, Isis stopped, her mind focused like a laser.

Before the door swung closed behind her, she eyed the many glasses, bottles and neon beer signs behind the bar, and pushed her intentions with the entire power of her mind.

As the running men drew beside the bar, every glass, bottle and sign flew from their racks, shattered in mid-air and came crashing down on top of the men, taking them down mid-run.

Isis turned and ran toward the door, the huge, commercial refrigerator tilting on its own behind her and slamming onto its side in front of the door.

She burst outside and saw Max and Charlie by the dumpster again. She ran to them.

"What did you do in there?" asked Charlie.

"I pushed as hard as I could," she said. "Max, it worked."

"Wow, Isis," he said. "Wow."

Charlie just stared at her.

"We need to get to the jail now," said Isis. "The Hybrids are there, and we now know our family will be there before long."

Staying low, they headed for the deepest shadows and made their way south, toward the jail.

*****

Charlie watched the women moving around the basketball court, her eyes falling upon the corpse wired to the net and backboard. "Wow," she whispered. "Incentive to behave?"

"Incentive to do what Maestro says," said Max.

"I can only find Beauty among them," said Isis, scanning the many women wearing orange jumpsuits from the Department Of Corrections. "They're all here, but I can't put my eyes on Alyssa and Megan."

"That's not good," said Max. "I don't see them either."

Charlie's mind again turned to her captive husband and friends. Gem had lost her son, and if Charlie knew Gem as well as she thought, that horrible pain of loss would manifest itself in every emotion from sadness to anger to unadulterated rage.

Flex, Gem and the others needed to be freed, but if that was an immediate impossibility, she at least had to find ways to protect them until it became possible.

"Guys," said Charlie. "I don't know how, but we have to get some WAT-5 to everyone. If I was expired, they either are already or they're close."

Max snapped his fingers. "If we can get inside the cells before they get here we can figure something out," he said. "Come on."

Charlie and Isis followed Max, who cut to the southwest and skirted along the west side of the police station. The street in front was still deserted, and no candles or lanterns glowed within the dark station windows. Max moved to the front door and tried it.

It pulled open. He went inside. Charlie followed and Isis came in last.

They stopped in the lobby of the police station, standing still. No voices or snarls from inside. Charlie removed a headlamp from a pocket and put it on.

Using the more inconspicuous red light, she followed the soft glow toward a door in the rear that she believed would lead them to the cellblock.

"It's propped," she said. "Whew."

They all entered. Nobody was in there, but in two of the far cells, skeletal remains lay on the floor, the clothing in tatters.

Max pointed at them. "Must've had Hungerer roomies," he said.

"I want to leave them a radio," said Charlie. "We need to find a way to stash one for them."

"We have no way to know which cell they'll put them in," said Max.

"There are seven of them," said Isis. "They'll have to use more than one cell.

"These are open," Max said, motioning to the three cells to their left. "The four on the back wall are closed." He walked quickly back and pulled on each door. They did not budge.

"We put the radio in the center cell, close to the third cell," said Charlie.

"Why?" asked Max. "That first cell's open. They might just stuff them all in there."

Charlie walked over and pulled the door closed. "Not anymore. If they don't have the keys handy, they'll just put them where it's convenient."

"Hurry," said Isis. "They'll be here any moment."

Charlie looked around and found an old newspaper. She picked it up, wrapped the radio in a piece, and in another thought, reached into her pocket and removed the baggie holding the WAT-5 wafers. She quickly counted off sixteen of them and wrapped them up with the radio.

"This will get them through the next ten hours," she said. "I hope."

She placed it in the corner of the cell and lay another piece of torn paper over it. There were other pieces of trash within the cell, so it did not appear out of place.

"Okay, let's go," said Max. "Isis is right. We get caught here, there's no back way out."

Charlie stopped him. "What about leaving a gun?"

"No," said Isis. "If they do search the cell, maybe the radio won't raise too much suspicion. As for the WAT-5, they won't have any idea what that is. A gun would alert them too much, I'm afraid."

"They're still going to be transported from here to the pen where the Mothers and Hungerers are kept tomorrow," said Max. "Once they get into the cell and find the WAT-5, they'll figure out that they don't need to take it right away. They can take it in the morning, and we can fill them in on our plan with the radio."

They hurried back outside and Charlie turned her headlamp off as they exited the station and closed the door behind them.

"Let's head back over to the court," said Isis. "We have to speak with Alyssa, Megan, and Beauty."

307

Once again, they ran around the west side of the station, took a course through the tall weeds and moved to their original rendezvous point with the Hybrids.

This time, Beauty stared directly at them.

"She sees us," said Isis.

Beauty disappeared into the group, which Charlie estimated to be anywhere from thirty-five to fifty.

Charlie saw the girl emerge from the crowd. Behind her were two who appeared older than the rest.

"Charlie," said Isis. "Move back into the grass for a moment, okay?"

"Sure," she said, though she did not want to. She had been separated from her son once, and did not intend to put more than a few feet between them again.

She watched as the women drew near and stopped, facing one another as though stepping aside to have a private conversation. It was clear they were pretending that they were not speaking to anyone else.

"You are back," said Alyssa.

"I've brought you something," said Isis.

"It is not safe now," said Megan. "They are our daughters, but they are not devoted only to us."

"I am," said Beauty.

Alyssa and Megan nodded.

"I've brought Max's mother," said Isis. "Charlie, come out."

Charlie, smiling, emerged from the grass and crouched near the fence. "Hello," she said.

The Hybrids did not smile, but they did not appear worried.

"Do you love your children?" asked Isis.

"Love?" asked Alyssa.

"Do you feel a need to protect them?" asked Charlie. "I do, with Max. If someone tried to hurt or kill him, I would die in his place without hesitation."

"We are merely the vessel of birth," said Alyssa. "The children belong to Maestro."

"They're *your* fucking kids," said Charlie. She put her hand over her heart and added, "Sorry to be harsh, but they are your children and right here, deep in your heart, you should be willing to do anything to give them a better life."

"Better than what Maestro has done for you," said Isis. "As I told you before, I'm exactly like your mothers. While I was in her womb, one of the Mothers sprayed my mom with her vapor. When I was born, she died. What happened to your mothers?"

Alyssa looked at Megan, and they nodded. "Maria was my mother," said Alyssa. "Sofia was Megan's mother. Maestro killed them both as he took us in caged cars from our birthplace. He said our mothers were too dangerous."

"How did that make you feel?" asked Charlie.

"Angry," said Beauty interrupting. "Maria was the mother of my mother," she added, looking at Alyssa. Alyssa returned her glance, and while the look that passed between them was somewhat tender, Charlie felt it lacked any real depth of emotion.

"She was your grandmother," said Max.

"I had a special relationship with my own grandmother," said Charlie. "She was everything to me, and she taught me about a lot of the things that were special to her as a girl. When she died, it was devastating for me. I was only eight years old."

Isis reached into her pocket and withdrew the paper she had showed Charlie earlier. "Can you read?"

Alyssa and Megan nodded. "We can," said Megan. "Our mothers taught us. Maestro has forbidden our daughters from learning. He said there is no need."

Isis passed the folded paper through the fence. "This document was written over 250 years ago," she said. "The country in which we live is called the United States of America, and they were once ruled by King George III of Great Britain. He made their lives so miserable that they felt they must break free of his tyranny."

"What does this have to do with us?" asked Alyssa.

"It's called the Declaration of Independence," said Isis. "Part of it says, 'We hold these truths to be self-evident, that all men are created equal, that they are endowed by their Creator with certain unalienable Rights, that among these are Life, Liberty and the pursuit of Happiness.' That is how this applies to you."

"Happiness?" asked Beauty. "Liberty?"

Alyssa looked up from the page. "Are we … the governed?"

"Does Maestro control every aspect of your lives?" asked Charlie. "Is there a time when you laugh and sing and play and enjoy your lives together, able to move freely around Hoisington?"

The three were silent.

"How many of you are there?" asked Charlie.

"There are we three and Magas through forty-one," said Beauty. "As you know, I was Maga 7 before you called me by this name."

"An entire independent country was created by the introduction of this document," said Isis. "People fought and died for this freedom, and millions of people have been inspired by the very document you hold in your hand."

Charlie spoke up. "What Isis speaks of she read in a history book," she said. "I lived that freedom. I lived in

310

that world, and we have a little piece of it right now, not very far away."

Charlie took a deep breath. "Freedom is such a powerful thing, I can't stress it enough. People died just trying to get to our shores. Right up to the time this horrible disease struck the world, people fought to come here to experience true liberty."

Isis said, "You are powerful, and you have the ability to gain your independence from Maestro with a strong will and a distinct purpose."

"What would you have us do?" asked Megan.

"I've been thinking of something," said Charlie. "Isis, if we can put all of the Magas to sleep except Alyssa, Megan and Beauty, what would that do?"

Isis touched her shoulder. "Charlie, that is an excellent idea. It will relinquish the control of the Mothers and Hungerers to us," said Isis. "Freedom is a powerful emotion. Alyssa, please let Megan read this. Read it aloud to Beauty."

"I would like to read this sentence aloud, for it rings of familiarity," said Alyssa. "He has plundered our seas, ravaged our coasts, burnt our towns, and destroyed the lives of our people." She looked up at them with something akin to guilt in her eyes. "The people of Great Bend might have written something of this nature following our visit to their city," said Megan. "It is what *we* did to *them*, at Maestro's command."

"Okay," said Charlie. "Do you have anywhere you can hide this?" She reached into her pocket and pulled out all of her remaining WAT-5. She took two from the baggie and put them back in her pocket.

"What is it for?"

"Can you crush these up and mix the powder into the other Magas food?" asked Charlie.

311

"What will it do?"

"It will put them to sleep indefinitely," said Isis. "They will be okay."

"Sleep? We do not sleep."

"There's a first time for everything, ladies," said Max. "I only wish you'd get to experience it. I did, once or twice. It's a trip."

"We are brought meat once each two days," said Beauty. "Always just before dawn. Maestro realizes that we must maintain our strength in order to control the Mothers."

"When is your next feeding?" asked Isis.

"This pre-dawn," said Alyssa.

"Then with Alyssa and Megan's consent," said Beauty, "I will help distribute the powder into the food."

Alyssa and Megan nodded.

"It's very important that you three not consume this," said Isis. "You must be awake to work with us to control the Mothers and Hungerers, and you will need your strength. Will you be able to separate your food out before tainting the remainder?"

"You used the word *tainting*," said Megan. "Will they be harmed?" she asked. "Because we can do nothing to harm them."

"The harm you speak of is being inflicted upon you now," said Isis. "No, your sisters and daughters will not be physically harmed in any way."

"There's lots more to figure out, guys," said Charlie.

"I know," said Max. "Still, we need to knock his army of Hybrids out before we stand a chance. This was a good idea, mom. Really good."

"It better be," said Charlie. "When it comes to WAT-5, we're really blowing our wad." She looked at the three. "When this is over, will you come back home with us?"

312

Doubt crossed the expressions of Alyssa and Megan, but Beauty said, "Yes, I will come. I must know this freedom."

"We will come, too," said Megan. She turned and said, "Alyssa?"

"Yes," Alyssa said.

"I promise you it will be the true beginning of your lives," said Isis. "To experience actual freedom is the only way to understand the power of the document in your hands."

"We will declare our independence?" asked Alyssa.

"You bet your asses you will," said Charlie. "And ours."

*****

CHAPTER SIXTEEN

The walk from the Applebee's to the jail was not far, and as Maestro's men pushed them into two of the trash-scattered cells, Flex secretly feared they would not survive this critical error.

Trina, Gem and Taylor were all put in the middle cell, and Punch, Nelson, Flex, Dave and Hemp were all installed into the first open cage.

The four men who had led them there were nursing several lacerations and punctures from the exploding glass from the restaurant's bar. There had been some delay in leaving the restaurant for need of patching them up with a first aid kit found in the kitchen.

The guards left a kerosene lantern hanging on a hook across from their cells, providing a low, flickering illumination in the cellblock.

After the men left the cellblock area, everyone gathered in the corner where the two cells connected. Flex said, "Can we assume that was Isis and Max back at the restaurant?"

Hemp looked perplexed. "I've never seen any indication of telekinetic abilities in either Max or Isis," he said. "But all that means for sure is that it was not Charlie."

"She could have been there," said Gem, her face resting against the bars. "They still had their radios, so as long as they remembered each other's numbers it wouldn't have been too much of a feat finding one another."

"I hope so," said Hemp. "I'm locked in here while my wife and son are out there battling who knows what."

"They may be the lucky ones," said Dave. "No offense, but I'd rather be with them right now," he said.

Flex kicked at a piece of newspaper at his feet. His toe hit something hard, and it hit the wall and bounced back. A piece of plastic and a 9 volt battery slid across the floor.

Nelson bent down to retrieve it. He put the poles on the battery to his tongue and jerked it away suddenly. "Holy moly, dudes! This battery is hot!"

Flex swiped at the newspaper. Something was under it. He picked it up. "A fuckin' radio," he whispered.

"Quick, Nel," he said. "Give me the battery."

"This plastic piece is the battery cover," said Nelson, giving both to Flex.

Flex reassembled the radio and turned it on. The numbers lit up.

Everyone smiled, and Flex put his finger to his lips. "We don't know how many guards are stationed out there, and we don't need them hearing a celebration."

"It's that awkward moment when you're trying to think of some clever way to say …" Dave Gammon's voice trailed off and he simply held up a baggie.

Punch said, "Is that WAT-5?"

"Yep," said Dave. "Looks like Charlie was here," he added.

Flex shook his head. His friends were the best and most dedicated he could ever have hoped to find. When he thought of Charlie holed up in that hospital linen room aiming that crossbow at him and Gem, it would not have entered his mind that almost fifteen years later they would still be together.

Hemp could not stop smiling. "Okay, everyone," he said. "Any idea what time it is?"

"I tend to keep a running clock in my head," said Nelson. "It's around three in the morning."

"Okay, that means we're looking at light within three hours, three and a half at the most," said Hemp. "There's no need for us to take the WAT-5 yet, but as we are all beyond our five hours, we'll need to take it once we've secured our freedom and in a secure place."

"I could use mine now," said Gem. "I'm wiped."

"It gets better," said Punch, holding something behind his back. "Hemp, how much do you love me?"

"I suppose that depends on whether you're hiding a bouquet of freshly-picked Freesias behind your back or not," said Hemp, smiling. I knew he was still floating on air with the knowledge that Charlie was okay.

At least it seemed that way.

Punch swung his hand around in front of him and opened his palm.

"That's Max's lock pick kit!" he said excitedly, trying to keep his voice low.

"Uncle Hemp, can you get us out of these cells with that?" asked Taylor.

"Absolutely," said Hemp. "We have to be prepared to take out any guards out front."

"Maybe we can radio Charlie, dude," said Nelson. "She can recon the lobby for us. Wonder if she's got her crossbow still."

"If she has to take them out, it would be the best method," said Punch. "Quiet."

Flex said, "Okay, guys. Our prospects just got a hell of a lot better in the last five minutes. Let's structure a plan and execute the shit like yesterday."

"Dude, that would require advanced technology and building a time machine," said Nelson. "We're just going to have to work in the now."

Everyone in the two cells stared at Nelson.

"Dudes, seriously? You don't know a joke when you hear it?"

"Nelson," said Hemp.

"Yeah, bro?" he said, still smiling.

"That's it, guys," said Hemp. "Nelson!"

Hemp was obviously trying to contain his excitement and keep his voice low.

Nelson stared at him, his arms out. "Yeah, dude? I'm Nelson, so what? This should not come as a surprise to any of you who've known me over the last several years."

"Nelson's Subdudo!" whispered Hemp, turning to Flex. "I've got a plan."

"We call Charlie, Max and Isis?" asked Trina.

"No," said Hemp. "We escape first and contact them when we're prepared to meet them."

"No way," said Gem. "Hemp, at least call them and let them know what we're about to do," she said. "If anything goes wrong, we might need backup."

Hemp nodded. "Good point, Gem."

Hemp went around to the cell door and unwrapped the lock pick kit, exposing its many tools. He removed what Flex believed were the largest devices in the kit and put his arm through the bars, working his way to the lock.

As he worked on it, he looked at everyone, his tongue sticking out of the corner of his mouth as he concentrated.

"It's more difficult ... without visuals," he said. "The ... sounds ... are all you can ... go by," he said, as the door clicked open.

Everyone's arms went in the air in a silent cheer.

"I haven't see this many teeth since we were locked in that fuckin' pen," said Flex. "Okay, Hemp. What's next, brother?"

Hemp moved to the corner and said, "Everyone huddle around me. I'm calling the kids. I need your bodies around me to muffle the sound."

Hemp knelt down in the corner of the cell, and Gem, Taylor and Trina huddled around him in the other cell, and Punch, Flex, Nelson and Dave created a wall on his other side.

He turned on the radio. Flex looked down and saw it was already turned to Channel 2.

"Hemp, buddy," said Flex.

Hemp looked up, smiling, tears in his eyes.

"You know what I was gonna say."

"Yes," he said. He pushed the button. "Charlie," he said. "Charlie, come in."

"Baby?" came her voice. "Oh, my God, it's you."

"It is," said Hemp. "Charlie, are you okay?"

"I am," she said. "I'm with Max and Isis, and they're both fine."

"Okay, darling," said Hemp. "Tell Max thank you for the lock pick kit. We've already got the cell door open and we've formulated a plan. We still need to get out of this building and to where you are."

"We've got a plan underway, too," said Charlie. "Baby, these are second-generation Hybrids. We've made friends with three of them. The matriarchs, essentially, and one of the daughters."

"How can they help?" asked Hemp.

318

"By putting the other Hybrids to sleep," said Charlie.

"Where are you?"

We're staying in a sheet metal, aluminum siding shop across the street from the Applebee's where they interrogated you guys."

"Was that you behind the bar?" asked Hemp.

"Yeah," she said. "Max was being Max. We're all fine."

"I need to ask about the flying glass," said Hemp. "But that can wait. We'll execute our plan in fifteen minutes. How long will it take you to get back over here?"

"We can be there in five," said Charlie.

"Okay," said Hemp. "Charlie, I think we should leave here immediately. Get everybody back home. We can deal with this Maestro later."

"Dad?" came the voice on the radio.

"Max!" said Hemp. "It's good to hear your voice, son. Are you alright?"

"I am," he said. "I screwed up in the bar, but we're all okay. Anyway, dad, I don't think we can leave this guy alive. He's doing some crazy things here. Stuff that can come back to hurt us in Kingman."

"What do you suggest?" asked Hemp.

"I've got an idea," he said. "I need the lock pick kit the minute you guys get out of there. Charlie told me where all the packs are hidden, plus, I need to do something else on that side of town."

"Max, there's no need," said Hemp. "We only need to pile into a vehicle of some kind and get out of Hoisington."

"I disagree, dad," said Max. "You'll understand later."

"Max," said Hemp, sounding defeated.

"Dad, don't worry," said Max. "We'll be fine."

"Alright, son," he said. "I'm trusting you."

319

"I fucked up once tonight," he said. "I won't do it again."

"Language," said Hemp.

Trina and Taylor laughed softly.

"We're down to twelve minutes," said Max. "Get going. We'll be outside of the jail in three more minutes."

"Got it," said Hemp. "Out."

"Nel, stand by the door there while Hemp picks the other cell lock," said Flex.

"Better stay low, buddy," said Punch. "They might spot you through that glass."

"I will," said Hemp, kneeling beside the cell door. Gem, Trina and Taylor crouched directly behind the door, waiting.

Nelson stood to the side of the entry door, shaking out his arms. He took four practice kicks as he waited. Flex watched him, smiling.

The guy was just as skinny at 38 as he was at 25, but his muscles were highly toned and if he ever wanted Subdudo to inflict damage, Flex had no doubt it would take no more than minor adjustments to snap some bones.

"Got it," said Hemp, and the door clicked open a half-inch. Gem pushed on it and left the cell. She immediately walked over to Flex's cell and embraced him.

"It's alright, babe," he said. "We're gonna get out of here. All of us."

"I know," she said, looking into his eyes. "Somehow I never really have any doubt." She turned her face down again and put her head against his chest.

"Gem," said Flex.

When she looked up again, her eyes were misty and sad. "Oh, Flex," she said. "I miss Flexy so much."

"So do I, Gem," he said, pulling her tight against him. There was nothing else to say.

She wiped at her eyes and pulled away, turning toward Trina and Taylor. To Flex's relief, they both saw her pain and went to her. The three embraced while Hemp approached Flex.

"Next step," said Hemp. "We need to call the guards. Everyone back into the cells. You too, Nel," he whispered.

Once they were back inside, Punch picked several pieces of newspaper from the floor and wadded them up. He then stuffed them tight into the latch receiver of their cell door and gave another wadded ball to Gem. "Do the same with yours, then pull them closed so they look latched."

She did. The cell doors appeared to be closed and locked, but a light push would open them.

"Help!" shouted Punch. "We need help in here!" he called again.

A moment later, a face peered through the glass, turning to look toward the cells. The window in the door was not ideal for getting a good view of the entire cellblock, but before the epidemic, they likely had video surveillance.

The sound of a key in a lock, then the door opened. Two men walked in with guns. One stood back with his weapon in firing position.

"I gotta take a shit like no tomorrow," said Flex. "Toilet's plugged."

Both of the guards' eyes went to the stainless steel toilet protruding from the wall. From the corner of his eye, Flex saw Gem push open her cell door, which swung outward without a sound.

"It's fucked, dude!" shouted Nelson, walking over to the toilet in an excellent bit of acting. He pointed into the bowl. "There's a dried out turd in there from 2015 or so, and no matter how much we pee on it, the thing won't budge. These conditions are deplorable! We demand to see the Conductor!"

"You idiot," said the guard standing back. "It's Maestro."

He did not see Gem's foot coming toward his groin. His eyes had been peeled on Nelson as she had crept out of her cell, and Gem had stayed on her hands and knees until she reached the guard. By the time she shot up from the ground, her foot was already flying.

He emitted a choked cry as the gun fell from his grip and clattered to the ground, both hands instinctively covering his testicles, which were no doubt throbbing.

Gem snatched the AK-47 from the cellblock floor, rolled onto her back and aimed it directly at the other guard. "One fucking move and your head will explode like a paintball," she growled. "A bright red one."

He raised his hands. Nelson flew out of the cell and snatched the weapon from him. Punch had come out behind him, and Nelson tossed the weapon to him and quickly administered several kicks and chops to the guard. Flex and the others watched in amusement until the man was down on his back, staring at the ceiling in confusion.

Nelson approached the other guard, who held up his hand and said, "No, no, please. I'll cooperate."

He was in his mid-twenties and looked like a firefighter who might have made their annual fundraising calendar. Still, Flex had no doubt that Nelson could have spun the guy around like a top.

Now everyone was out of the cells.

Flex went to the muscular guard on the floor beside Gem. "Get up, get into the first cell," he said.

The guard got up and held his palms outward as he stepped into the cell and moved to the back wall.

"You now," said Flex, indicating to the other guard. He did the same.

Punch removed the wadded paper from the lock and held out his hand. "Keys."

The guards looked at one another, then back at Punch. Punch waited for a two second count before rushing inside, grabbing the biggest guy by the neck and slamming his head against the cinderblock wall behind him. "Fucking keys, now!" he shouted, spitting into the man's face.

"My left front pocket," he said.

Punch reached down, jammed his hand into the man's pocket, and pulled out a ring of keys. He held them up. "What are these keys for?" he asked.

"Maestro's house," The man said.

"And where might that be?" asked Punch.

The man stared at him but did not answer.

Punch reached down and grabbed his crotch, twisting hard, his left hand still pushing him against the wall.

"That is what I'd call a painful grimace," said Flex, smiling. "Former United States Marine right there," he said. "If you don't wanna go through the rest of your life as a gelding, I'd say you should answer Punch's question."

"He's over on the corner of West 1st and North Vine," he said. "At the Living Joy church. It was set up with good sleeping quarters for the guy who ran it."

"And the irony keeps coming," said Gem.

"There's plenty of homes available," said Punch. "Why live in a church?"

"I don't know, man," he said. "It has a propane-powered kitchen and a good diesel generator. Community used it for a shelter. Basement, too. Maestro's been there from the start, because it's close to the pen and the main exit from the town."

Punch released the man's neck.

"What's your name?" asked Punch.

"Walter."

"What kind of guards does he have over there, Walt?"

"At any given time he's got at least ten."

"Defenses?"

"Just guns. He does have surveillance."

Punch nodded. "Does he have surveillance here?"

"No," said the frightened man.

What's your name?" he asked the other.

"Brian," he said.

"What have you got to offer?"

"That's pretty much it. We just do what the guy says. He'll kill us otherwise."

"Everyone seems to have an excuse for being an asshole," said Punch. He turned to Hemp. "I'm letting these guys split a WAT-5."

"Good idea," said Hemp. Everyone else, take yours, too. I'll go last. These two first."

Punch took a wafer from the baggie and snapped it in half. He gave half to Walter and half to Brian. "Eat this. Now."

"What is it?" asked Walt.

Punch glared at him, his right hand twitching.

Walt popped it in his mouth. So did Brian.

"Oh, shit!" said Punch. "Flex, catch the guy!"

Flex shot forward and grabbed Brian, mid-fall. He eased him to the concrete floor, even as Punch assisted Walt with his downward slide against the wall.

They locked the two sleeping guards in the cell and left the police station.

They had not taken twenty steps when Max and Charlie shot out of the night and nearly plowed into Hemp, scooping him into a long, hard embrace.

*****

324

"Did you find the WAT-5 in the cell?" asked Charlie.

"Got it," said Punch, holding up the baggie.

Isis saw the relieved look on Charlie's face. The crow's feet around her eyes had become more pronounced in the last three or four years, and some wisps of gray hair had begun to creep into her blond.

Isis had loved her since the day they met, just as she had bonded with Max, whose birth she remembered vividly.

"We need to get away from this jail," said Hemp. "Charlie, you said something about an aluminum siding place you stayed in?"

"Yeah, it's about a quarter mile from here."

"Let's go then," said Hemp. "Isis, do you have any objections?"

"No," she said. "It's a perfect midway point. Did you learn from the guards at the jail where Maestro is?"

"He's at a place called Living Joy Church," said Nelson. "On West First and North Vine. Guard said it was near the main town exit."

"I'm guessing it's not the entrance we came through," said Dave. "No mazes, I'd assume."

"Glad you remembered the location," said Flex. "I heard it, but it went in one ear and out the other."

"Go figure," said Gem. "You're almost sixty years old." She winked at him and took his hand, and the slight smile that found her lips for a moment disappeared as quickly as it had come.

Isis knew why; Gem's son had died the day before. Any attempt at being happy would be slapped back down by the sorrow that had not yet run its most intense course.

Still, even in times of great sadness and stress, Flex and Gem managed to keep up their playful banter. Isis glanced at Max, considering the feelings that occasionally surprised her when it came to him. With every passing month, they had grown closer, and she felt more strongly about him. He looked so much more like a man than a boy now, and she was pretty sure he wanted to be with her.

If the time came when she was convinced Max would make her as happy as Flex made Gem, she would ask *him* to marry *her*.

"We'll lead the way," said Isis.

*****

In ten minutes, they had made it safely back inside the dark aluminum siding building and everyone sat on the linoleum floor.

Charlie illuminated the red lights on two different headlamps and directed their soft glow upward. The result was hardly enough to read by, but allowed them to see one another's faces.

Trina and Taylor leaned against the wall and were out within seconds of entering.

Punch got up and went to them, kneeling down beside them. Shaking them gently awake, he removed two WAT-5 wafers from the baggie in his pocket and gave them each one. "Just wake up long enough to take these," he said. "We'll wake you when we leave."

"I didn't mean to fall asleep," said Trina. "Sorry, Punch."

"Not a problem, kid," he said. "I'm wiped, too."

"I'm out," said Taylor, popping the wafer in her mouth. She chewed, swallowed, and her eyelids closed as her head drooped.

"Fuck it," said Trina. She ate the WAT-5 and went out. Punch steadied her until she leaned into Taylor and they supported one another.

"Max, Isis, what are you up to?" asked Hemp. "I trust you, but I still worry."

Max shook his head. "Look, it's a preliminary plan, and we –"

"Max, just spill it." Charlie stared at him.

Max was hesitant and Isis was tempted to interject, but for the moment, she only watched. She and Max had discussed the beginnings of their plan in Charlie's presence, but it had been finalized when Charlie had slipped away for a moment to relieve herself. They had not yet filled her in on the details.

"Okay," said Max, with a sigh. "They feed the Magas early in the morning, typically just before dawn. We've given Megan, Alyssa and Beauty what we believe is enough WAT-5 to put the rest of them to sleep. They intend to pulverize it and mix it in with the food."

"Then what, dude?" asked Nelson. "The Magas aren't the threat, are they? I mean, you and Max are cool, and you're one of them."

"They are a threat, Nelson," said Max. "They've lived their entire lives under the control of this asshole. The guy's like a freakin' warlord or something. All those women know is the dark side of life and they fear Maestro. That's a great motivator to follow his instructions."

"Right," said Nelson. "Good point."

"Uh huh," said Max. "So that's why, once the other Magas are out, Megan, Alyssa, Beauty, Isis and I have to take control of the Mothers."

"Okay, so what's next?" asked Charlie. "I knew up to that part, but I think I had to go pee. By the time I got back you guys were done."

"TMI, mom," said Max. "Truth is, we weren't sure we were going to share it with you."

"Whatever," said Charlie. "You are now."

Isis felt it was time to assist Max. "Tonight we must get the gate not only unlocked, but unlatched so that it can be easily pushed open. Before we have any chance of doing that, we will need to replace the two guards in the towers."

"Replace them with what?" asked Nelson.

"What gate?" asked Hemp, his expression confused.

"You know that pen, Dad," said Max. "The one you were all locked in last night."

"No," said Hemp, standing. "You'll be unleashing that massive horde on this place and any settlements nearby as well."

"You know what almost happened to us inside that pen, right guys?" asked Charlie. "Plus, they're all freshly fed in there. We *saw* them eating. They'll have every offensive mechanism in their arsenals primed and ready."

"They won't get that far," said Max. "We'll be controlling them, so they won't be in feed mode."

"So that's the start," said Gem. "What's next? Where are you directing them?"

"Wait a minute," said Dave. "Won't the ghouls in the cage go nuts when Nelson and whoever else tries to take out the guards?"

"We still have some remaining WAT-5," said Isis. "Nelson, you can take a man down quickly and quietly with your Subdudo. You can bring a knife if you don't have sufficient room to use your technique. I'd say you could take the suppressed Walther, but there's only one of them, and whoever takes the other tower will probably need it."

"If they weren't caged up there I could use my crossbow," said Max.

"Or me," said Charlie.

"I got this," said Nelson. "These are bad guys, man, and I may not like it, but I'll do what I have to do." His face was more serious than Isis had ever seen before.

"This is the preparation to be done before daybreak," said Isis. "As you know, the commands we're capable of issuing to the Mothers can be of a directive type or just a call. The latter draws them to our doorstep, and it's the simpler of the two. It's what we use in Kingman to draw them from miles around into our pit, and the call includes a command to ensure they move the Hungerers along with them, even though they kind of do that naturally. The other directive is more complex and involves a long-term connection with them and the ability to guide them to a location other than where we are."

"You're going to sic them on Maestro," said Punch. "Once the Magas are countin' sheep and the gate is breached."

"Yeah," said Isis, "but our work starts way before then. The Magas will be asleep, and we have to be there, outside their enclosure, at that very moment so we five can combine our control of the Mothers."

"Yeah, that's a lot of red-eyes to take on," said Charlie. "Can you do it, Isis?"

"Whether we're strong enough to control all of them or not on a long-term basis, we have to try," she said. "The only alternative is to escape this place and go back to Kingman. That man will come after us, I don't doubt that."

"Isis, we stopped the vibration at the football field," said Max.

"Sure, but only for a few seconds, Max," said Isis. "We're talking a bigger undertaking than that."

"So you'll push them to the Living Joy Church," said Flex.

"Exactly," said Isis. "We'll breach their building's security and let the horde inside."

"Bye-bye, Maestro," said Dave.

"That's a viable plan," said Hemp. "Anything else is too risky as long as the Magas are under Maestro's control."

"Yeah," said Max. "We pretty much know that, Dad. Anyway, we don't need many guys. Flex, Punch, Nel, that's about it. The rest of you guys need to get back through the maze, and go get the cars. We don't want to have to hoof it to the vehicles if something goes wrong and we're in a hurry."

"What about me, Max?" said Charlie, moving her crossbow around in front of her.

"Mom, you're not coming. You're too damned protective."

"I'll protect you right into next week," she said, her mouth straight and serious.

Max shook his head. "We're wasting time. Nelson, what time is it?"

"Around 3:45, dude," said Nelson.

Suddenly Isis felt an intense rush of agony ripple through her body. Her skin erupted in gooseflesh and she felt the scream rising in her throat, no way to stop it. It came out of her, high and shrill.

Her body flopped back onto the linoleum floor and all of her limbs convulsed, as though involved in a full-body seizure.

She felt someone beside her. A split-second later, a hand clamped over her mouth, and she instinctively knew it was Flex. She vaguely heard Max's screams, sounding as though they came from a great distance.

Charlie's comforting voice met her ears and Max quieted.

Isis hyperventilated, her body suddenly drained, the pain gone as quickly as it had come. She opened her eyes and found she could sit up.

"What the fuck was that?" asked Gem. "Isis, Max, are you guys alright?"

Isis shook her head. She composed herself and leaned forward, taking Max's hand. "Max, what did you feel?"

"It was … horrible, Isis," he said, his voice weak and unsteady. "I felt like I died."

"Are you okay now?" asked Flex, his arm still around her shoulder. "Max? You alright, buddy?"

"I think so," he said.

"I … don't know the source of what we just felt," Isis said. "It was an intense pain, partly physical, but almost more emotional."

Max breathed hard, but managed to say, "Isis … that was no … ordinary pain. It wasn't just … I don't know, like you said, physical."

"No, Max," said Isis. "It felt like the emotional end of a life."

"I couldn't describe it any better," he said. "It's passing. I hope I never feel that again."

"That goes for all of us," said Gem. "No idea what caused it?"

"None," said Isis. "But the implications cannot be good for us and what we plan to do. *That* I know."

Gem said, "Are we getting ready to do this?"

Standing up and shaking it off, Isis said, "You all need at least another hour's rest. You'll endanger all of us if you're dead on your feet."

"I hope that is the very first joke I've ever heard you crack," said Punch.

"No, Punch," said Isis. "But that's exactly why I avoid wordplay. Now rest."

*****

331

Maestro stood over the body of Alpha, a blood soaked piece of paper in his fingers. The rest of the Magas cowered in the far corner of the enclosure. His knife still jutted out from her head and she lay sprawled on her back.

He stood there shirtless, his demonic skull face and tuxedo tattoo an illustration of the power and darkness he needed to convey in order to maintain his power over them.

"What you just felt will be nothing compared to the pain you will feel when I mutilate and kill the next traitor," he growled. "It will be what you feel when I kill your newborn boy children. I despise the time wasted when you give birth to them, but I cherish the moment of their deaths, for your pain is only ecstasy to me."

When he had arrived, Alpha had been standing in the near corner of the fenced court, her eyes turned down, looking at something. Only when the other Magas reacted to his arrival did she look up; too late.

He had entered the cage and moved directly toward her, his eyes never wavering. When he reached Alpha, she had stuffed the paper into her mouth. He grabbed her by the jaw and forced his fingers in to keep her mouth open, but had only been able to retrieve a single corner of the page. The rest she had frantically chewed and swallowed, even as he clawed at her face, trying to stop it.

He stared at it. Maestro could make out only four words of the neatly printed text: *our lives, our fortunes.* This was obviously only a portion of a sentence, but the words were foreign to Maestro.

His torture of Alpha had been swift. She broke easily, saying that two women and a man had arrived, trying to convince her to talk the others into helping them. Their friends were in the jail, they said, and they were from a place called Kingman.

Maestro turned to Wesley, one of his most trusted men and one of the strongest guards in his contingent. "Get to the jail now, and check on my guards and the prisoners. Wait for me there."

"Yes, Maestro," said the man.

When Wesley ran off, Maestro turned back toward the cowering Magas. "Come here. Now."

They all obeyed, stopping just feet in front of him, their eyes turned to the ground.

"I want to know who else was involved. Alpha said the rest of this paper is gone. Do any of you have it?"

All heads shook. No.

"Did you see them?"

"Yes, and we would have told you, Maestro," said Maga 40. "We had only to await your arrival."

"She asked me to help her," said Omega, stepping forward. "As we were equals, she felt I would be sympathetic. I stood with her for a few moments, but I would not hear their plea. I told her I could not, for to deceive you would be to risk the lives of us all."

"She also asked me to join her in convincing the other Magas to guide the Mothers and Hungerers to your door," said Maga 7. "I, too, refused."

"Do you know of this paper?" he asked.

"She did not share it with us," said Maga 7. "Perhaps Alpha believed it to be pointless after we refused to consider her request. We only waited for you to arrive so that we could tell you what had taken place."

Maestro considered this. Had they wanted to, any one of them could have pushed the information to his mind, but he had forbidden that long ago. It was unsettling to him, and despite the value it may have, it made him feel they had control over him.

"Maestro!" shouted Wesley, running toward him. "Our men are locked in the cells and the prisoners are gone!"

Maestro stared at Wesley for a long time before turning and leaving the enclosure. He locked the gate behind him and walked calmly toward Wesley. Together, they entered the police station cellblock. The two guards sat on the floor, their backs resting against the wall. They were dead asleep.

Maestro clapped his hands. Neither man moved.

"Are they alive?" he asked.

"They're breathing," said Wesley, a large, black man who had been with him from the beginning.

"Do you have the key?" asked Maestro.

"Yes, sir," said Wesley.

"Dismember them," he said. "Start with their fingers, then their hands, then their arms and legs. I want them alive as long as possible."

"Y-yes, sir," stuttered Wesley. "I'll … need help. Mind if I call Sedat to help me?"

"I don't give a shit who helps you. I want these men dead and I want them to feel every cut."

Maestro moved toward the door and stopped.

"Yeah, Maestro?" asked Wesley, jangling the cell keys.

"When you're done, get to the maze and apply configuration six," he said. "I'm moving the Magas to my quarters right now."

"Why, sir?" asked Wesley.

"I'll fill you in on the rest when you're done here. Kill them fast and get to the maze. I want you at my place within half an hour."

*****

334

Flex slept for maybe thirty-five minutes and awoke feeling more refreshed than he had a right to feel. He stared at his wife through the gloom, wondering if her dreams were all of their son like his had been.

His cheeks were still wet.

Isis apparently felt their rest was important. An hour and a half had passed by the time she stood and began to nudge everyone awake.

"The sun will be coming up in an hour," she said. "Punch, Flex, Nelson? Will you work with us while the others head for the vehicles?"

Flex looked at Gem before answering, and Isis knew why. He loved her with every synapse and sinew in his body, and there was nothing he wouldn't do to make her happy, even when the sadness within her made it impossible.

"Are you going to be well armed?" Gem asked, her voice still thick with sleep. "God, I really went out."

"You probably needed it," said Flex, touching her arm.

"We'll need to get Flex's and Punch's packs before we take on the guards," said Nelson. "Mine's stashed by the maze. Charlie, where'd you put them?"

"They're pretty near the zombie pen," said Charlie. "Just get to 9th Street, just east of the pen. On the north side you'll see a little yellow house with a detached garage. The door's unlocked. Just slide the garage door open and they're on the right side in a pile."

"You guys be sure to stay out of sight on the way up, and when you get near the pen, detour around," said Isis. "If the Mothers and Hungerers detect you and alert the guards, our plan might all go out the window."

"Sure you guys can't use me?" asked Dave.

"To get the vehicles, Dave," said Max.

"It's that awkward moment when you check your back for a bra strap," said Dave Gammon.

"Dave, buddy, it's not that you're not a threat," said Flex. "You run nearly as well as Lola. If anybody peters out on the way to Great Bend, you can just run ahead. How are you with mazes?"

"I suck at puzzles," Dave said.

"You guys have the directions written down, right Gem?" asked Nelson. "Just reverse them and you're through."

"You guys need to go now," said Max. "Daylight's coming and all of this is better done way before that."

*****

"It's not far to the house," said Charlie. "We should be able to get the packs and get through the maze in a half hour. Nice little ten-mile run and a drive back, we should be waiting for you in less than two hours."

"Is this the last of the WAT-5?" asked Punch.

"It's all I have. Max and Isis have some," said Charlie. "I took everyone else's except Nel's."

"My pack's stashed over by that auto parts store," he said. "I got about eight hits in there."

"Well, if you haven't already, dose up everyone. This is it, folks," said Punch. "Execution time."

"Meaning executing our plan, right?" asked Trina, with a yawn.

"Absolutely," said Punch.

"Good," said Taylor.

Once everyone was protected by WAT-5, they separated into groups.

Gem went to Flex and hugged him. She did not let go of him until everyone else had said their goodbyes and moved toward the door.

"Radios on, please," she said, letting her arms fall from Flex's neck. "When we get back and I call you guys, I want to get a response."

"I hear you, girl," said Flex. "Loud and clear."

"Plug up that other ear so it doesn't fall out," she said, smiling again. With a last sad wave, Gem moved into the streets of Hoisington with the rest of their family.

Flex went to the loose panel and held it aside as he watched them walk away. Isis did not rush him.

He turned with a big sigh and said, "So Max, now that they're gone … is this plan kinda fuckin' crazy, or is it just me?"

"It's you," said Max. "Let's get to the pen. Punch, ever use a crossbow?"

"If something shoots out of it, I can handle it," he said. "Now let's go pretend we're guards."

*****

Gem, Dave, Taylor and Trina crouched in the nook of a building as they watched Hemp and Charlie move across the street, successfully reaching the opposite corner and disappearing into the shadows there.

Gem stood up. "Trini, you and Tay come with me. We'll go a little west so it doesn't look like a goddamned zombie crossing, and Dave, why don't you go now. Just cross where Hemp and Charlie did."

"Sure, I'm just a poor, lonesome rotter with no friends," said Dave.

337

"You can get some hug therapy later," said Gem. "We're all gonna need a few days of that when we get back home."

"None more than you, Gem," said Dave. "So much has happened since we got here, I forget what you're dealing with. You're strong."

"I'm barely holding on," said Gem. Trina took her hand and squeezed it and she felt the tears come. She felt Taylor's hand on her back and smiled at her.

"Stop it, mom," said Trina. "You're gonna have glow streaks down your face."

Gem wiped at her eyes. "Got it. Dave, go."

With that, she, Taylor and Trina moved down the street. They met up on the other side and could still see the others ahead. So far, all were safe.

*****

They reached the building and everyone situated their packs. They would keep the rotten clothing on until they were clear of Hoisington. They agreed to move back toward the high school, staying clear of the main part of town. From there, they would head south, taking the same course they had taken to the football field.

Charlie said, "Everyone ready?"

"More than," said Hemp. "I hate leaving Max and the others behind though. Gem, do you have your turn list for the maze?"

Gem pulled it out. "Right here. And I wouldn't worry too much, Hemp," she said. "Isis is a tough cookie. She said she's got tricks she hasn't revealed to even us yet."

Hemp shook his head. "Unfortunately, this Maestro fella has dozens like Max and Isis, only second generation versions," said Hemp. "If we don't even know Isis and

Max's full capabilities, we certainly have no bloody idea what they're capable of."

"Yes, and we don't know if they're lying to them about helping, either. On top of that, there's that weird episode with Max and Isis when they felt that pain at the siding shop."

"I don't know what that was," said Charlie. "But Dave, believe me. I met Beauty, Megan and Alyssa, and they're not lying. Alyssa and Megan are the matriarchs. I got a feeling they were fully aware at how tentative their existence is under Maestro's thumb."

Taylor fidgeted. "Can we go? I want out of these shitty clothes and I want back in Kingman like yesterday."

"Gem, you lead the way and I'll be right behind you," said Dave.

The group set out into the early morning of Hoisington, Kansas.

*****

CHAPTER SEVENTEEN

Gem and the others reached the maze in fifteen minutes. They split into three groups and took separate routes there, keeping an eye out for sentries.

Charlie and Hemp came up behind Gem, Dave, Trina and Taylor.

"What the hell is this?" asked Charlie.

"Can you read your turn list and kill zombies at the same time, mom?" asked Trina.

Shambling zombies filled every square foot of the maze. They dragged their feet from section to section, some filtering into the town, others managing to make it through the puzzle and emerge on the outside.

"We're on WAT-5, so this shouldn't be an issue," said Hemp. "Unless there are Mothers among them, which I'm sure is part of Maestro's defense plan."

"But why do this?" asked Dave. "Why not just use the maze itself, reconfigure it and post snipers to pick off anyone trying to get through?"

"Ours is not to question why," said Trina. "Ours is but to get our asses through there."

"I can't stand rubbing up against them," said Taylor. "Everyone, make sure your sleeves are down and secured."

It was to prevent scratches, which were always possible and only sometimes dangerous.

"Charlie," said Gem. "Use your crossbow and your knife where you can, even if you just stab the bastards in the head with the arrows. Everyone else use your knives. We don't want to use guns and have it sounding like a fucking Wild West show over here tonight."

"I still don't get this," said Dave. "Looks like a hundred or more."

"Perhaps he has more abnormals than he has personnel," said Hemp.

Movement from Gem's peripheral caught her attention. She turned to see another horde of approximately equal size moving toward them from the west.

"Go, go go!" shouted Gem. "Into the maze, now!"

Everyone looked as they ran across with Gem in the lead, watching the band of rotters staggering up West Railroad Street.

"Jesus, is that the whole pen?" asked Charlie.

"Keep moving!" shouted Dave, taking Trina and Taylor by the arms and pulling them right behind.

As Gem reached the maze and pushed herself between two male rotters, she stood aside to let the others in while she stopped to look again. Walking alongside the massive group of abnormals were four women, two per side. Even from the distance, Gem could see their glowing red eyes.

In front of the horde were two more red-eyed females, but these had corn silk-straight hair and walked with shuddering gaits.

Hybrids on the outside, commanding the Mothers. Mothers in front, commanding the Hungerers.

"WAT-5 isn't going to help us with those Mothers," said Gem. "We need to push our asses the hell through this maze, now!" Gem was acutely aware of their disadvantage without being able to utilize firearms.

"Mothers?" asked Dave.

"We got Hybrids on both sides and Mothers in front," said Gem.

Dave guided Trina and Taylor into the packed maze beside Gem, and Hemp and Charlie pushed in next. Gem looked up to see Dave staring at her.

"They're moving now, Gem," he whispered. "*Really* moving."

"The Mothers will tell them to attack us despite the WAT-5," said Hemp. "Everyone, blend in among the ones inside the maze and let's move through it as quickly as possible."

Gem glanced back before the stinking masses engulfed the entrance and left only one possible choice.

Get through.

The advancing pack, led by the Hybrids and Mothers, was now less than a hundred yards away and closing.

"Keep a sharp eye out for Mothers in here, too," said Hemp. "I'll go first, Gem, you follow me, and tell me which way to turn. Everyone else have your knives ready."

Dave had left his suppressed Walther with the others, so had only his EB-tipped knife to grip. Charlie's small crossbow would not be effective in the tight quarters, so she had a 9mm Glock in her right hand, and her EB-tipped knife clenched in her left fist.

Gem said, "Charlie, remember. Don't fire the gun unless you don't have a choice."

"De-fucking-fine choice," said Charlie.

Hemp nudged unceremoniously past Gem. "Hurry, Gem. Which way?" he whispered, his voice more frantic than Gem recalled hearing before.

She knew why, of course. His adopted daughter, Taylor was here, along with his wife. His son was back with the others risking his life. The lives of everyone he loved were on the line.

Gem looked at the list and started at the end, reversing the turns. "Okay, make your right, then the second left."

The smell was horrific. The zombies within the maze reeked of death and deterioration as they pushed against Gem and the others, their flaking, mottled skin rubbing against them.

"Gem," said Hemp, his voice rising. "We hit a wall here."

"Shit," said Gem, looking at her list. She took a quick glance back up. Something wasn't right.

"Fuck!" she said, realization striking her smack in the face. "Hemp, they've reconfigured the walls!"

"Turn around and find another path then," he said, stopping. "We'll have to do this the old fashioned way."

Gem turned around and quickly pushed Trina and Taylor's shoulders, spinning them. "Go, go!"

They moved, and Gem and Hemp once again took the lead. It did not matter anyway. Their inability to see beyond the rotting bodies meant they were walking blind. They had no idea what lay ahead and no way to tell if the path they were taking was one they had taken before.

A hand brushed Gem's neck, and she swiped at it, feeling the scaly flesh against her skin, making her want to vomit and kill it at the same time.

They took turn after turn, each time running into dead ends.

"Jesus Christ," said Dave. "Guys, this is taking too long. It looks like the sun is ready to come up. We need to get through this damned thing!"

Gem looked, and sure enough, the dawn was ready to break.

"Shit, I forgot!" shouted Charlie, whipping out the bottle of urushiol. She raised the sprayer and pumped it into the air over their heads.

"Good, Charlie!" shouted Gem. The effect was instantaneous. The bodies around them began popping and hissing, the creatures falling away. As they fell and bubbled into oozing piles of muck, Trina called, "Watch your feet, everyone! Stay away from their teeth!"

Even as the oily liquid hit their emaciated bodies, they gnashed their teeth at what seemed to be double and triple speed, still following the commands of the nearby Mothers to attack us even as they melted and died. The little clump of shriveled brain within their skulls would have to dissolve before the Mothers' control would wane.

"The other ones are entering now!" shouted Hemp. "Gem, keep moving, and everyone else, keep up with us!"

Gem glanced over her shoulder. The horde had indeed arrived, and now they pushed into the maze. Gem realized they had not gotten far enough inside. If they got lucky, two turns and they would reach them.

The bodies of the dozens of dead zombies had congealed at their feet, and now it was like walking through two feet of thick honey. Gem made a turn and advanced through the maze, pulling her feet out of the mess with great effort. She turned again, and found herself at another open path.

"Charlie, I found a way through!" she called. "Give me the bottle!" she shouted, her hand in the air.

"Here, Gem!" shouted Charlie, tossing the bottle over the crowd. Gem watched it sail just over the reaching arms of the still-standing rotters and snatched it from the air. In her hand, she adjusted her grip on the bottle and pumped the liquid out into a fine mist in front of her.

Three bodies directly ahead of her blistered, the skin pulling back from their eyes and teeth, creating ghoulish skulls atop dripping bodies. Ultimately, they fell away from Gem, adding to the now flowing goo at their feet.

Gem felt something close on her foot and looked down to see what appeared to be nothing more than a skull biting down on her leather boot. She kicked at it, then raised her foot, bringing it down hard atop the thing, shattering it into fragments that immediately disappeared into the slime coating the asphalt street beneath her.

As she pulled her foot from the muck and looked up, a Red-Eye stood in front of Gem, three feet away. She stood stock still, her blazing, crimson eyes locked to Gem's.

Red-Eyes. Mothers. Whatever they were, they were what gave the Hungerer masses focus beyond their ravenous craving for human flesh. They told them that even if you could not smell them, all living humans were food.

This one stared at Gem with great intensity.

She killed my son, thought Gem.

Gem wanted to reach for her EB-tipped knife and jam it straight through the monster's eye, but when she tried, she realized she could not move. Her limbs were paralyzed.

The Mother's eyes remained locked on Gem's as she closed the gap between them, pulling her feet from the goop with relative ease and a deep, sucking sound. The advanced creature stretched its jaws open wide, its teeth not brown but ivory, its skin not flaking away, but vein-riddled and smooth.

Move! She thought, but the word had no effect on her frozen muscles.

"Gem, duck!" shouted Dave behind her, but she found she could not. She could not answer Dave, either.

The Mother's arms reached out and took her shoulders, jerking her forward. Gem could only watch as the urushiol bottle fell from her hand and the Mother moved in, her mouth stretched open wide.

*****

Isis, Max, Punch, Flex and Nelson stared, analyzing the space in silence.

Inside were dozens of sets of remains, and with all of the Mothers and Hungerers gone, the bloodstained concrete became more obvious at a casual glance, even in the early morning gloom.

"Where the hell did they go?" asked Flex.

"I think maybe Maestro had a plan we were unaware of," said Punch.

"Think he still thinks we're in jail?" asked Nelson.

"We need to get back to the basketball court," said Isis. "Now."

They ran.

*****

The basketball court was empty. The cots were there, but the gate was open and all of the Hybrids were gone.

"Think there's any sense in going to Living Joy church?" asked Max.

"He's gone," said Isis. "I don't know how he found out. Perhaps we were deceived after all."

"No, Isis," said Max. "I looked into Beauty's eyes. She was telling the truth. I could see a longing there."

"He's sure as hell taken them all somewhere," said Flex.

"Do you feel them?" asked Max. "I feel something. There are Mothers and Hungerers here still."

"I feel it, too," Isis said. "Powerful. They're nearby."

"Not all of them," said Max. "Not near."

"Then we need to get to the maze," said Nelson.

"Let's go," said Flex.

Punch said, "Wait, guys. Let's check on the guards. We don't know if they had the key, so they might be there. If we can get some information out of 'em it could really help us track this bastard down."

Isis recalled that Punch was always the military man. He knew interrogation and he knew strategy.

"He's right," she said. "Let's hurry."

They ran around the corner of the block building and ran for the open door. Inside the front lobby area nothing looked different. Once they opened the door to the cellblock, that changed.

Flex drew back and gagged. "Oh, God," he mumbled.

Isis stared. The cell doors were indeed open. The two guards were in pieces. Not by the Hungerers and not by the Mothers.

"This was Maestro," said Isis. "It's his punishment for them letting us get the better of them."

The heads were jammed into the stainless steel toilet. The torsos were in the area just outside the cells, and the arms and legs were everywhere. All of the fingers had been severed from the hands, and it appeared that all twenty of them lay scattered throughout the cellblock.

"Dude, it's like a zombie all-you-can-eat buffet in here," said Nelson. "I gotta get outta here, like yesterday."

They left the building and ran toward the maze. Punch led the charge with Nelson behind him, Isis and Max followed them, and with Flex's injured ankle, he hopped along behind them, barely keeping up. Isis kept her eyes and ears peeled as they worked their way toward the maze.

They rounded the corner on West Railroad Street and Main Street came into view.

"Holy shit," said Punch, stopping sharply and holding up his right fist. "Guys, wait."

"That is not all of them," said Isis.

"Not near," said Max.

"I sense Maga are among them," said Isis. "And Mothers."

"I can't see into the maze," said Flex. "Anyone?"

"Nah, bro," said Nelson. "Just a couple yards in. Maybe they're through already." Nelson continued staring at the maze for a moment. "Wow," he said.

"What?" asked Flex, looking at Nelson, then back to the massive horde.

"That maze is different, dudes," he said. "You're supposed to go in and make the first left, but I can see from here that leads to a dead end."

"What does that mean?" asked Flex.

"It means," said Isis, "that Maestro always had a contingency plan in place. I don't know whether he was informed by Alyssa, Megan and Beauty or not, but he's reconfigured the maze and released these Mothers and Hungerers to stop us from leaving the city."

"Why would he do that?" asked Nelson.

"Because he wants to get to Kingman before us," said Isis. "Charlie unintentionally revealed the name of our city to them."

"Fuck!" shouted Flex. "If everyone is caught in that maze, we need to go now!"

348

"First let Max and I go," said Isis. "Max, come on. We need to hurry."

She and Max ran toward the crowd, splitting up and flanking them on both sides. Isis saw two women standing outside the maze against the fence. They were not shuffling or staggering; they simply stood there. Isis grabbed her radio, turned it on and made sure it was on channel 15.

"Max, there are two Hybrids at the fence," she whispered. "They may be commanding those inside the maze."

She had the volume low as Max's voice responded. "Yeah, Isis, there are two more over here. It's the same thing. They're just standing there, staring into the maze."

"Make sure it's not Megan, Alyssa or Beauty and kill them, Max," she said.

"Isis," he said. "I've never killed … anything alive before. They're innocent."

"They're definitely not innocent, Max," said Isis. "Whether they would've been if they'd never met Maestro is one thing, but we have to go by what we know, and we know they do his bidding."

"But Isis," said Max.

"Do it, Max," she radioed. "Save your family."

Isis tucked the radio away and started a slow jog. She slipped into the crowd of rotters to the left of the hybrid and drew even with her. She remained concealed behind a dozen rotters, working her way to within three feet of the Hybrid.

A shriek came from the other side of the crowd, somewhere out of Isis' view. She felt the scream in her mind, and tears immediately came to her eyes. Her breath caught in her throat and her heart rate increased to quadruple what it had been moments earlier.

Max had killed one of the Hybrids. The severe pain Isis felt wasn't drawn out like her earlier pain; it was stabbing, emotionally intense, then gone.

Had it been Max killing the Hybrid, or the Hybrid turning the tables on him?

Isis burst from the crowd and hooked her left arm around the hybrid's neck, dragging her to the pavement.

Suddenly Nelson appeared, and as Isis dragged the Maga to the ground, he jumped on top of the Hybrid, his knee on her neck, his knife pressed against her forehead.

Isis got on her knees beside Nelson. A moment later the Maga blinked twice and her red eyes stared up at Isis and Nelson. "Why?" she asked. "You are as Alpha and Omega."

"You mean Alyssa and Megan," said Isis. "And you are as the Magas," said Isis.

"I am Maga 23, and you must die," said the Maga. "You are not one of us."

"What are your orders?" asked Isis.

"I cannot reveal them," she said.

"I'll kill you," said Isis, pulling the Walther from her pocket and pressing it against the young woman's forehead.

"*Mothers,*" said Maga 23. "*Come.*"

"I'm so sorry," said Isis. "In Kingman, you could've been called Maggie if you wished." She pulled the trigger and the Walther's suppressed discharge was subdued in comparison to the destruction the bullet did to the young woman's face. The blood sprayed out on the asphalt and the feet of the rotters surrounding them.

The shriek came again, this time accompanied by the worst pain that Isis had ever experienced. She looked up to see two Mothers advancing on her, now five feet away. Nelson jumped up and charged them, reaching into his pocket at the same time.

350

"Move, Nelson!" shouted Isis, but he did not. She held the Walther out in front of her so that if Nelson were to drop down, she would have a clean shot at the Mother's head.

His arm came back, and the morning sun, now well above the horizon, glinted off the flying brass star, allowing Isis to follow its flight until it embedded deep in between the eyes of the first Mother.

"Got it!" he shouted.

The pregnant female toppled forward, its eye shine fading to black as she dropped.

Nelson saw the other advancing Mother and grabbed a staggering rotter by the shoulders, practically tossing his emaciated body at her.

It slowed, but did not deter the Mother. She caught the long-dead man, lifted his wasted body into the air and heaved the Hungerer into the middle of the crowd. Her eyes never left Isis, glowing as deep and vivid a red as Isis had ever seen.

Out of the blue, something struck the Mother.

It was an arrow. It entered above her right ear, and came out in the same spot above her left ear.

She stopped, teetered from side-to-side for a full two seconds before several shambling Hungerers knocked her to the ground.

Nelson reached the other hybrid and used his Subdudo, taking her easily down. At that moment, another shriek came in Isis' mind, and this time she found herself breaking down into sobs, even as she approached the last hybrid.

She was the last, for Max had just killed another. It was horrible. The pain lingered, blurring her vision and dashing her concentration for a few brief, critical moments.

351

Isis prayed they would not have to kill the other Magas. The emotional damage it might do to her and Max might never be repaired.

She knelt down before the Maga. It was Beauty.

"Beauty!" said Isis. She held her down on the ground for the moment. "Beauty, where are Megan and Alyssa?"

"They have not been Megan and Alyssa since Maestro came to them again," said Beauty. "At that moment they again became Alpha and Omega."

"Where are they," asked Isis, fearing the answer.

"Megan is in the cage car," she said. "She is going to Kingman."

Isis hesitated at the omission of Alyssa, but before she could ask about it, a distant engine roared to life. Flex ran up, breathing hard. "Everyone get back, now! Punch found a back hoe!"

The diesel engine revved in the early morning, and Isis heard Punch grinding the gears and he worked the machine.

"Beauty, are you still with us?" asked Isis, holding the pistol to her head.

"I am," she said. "I was commanding nothing here," she said. "I was only waiting for you as I promised."

"Okay, get up."

"What was that horror in my heart and mind?" she asked, as Isis pulled her from the street.

"It was your sisters – no, it was *our* sisters dying," said Isis. "I'm sorry."

They moved aside as Punch accelerated, the scoop four feet off the ground.

He drove straight toward the fence to the west of the maze at full speed.

*****

352

Maestro had taken a different route on his original run to Hoisington, all those years ago. Now he had his sights set on Kingman, Kansas. It was a town he had missed on his trek north.

"How far are we from Kingman?" he asked. "Damned roads are getting worse by the month."

The driver had gotten little sleep the previous night. Maestro had been pacing all night, issuing commands. This ramped up when he discovered the contents of his jail had gone from his prisoners to his two guards.

There was only one way that could have happened; they had more friends in the city, as he had assumed from the start.

"Got about thirty miles to go," said Jerry Lee. The cage trailers were narrow and tall, so had to be pulled with care. Unlike a train, there were no tracks to keep everything in line. A deep pothole – of which there were many these days – could send one trailer toppling onto its side, taking the others with it. With all the grass and weeds growing up through the streets, Maestro knew he would need his patience for his driver had to be watchful.

"At this pace it'll take us two more hours," said Jerry Lee. He scratched his rough beard and blinked his eyes. "I miss coffee."

"From what they told Omega, they've got quite a setup down there," said Maestro. "Once we're through with them, I'm sure you can get whatever you want."

The driver nodded, but did not answer. Maestro did not expect it. He and all of Maestro's men knew he was a man who conversed on his own terms and who did not appreciate idle chatter.

"Speed it up."

"Maestro, the –"

"Speed it up!" he shouted. "There was something about those folks. I'd have rather killed them before we started out, but they're probably dead by now anyway."

"I don't know, boss," said Jerry Lee. "They survived this long."

Maestro punched Jerry Lee hard in the side of his face, his head slamming against the side window as Maestro grabbed the steering wheel to steady the tractor-trailer rig.

"Control this fucking vehicle!" shouted Maestro, and Jerry Lee, his face red and already swelling, gripped the steering wheel hard as he worked his jaw back and forth with tears running from his eyes.

Maestro saw a sign ahead. It said, Kingman – 25.

*****

As Gem felt her body jerked forward, unable to defend herself, she thought, *Is it something she's doing to me, or have I frozen up? Have I given up?*

She did not know the answer. A moment later, it didn't matter.

"Gem!" shouted Dave.

His arm arced down and his knife blade rammed into the Mother's head all the way to the hilt.

The moment the steel penetrated the Mother's brain, Gem collapsed, her muscles suddenly free, and her mind not yet ready to take control of them again.

As she stared upward, she saw Dave pull his blade forward, the sharp edge cutting through skin and skull, cutting clean down to the Mother's eye socket. He then pushed the blade backward, sending the now dying zombie falling away from them.

As she crumpled backward, Dave held onto his blade, withdrawing it.

He reached for Gem and pulled her from the sticky pool of biological juices, holding her up by the shoulders.

As she stared at him, still dazed, Dave said, "Hold on, Gem! Watch out!"

To their right, the engine noises peaked as the fence beside them bent sharply outward, pulling the maze hard to their left, all of the steel uprights and barriers moving with it.

As Gem fell again, she saw everyone within the maze had been knocked to the ground as well. Clinging to Dave, they both managed to scramble back to their feet.

"Everybody, stay clear of the uprights!" shouted someone. Gem realized it was Punch's voice, and she turned to see him driving a backhoe of some kind toward the maze.

He lowered the bucket and tried to wedge it beneath the steel beam at the base of the barriers, but the machine revved, the bucket lifted, and skipped out, jerking away. The gap between the lower beam and the concrete to which it was bolted was too narrow for the thick scoop to wedge beneath it.

Gem realized she and her friends could not move forward, nor could they move back. More zombies poured in, and ahead of them were piles of bodies, writhing and scratching.

Suddenly, without warning, there was a smell in the air. It was hot, industrial and familiar, but Gem could not place it.

"Gem!" said Dave. "Move your feet!"

Gem looked down and saw why. The steel base of the fence now glowed red hot, and as she watched in amazement, the entire maze lifted skyward.

"What the hell is happening!" shouted Taylor, clutching at Charlie, who also stared at the eerily floating maze, the bottom crossbeam now so hot that molten steel dripped between them, hissing as it met the cooler slime.

In a flash, the entire, hovering maze shot to the north. Gem could not help but watch it fly away, as if it were the house in The Wizard of Oz, swept up by a tornado and carried to the wind.

Only it was windless, and the maze was not aerodynamic.

The mass of steel walls slammed hard into the old auto parts store roof as welds snapped, creating dozens of twisted, steel pieces. Soon, the still red hot steel caught the structure on fire.

Gem turned back.

"Gem, Dave!" shouted Hemp. "Come on, now!"

Gem looked, and saw everyone else but she and Dave stood in the street, their weapons at ready, but out of immediate danger as no Mothers were closing in on them.

"C'mon, Gem," said Dave, pulling her by the arm. She staggered along behind him, realizing she was walking atop melting meat and bone with bare feet. Her canvas shoes had become the victims of the gelatinous pool that had formed beneath them, sucked off during desperate steps taken of which she had no memory.

Gem reached the others and fell into Trina's open arms. "It's okay, mom," she whispered.

Gem turned. "Flex," she said, her heart ramping up as the thought hit her. "Where's Flex!"

"He's right there, mom," said Trina, pointing.

Then she saw him. He was behind several of the rotters, standing with a girl in an orange jumpsuit. Max and Isis were with him, and the four of them pushed through the dozens and dozens of remaining rotters as they worked their way through the sticky gunk, now spreading out and becoming easier to walk through by the second. The walls of the maze had allowed it to build up quickly.

Nelson emerged from behind them, and with his slight build and lanky body, he leapt like a gazelle over the cesspool of melted bodies, reaching them before the others.

He panted as he said, "Dudes, I could use a huge bowl right now!"

Gem looked at him and a smile found her lips. Slime coated his hair and his gaunt face held what some might consider a blank expression. Gem knew better.

Her eyes moving between him and her husband, she said, "Nel, I'm glad you're okay."

"You too, Gem. You see what that Maga did with Max and Isis?"

"That was them?"

Nelson didn't have time to answer. Flex reached Gem and pulled her into his arms, holding her to him.

"Babe, are you alright?" he asked.

She shook her head. Words would not come. Flex put his hand on the back of her head and held her to his chest.

As she allowed Flex to hold her, she heard Hemp say, "Max, Isis. Was that you? With the maze?"

"Let's go," said Taylor. "And please allow me to say thank you again for WAT-5, dad."

Everyone stared at the receding horde for a few seconds. They stood just thirty feet south of the space the maze once occupied, smack in the middle of Highway 281. They all seemed to stare toward Hoisington, the zombies mulling aimlessly about, spreading out. Some of them wandered north. The burning buildings around them had begun to blaze with intensity now, shooting wild flames high overhead.

"Start walking, everyone," said Hemp, his arm around Charlie. She had her crossbow on her back and her pistol swung freely by her side.

The crowd began trudging slowly down the middle of the highway. Gem's feet were tender, having been softened by comfortable shoes for so long.

"I might have you carry me in a bit," she said to Flex.

"Fuck that," he said. "You can ride in Punch's Tonka Truck."

She was confused for a moment, but realized the droning sound that she had vaguely associated with the general environment was, indeed, a diesel engine running.

The backhoe was twenty feet behind them, and Punch sat atop it, eyeing the road ahead of them from his vantage point.

"Awesome," she said.

Flex waved Punch down and he accelerated, pulling up beside them.

"Tank's full on this thing," said Punch. "Guess Maestro liked building shit."

"Or tearing shit up," said Flex. "Buddy, my girl needs a ride," he said. "Maybe a couple of these others, too."

Punch gave her a hand, and she hopped up, sitting sideways on the seat as she stared back at the devastation in Hoisington, Kansas.

He ground it into gear and the backhoe jerked forward. The auto parts store had ignited several stacks of tires between that building and a shop whose sign identified it as Willie's Tire Service. Gem could see a third building now catching.

The smell of pungent rubber filled the air, blending with the rotten smell of decay to create something Gem had never experienced before, and did not want to partake in for long.

"Why aren't they coming after us?" asked Taylor. "Even on WAT-5, they follow moving stuff."

"Ask Beauty," said Max. "Pretty sure she's got something to do with it."

"Can you turn this thing off a sec?" asked Gem. "I need to hear this."

"Sure," said Punch. He cut the engine. Silence engulfed them.

The former Maga 7 spoke, known to Gem and the others as Beauty: "They have been so long conditioned to following the commands of the Mothers that they no longer have the instincts to feed on their own."

Hemp released Charlie's hand and walked toward Beauty. He stopped and touched her arm. "You are Beauty?"

"I am," she said, her intense, green eyes meeting his directly.

"You say they've been conditioned?"

"Yes," she said.

"By the Mothers."

"The Magas have commanded the Mothers and they have commanded the Hungerers," said Beauty. "Without the guidance of the Mothers, they walk without purpose."

"In the pen," said Hemp, "had we not been on WAT-5, would they have attacked?"

"In such close proximity, I would imagine their hunger would overtake them in time," said Beauty.

"But in the open," said Hemp. "Without humans so near them. Will they eventually follow their instincts to feed again?" asked Hemp.

"Yes," she said. "They are starved, having fed not by their will, but only at the Mothers', and only at our command."

"How soon?" asked Hemp. "How long before their hunger drives them toward food again?"

"Hours," she said. "Not long."

"How can she know that?" asked Punch.

Beauty looked at Punch. "It is among the things I have always known."

"Can you call them?" asked Hemp. "The Hungerers?"

"Not as the Mothers can," she said. "Mine is a manipulation of matter. Like your Isis and Max, I can manipulate them only as we manipulated the maze. Forcing matter to move with great mental concentration, but only when they are visible to us."

"So you need line-of-sight," said Hemp.

"Exactly," said Beauty.

"Yeah, dude, that was amazing!" said Nelson. "I saw you guys holding hands, but I had no freakin' idea the whole maze was gonna fly into the air!"

Gem smiled. Nelson had found his pipe. He looked happy. Tired and happy.

"So when you manipulate the Hungerers, it's like moving an inanimate object," said Hemp. "And the Mothers? How is that different?"

"The Mothers is a connection with the encephalon."

"With the brain?" asked Hemp.

"Of course," said Beauty. "We can draw them to us or repel them, but we cannot send them in a particular direction."

"But you can command them to send the Hungerers in a ... particular direction?"

"Yes," she said. "I believe I understand what you are asking, and yes. I believe that is true."

"Are there more Mothers?" he asked.

"They number eighty-four."

"I was going to ask if that includes the eight or so we killed here, but with those kinds of numbers, I guess it doesn't matter much," said Gem.

"They are all with Maestro," said Beauty. "With them are 1,762 Hungerers and thirty-seven Maga."

"The fuck you say?" said Flex.

"What happened to Alpha and Omega?" asked Charlie, moving beside Hemp. "Are they with him?"

"Alyssa," Beauty said, with true reverence in her voice. "*Not* Alpha. Alpha is not a name. It is not a person. Alyssa is the name given her by Isis."

At that moment, a light breeze touched Gem's skin. The crackling sound of the fire was carried north, away from them, and the silence that ensued allowed her to hear every word Beauty said.

The young Maga turned her eyes toward the sky, the stars shining brightly in a world no longer generating pollution, and with no bright, city lights to diminish their brilliance.

"Alyssa was my mother, and she is dead," whispered Beauty. "She was murdered by Maestro, as her own mother, who was my grandmother, was murdered so long ago. He took her life while he tortured her to learn of your city, Kingman. Our other matriarch, once Omega, now Megan, remains alive."

"Why didn't she turn you in?" asked Flex. "and Megan?"

"Because the words of freedom shared with us could be understood, even by those in captivity," said Beauty. "She wanted that for me. For all of us."

Charlie threw her arms around Beauty and held her. The girl's arms hung limply at her side, but she did not pull away.

361

"Your mother was brave," said Charlie. "This Maestro is a sadistic killer. We'll make sure you know freedom."

Beauty nodded. "Alyssa fought the pain as long as she could before telling him."

Hemp nodded. "We're so sorry, Beauty. I cannot express how much. Now please, tell us. When did they leave here?"

"Eighty-seven minutes ago," she said.

"Punch, start this thing up and move," said Gem. "Everyone, climb in the bucket, get the hell up here, ride a fender. We need to get our asses to the vehicles and we need to do it now."

Everyone scrambled to find a seat. Punch jumped down to the floor and found something. "Flex, you're back there," he said. "Is there a tray of tools or something back there?"

"Yeah, right behind your seat. Whatcha lookin' for?"

"Big screwdriver. Flat or Phillips, doesn't matter."

"Flat then," said Flex, handing it to him.

Punch jammed it beneath the accelerator pedal and pried, his face wrinkled up. Something snapped, and he reached down, picked a piece of metal up, and tossed it into the street.

"Governor," he said. "We don't need no stinking governor."

He eased into it, but now the machine really moved. They burned up the almost ten miles in less than twenty-six minutes.

*****

362

CHAPTER EIGHTEEN

The train of vehicles consisted of two forty-foot trailers, each towing a thirty-foot cage car – the original circus cars that Maestro had acquired in Texas, and the lead vehicle, in which Maestro rode. Behind them, they towed the largest, most heavily stocked trailer.

Maestro closed his eyes and put another garlic tablet in his mouth, his face distorted as he chewed it up and swallowed. He followed it with a quick swig of water from his canteen.

He was not sure whether the intruders had lied about garlic providing protection, but there was no harm in taking the supplement. It may not help, but it would not hurt him, either.

Maestro took a deep breath and unbuttoned his shirt, slipping it off his shoulders. It was a part of his ritual.

His arms lifted into the air, his hands directing an unseen orchestra, he smiled.

He reached up and flipped the sun visor down, pleased that there was a mirror there. He moved it so that he could see his face and chest, where he saw the skeletal face of his symphony conductor, head raised, arms guiding each rise and fall of a requiem of death that he, and only he, would know.

He had written the aria in his mind; it was filled with great crescendos and soft, brooding cellos, and there was not a doubt in his mind that he would one day force someone to learn it note for note and play it for him, flawlessly.

"Everyone will hear it soon enough," he said aloud.

The driver drove on in silence.

"Stop the truck," he said, turning off the music in his mind and lowering his arms. He slipped back into the shirt and reluctantly buttoned it.

Jerry Lee put his foot on the brake and Maestro closed his eyes again. He could already smell the coppery scent of blood in the air; hear the screams of the dying citizens of Kingman, Kansas; the slurps of the Hungerers feeding.

The Mothers would eat the babies. He loved seeing that. He would have the Magas command it.

"Feed the Magas," said Maestro. "They're going to need strength. There are many people in Kingman, or so I'm led to believe."

"We really do need radios," said Jerry Lee, opening his door. "We wouldn't even have to get out of the truck."

"I've told you a thousand times," said Maestro. "I don't trust you to keep quiet. I don't like people to expect our arrival."

Jerry Lee nodded, his gaunt face stubbled and scarred. The scars were reminders from Maestro that his orders were not to be questioned.

His Magas were the true threat, but if Maestro were not allowed to wield his personal, physical violence on someone with regularity, he would go mad.

"Hurry!" said Maestro.

The other drivers exited their vehicles, as was the standing command when the vehicle containing Maestro came to a stop. Behind them all was an old ice cream truck. Maestro had converted it for his purposes several years earlier. The old speaker was still mounted to the roof, and the faded pictures of Bomb Pops, Fudgsicles and Push-Ups remained plastered on the sides of the heavily rusted truck.

The freezers had been turned down, and now only provided refrigeration for the meat he fed the Magas when traveling. On the west side of Hoisington was a well-fed herd of cattle. Raw meat for the Mothers and Hungerers when necessary; cooked for Maestro's people.

*****

When the vehicles stopped, Megan knew what to expect. They were going to destroy a town, and the Magas had not eaten for days.

Megan pushed her way to the front of the car. Her hands shook from watching Maestro torture Alyssa, but still, she had to try to do what was right and to gain the freedom about which she had learned from the ones called Isis and Max.

Megan reached the front, standing ahead of the others, just behind the door. They did not know of this freedom, nor would they likely believe it existed. She would be the one to serve the Magas today.

Maestro never allowed his men to serve them; they were women, after all. According to Maestro, women evolved on the planet only to serve men, and it would never

Eric A. Shelman

be otherwise. Anything else was unnatural and unacceptable.

The door opened and two of Maestro's men stepped aside. "C'mon," said the one called Ray. "Chow."

Megan eyed him as she stepped down. There were murmurs behind her, and she again wondered why none of them had reported her to Maestro. One of them – at least one – had reported Alyssa. The others had protected them, as sisters should.

Megan wondered if the reason was not so much a feeling of obligation, but rather one of self-preservation. When Maestro felt one of them had deceived him, he often took several of them out to torture, just to be sure the deceit was not widespread.

Megan jumped down from the car and felt the baggie tucked into her waistband. She had been working the wafers called WAT-5, crumpling the bag and disintegrating the wafers within into a near powder. Now, as she felt the baggie, it felt like the consistency of the sand she found in the dry fields of Hoisington.

They transported the meat for her and her sisters in large, stainless steel bowls within the chest freezers of the ice cream truck. She climbed inside and slid the top of the chest open. The guards waited outside as usual.

Her eyes darting back and forth between them and the food before her, she carefully unzipped the front of her jumpsuit, turning her body away from the rear door so nobody could observe her should they turn around. She slipped her hand in and withdrew the baggie.

The guard did not rush her. Megan knew, from watching the men in the past, and from pure instinct, that they did not rush headlong into each new slaughter. They took their time at every juncture; but only enough time that Maestro did not grow angry.

366

That was a death sentence. Maestro could replace any of the men at any time with new men from the towns they destroyed. When it was cooperate or be eaten, the choice was obvious for a clear-headed person, Megan knew.

She opened the bag and sprinkled the fine dust over the entire top of the bowl, like fine pepper. She pushed that bowl aside and slid another, equally filled bowl in front of her, repeating the process with the baggie. One more, but with this one, she took a piece of wax paper from a rack on the wall and placed it in the freezer beside the bowl.

Megan scooped her hand into the bowl of meat and moved a mound to the wax paper. She did it twice more until her portion was separate from the rest.

She then sprinkled the remaining WAT-5 into the third bowl.

"C'mon, unless you want Maestro to cut off your fuckin' head!" shouted Ray, clearly becoming nervous at the delay.

Megan kneaded two hands in two separate bowls, mixing the raw beef and fine dust together. She then plunged both hands deep into the bowls of raw meat, mixing it around thoroughly until no trace of the WAT-5 was visible.

When she finished, she placed her portion on the top of the last bowl. She would take it out before passing the bowl along.

She carried the first bowl out and hurried to the car. Megan passed it up to the Magas who waited, eager anticipation of their first meal in two days, peaked.

She almost ran back to the ice cream truck to get the second bowl. She got it to the trailer where her sisters waited, then hurried back to the ice cream truck to retrieve the last bowl. When she got it, and turned to run again, the guard, whom she knew as Henry, grabbed her arm.

367

Eric A. Shelman

"What the fuck is this?" he asked. "You take forever in the refrigerator truck and then you run?"

"Ray said to hurry up! He's afraid Maestro will be angry!"

He did not answer her, but did release her arm, giving her a little shove toward the trailer. Megan walked more slowly, but when she reached the truck, she nearly leapt up inside. The door slammed immediately.

She put the last bowl on the floor and took her separated meat. It was crowded in the car, but she found an empty corner, tucked her back into it, and watched the others consume the tainted meat.

Nothing was happening. She watched them, her heart pounding beneath her orange DOC jumpsuit.

One of the large, stainless bowls hit the floor as the car began to move again. Megan steadied herself and watched as several of the women became wobbly on their feet, staggering into one another and falling to the floor.

One by one they fell, piling one atop the other.

"What is happening," began Maga 35. She did not finish the sentence. She crumpled atop her sisters.

Megan focused on her meat. She ate every last piece, keeping her eyes down. When she finished, she looked back up.

They all slept. She was alone.

She relinquished her last bit of control over the Mothers; it was a conscious effort to do so.

When she heard the sound, seeming to come from all around her, she knew exactly what it was.

The Mothers were entering their destruction mode.

They were operating independently.

*****

368

The caravan had resumed its progress toward Kingman, Kansas.

"What is that sound?" asked Maestro, but he need not ask the question. He had ordered the Maga to command it of the Mothers many times. He used it when his prey hid inside buildings. He used it to gain access anywhere he wanted to go.

Because there was no place Maestro could not go if he wanted to. He would do whatever he wanted to do, just as he had since the day he escaped his mother's cage.

"Stop the goddamned truck!" he said. Kingman was around two miles away, and he did not need any disruptions to his plan now.

Jerry Lee put the engine in neutral and left the diesel motor running. Maestro jumped out and stopped.

Before his eyes, the walls of the trailers, just thin aluminum over lightweight uprights, pushed outward. The impression of hands from end to end were easily discernible, and as he watched, the intense, almost sonic vibration snapped every weld and spun every nut and bolt free that once held all of their equipment together.

On his initial run north, he had left the cage cars exposed; now, as he moved toward a town of unsuspecting victims, he thought better of it and ordered his men to put thick tarp flaps down over the cages.

By the time Maestro unveiled what waited within to greet them, it was too late for the idiot townsfolk to mount an offense or defense. If they did, it would be their last stand.

As Maestro and Jerry Lee stood by the 40' trailer staring at the line of stopped vehicles behind them, the floor suddenly dropped out of all the cage cars simultaneously, each one containing 150 or more of the creatures. With each one that disintegrated, a cloud of thick, red vapor blew forth like a horizontal mushroom cloud, spreading low over the asphalt before drifting slowly upward.

"Maestro, this shit is getting out of hand!" shouted Jerry Lee.

As if on cue, the 40' long trailer beside them began pulsating, too. Maestro's men had stuffed nearly seven hundred of his army into that trailer, his Magas instructing them to lie on their backs, to be stacked up like cordwood.

As Maestro looked, he saw that the only vehicle that was not vibrating into rubble around them was the smaller truck that held his Magas; his controlling force.

"Where are the Magas!" Maestro shouted. "Why aren't my Magas stopping this!"

Now the rotters crawled from beneath the collapsing trailers. The leaf springs and U-bolts popped apart and became projectiles, flipping in the air and into the crowd of zombies rising en masse from the ground, finding their footing.

Jerry Lee said, "I don't know, Maestro, but we need to get the hell out of here, either way! If your Magas *are* controlling this, they're rebelling, sir. If they're not, they've lost control of these things."

"Go to their truck and open it."

"I ... Maestro ... we need to go!"

"Do what I said!" shouted Maestro.

Jerry Lee didn't move.

Maestro ran back to the truck and pulled a machete from beneath the passenger seat, charging back toward Jerry Lee. He held it over his head, his eyes blazing at the man. "Open the goddamned truck! Now! Now!"

The driver eyed the Mothers and Hungerers moving toward them before looking again at the machete held high in Maestro's hand.

Jerry Lee bolted toward the tall weeds on the side of the road. Maestro knew if he made it there, he could disappear.

Jerry Lee reached the grass at full stride and his body suddenly stopped its forward momentum and bounced backward. The middle-aged man screamed as he struggled to keep his feet beneath him, staggering back five or six steps before losing his balance and falling onto his back, where he slid to a stop on the gravelly blacktop.

Maestro was confused at first, but then he saw the dozens of puncture marks on the man's front side.

Barbed wire. The entire I-281 from Hoisington to Kingman was bordered with it. The tall grass had obscured it.

Maestro smiled as he stared down at his former driver, blood spreading over his clothing and running down his cheeks. Puncture marks adorned his face, body, arms and legs, and now Maestro really could smell the metallic scent of blood, so familiar to him, and so arousing.

"Oh, no you don't," he said, looking up to see several Hungerers moving toward him, their snarls exciting and frightening him at the same time. He saw that his other men had tried to seek cover in the cabs, but turned to run instead, finding the deterioration had turned them into crumbling death traps. Oil, diesel and water poured from the engines as they, too, vibrated into nothingness.

They had nowhere to hide. Some of the horde went in their direction.

A male drew near, his mouth agape, his black tongue flitting from his mouth. Maestro thought briefly of the garlic, letting the thing get a bit closer. When it stumbled within two feet of him, he drew his arm back and threw it forward sideways, slicing the Hungerer's head from his body.

More were behind him. Maestro saw two Mothers advancing from twenty-five feet away.

He ran, cutting into the grass on the west side of the road, between the fence and the now crumbling shell of the trailer. He would be careful to stay far enough away that he did not make the same mistake Jerry Lee had.

He ran alongside the now flimsy trailer, leaping over the semi-rig parts that had fallen away from the once powerfully strong Peterbilt cab, skirting by the truck in which the Magas traveled.

Behind him, he heard a loud crash and turned to see the 40' trailer had now fallen to pieces, its undead passengers crawling out and filling the street.

He did not have the key to the Magas truck and did not know where Henry was to retrieve it.

Frantic, he rounded the corner of the now collapsing trailer, and saw his way out; the ice cream truck parked twenty feet behind the Maga vehicle.

Maestro ran. The engine of the small truck was already running when he yanked the door open. He jumped in and slid into the driver's seat, pulling the door closed behind him.

"Maestro," said a meek voice from the back.

Maestro jerked his head around to see one of his men cowering there, looking terrified. "Henry," he said.

"You better hurry, Maestro! They're right there!" He pointed frantically to the advancing horde visible through the windshield.

"Have you been hiding in here?" he asked.

"Yeah," said Henry. "I got around the backside of the trailer. They never even saw me."

Maestro leapt out of the chair, his fingers curling around the handle of the machete between the front seats, and with a powerful blow, brought it down atop Henry's head. It cracked the skull and sliced cleanly down to his shoulder blades.

He had always insisted his men keep his cutting tools razor sharp. If done correctly, they would slice tissue.

Henry had never seen it coming. His body convulsed three quick twitches before falling still.

Maestro slid the machete out and tossed it back between his seats. He cursed to himself as he scooted past the corpse, grabbed Henry's boots and dragged the coward to the rear of the truck. He glanced out the filthy back window to make sure it was safe before turning the handle, kicking the door open and heaving his former guard's body into the street.

His warm flesh and innards would keep some of them busy for a time.

As Maestro pulled the door closed, he saw a horde come into view, their eyes on the dead man's meaty corpse.

Maestro ran to the driver's seat, threw it into drive, and floored the accelerator, spinning the panel truck around. As he turned, his eyes fell on the Magas trailer, still intact. Maybe they were all dead somehow. There was no time to find out, as his former army was now pouring into the street, and he knew that without control, they would attack and tear him to pieces.

He threw the wheel sharply to the left and right to maneuver between two staggering rotters, solely to avoid damage to his only means of transportation. When he was past them, he floored it.

Maestro, for the first time in many years, did not have a plan. He did not like that. He needed to regain control of his army.

*****

Inside the car, Megan waited. She waited until the sounds were only those of the Mothers and Hungerers. She heard the sound of an engine recede in the distance.

She closed her eyes and reconnected with the Mothers. No. Just one Mother. It was all she needed.

Come to me, she pushed.

Megan waited. She pushed the command again.

A sound came to her from just outside the door.

Lift the padlock and drop it, she pushed.

A moment later a *thunk!* sounded. Megan moved to where she heard it.

Repeat it, she pushed.

Again, the sound came, and she re-adjusted. She held her finger on the inside wall at the exact point.

Megan closed her eyes and concentrated. Her first command was, *Go now. Leave this car.*

She did not know for certain the Mother would follow that command, but she then turned her thoughts to the padlock.

Squeezing her eyes closed, she again focused her mind. Thirty seconds. She smelled rubber burning.

Steel melting. Hardened steel, pungent as it softened and became molten metal.

Another sound came at her feet. The lock had melted away. All she had to do was open the trailer.

Instead, she remained there, standing amidst her sleeping sisters, silently waiting.

For what, she was not certain.

*****

The cars were where they had left them. Beauty rode in the Hummer with Max, Isis, Trina and Taylor. Trina insisted on driving.

Gem smiled, thinking back to when Trina was very young, sitting in Flex's lap, steering his truck. He had taught her how to drive and she was damned good.

Flex rode beside her in the passenger seat of the Crown Victoria while Gem pulled it between the idling GTO and Hummer.

"Should we stop and get the sole survivor of Great Bend before we leave town?" asked Nelson, his head hanging out the window of the GTO.

Dave shook his head, answering before Flex could. "No way. We don't know what we're up against when we catch Maestro, and Irene doesn't need to be there."

"Good point," said Flex. "She was all set with food and water for a while, right? We'll send a party to pick her up and search for other survivors once we get past this. Let's fly."

Gem drove, with Punch following close behind him in the grape GTO, and the Hummer bringing up the rear. Gem kept the speed up to sixty miles per hour, but occasionally had to slow as the zigzag between cars demanded it.

Everyone kept up. They drove an hour, and had gone fifty-three miles.

"If he's hauling trailers he can't be going very fast," said Charlie.

"I feel like a dog chasing a car," said Hemp. "What do we intend to do when we catch him?"

"We gotta play that by ear, buddy," said Flex. "I'm fuckin' wiped, though. That hour at the shack didn't do a damned thing for me."

"Good thing I'm driving," said Gem. "I'd need five Quaaludes to sleep."

"Nelson might be able to hook you up," said Charlie. Flex could hear the smile in her voice.

The banter stopped. Gem drove the car more slowly, but it was necessary. There had apparently been a slight traffic situation exiting Kingman back when the gas started bubbling out of the earth, and while they had been pulled off the road by various travelers' winches, it was still a zigzag proposition.

They passed a sign that said, "Kingman – 3 mi".

"Get on the radio," said Flex. "Charlie, see if you can get someone from town. We might be close enough."

Behind him, he heard a click. Charlie said, "Kingman, it's Charlie. Come in. Kingman, it's Charlie Chatsworth."

There could not have been a ten-second pause when a voice came on the line.

"Charlie! Oh, my God! It's Vikki Solms. Is everyone with you? Are you guys okay?"

"Yes, yes, Vikki," she said. It was one of the three sisters. "We're okay. But someone is headed there, and he is not fine. Definitely not fine."

"We're not fine, either," she said. "Two babies were born, and both of their moms had agreed to be exposed to the vapor of the Mothers."

"Yeah, and what?" asked Charlie.

"They're sirens," said Hemp, beside her.

Charlie absorbed what he said as Hemp touched Flex on the shoulder. "Bloody hell, Flex. We left them at the worst possible time."

"Yeah, well, we didn't have a choice," said Gem. "The foursome in that car behind us made sure of that."

"Doc Scofield said he thinks they're all coming from Wichita," said Vikki. "Red-Eyes and rotters. A few hundred of them over the last day and a half."

"Ready for around fifteen hundred more?"

"No!" cried Vikki. "We're really not! We can barely keep the pit clear as it is!"

"Fortify and get as many people with guns to the town entry as you can," said Flex. "The word we have is there are multiple, large semi rigs and trailers filled with them, along with some old, circus cage cars."

"Can't you stop them?" asked Vikki, desperation in her words. "I'll let them know, but I ... how close *are* they?"

"We're not sure, Vik, but likely any minute," said Flex. He turned to Hemp. "Hemp, anything you can offer?"

"Maybe," he said. "Give me the radio."

Flex passed it to him.

"Stop the car Gem!" shouted Charlie, and Gem looked back to the roadway ahead to see truck wheels, steel and other debris blocking the road. She slammed on the brakes and threw everyone forward as the Crown Vic slid to a stop.

The radio in Hemp's hand clicked again, but it was not Vikki.

"That debris is what is left of the cage cars and other tractor-trailers." It was Beauty's voice, transmitting from the Hummer.

"Were they filled with Mothers and Hungerers?" asked Hemp.

"Yes," Beauty said.

"Fucking zombies," said Gem.

"That is what you call them," Beauty said. "Isis, Max and I feel the horde again. They are nearing Kingman."

"Beauty?" asked Gem, her voice calm.

"Yes, Gem?" she replied.

"Where is Maestro?"

377

"I do not know this," she said. "But that," she said, pointing, "is the car in which Magas usually travel. The only one still intact."

Flex picked up the radio. "Everyone get out and have your weapons ready. We need to investigate what went on here."

*****

The group of eleven spread out as Isis, Max, Flex, Gem, Nelson, Trina, and Dave approached the car. Beauty came behind them.

Flex couldn't help the feeling that they had been playing catch-up since Maestro reconfigured the maze and left town. The people of Kingman could be mere minutes from doom.

"What now?" asked Flex.

Hemp, Charlie and the others walked around, picking through the debris inspecting the devastation.

Isis said, "This lock is melted away."

"What the hell?" asked Punch.

Isis lowered both of her arms, her hands splayed open at her sides. As she swept them backward together, her eyes glowed bright red and the door of the trailer swung outward.

"I'm not gonna lie," said Gem. "Isis, I've known you since you were a baby, and that just gave me chills."

"Megan," said Isis.

The Maga stood inside the trailer, directly in the center of the open door, facing them. Her expression, while subdued, was one of relief. Behind her appeared to be a stack of dead bodies, but there was no stench from within.

"Isis, Max and Beauty," said Megan. "I was able to feed them the WAT-5."

378

Flex glanced at Gem and waved Hemp over. Flex did not want to call out, as he saw the many Magas sleeping on the floor of the trailer behind Megan, and he did not want to awaken them until a plan was in place.

Hemp reached them and looked inside the trailer, holding a hand out to Megan. She looked at him, then at his hand for a long moment. Then she simply crouched down and made the small leap to the ground without acknowledging Hemp's offer to help.

He lowered his hand, looking somewhat perplexed. "How did you manage this?" Hemp asked. "We assumed that plan was dead once we were outsmarted by Maestro."

"Alyssa was able to transfer the wafers to me before she was interrogated," said Megan.

"Beauty told us she was killed," said Gem. "If that is true, we're so sorry, Megan. It wasn't our intention to come here and put your family and friends at risk."

She nodded. "Alyssa's ending did not come quickly, nor was it easy for her to endure," she said. "Maestro does not tolerate deceit." Megan looked at Beauty for a moment before turning back to Gem.

"I understand that what you have done is to release us," said Megan. "As sacrifice was made by your founding fathers, our own sacrifices must be made to gain our freedom."

Dave whistled. "It's that awkward moment when you realize women raised in cages understand our framers' intentions better than the American voters did."

"Why did you use the WAT-5 here?" asked Hemp.

"Because they stopped to feed us," said Megan. "You see, there is never a time when we do not assert our will – or Maestro's will – on the Mothers. It is what prevents them from entering their destructive mode. Should we cease our efforts, they recognize only that they are imprisoned and they must escape. Only our imposed will allows them to exhibit a sense of calm."

"So you're saying that anytime they're trapped, they start that crazy vibration thing?" asked Nelson.

"Yes," said Beauty. "Unless it is quelled by our commands. As for why Maestro ordered us to be fed when he did, it is because he realized we would need our maximum strength to control the Mothers for the Kingman slaughter. It is only because of you and learning of Kingman that he felt it was necessary to go immediately in case you had all escaped Hoisington. He feared you would alert Kingman to his existence.

"Hells yes we'd alert them," said Charlie, who had come over to listen. "And we'll fight him together. We're a tight group. A guy like Maestro can't be allowed to live as long as he threatens our existence."

"Maestro is dangerous, no matter whether he is alone or with others," said Megan. "He knows that even when the Mothers are merely idle, they fight us. They fight us for control over their abilities.

"I tainted the food, but if I had possessed the paper containing the words Isis had re-created, I might have been able to convince the other Magas that Maestro does not have any right to wield power over them or anyone else."

"She gave the words of freedom to me," said Beauty. She held up the paper and looked at each of them.

"I had only your wafers," said Megan. "I carried out the plan here. I felt it was better to release the Mothers."

"How long have the Magas been sleeping?" asked Gem, nodding her head toward the sleeping young women.

"I do not have a concept of time," she said. "Not long. When they went to sleep, they released the Mothers." She looked around the scene with the deteriorated big rigs and trailers. "They used their destructive powers."

"Yeah, Max was born in the middle of one of those sessions," said Nelson. "I'll never forget that."

"We're only three miles from Kingman according to that sign," said Flex. "Hemp, any ideas? Do we let them sleep or chance waking them and have them re-join Maestro, wherever he is?"

"Beauty, do you know where Maestro is? Is he with the Mothers and Hungerers?" asked Hemp.

"The Mothers would have killed him without the Magas controlling," said Megan. "Unless you find his body among this devastation, he is alive. I heard the sound of a smaller engine departing. I do not know if it was Maestro."

"Let's assume it was," said Punch, walking up. "Most of them are eaten, but I didn't find any remains with that fuckin' crazy conductor tattoo of his."

"It is better to assume he lives," said Megan.

"Agreed," said Isis.

"Do you believe we can convince them to help us?" asked Flex. "If we wake them up?"

"Megan, Beauty," said Max. "You guys know them best. What do you think?"

"Almost half of them are my offspring," said Megan. "One of them told Maestro of our consorting with you. I know not which one. She cannot be trusted."

"But dudes, maybe she can be convinced," said Nelson. "Maybe with the threat of great bodily harm."

"Nelson!" said Dave. "What the hell's gotten into you, buddy?"

Nelson threw Dave a sideways look. "Dude, I don't mean for real, 'cause I'm not like that. Just to throw a scare into them, bud."

"Who would be most believable?" asked Dave. "Not me. We need someone imposing."

381

"I say Punch," said Nelson. "He's got the whole U.S. Marine badass thing going."

"I'll do it," said Taylor, walking up with a partially burned sword of some kind. "Someone got the better of a Mother," she said. "Found this sticking out of one of their heads over there."

"That sword once belonged to Maestro," said Beauty, her eyes fixated on the rusted, bloody blade. "That weapon was often used at the killing tree at our birthplace, so is well known and greatly feared by the Magas. But you are not adequate, Taylor. Maestro, a man, has dominated us since the days of our births. The Magas will be more easily convinced they are in danger of losing their lives if a man wields that weapon."

"I got this," said Punch. He pulled off his shirt revealing a large tattoo of a coiled Cobra in mid-strike, emblazoned on his chest and abdomen. "Gimme that machete. It ain't no demonic symphony conductor, but it's got its own evil charm."

"We must make sure they are secured within the container before making our appeal. Do we have light?" asked Megan.

"Hold up," said Punch.

He ran to the GTO and opened the door. He leaned in, and when he came back out, he held his tactical shotgun.

Jogging back to the container, he said, "Get ready." He then ran alongside it, firing the shotgun at an upward angle, peppering its length with buckshot holes that punched through the upper side and the roof, sending shafts of silver sunlight poking through the darkness within.

"Some of them are stirring," said Flex. "Punch, best get inside. Bring the sword and that bear of a shotgun. Who else goes in?"

"Us," said Isis, indicating to Max, Megan and Beauty. "If we can't convince them, we'll have to kill them, as painful as that will be for us. Flex, bar the door once we go in, would you?"

Flex felt a shiver run down his spine. The girls, known as Magas, were all in their teens and pre-teens. While most of them looked like young women, they were essentially children.

But they were not Isis. They were not Max. They had not been raised with love, but hate. They had not been taught to protect, but to command death.

Isis was right. If they did not comply, they were as dangerous as the Mothers and Hungerers.

When the door swung closed, Flex picked up a downed fencepost and jammed it against the door.

He looked at Gem and the others. None of them said a word. "Even if it's not somethin' you normally put on your checklist," said Flex, "it might be a good time to pray."

*****

The sun was high in the sky. The Magas, along with Isis, Max and Punch, had been inside for nearly half an hour. God knew where the Mothers and Hungerers were at this point.

Nelson, Taylor and Trina used the Hummer's winch to pull the scattered debris out of the road enough to make a path. Once it was clear, the travel trailer holding the Magas could be dropped onto the hitch on the Hummer. Everything was still intact on that trailer, but the truck that had pulled it was deconstructed.

The roads had been cleared in twenty-five minutes, but somehow, convincing a group of frightened but powerful women to help them was taking longer. Flex checked his watch again. Forty minutes since they went inside. They needed to get to Kingman.

"Can't wait anymore," he said, shaking his head.

He kicked the post away and pounded on the door, but as he drew back his fist to hit it a third time, it pushed outward.

"I think we got through to 'em," said Punch, jumping out. Beauty, Isis and Max followed.

Punch pulled the door open wide, and the rest of the Magas walked to the edge to exit the trailer.

As Flex, Dave and Punch moved to take their hands and assist them, the Magas pulled away from them, fear on their faces.

"What's wrong?" asked Nelson.

"They are not accustomed to being helped by men," said Beauty. "In their lives, men have never once been subservient to women."

"It's not being subservient," said Dave. "It's called being a gentleman."

"Please," said Megan. "Allow them to exit on their own. They may eventually understand what your world is like, but this will only delay our mission."

Over the next fifteen minutes, they discussed what would take place. It was agreed that the Magas would call the Mothers back and order them to move the Hungerers as well, but if their proximity was too close to the newborn sirens in Kingman, it could be fruitless.

"Okay, Magas," said Isis. "Begin."

It was not something that could be seen; the call of the Magas to the Mothers was a matter of a mental decision. It was an opening of a mind gate.

It took no more than fifteen minutes before Maga 11 said, "They do not come, Isis."

"This is Déjà vu all over again," said Gem.

384

*****

CHAPTER NINETEEN

The many young and powerful women with glowing, red eyes, stared toward Kingman, silently, fruitlessly calling to the Mothers.

"I feel them," said Isis. She felt them as she had in Kingman. They were there, but they were not responding. Isis knew there was one thing she could not feel, but that she understood.

"We have called them for the better part of an hour now," she said. "They do not come."

The Magas appeared confused. There had not been a time when the Mothers did not respond to them.

Isis said, "Megan, Beauty. I have an important question."

Both raised their eyebrows in anticipation.

"Do your Maga babies call to the Mothers unintentionally? This is what our Maga infants do."

Megan shook her head. "That is what I did as an infant, and Alyssa as well. It has not been an issue with our offspring. It may be an evolutionary change, but while the ability to call them is powerfully strong in infancy – at least a hundredfold stronger than any adult, first or second generation – they must be told when to initiate their summons."

"Not so with ours," said Isis. "They call from birth until they learn how to cease their call."

Beauty's eyes grew concerned. "How many babies are in Kingman calling to them?"

"Two as far as we know," said Charlie. "Is that enough to outpull all of you?"

"Yes, Charlie," said Megan. "If there was ever a question, there is none now." She extended her arm, palm open and swiped it in the air toward the many Magas who stared at them in silence.

"Wow," said Nelson. "Two babies against like forty-something Magas. Will proximity help? If you're like right there near them?"

"Our control over the Mothers has never ceased before now," said Beauty. "We have never had to experiment with such things."

Flex jogged around to the front of the trailer, then ran back, winded. "Everything's intact on that hitch," she said, wheezing. "Let's get it hooked up and get going."

Charlie looked at Megan and Beauty and spoke in a conspiratorial tone. "Can we trust these women?" she asked.

Megan smiled. "As I said before, half are my daughters, though that word does not carry the same emotional connections as it clearly does with your people. We have been born to all of this, therefore, our understanding of love and this family bond you speak of is almost incomprehensible."

"You know the meaning of incomprehensible, but not love," said Charlie. "To me, that's incomprehensible."

*****

When the Mothers and Hungerers escaped, Maestro did not have the key for the trailer containing the Magas. They had stopped controlling them for a reason unknown to him, and even as he ran to escape, he knew that with one look, they would comply with his commands again and quell the uprising.

Jerry Lee, who he watched being eaten alive by the undead creatures had one of the keys, and another of his men – who had fallen quickly to the ravenous humanoids – had the other.

None of that was clear in Maestro's head at the time because he was running for his life.

As it was, he had nothing. The Mothers and Hungerers were out of his control without the Magas, and he had begun to follow them to where they were drawn.

At the obvious epiphany that the powerful creatures were out of his control without his Magas, he knew he had no choice but to go back and retrieve them. If they had to walk into Kingman, they would.

But when he arrived back there, they had been gone. The entire trailer.

Telepathic power entered his mind; Maestro had seen the Magas do many amazing things since the very first one had been born. *Perhaps they ... transported.*

After discovering them gone, he took dusty side roads. As clearer thoughts prevailed, he became certain who the real culprits were: The group that had invaded his city had taken them.

He would regain their allegiance. They loved him.

I can be sidetracked, he thought. *But I can never be stopped.*

He floored the old truck, eyeing the fast-dwindling fuel gauge, and turned left on NW 10th Avenue, just short of the Kingman city line. From there, he drove a short distance north and hung a right on West Kansas. In five minutes, he came to a high, steel fence rimmed with coiled razor wire.

The fence was not one he could gain a foothold to climb. He put the old ice cream truck in park and got out, leaving the engine running for the moment. If he had to take off, it would be unfortunate if it did not start.

Maestro walked along the fence line, pushing weeds back as he went, looking for a weak point or somewhere he could dig underneath.

Nothing.

"Damnit!" he shouted, staring at the town beyond. He could see people, so he ducked down a bit. They were far away and seemed focused to the south. It was where the Mothers and Hungerers would be entering, that he knew.

Maestro looked again at the truck. It was his only chance. He got back in the ice cream truck and put it in gear. He drove slowly forward until the front end touched the fence.

If Maestro assumed correctly, the fence was built to keep the walking dead out of the town of Kingman; it was not likely built to withstand a makeshift battering ram.

The truck bounced off it. He started a foot out. When he accelerated, he swore he felt it move.

"Yes!" he said, backing up two feet this time. He pulled forward again and this time he definitely felt the base give way a few inches. He threw the truck back in park and got out.

He knelt by the fence to see an approximate four-inch gap at the base. It had pushed inward for a width just about three-quarters as wide as the truck. Yes, the fence had been built strong and well, but this was just too easy.

He jumped back in and tried twice more, this time feeling it give almost a foot.

He grabbed the machete and jumped out of the truck. Maestro got down on his belly and crawled beneath the fence, utilizing what could not have been more than an eleven-inch space through which to crawl.

Once through, he reached back in, grabbed his machete and stood. There was a high ridge surrounding the town that appeared to be fabricated, and it was atop this raised area that the fence had been constructed. He glanced down its length and saw there was a trail there, probably for perimeter checks and fence maintenance.

Maestro guessed it would take him all the way to the south border of Kingman.

Maestro ran south. He would find a way to take this town.

*****

The caravan rolled on, with Flex and Gem taking over the piloting of the Hummer with the large trailer attached. Trina was not up for driving such a rig, and jumped at the chance to drive the Crown Vic instead.

"Do we have a plan when we get there?" asked Flex, looking at Gem.

"I guess that depends on this bunch of Hybrids," said Gem. "If they're really with us."

"I feel bad leaving them in the trailer," said Flex. "I mean, they agreed to help us and we haul 'em around like Maestro did."

"I think they get we didn't have a choice," said Gem. "Megan stayed with them, anyway."

390

"It's a good idea," said Flex. "Don't want to give them too much time alone to change their minds. Gem, get on the radio to Kingman. See what's going on."

Gem took the radio from the glove compartment. "What channel was Vikki on earlier?"

"Try 15."

Gem did. She did not have to wait, because Vikki was already talking to someone. Next, they heard Hemp's voice: "Tell them to add some fresh diesel from the tank, Vikki. They must get that generator started to pump the urushiol and estrogen blocker into the pit and activate the shafts!"

"Add more diesel," she said. "Okay, I'll tell them, but they're thinking it's electrical or something, and the damned thing just won't fucking start! Hemp, the pit has more zombies in it than I've ever seen in one place, and that includes in Concord. Hurry!"

Gem looked at Flex. "I didn't see a need to say anything," she said. "I think we heard all we need to know."

"Gimme that radio, would you?" asked Flex.

She did, and he pushed the button again. "Hemp?"

"Yes, Flex."

"I guess you guys have been talking. Tell me Isis has a plan. We're less than a mile from the entrance to the pit."

"She's worried about Maestro's whereabouts," said Hemp. "She says he's the only wild card."

"Does she think the Hybrids are solid?" asked Flex. "That they'll stick with us?"

"I'd be more comfortable with Maestro dead," came Isis' voice over the radio.

"She is right," said Beauty from the back seat. "As long as he lives, we're in danger."

391

Eric A. Shelman

"I get that," said Flex. "I mean, I get you feeling like that. He's just a man now, though. He's out there alone."

Punch sat beside him. "Yeah, even if he finds the horde, he can't control them at all with out those Magas, or Hybrids, or whatever we're callin' 'em these days."

"Wait!" said Gem.

Flex jumped in his seat and looked at her.

"Flex, turn here! Make a left!"

"Why, Gem?" he asked.

"Because, look!"

Flex had not been using high aim steering, or he would have seen the massive horde filling the roadway a half mile ahead, clogging up the road into Kingman. Like a colony of ants, they flowed like liquid toward the town, and they appeared to be only a quarter mile out now.

"Shit," said Punch. "At that pace, they'll be at the pit in less than half an hour."

"Which means … shit." Flex pushed the button again. "Vik, you listening?"

"Yes. Did you just say we haven't seen your zombies yet?"

"That's right," said Flex. "The ones you're seeing gotta be from Wichita and all the other points of the compass, because they ain't from Hoisington."

"What's your plan, Gem?" asked Flex.

Gem sat up, excited. "Okay. Take the 11 to the 20 and head east. We'll drop into town down Main Street. Push that button," she said.

Flex depressed the transmit button. "Vikki, it's Gem. Get some people at the Main Street gate on the north side of town. All the freaks are coming in along I-400 toward the pit."

392

"I know it's big, but how are we going to be able to fit them all in?" said Vikki. "I'm telling you, we might have to stack them!"

"Are there Mothers there?"

"Hell yes, there are Mothers here!" said Vikki. "Don't get me wrong, I love babies, but *these* damned babies are going to get us killed!"

"Just do it," said Gem.

"I have an idea," came Hemp's voice from the GTO.

Flex pushed the button again. "Give it up, Hemp."

"Vikki, can you hear me?"

"Yes, yes. Go on, Hemp," she said.

"Have some men go to our lumber storage and cart at least twenty-four of the twelve-foot by two-by-ten inch boards to our water trough," he said. "Make sure they are positioned at the point closest to the pit."

"You want twenty-four, 12-foot 2x10s at the trough as close to the pit as possible," she said. "I got that, right?"

"Yes, and there's more," said Hemp.

"Okay, but everyone in town's at the freaking pit! I don't think they know what to do, but they're there in case they think of something!"

"Tell them we ordered them to do this and tell them it might save their lives, Vikki," said Hemp. "Now, I also want someone to get to the urushiol plant and load up two drums of pure oil. Position them with the lumber, and remove the bung caps on both."

"Okay, Hemp. How long until you're here?" she asked.

"Fifteen minutes at the maximum," said Flex. "We're haulin' ass, darlin'."

"Hurry!" said Vikki.

"Quickly," said Hemp. "Vikki, get everyone working, and remember, try some fresh diesel in the generator and have someone check if the fuel injectors are clogged up. Most of this will be unnecessary if we have that damned generator working!"

*****

Maestro crouched as he ran, for here and there, people would appear, running in the streets below him in the town proper. The weeds on the hillside had grown tall, though, and provided him much needed cover.

In the distance, he saw something that at first confused him. It appeared to be a giant cage, but it also had a lid. It looked like an enormous, round aviary. He could see large crowds gathered on the outside, so could not see past the fence.

Maestro ran faster, his aching lungs protesting with every footfall and breath he took. He was now within an eighth of a mile of the structure and could make out some activity within what now appeared to be a caged pit of some kind.

As the crowd parted, he could see inside for brief spurts. Areas within the cage were crammed with people, pushing against one another, shifting and bumping. It was not full by any stretch of the imagination, but there had to have been six hundred or more men and women there, and a line continued to push in.

He ran further, and as the structure grew larger in his vision, he saw that they were not people. Their clothing was filthy and ragged. They were not alive. They were the Mothers and Hungerers, perhaps from Hoisington.

"Wait until I take control of the Magas," he said aloud.

Just then, something caught his eye; a man in the street just below him, working behind a cart. His back was to

Maestro, but as he shifted from foot to foot, bending down to scoop something out of a bag, Maestro could see he was loading up magazines with ammo. Maestro could make out several pistols on the top of the cart as the man stuffed magazine after magazine with live rounds.

Maestro looked to his left, finding a path down from the ridge. It was only fifteen feet or so to the bottom. He sidestepped down the hillside, working his way north a bit to stay out of open view of the man.

He reached the street and approached the corner of a building, where the man came into view again.

Maestro's machete in hand, he stepped into the street and took slow steps toward him, his machete raised.

"Hey, you wanna take these and I'll go get more magazines? They think they'll need them at the pit for some reason." He turned to stare into Maestro's face.

Maestro smiled at him and kicked him hard in the groin. The man buckled forward and when he dropped to the ground, Maestro brought the machete high over his head with both hands and brought the blade down hard, slicing cleanly through the man's neck with one deadly blow.

His head rolled away, coming to rest against the bump of the nose. The mouth worked two more pointless attempts at a breath before falling still. The arms and legs jerked and twitched, but Maestro grabbed the headless corpse by the shirt and pulled upward to keep the clothing out of the now flowing blood.

He tugged the body aside, away from the crimson pool, then walked around and grabbed the feet.

He muscled it behind the building and stripped the corpse, glancing around him often to make sure he was still alone. Maestro stuffed his own clothes into the tall grass and zipped up the hoodie he had taken from the dead man's corpse.

Afterward, he went back to the table and snatched up two 9mm pistols with as many magazines as he could stuff in his pockets.

He pulled a plastic sheet from the top of the table and dropped it over the sticky pool. There was no reason to alert passersby that something had gone terribly wrong for a citizen of Kingman.

If Maestro had his way, it would be the first casualty of many.

*****

The gate swung inward and the three vehicles charged through. Flex drove the lead vehicle and piloted the Hummer straight down Main Street toward the pit.

"Get Hemp," said Flex, his eyes on the road ahead. People ran south down Main with no exceptions. Most had weapons and spray bottles. Flex wondered if none of it was enough. They had the weapon that would stop all of this.

The Magas. The Hybrids.

Gem pushed the talk button. "Hemp, Charlie! Do you read?"

"Yeah, Gem," said Charlie. "Hemp says head down to the trough nearest the pit. If the stuff is there, we need to get started."

"Okay," said Gem. "Have you heard from Reeves?"

"We caught him on channel 22," said Charlie. "He asked for help distributing guns on the southwest corner of the pit."

"Yeah, so who's doing that?" asked Gem.

"Dave and Nel are going to drop Trini and Tay off with a bag of ammo, along with an extra shotgun filled with urushiol-soaked flechette rounds," said Charlie.

"Jesus," said Gem. "Can't Dave and Nel switch with them? I'd rather they're near us."

"They insisted, Gem," said Charlie.

The pit was now straight ahead, and the crowd filled the street. "I need off this road," said Flex, easing the Hummer and trailer left at the next intersection. He made the turn smoothly, and at the second intersection, turned right. The trough ran along this road, called North Spruce. When he reached the stack of lumber and the drums, he eased onto the brake and pulled the Hummer to a stop.

"Okay, Beauty, let's see what's happening at the pit and you let me know how you think we should best use your sisters."

When they got out, Isis and Max were there, frantically waving Beauty over.

Gunfire, both single-round and rapid-fire barrages rang out over the cacophony of sound that rose from the throngs of citizens and undead, and Flex wondered briefly if this was what it sounded like to the soldiers during some of the great battles of the U.S. Civil War.

Dave Gammon and Nelson Moore ran up, breathing hard, weapons strapped over their shoulders.

"We saw my uncle over by the pit!" shouted Dave. "Nel and I are going to see what we can do to help them start that damned generator!"

Before Flex could acknowledge them, they were off and running. The noise was insane. The crowd was animated and frantic, and the pit continued to fill with moaning, gnashing, snarling Hungerers. The Mothers were more elusive, typically blending in until they were in your face and it was too late.

Flex lifted his left leg and rubbed his ankle. The boot was working fairly well, but the pain was beginning to work its way into a throb.

"George!" shouted Hemp, at one of the men stacking a last piece of lumber near the trough. "Come here, please!"

He stood by the rear of the Magas trailer, and Flex ran up beside him and Charlie. Gem moved behind the trailer with Max, Isis and Beauty.

"George," said Hemp. "I need you to use the lumber you brought to build a diverter trough," he said. "Just nail the boards to one another at the ends, and make at least a three-foot wide trough. Nail the ends to the side of the main trough, and when you're done, make sure it reaches all the way to the pit."

"So you want me to create a channel from the main trough to the pit?"

"Exactly. I don't know if we'll need it, but also get a rechargeable reciprocating saw and be ready to cut the side of the trough away where our channel branches off, allowing the water to flow down to the pit."

"What good will water do?" asked George.

"I think that's where the drums of urushiol oil come in," said Flex. "Hemp, you want 'em to dump it in the water?"

"Exactly," said Hemp. "If we can't get the overhead sprayers and the shafts working, we can at least kill the Hungerers in there. The Mothers will be a different challenge."

"Go, go!" shouted Flex. "Get two teams working on it fast, George!"

Flex ran to the rear of the Magas trailer, arriving as the doors swung open. Megan stood staring down at them. "We're ready," she said.

"Let's get you all out of there," said Flex, standing back.

The Magas climbed out. Their eyes never met Flex's, and he silently hoped that one day he would gain their trust.

When they were all out, Isis said, "Let's do this, ladies."

"And gentleman," said Max, smiling at Isis.

Flex saw something flash in her eyes; something he had never noticed before. It was almost a twinkle, accompanied by the slightest smile.

"Turn it on, girls," said Gem. "Now would be good."

The Magas, as one, closed their eyes. It was, Flex thought, similar to watching a huge flock of birds dart in a new direction all at once, or watching a school of fish do the same.

They were one.

They opened their eyes. All told the same story.

"What's wrong?" asked Flex. "Nothing's changed. Are they … I don't know … *commanding* them or something?"

Hemp looked at the pit. "They still appear to be out of control. Isis, what *is* happening?"

"We're issuing the commands," she said. "They're just not responding. They're drawn somewhere else!"

"It is the babies," said Megan. "They call a thousand times louder, which only causes the Mothers to want to escape their bonds and find them. We cannot defeat them."

"Where are these children?" asked Beauty.

Gem took the radio from her belt, switched the channel and pressed the button. "Vikki! Vikki, where are you?"

"I'm helping distribute water!" said Vikki. "Why?"

"Where are the newborns?" asked Gem.

"They and their mothers are with Victoria and Doc Scofield at the clinic," said Vikki.

"Both of them?" asked Gem.

"Both?" asked Vikki. "Oh, no. You didn't know. Another was born an hour ago!"

"Is she a Hybrid?"

"Yes, Gem," said Vikki. "The recruiting Max and Isis did before they left really touched a nerve. More stepped up later."

Isis suddenly turned, her eyes flashing. "Give them WAT-5. Do it now! It's the only way to stop their call!"

Gem responded immediately. "Vikki, tell Doc Scofield they need to take WAT-5 now. Right now. Just shave some dust off and put it in their mouths with your fingers. Hurry!"

"Got it!" said Vikki. "I'll let you know when it's done."

There was no need for notification. In less than a minute, the crowd died down. The gunfire continued for several minutes afterward, but as the Magas stood facing the pit, the Hungerers and Mothers within stood perfectly still.

All at once, they slowly shifted, rotating as though by command. As Flex stared at the crowd, he saw they all now stared as one toward him, Gem, Hemp, Charlie and the Magas.

And the single Mago. Max.

*****

CHAPTER TWENTY

Trina and Taylor neared the point that Kevin Reeves, the former mayor of Concord, New Hampshire, had told them to bring the rounds.

As they ran by an alley, Trina looked to her right. A man stood there, magazines on the ground at his feet. He wore a dark hoodie and was picking the mags up from the ground and stuffing them into his jacket pockets.

"Hey, Tay," said Trina. "C'mon. That guy dropped his stuff."

Taylor looked over at the man. "We're going to meet Kevin. You need help?"

"Yeah," he said. "Arm's hurt and I dropped this stuff."

They hurried over to him and bent down, grabbing magazines along with him."

"Where you taking these?" asked Trina.

"To the cage," he said.

"Cage?" asked Trina. "What ... the pit?"

"So that's what you call it," said the man. He stood up and looked Trina in the eyes. He held a 9mm Glock in her face.

"Did you really think I'd just go away?" he asked, smiling.

"You piece of shit," said Taylor, reaching for her holstered gun. The man the girls knew as Maestro turned the barrel from Trina to Taylor and fired, knocking Taylor backward into the street. She lay still.

"No!" shouted Trina, her heart racing as she watched blood flowing from her childhood friend's supine body, now motionless.

Maestro grabbed her by the neck and jammed the hot gun barrel to her head. "Drop all of your weapons," he commanded.

Trina reached down and removed her gun, dropping it on the ground. She withdrew her EB-coated knife and another small revolver from her back pocket. Last, she slung the pack off her shoulder, containing all of the full magazines.

"Now you'll come with me, you pitiful bitch," he said, pushing her ahead of him. "You go first."

He pushed Trina up the hillside, his gun pressed against the base of her skull. "If you even slip," he growled, "I'll happily put a goddamned bullet into your brain."

Trina staggered, leaned forward to steady herself with her hands, and clawed her way up the hillside to the fence trail. She considered trying to kick straight out behind her, but the 9mm was pressed firmly against her. Too risky.

What have I done? she asked herself, knowing the answer. *I've given the sadistic bastard leverage.*

*****

402

Maestro pushed the girl along the trail; now he could see clearly into the cage.

The pit.

Inside were Mothers and Hungerers. They had all turned in one direction, and Maestro immediately knew why.

The Magas. His Magas. They were in control again. Soon they would again be in his control and under his command.

He pushed the girl closer and closer to the southwest corner of the fenced city of Kingman, Kansas, standing high on the hill overlooking the pit.

*****

Gem stared at the orderly zombies in the pit and was again amazed at all of their discoveries. The bad and the good seemed to come one on top of the other.

She thought of Flex Jr. and how much he loved to come down and work on the shafts; he would use a file to keep them razor sharp, and he never shied away from a day of hard work. His father had been a good example of that.

"Position the Magas on top of the catwalk," said Hemp. "They will continue to draw them into the pit."

"How many more can it handle?" asked Charlie.

"We can pack them in," said Flex. "I don't give a rat's ass if they're a little uncomfortable. I wonder how Nel and Dave are doin' with that goddamned generator."

"Hemp, will the catwalk support the weight of all the Hybrids?" asked Gem.

"Absolutely," said Hemp. "The fence is just fencing, but the rest is all thick gauge, cold-rolled steel. It will support them and more."

403

Isis raised her arms and the Magas stared at her. "Follow me," she said, turning and walking quickly toward the steps to the pit's cage catwalk.

The Magas followed.

The men working on the diversion trough were making progress. They were two board lengths away from reaching the edge of the pit.

"When you get it there, use nippers to cut away enough of the fence to be sure the water runs in unhindered," said Hemp. "When that's done, have the Sawzall ready and waiting. If the time comes, I'll order you to cut the hole and start the flow."

The Magas reached the edge and began climbing the narrow stairway leading up to the catwalk. The two stackable resin chairs still sat in the middle, but as Isis reached them, she kicked them onto the cage itself and continued crossing to the other side, closest to the large urushiol and water tanks and the failed generator.

"Wow, Flex," said Gem. "Like shooting fish in a barrel. Now all we have to do is finish them. It's so quiet."

"Our equipment needs to work before we can do that," said Flex. "Nothing would've happened with that electrical system that I can think of, so they either got an injector problem or a fuel issue. What a time for all this shit to bite us in the ass."

"I'm afraid to get through this," said Gem. "Worried about how I'm going to handle ... you know. Once I don't have anything else to think about or do I'm going to be an unbearable mess."

Flex put his arms around her. "We'll be unbearable messes together, Gemina. I love you, and I've still got you and I still have Trina. As for Flexy, he made us better people. There's no way in hell any part of his life was in vain."

Gem nodded, her face pressed into his chest. "Let's get this over with then," she said. "I think I'd like to lay down with you and cry for a few days. Then I'd like to sleep for a few weeks."

*****

Isis moved as far to the south edge of the pit's catwalk as she could, allowing Max, Beauty and Megan to move in beside her. Looking down, she saw a line of zombies flowing up the road, pushing their way through the spring-loaded gate. It looked as though nearly all of the Hoisington Mothers and Hungerers had entered, none of their singularly-focused minds recognizing it as a killing machine.

Isis saw Nelson and Dave below her in the equipment area, hunched over the generator. Dave had the air intake removed and pushed the button, engaging the starter. It turned and kept winding, but the engine never started. The smell of diesel fuel wafted into the air as the pit reached capacity.

Ten minutes passed. It seemed that once they either opened the trough or started the generator, the nightmare of the moment would end.

Isis looked again at the roadway entering Kingman. The incoming line of Mothers and Hungerers had now dwindled to nothing, indicating the capacity of the pit was somewhere around 2000 bodies.

Isis turned to see Hemp standing beside Charlie near the trough and the mouth of their inoperable diverter channel. Staring at him and concentrating, she pushed, *They can't start the motor, Uncle Hemp. Dump the urushiol into the new channel and open the trough to get it into the pit. We'll take care of the Mothers afterward.*

She did not need acknowledgement to know that Hemp had received her communication. He put a hand to his head and turned to stare up at her. Isis smiled and waved.

He moved the radio to his mouth and she heard "You never cease to surprise me, Isis."

He turned back and gave the command to George to start cutting.

She heard the whine of the reciprocating saw's blade chewing wood off in the distance.

*****

Gem's radio crackled. She heard a voice that she did not recognize.

"Anyone … anyone. Can you … hear me?"

It was a female voice. Gem pushed the button. "This is Gem Cardoza. Who is this, please?"

"It's … Tay."

"Tay? Tay, where are you? What's wrong?"

Gem glanced back at Flex, her eyes searching the streets. He was focused on the work on the diverter channel. She remembered the girls told them they were going to get more ammo to Kevin Reeves.

After a moan, Taylor said, "I'm … I've been shot, Aunt Gem. Trina was with me … he's got her."

"*Who's* got her?" asked Gem, frantic. Forgetting Flex, she started running west, toward the path the girls had taken.

"Maestro," said Taylor, her voice frightened and weak.

Gem ran faster.

"Gem!" called Flex behind her, but she did not stop.

406

"Tay, tell me where you are! I'll get someone to you!"

"I'm on … Sugar Street, I'm pretty sure," she said. "Gem … hurry. I can't … push …"

She stopped talking. Gem pushed her transmit button again. "Taylor!"

There was no answer.

"Where the hell are you going?" asked Charlie from behind her. Gem spun around.

"Charlie, Charlie!" she shouted. "He has Trina! Tay's been shot!"

Charlie's eyes lit up like hot coals. "What? Who shot her? Is she alive?"

"Yes, on Sugar Street," said Gem. "Come on!"

The two ran full tilt along W E Avenue. As they ran, Gem saw Charlie pull her crossbow from her back and load up an arrow without slowing. She caught up with Gem as they reached Sugar Street. They both looked both ways.

"There!" shouted Gem. "On the ground by that alley!"

They ran to where she lay and crouched down beside her. Charlie lifted her head and lightly slapped her cheek. Her eyes fluttered open.

"Mom," she said.

"Tay, where are you hit?"

"My … chest, Mom. Mom, he has Trina!"

"Shh," said Gem. She pushed the button. "Jim, I need you at Sugar Street near the old bicycle shop. Tay's been shot. Push a gurney over, please! Hurry!"

Vikki came on. "He's in the other room, Gem," she said. "Is she alright? Oh, my God!"

"She's alive," said Gem. "We need the rolling gurney now!"

"I'll get it and get Doc and we'll be there!" she said. "Just stay there and wave us down if you see us!"

"Charlie will wait for you," said Gem, her eyes on Charlie.

Charlie returned her gaze for a long moment. "Gem, what about Trina?" she asked.

Gem looked down and touched Taylor's face. "Tay, baby, which way did the man go with Trina? Do you know?"

Taylor opened her eyes and said, "Help me … lift my head."

Charlie did.

"That trail," she said, her eyes staring toward the hill. "I just saw them go up that trail before I passed out."

Gem ran.

*****

Maestro had reached the highest point on the trail next to the fence line, almost dead even with the pit. There was a clearing where he could stand, but for now he crouched down, the feisty, young blonde girl's hair balled in his left fist and his gun's barrel pressed firmly into her head with his right.

"You the type to do what a man tells you to do?" he asked.

"Oh, I'm way compliant," said Trina. "A man speaks and I just listen. He says jump and I ask him, "How fucking high, asshole?"

Maestro drew back his hand and knocked her in the temple with the butt of the 9mm. As he watched, her eyes rolled back and her body went limp.

The Magas – *his Magas* – had been walked onto a catwalk that ran from one end of the caged pit to the other, and now just stood there, calming the Mothers and in turn, ordering them to calm the Hungerers. The reasoning for the catwalk was unclear, but it did not matter anyway.

He was ready to take them back.

Maestro unzipped the stolen hoodie and pulled it over his head. On his face, Maestro felt the sticky wetness of the blood that had leaked from the sweatshirt's former owner onto the light jacket. He breathed deeply, hoping the metallic scent of blood would strengthen him.

He removed his pants and underwear, too. He would show all of them that he required nothing but that with which he was born in order to resume his role as Maestro.

Maestro bent down to check the girl again. She was unconscious. Perfect.

He moved into the clearing and stood tall, facing the row of Magas high on the catwalk. They would have the best view of him, high above the melee below.

"Magas!" he shouted at the top of his lungs, raising his arms high over his head as a symphony conductor might do as the musical composition reached a final crescendo.

As he watched, all of the Magas looked up to see him. Three-quarters of them fell to their knees.

"I command you!" he shouted, not knowing whether they could physically hear him or if they had again tuned their minds to his.

"Allow the Mothers to destroy their bonds!" he called. "Let them break the fence in which they are imprisoned!"

Maestro closed his eyes and moved his arms and hands, conducting what he hoped would be the deadliest aria of his entire life.

*****

The vibration began beneath Isis's feet and at first, she didn't realize what was happening. When she glanced down into the pit, the dozens of red eyes staring back up at her answered her question. They were in their destruction mode, and it did not take long for the dirt walls of the pit to begin powdering away.

The Magas then fell to their knees.

"What are you doing?" called Isis. "You were told of freedom! You promised to help us!"

One of the Magas who had not dropped to her knees pushed to Isis, *He has again taken control. He has always been a malevolent God to us. Others and I still resist him.*

Isis followed her gaze and saw him. Maestro. He had again seized control of the majority of the Magas. Not all of them, but it was enough.

Maestro stood almost directly across from her approximately two hundred feet away, perfectly nude, his arms raised and moving.

As his arms danced in the air over his head as though conducting a symphony, the image of his demonic Maestro conjuring an orchestra of demons. It was very clear what his intention was.

There were not enough of the brave, defiant Magas to overpower those who had succumbed again to Maestro's control.

"Magas!" Isis shouted, looking at the many kneeling followers of Maestro. "Remember the freedom we told you of? This Maestro is powerless without you! He will not hurt you again, ever! Resume the calming of the Mothers and you shall know freedom!"

The words pushed into her head so thick that Isis felt her own brain would rupture. All were thoughts of fear and submission, excuses for being certain that to disobey

Maestro would be to die or feel the agony of the deaths of others.

Gunfire erupted and Maestro ducked down again, behind the grass to his right.

The pulsation grew stronger. The Hungerers within the pit pushed toward the edges and clutched at the fence just above the five-foot tall dirt walls of the pit. Men and women stood on the outside, firing guns into their rotting faces, some using swords and machetes, others using sharpened rebar, an idea Dave had brought back from his trip to California.

The fence began to collapse, section by section. The catwalk shifted under Isis' feet and she shouted, "Max, Beauty, Megan! Follow me!"

As the catwalk's last weld vibrated to oblivion and snapped, the steel platform itself snapped and crashed onto the thin fencing beneath it. Square foot by square foot, the fencing sagged downward beneath the weight of the heavy steel, and the side walls above the hole bent inward, ready to fold.

Isis leapt the fifteen feet to the ground and landed hard in a muddy patch of grass and weeds, and looked up to see Max trying to climb his way down instead. He scrambled down the side, and Megan stood at the edge now.

"Megan, jump!" shouted Isis.

She did not. She stood there and stared down.

Isis dropped her hands to her sides and swept them backward. Megan flew from the edge and behind her came Beauty, who had seen Max's climb and duplicated it.

Megan had landed face down and Isis helped her up.

"Are you alright?" asked Isis.

"I am," said Megan. "I think. Maestro must be stopped!"

"We've lost your Magas," said Isis.

"More than we could afford to lose anyway," said Max. "That damned fence isn't gonna last much longer!"

*****

Maestro rose again after dropping back down at feeling the live rounds whizzing by his head. He had them now. It was no time to take a bullet.

He moved to a different clearing further to the south and stood up again, his arms directing the destruction below.

"Destroy this cage in which you are imprisoned!" shouted Maestro. "Magas, the Mothers have the power to bring it crashing down!"

Something stung his cheek and he put his hand up to his face and felt a warm stickiness.

He tasted it. It gave him power.

An entire section of fencing fell and his Magas directed the Mothers to send the Hungerers to the opening.

*****

Flex saw men running toward where Maestro stood, weapons in hand. One or two would stop and fire at him, but he was a small target and he was high on the hill.

He said, "Jesus fucking Christ, George, get that goddamned thing cut already! They're destroying the pit!"

The creatures climbed from beneath the fallen fence on the north side of the pit. The top was also pressed against the dirt making it difficult for them to crawl from beneath it, but dozens were making progress and getting through.

As they did so, they attacked the unprotected citizens of Kingman. When magazines ran empty the rotters were there to take advantage, their jaws open wide, ripping at the flesh of the unprotected men and women.

Urushiol bottles in disrepair because of the safety people had lived under for so many years.

Flex realized they were wholly unprepared for a full scale invasion of the walking dead.

To his horror, Flex spotted Kimberly near the pit, struggling with a small pistol.

"Kimberly, run!" he shouted, but the cacophony of sound was too much. She could not hear. Behind her three rotters had escaped the fence and now moved toward her.

"Kimberly!" shouted Flex, but he was too far away to take a shot without hitting other citizens.

The monsters reached her. They clawed at her thick, blonde hair, pulling her backward to the ground where they fell upon her, immediately tearing her open and feasting on her warm innards.

Flex turned and vomited. She had been with them for so many years, and had proved her heart and courage many times over.

Kimberly lost the battle, her body now only moving from the motion of her attackers feeding. Flex stole a quick glance further along the fallen cage. He spotted Lolita Lane and Rachel Reed working alongside Serena, two of the three resorting to close-combat weapons in the form of the sharpened rebar spikes they had reported seeing the children of Dunsmuir, California use so effectively. Lola, the sole holdout, used her favorite six-inch blades of choice, and in each hand Flex saw the blood-stained metal flashing as she combined kicks, spins and thrusts, stilling the walking dead predators for the last time.

For the moment, the women had the upper hand, taking each abnormal out as they tried to crawl free of the fence, their mounting dead bodies becoming further barriers to those behind them still trying to escape and feed.

Flex witnessed six kills in his short glance, equally distributed between the three determined Hungerer slayers.

Down the line to their left and right, several other Kingman residents engaged in similar battles. There were not enough of them though, and Flex could see with a glance that everyone was exhausted.

The Sawzall's charge had depleted. Flex pushed George aside. He kicked at the wood, but the cut was not deep enough yet. He gave it two more good kicks and a four-inch chunk broke free, allowing some of the channeled river water to begin flowing into their new trough.

"That's not enough, Flex!" said Hemp, who was busy manipulating the drum dolly, preparing to dump the urushiol into the trough. "The flow is so minimal it's just running out from beneath the boards."

"Does anyone who can hear me have a hatchet!" shouted Flex.

A man ran over, wielding a pickaxe. "This is the best I can do," he said. "Trade you for a gun."

Flex nodded, gave him a Glock from one of his drop holsters, and grabbed the pickaxe. He moved in and hacked away at the wood, slowly breaking piece by piece away until the flow actually began to work its way down toward the pit rather than leaking into the streets.

"Still too slow!" shouted Flex, swinging the pickaxe for all it was worth. His ankle screamed as he hacked frantically at the wood.

Charlie ran up, breathing hard, her face white. "Where's Gem, Flex?"

He looked up at her, his lungs burning. "Gem? I thought you went after her!"

414

Charlie shook her head. "No, Flex! Taylor was shot," she said. "Gem and I got Vikki and Doc Scofield on the radio and I waited with her, but Gem took off. Maestro shot Tay!"

Flex looked up and furrowed his brow. "Jesus Christ! The bastard's right up there and I don't see Gem anywhere."

"Hemp! Take over here!" he shouted, dropping the pickaxe and hobbling on his bad leg in the direction of the demonic conductor on the hill, swinging his Daewoo around to kill position.

*****

"It's useless, dude!" said Nelson. "It's dead!" He pulled out a star and flung it, scoring a bulls eye in the forehead of a Hungerer that had just broken free of the cage.

"We're fucked," said Dave, pulling out his gun. He ran to the fence and fired several shots into the horde, but even as they fell, the number never appeared smaller.

The rotters rushed the fence on his side now.

Another section of fence fell to the east of them, and zombies again tried crawling from under the chain-link roof.

The Magas that had tumbled onto the fence from the catwalk now sagged so low that the Hungerers reached up, their clawing, dirty fingernails scratching and ripping at their skin, but each of them struggled to keep their eyes on Maestro, who amazingly, had avoided being struck by any rounds yet. He stood there like a specter, ordering the mayhem below.

Isis approached the generator. She put her hands on top of it and closed her eyes. Knowing from the many volumes of encyclopedias she had read, she understood the functions of a diesel engine. All this needed to do was turn, though. They were not generating power; the rotation was only necessary to turn a pump and create hydraulic and pneumatic pressure.

She envisioned a rotation in her mind. Clockwise, turning, turning. Increasing in speed, faster and faster. She felt a new vibration under her hand. Not the Mothers destroying the cage, but the motor turning at her command.

As she felt her success, she relaxed, and pictured the turning motor in her mind, coupled to the pump that powered the hydraulic shafts buried within the pit and pressurized the lines through which the urushiol flowed.

"Isis!" shouted Dave Gammon. "Isis, it's coming out!"

"The shafts!" said Nelson. "Faster, Isis! We need that to go a lot faster!"

Megan and Beauty dropped down into the mud beside Isis and lay their hands on the motor. All of their hands touching one another, Isis felt Beauty and Megan connecting with her thoughts, and now the three of them issued the same commands.

Turn, turn, turn, faster, faster, faster.

The motor spun up to an ear-piercing whir, the bearings within singing as it spun up to a speed far beyond what even the motor would have generated.

The shafts jabbed out of the ground, and bodies jerked upward over every inch of the pit. Liquid flowed from the sprinklers that criss-crossed the pit's lid, and now the inside of the pit looked like a Mixmaster with hundreds of sharp, steel shafts engaging and disengaging, spiking through heads, legs, arms, faces and bodies without discretion.

Suddenly the entire top crashed down atop the dying zombies inside, and the spikes now protruded into the bodies of the Magas still atop the fence.

Isis saw this, but was unable to prepare for the emotional and physical agony of the many dying Hybrids; Max screamed beside her, and the cries of Beauty and Megan added to her emotional terror and pain.

The motor wound down and stopped. Concentration was impossible as their sisters died just yards away.

Max, Isis, Beauty and Megan lay writhing in emotional and physical agony, powerless to do any more.

*****

Gem saw Maestro ahead. He stood, his arms raised, his eyes scanning the destruction and death below, a demonic smile on his face. Gem had taken brief looks at the activity happening in and around the pit, but she was not sure if the townspeople of Kingman were winning or losing to the lunatic on the hill.

She saw a mound in the trail ahead and hurried to it. It was Trina.

Gem felt her neck for a pulse, looked for blood. She found a heartbeat and saw no blood except for a bit running from a cut on her head. She was alive.

She glanced back up. If Maestro looked to his left, he would see her.

Gem touched Trina's cheek and scrambled up the hill toward the fence, hoping the noise below was still loud enough to provide cover.

Taking slow steps, she drew even with the man below and began sidestepping down the hill, directly behind him.

Ten feet away. Five feet. Three feet.

She began to reach for her knife, but saw something more satisfying at his waist.

A machete. Dropping her knife back into its sheath, she eyed the handle and reached out to take it.

*****

Many of the Magas lay sprawled on the fencing, their bodies pierced by the finely sharpened shafts that projected from the floor of the pit.

Many others had been severely injured, but not killed. Isis stood again, the agony of the Magas echoing through every nerve ending in her body and every synapse in her brain.

She stared at Maestro and noticed movement from up the hill. It was Gem, sliding down the hill directly behind him.

Isis held her breath. She pushed, *Aunt Gem, he doesn't know you're there. Avenge the Magas he killed and let him draw his last breath.*

Upon seeing Maestro there, Isis had considered using her telekinesis to ignite him like a human torch, leaving nothing but charred bones in his place.

Instead, she would let Gemina Cardoza, who carried within her a fire that Isis had long recognized, kill Maestro.

*****

Flex climbed the trail, his ankle screaming.

As he came around the corner and cleared the tall weeds, he saw a body lying in the trail twenty yards ahead.

It was Trina. He called out to her but she didn't move. As he crested the hill, he stopped.

Maestro stood on the trail beyond Trina, nude. On his face was a Cheshire grin, and as Flex stared, taken aback briefly, Maestro's arms went up and he said, "I orchestrate yours and the death of everyone you love."

Movement behind him caught Flex's eye, and he saw Gem sidestepping down the hill behind Maestro.

Flex ran toward Trina, but his ankle folded beneath him and he fell forward.

Maestro saw his weakness and bolted for Trina. When he reached her, he slapped her hard in the face, waking her, and yanked her from the dirt, wrapping his arm around her neck and placing his other open palm on the side of her head.

"Would you like to see me snap her neck?" he asked, his smile even wider than seemed humanly possible.

"Let her go," said Flex, struggling back to his feet. "She didn't do anything to you. We'll let you take your girls home and whatever else you want. Just let that girl come to me."

"He's crazy, Dad," cried Trina. "Don't give him anything!"

"Be quiet now, Trini," said Flex. "Maestro ... I think that's what you like to be called ... we never meant to hurt you. We came into your town to kill some zombies, that's it. Nothin' more, and then you showed up. We can fix this."

Gem was on the trail now, ten feet behind him. Flex held his breath, using every bit of power within him to keep his eyes on Maestro and off Gem.

"All I really need to do – and mind you, I don't have most of my best tools here now – but if I just hold her neck in place and press firmly with my right palm, it's actually quite easy to snap a neck. The death varies from very fast to agonizingly slow, which really depends on how the neck snaps. While all the same, they are all different, you know, like snowflakes."

"Trina, just stay calm, baby," said Flex, seeing Gem was five feet away. "He knows he's dead the minute he hurts you."

"Everything is a bit fucked right now," said Maestro. "I was building my army up there. I've been creating these amazing slaves – so powerful and obedient – for years. Perfecting them, really. You can see how they serve me."

"They fear you, Maestro," said Flex. "I don't know that there's any love there. No admiration. Just fear."

"Sometimes that's enough," he said. "Let me show you now what I was –"

Gem pressed the razor-sharp knife against his wrist and yanked it backward, slicing through the tendons as his right hand went slack, releasing Trina's head. After administering the first cut, she put the blade to his neck and said, "Let her go or I'll slice your throat and you'll choke on your own blood."

Maestro slowly released Trina, who immediately ran two steps forward and spun around. She reached into her other boot and pulled out a small .380 Automatic. Now she trained it on Maestro, sure to keep Gem out of her sights.

Gem reached down and slid the machete from Maestro's belt and kicked him in the back of his knees, dropping him onto his back.

His head hit the dirt trail hard and his teeth bit into his tongue. "Fuck," he said, spitting blood that spattered his chin and chest.

Trina did not move. She stood there, holding the gun on him with both shaking hands.

"Trini, c'mon," said Flex. She turned to glance at him, and Flex saw that it wasn't fear that caused her to shake. He could see the rage in her eyes. She turned back toward Gem and Maestro.

"Just go to Flex, Trina," Gem said, her eyes never leaving Maestro. "He looks like he could use some help."

"Not fucking yet," said Trina, glaring.

"Trina," said Gem, her voice stern.

"Mom, you told me a long time ago how you and dad pulled Tay from a stack of bodies in a house in Atlanta when she was a little girl. That was the day I met her, and she was a mess like I was after seeing what happened to my family. *This* son of a bitch imprisoned women and girls. I need this."

Gem nodded. "Maestro, I believe Trina has a score to settle. You might want to prepare yourself."

He laughed. "Fuck you, fuck her, and fuck the useless whore I shot."

Trina rushed toward Maestro and dropped down beside him, the gun pressed against his right shoulder. "Where'd you shoot my friend, asshole? Here?" She fired the gun and Maestro's body convulsed as he screamed.

"Aw, crap," said Gem. "She put a hole in your stupid ink suit. Maybe you can have that shit tailored."

Trina wasn't finished. "You know, I didn't really see the shot very well because you had a fucking gun in my face. Maybe you got her in the knee?" Trina moved the gun and pressed the barrel against his right kneecap. She fired again.

Maestro's body convulsed and Flex swore he heard the crack of bone beneath the gun's report.

He cried out in agony now, his eyes squeezed shut.

"I'm done," said Trina. She turned and went to Flex, who put his arm out. She slid beneath it and provided support.

Gem straddled Maestro, the knife in one hand and the machete in the other.

"I shouldn't give a shit, but what made you this way?" she asked.

"Gem, he is what he is," said Flex. "Kill him."

"Tell me," said Gem.

"You made me this way," spat Maestro. "Bitches like you. You belong … in cages because you're goddamned animals, and you gotta train animals if you're gonna let them live."

Flex was transfixed as Gem stared into his eyes. His breath rose and fell quickly, and as Flex looked on, Maestro got an erection.

"Gem, he's a sick fuck," said Flex. "Don't let him take another goddamned breath!"

"Mom, the fucker has a goddamned hard on!" shouted Trina. "He's enjoying this!"

Gem turned to see, and Flex watched her expression turn from anger to disgust. She got up and stood beside him, the fingers of her right hand opening and closing on the handle of the machete.

Maestro either could not, or did not bother trying to move.

"You created those young women down there to be your slaves. They were born into captivity and you kept them in cages."

Maestro managed a weak laugh. "My daughters," he said. "My legacy."

"Yeah, there's that," said Gem, stepping back and raising the machete over her head. She stared at his erect penis for a brief second before bringing her arm down in a sweeping arc.

His severed manhood balanced there for a moment after the sharp blade exited his flesh, then toppled into the dust beside him.

His scream echoed across the town of Kingman, silencing many of the voices from down below.

Flex cringed and closed his eyes. He didn't blame her, but that didn't make it any easier to watch.

"Yeah, mom!" shouted Trina, stomping her foot in the dirt.

Gem dropped to her knee and jammed her knife into the small of Maestro's throat and pressed it straight down. Blood bubbled up from the wound, but she twisted it back and forth until his gurgling ceased and his eyes stared open and blank toward the cloudy sky.

Gem Cardoza stood and stared down at the dead man, for Flex knew that Gem was aware he was nothing more than that now.

She looked at him and Trina, tears pouring down her face.

"Help me," said Flex, moving toward Gem. Trina put his arm over her shoulder and they stumbled toward where Gem stood. As she passed Maestro, Trina grimaced and kicked his severed penis off the trail and down the hillside.

They reached Gem and the three of them embraced, holding one another for a long time.

"I know good work when I see it," said Charlie.

They looked up and saw Charlie standing at the base of the trail. She threw them a wave, her crossbow in her other hand. "I was down the hill trying to get a shot, but you guys were pretty much in my way. Glad you got it done."

Gem waved her over. "Come here," she said. "Is Tay okay?"

Charlie walked over, saying, "She's going to be fine. Nice touch with the whole dick thing."

Despite herself, Gem laughed, and Flex found a smile on his face, too. It was probably just shock and relief, but

423

soon Trina was laughing. All of their laughter turned to tears, and by the time they headed down the trail, the dead man behind them was already becoming a distant memory.

Flex knew they would not waste any time thinking about the dead tyrant.

Soon they would have time to mourn their son.

*****

The battle raged below, with the Mothers pushing the Hungerers into a frenzy within the compromised enclosure. The surviving, uninjured Magas were paralyzed with emotional pain and terror, as seventeen of their sisters had been impaled by the hammering hydraulic shafts or torn apart by the driven flesh-eaters.

Isis heard Hemp's voice from across the pit, but she could not spot him or Flex, to whom he called, "Dump it, Flex! Dump it!"

Water had been flowing into the pit, but it had no effect; there was no urushiol mixed in.

Now, as Isis saw the rush of water change in appearance, the creatures near the inflow seemed to blend with the water and disappear. More and more of them escaped over the north, south and east sides of the fence pouring into the town. Mothers were among them, directing the battle.

Isis climbed back up the side of the fence to where the catwalk once stood, and clung there, holding out her hand. Max saw her, climbed up behind her and passed her, crawling out onto the fence where the Magas lay, clinging to the chain link just out of the grasp of the reaching creatures below.

One by one, they helped them to the edge, and eased them down to the ground, where Megan and Beauty had recovered enough to receive them.

Many were dead or dying. When those in condition to survive were all safely away from the caged pit, Isis stared down inside, most of the pit still dry and teeming with the ever-hungry dead things.

Isis remained on the fence, staring down at the now oily water within the pit. Her eyes grew redder as her focus increased. She vaguely heard the screams of dying townspeople, and it was the last straw.

The pool of urushiol and water exploded into flame below her, the sudden flash shocking Isis, sending her flying backward from the fence. Dave and Nelson had been watching and charged to a position to catch her, but in the end all three went down.

The burst of heat had been so unexpectedly powerful that even Isis was not sure what she had done.

Scrambling back to her feet, Isis shielded her face from the firestorm within the pit. Every creature was aflame; not just the ones within the pit itself, but also the monsters that had already escaped. They ignited mid-step, falling and burning as hot as jet fuel. The Mothers exploded into torches and burned a vivid blue, then a dazzling white.

Then they were scorches on the asphalt.

In twenty minutes, it was all over.

It was time to count the dead.

*****

EPILOGUE

Six Months Later

The killing pit had been rebuilt, and the motor supplying rotation to the hydraulic and pneumatics was converted into a magnetic-driven, energy-free design that Hemp and Flex had been experimenting with.

Flex had a lot of input, as years earlier, he had enjoyed toying with magnetic motors, always with the hope that he would invent one that could be brought into the mainstream. Free power. Who wouldn't want that? He knew it even before the true need arose.

Taylor's gunshot wound had been clean through and missed any major organs, but it struck a nerve running from her spine, which caused her to lose the feeling in her left, lower leg. Her gait was noticeably off, but if called upon to do so, she could muster a run.

Doc Scofield told her she was lucky. Another quarter inch, and she might have been paralyzed. She had begun medical training under Scofield, and was becoming quite a nurse practitioner herself. Her dexterity was not affected, and she had good hands, or so Doc told her.

All in all, twenty-two citizens of Kingman had been killed in the onslaught driven by Maestro's need for power; many of them by head shots administered by other townsfolk.

The many funeral services were well-attended, including that of Kimberly. Her sisters, Vikki and Victoria, sobbed uncontrollably as several patrons of Three Sisters Bar and Karaoke Lounge spoke about her and her caring ways.

The service for young Flex Sheridan Jr. was held a week after the death of Maestro. It had been necessary to cremate his body well before that, but the condition the Mother had left it in was not suitable for an open casket anyway.

At the service, Gem and Flex sat in the front row of the small church beside Hemp, Charlie, Trina, and Taylor.

The statue of Jesus Christ on the cross stared down at them, and Gem wondered for the millionth time if she had just believed or disbelieved with more conviction, if anything would be different today.

If all of humankind had believed in this God, might he have spared them this horrible apocalypse? Were the non-believers and the sinners to blame?

Gem did not know. Her son was gone. It didn't really matter now.

Isis and Max, two of Flexy's greatest friends with whom he had grown up, spoke at the memorial.

"Flexy and I were tight," she said. "I remember every second growing up with him, and when I say that, I think most of you know I remember literally every second."

The crowd laughed at this, even as they wiped away more tears.

Isis continued: "There were lots of mornings when I'd look in the mirror and curse how fast I was maturing because I had such a crush on him it was stupid. I knew, without anyone telling me, that because I was aging twice as fast as he was, we never stood a chance other than to be close friends, which is what we were. I know he never really accepted it, but in time, he would have. It wasn't like he didn't have plenty of girls in Kingman chasing him, because he did. I would have been one of them had things been different."

She paused a moment, looked like she was ready to speak again, and took another few second before reaching down and holding up a picture that Gem had given to her.

"Gem gave me this," she said. "Flexy drew it of me the morning he died. You know how you see yourself a certain way? Maybe you ignore certain qualities in yourself and you only see the faults and blemishes?"

Tears streamed down her face now. "When Gem gave this to me, I looked at it and I cried. Flexy saw me this way," she said. "He thought I was beautiful, and I'd never seen myself that way."

She looked out across the silent, tearful audience. "I thought he was beautiful, too. I'll miss him every single day."

Nobody had ever seen Isis cry before that day. Nobody has seen it since.

Max stood and walked to the front of the church.

"Obviously Flexy was just a little older than me, but I have the same physiological condition that Isis has, so he always seemed more like a cool kid brother to me. I considered him my best friend."

Max looked up at the sky and said, "Flexy, buddy, if you can hear me now, I want you to know something without any doubt in your mind." He pointed at Isis and said, "I've always seen Isis as beautiful, just like you. I'm pretty sure you and I talked about it a few times. I sensed her inner beauty from the time I was born, and she's only gotten prettier since."

He stopped and looked at Isis for a long time and she smiled at him, her face red. Max nodded and turned his face toward the sky again.

"I'm telling you right now buddy, I'm going to marry Isis one day, and we're going to have a kid. Come hell or high water, that kid is gonna be a boy, and his name is gonna be Flex Chatsworth. If the first one isn't, the second one will be, and if the second one isn't, the third one will be. And Flexy, he's gonna be a Hybrid 3.0, so you can rest assured that your namesake will be the kinda guy that my dad calls a John Wayne."

Max slapped the podium and pointed toward the sky. "Flexy, I kinda see that as coming full circle."

It was not only the first and last time anyone saw Isis cry; it was the first time anyone ever saw her blush, too.

When they were done, Gem was unable to stand and speak of her dead son. Her grief, and Flex's, was shared through their silent tears at the service and with close friends in private.

Kingman soon returned to normal. The program to create more Hybrids was discontinued, as twenty-one of the Magas had survived Maestro's final onslaught.

Beauty had Maestro's child. The entire pregnancy lasted three months. She had a beautiful boy whom she named Travis. He is five months old and he is amazing. He's nothing like his father.

Together, the citizens of Kingman concocted a plan to send them out to strategic points across the country. It was voluntary, and once there, they were to develop a system to summon, then annihilate the Mothers and Hungerers. Logic dictated that if they were strategically located, every part of the continental United States, at least, would be reachable.

It was the only way that they could significantly reduce the numbers of the millions of rotters that remained in the country.

Life without Flexy was hard, but Flex and Gem still had one another, and they still had Trina and their family of friends. They knew there wasn't much time left for Gem, but they had not yet reached a decision about trying to have another child.

As a result of their great loss, or possibly just because they were so well loved in Kingman, Flex and Gem Sheridan also had lots and lots of requests to be Godparents to many, many Godchildren.

Kingman thrives.

THE END

(Keep going … there's news.)

YES, THERE WILL BE ANOTHER DEAD HUNGER.

Dead Hunger VIII: The Cleansing

Coming in early 2015

****

Other Books By Eric A. Shelman
And Dolphin Moon Publishing

Out of the Darkness: The Story of Mary Ellen Wilson
(1999)

Case #1: The Mary Ellen Wilson Files (2005)

A Reason To Kill
(2010)

Dead Hunger: The Flex Sheridan Chronicle
(2011)

Generation Evil
(2011)

Dead Hunger II: The Gem Cardoza Chronicle
(2012)

Dead Hunger III: The Chatsworth Chronicles
(2012)

Dead Hunger IV: Evolution
(2012)

Dead Hunger V: The Road To California
(2013)

Shifting Fears
(2013)

Dead Hunger VI: The Gathering Storm
(2014)

"Like" Eric A. Shelman's Author page on Facebook!
(On Facebook, Search "Eric A. Shelman, Author")

****

ONE LAST THING.

You clearly need chastising, my dear, stubborn reader. If you look above, you WILL see some books you haven't read before, like Shifting Fears and Generation Evil. This brings to mind a question: If you LOVE my zombie books, and you love the characters, can you PLEASE tell me why you ignore my other shit? I ask you this because I am a Dean Koontz fan and a Clive Cussler fan and a Ken Follett fan. I read EVERYTHING they write. I suggest you do the same with Eric A. Shelman and quit makin' me sad. 'Nuf said.